'*Everyone I Know Is Dying* is a strikingly honest portrayal
of mental health and young womanhood.
Emily Slapper's writing is sharp and uncompromising,
delving deep into Iris's struggles with depression, disordered
eating, and turbulent romances. She doesn't shy away
from uncomfortable truths, making the reader feel almost
intrusive at times. Yet, this unflinching honesty is what
makes the narrative so powerful and unforgettable.
Everyone I Know Is Dying is a book that demands to be read.'
Joe Gibson, author of *Seventeen*

'The writing is brilliant and so honest. I was
really invested in Iris's journey.'
Chloe Michelle Howarth, author of *Sunburn*

'*Everyone I Know Is Dying* paints an unflinching portrait of
a woman navigating the complexities of modern existence.
Emily Slapper's prose is drenched with such intense emotional
resonance that it's impossible not to think of Iris, George and
Patrick as real people. This novel delivers an absolute masterclass
in traversing fragile mental terrain; the writing is sharp and
witty and so delicately crafted. I read every page obsessively.'
Elvin Mensah, author of *Small Joys*

Emily Slapper grew up in Northampton before studying Cinema and Photography at the University of Leeds.

After graduating she moved to London to work in advertising whilst hoping to one day become a screenwriter. But wanting to write films turned into wanting to write books and so she started a Creative Writing MA at Royal Holloway. *Everyone I Know is Dying* is her debut novel.

In her spare time she loves walking around South East London with her dog, Tina.

EVERYONE I KNOW IS DYING

EMILY SLAPPER

ONE PLACE. MANY STORIES

HQ
An imprint of HarperCollins*Publishers* Ltd
1 London Bridge Street
London SE1 9GF

www.harpercollins.co.uk

HarperCollins*Publishers*
Macken House, 39/40 Mayor Street Upper,
Dublin 1, D01 C9W8, Ireland

This edition 2024
1
First published in Great Britain by
HQ, an imprint of HarperCollins*Publishers* Ltd 2024
Copyright © Emily Slapper 2024
Emily Slapper asserts the moral right to be identified as the author of this work.
A catalogue record for this book is available from the British Library.

HB ISBN: 9780008629144
TPB ISBN: 9780008629137

MIX
Paper | Supporting
responsible forestry
FSC
www.fsc.org
FSC™ C007454

This book contains FSC™ certified paper and other controlled sources to ensure responsible forest management.

For more information visit: www.harpercollins.co.uk/green

This book is set in 10.6/15.5 pt. Bembo by Type-it AS, Norway

Printed and Bound in the UK using 100% Renewable Electricity at CPI Group (UK) Ltd, Croydon, CR0 4YY

1

1

I hope the lights are on when we finally have sex, so he can see how young I am compared to his wife.

Ish is looking at me even though I'm not looking at him. Someone is speaking to him, they are having a one-on-one conversation, but he is looking at me. My shoulders are straight, but I stand up taller. I roll them back just a touch, as if I were readjusting, listening, processing the conversation I'm having with Sara.

He has two children at top private schools, so although he's successful you can tell he can't flash his cash as much as the bachelors in the room. His deep dark tan says, 'winter breaks in the Caribbean' but his watch says, 'and that's it'. To sleep with me he would be risking both his authority in the workplace and his marriage, but I know he'll do it anyway.

I make sure my conversation with Sara seems enjoyable and engaging. Her beauty enhancing mine. Nothing is more attractive than seeing someone content in themselves, living in the moment. I lean in and whisper something to her and we both laugh.

The pub is filling up with people. We are all here for the same reasons. The smell of spilt beer, cigarettes, aftershave, slices of lime. The white noise, regulated by the beat of the background music. The sight of everyone wearing what they've chosen to wear that day, trying to tell you something by the branding on their trainers or the tattoo on their ankle or the ring on his left hand that I see him caressing every now and again.

I am released from a keynote speech on 'the events of the day in the world of Sara' and move towards the bar. He moves towards the bar. This feels too easy, but I remind myself that he usually only talks to a few of the men from the management team and then leaves, looking at his watch, reaching for some gum, presumably to hide the smell of alcohol from his wife. If he stays this time, he's staying for me. The barman hands me my gin and tonic and looks at my décolletage. I turn to leave.

'Iris!'

I can't stop the brief smile which appears on my face at this moment of success. But I wipe it away, making sure I look indifferent before turning back around.

We talk about work, and then the weekend, and then our lifetime ambitions and I notice him switching focus between my eyes and my lips. I think about all the other people in the room he could be focused on. He seems to be relaxing, so I tell him I'm going out to smoke, no invitation. 'Great. I'll come out with you.' It's freezing outside and I know he doesn't smoke. These are the moments that do it for me.

Outside I slowly purse my lips around the cigarette and note that he has stopped checking his watch.

The alcohol has slowed my thoughts and I don't feel the evening's cool air on my skin anymore. I picture leaving now, walking to the train, satisfied with the knowledge of what I know he wanted. But it's too tempting. I want to see his desire. I wonder if he thinks I have the most beautiful face in the world.

I return to the conversation and touch his arm, laughing, resting my forehead on his chest for a second, stumbling back, apologising, maintaining eye contact, standing in silence.

In the taxi he sits in the front and I in the back, intensifying the illicit nature of what we are about to do. We don't speak, but I can see him in the rear-view mirror suppressing a grin and I can't help but smile a little too. His victory is my victory. But as the journey progresses I see his face relax and his eyes look up, thinking of something other than me. I lean forward and say, 'Sorry, I just realised I only put my address in. Could you drop him to another destination after?' But what I mean is, 'I'm not here to be forgotten.' The driver waits for him to say his address and I can see Ish pulsing his jaw. He takes a breath and cranes his head around to say something, in a casual hushed tone, about a quick drink at mine first. I relax again.

He slides my dress over my head and sits down on the bed, pulling me by the hips towards him so he can kiss my stomach. 'Your body's incredible.'

I can't help but notice that the waistband of his underwear is folded in on one side and suddenly I can see him getting ready in the morning and shouting at his children and falling asleep on his commute and spilling some lunch on his shirt and sitting down on the toilet and picking the skin around his nails and checking his bank balance and thinking about sleeping with me. I move around him and lie on the bed to try and curb the nausea. He's touching my body, and I almost think I won't be able to do it, but I close my eyes and think about the next time he has to have sex with his wife. My heart rate increases.

2

We all take a seat around the conference table.

'I know it's early and you all went out yesterday, so we'll try and make this quick!' Maggie beams around the meeting room. Her business-casual fitted blazer is making my hungover eyes throb.

'Shall I start then?' Dylan looks exhausted. He clearly hasn't washed his hair and the embarrassing t-shirt he's wearing with faded slogans all over it is wrinkled. That's how you manage to stay a junior for three years.

'Well, no, not yet, I think we should wait for Ish.' Maggie keeps leaning forward to look out the glass door. Why would you wait for someone who is ten minutes late? Usually I would say something, anything, to prevent a silence like this but for some reason I can barely keep a smile on my face let alone ask about the pointless and predictable things people have been up to in their spare time.

Maggie looks back to us. 'Did you lot have a good time last night then?'

Sara looks at me and smiles. 'It seems like some of us had a *great* night.'

My body freezes and I take a deep breath preparing to look unfazed, but then she turns to Dylan. 'Did you even sleep at yours, Dyl?'

Everyone can tell he did stay at his and I almost feel sorry for him as he goes bright red, but all I can think is, how hard is it to have a quick shower? He accidentally catches my gaze and I imagine how amazing it would feel for him if he got with me. I flick him a smile. It kind of makes me want to do it just for his sake, but the faux-distressed seams on his sleeves are one step too far.

Sara's thumbs are dancing over her phone and I wonder if it's that guy we were both speaking to at her friend's cocktail party. I try to focus on straightening the rings on my hand instead. After another excruciating lull Maggie breaks the silence. 'I get to see my nephew in a few days. He's just turned seven, bless him. Such a sweet age.'

It's so sad to me that a woman in her late thirties views seeing someone else's child as the highlight of her week, that I have to say something. 'Aw, that's so cute, I bet you're a great auntie.'

Her face lights up. The room falls silent again. I count to ten in my head to stop myself starting an inane conversation for the sake of it.

Maggie taps her pen mindlessly on the table. The noise is intolerable. She looks at me and I direct a forced smile in her direction. I wonder whether I should give up and rest my head on the table but then Maggie asks me, 'Anything you're looking forward to this weekend?'

I'm surprised that I have nothing to say and stutter, but Sara jumps in. 'Probably finding a man to take her somewhere fancy.'

Maggie leans forward like a school counsellor. 'You don't need a man to go somewhere fancy! Why don't you two go somewhere instead?'

Me and Sara glance at each other, our eyes doing the laughing. But before I have to think of an actual response Ish walks in. It's a relief to replace my last image of him with a more put-together, less intimate one. Although the blue jeans, black belt and smart shirt combo is harder to look at than I thought.

'Hello, ladies. . . and Dylan.'

'Come in. We didn't want to start without you.' Maggie admits. I don't know what's wrong with me but I find her meekness unbearable today.

'That's great. So where are we with the Blue Last spread? Are the designers finished with it?'

Dylan should answer, but he hesitates, so Sara saves him. 'They're nearly done but they're still working on that big feature for the sport thing-y.'

He raises an eyebrow at her. 'Adidas?'

'That's the one.' She giggles. I wonder if he thinks she's equally as attractive as me. Maybe there's something too faux-innocent about her, but if all he cares about is someone being young and beautiful, then I guess there's no difference. I wish I could say to her, why don't we both try then, and see what happens this time? But I'm sure there will be another chance to find out who is best.

Ish still doesn't sit down but rests his hands on the top of the chair, thinking. Maggie goes to speak, but he cuts her off. 'We need to make sure they're not eating each other's lunch. Sara, can I get a one-pager on the comms plan? Dylan, you help her. I'll ping you both later.' He flashes them both a brief smile. It's harder to feel the thrill of last night when I don't know how he sees me in comparison to her.

I can see the pulse in Dylan's neck as he looks at Sara making notes in her loopy handwriting. I decide to ask him to lunch later, and then the fact I even considered that makes me dig my nails into my knees under the table. *That's not who you are*, I remind myself.

'Is there anything you need me to do?' I ask Ish, the corners of my mouth turning up just slightly.

'I'm sure Sara will be able to give you something.' He gives a courtesy nod to Maggie and walks out.

I think Maggie sees I'm in a state of shock because she says, 'I've actually got something important for you to do. There's a meeting set up with a potential brand and I want to present them with a folder of some of our best work. It would be great if you could pull something together. Choose some things that you think might be relevant.'

Sara leans over and pinches my arm. 'If you finish the work I set you in time, Cinderella.'

The way she moves is so bouncy, her ponytail is still swinging when she sits back. Someone told me that Sara's dad left her mum for a twenty-eight-year-old trainee lawyer at his firm, and now her – ex-housewife – mum spends all her time renovating their empty house. For a beautiful girl with a trust fund, Sara works needlessly hard but she can't have it all. I will do everything I can to get promoted before her. I make a mental note to ask Maggie if I can attend the brand meeting.

'Maggie, is that a Pandora bracelet? You are *so* cute.' Sara reaches over to touch her wrist.

'Thank you.' She blushes, but I can tell it isn't because she's flattered. It's hard to have sympathy for her though. She makes her own choices.

'Right, is that it then?' I stand up because I feel a desperation to get back to my desk. I've had enough of people today. Either everyone is boring or fake and neither is a comforting thought. I decide it will calm me down to go and write a to-do list. Maggie looks at me with her big eyes as if she has no idea that she's the one who decides when this ends. I can't handle it anymore. Her life is depressing me. What is she getting from working here? I'm sure she would be happier if she just settled for some man she met online and became a mum.

I walk out. 'See you.'

Sara catches up with me along the corridor. 'What are you doing this weekend? Do you want to come out with me and Tash?'

'I don't think so.' I usually feel that being part of their little rich clique is an honour. But recently I've realised we're all aware that I will never, truly, be one of them. You can't compete with people who don't even see you as a threat.

'Oh, come on, what else could you possibly be doing?' Her question hurts because it's true. Since moving to London and making friends with Sara, I've relied on her too much. She brings me status and a social life and in return I bring her bug-eyed adoration.

'Something else.' I realise I'm being too real so I nudge her and smile. 'No, I'm only joking, there's nothing in my life but you!'

We get to my desk and I sit down, smiling at her to say goodbye. But she perches on my desk. Even though she's just wearing black jeans and a white blouse everything about her is gold. Her jewellery, her hair, her skin, even her eyes are a green-y gold. Rich people like to emulate precious metals, I've noticed. I've found it's a good way to tell what I'm worth, comparing myself to gold.

'You'll never guess what?'

I log back on to my computer hoping she gets the hint. 'What?'

'Freya is going to the BAFTAs.'

'Who's Freya? What's she in?'

'No, Freya, from Downe House.' I've known Sara long enough to understand she's usually referring to a particular school when she says something like that. I don't think she realises the only schools I know are from the tiny town I grew up in.

'Yeah, I think I know who you mean.' The rest of my team are pretending to work but I know they're listening. Since I've met Sara I can't help but fantasise that one day we will both be the same: so pretty that people will think 'Surely she's not successful though?', so successful that people will think, 'Surely she's not nice though?' And then the sinking realisation that, she is in fact, everything.

And even though I'm not a statuesque, privately educated, millionaire who has Oxbridge bankers escorting me to annual balls, I'm determined to make my own way in life. That's why right now my sole focus has to be the promotion. I don't want my team to associate me with this kind of inane conversation. I stand up and say I'm going to get a glass of water.

'I'll walk with you.'

We start walking all the way from one side of the L-shaped office to the other, where the kitchen is. Which means we will walk past every long table and everyone sitting at them. There isn't really a dress code, but I try to break it anyway. You don't get noticed if you don't put yourself out there. Today I'm wearing a slightly low-back top, but I look at Sara in her blouse and wonder if it looks better.

'She was at that club in Mayfair, and this guy was chatting to her, she didn't even like him that much, but he had this area cornered off so she sat with him. *Anyway*, turns out he's in that film about dreams or something? And he's like properly famous, but she's so stupid she doesn't watch films like that and had no idea.'

I stop at Sara's desk in the hope that she'll leave me here. She sits down and speaks in a loud-hushed tone because everyone else is quiet. 'Apparently he said she was so beautiful compared to all the fake LA girls. Like, naturally *so* stunning. She said she was only wearing a bit of mascara.'

I speak in a hushed tone back. 'That is mental. I'm so happy for her. Can't wait to hear about it.' Before she can say anything I add, 'Catch up with you later.' Give her a little wave and walk off.

In the kitchen, I fill up my large glass with ice-cold water and decide I should eat something so I can take the supplements back at my desk without the risk of stomach acidity and poor absorption. I choose an apple from the fruit bowl.

'Look at you being all healthy!' Maya the intern swans in. 'I need to get myself into that frame of mind. I had just come in here to grab a packet of crisps!' She's slim, neat, smooth-skinned, good-postured, the same age as me, but less successful, pulling her hand away from the crisp bowl without any crisps.

'No, seriously, this is all just for show. I had cookies for breakfast!' We laugh.

'Honestly though, I was just about to come grab a packet of crisps, but you've inspired me to get an apple instead.'

'Or why don't you have these nuts? That'll satisfy the savoury craving, but nuts are like, really healthy. They've got all that slow releasing energy.'

'Ooo, part-time nutritionist, is it?' She takes the nuts. 'Thanks! So glad you were in here.' She turns around to leave.

'Maya! Just while you're in here. I'm absolutely stacked, and Maggie said I could drag you in to help with this thing I've got to pull together for a new potential partner.' She is nodding eagerly, and I make sure not to smile.

'Yeah sure, that's cool – just send me over whatever you need help with and I'll get on it.'

'Nice one.' It's important she knows I'm not an intern. She walks out with an enthusiastic smile.

Whilst I'm cutting up my apple I think about all the fat and salt in the packet of nuts. It's likely she won't see that the packet is four servings and will finish it in one sitting. My shoulders relax. The day's back on track.

I put some apple in my mouth, but the sweetness hurts my tongue, so I spit it out and put the rest in the bin. I feel pride at the restraint. The only thing better than knowing other people are eating unhealthy food is not eating anything myself. I decide it can't be that bad to take vitamins without eating. My stomach aches with emptiness, but it focuses me. It drives me. I enjoy it.

3

My alarm goes off at 6.44 a.m. I chose 6.44 because I like knowing that I'm not one of those people that needs everything to be a round number. I get out of bed and walk straight to the bathroom before checking my phone. A healthy habit.

In the shower, I wash my face with an anti-acne medicated wash I got from behind the counter in a pharmacy. I don't get spots, and never have, but I like knowing that my skin is thoroughly clean. Fancy face washes are a rip-off; you're just paying for a bit of soap in some aesthetically pleasing packaging. The medicated stuff, in the brash packaging, has proper ingredients like salicylic acid. And at the end of the day, people are going to be looking at my pores, not my bathroom shelves.

I only wash my hair every two to three days because over-washing can make your scalp produce excess oil to compensate. Today is wash day. I use unscented shampoo as I don't think cleansing and scenting should be shoved together in the same step. Putting heavily scented products directly onto your scalp can cause irritation and you don't want that because it can lead to dandruff or itchiness. Body wash, unlike face wash, is worth spending the extra money on.

Exfoliating before shaving reduces ingrown hairs, prevents cellulite and creates an even skin tone. Some people just do their legs, but I always do my arms as well. Arms, especially in the winter, can become red and blotchy.

Most communication happens before you even open your mouth. So it's these extra steps that will make you stand out. People won't be able to put their finger on it, but they do notice. They get the sense that you're different to them. Better than them.

Lastly, I turn the shower to its coldest setting, wash out my conditioner and stand under the cold stream for a few minutes. Ending a shower like this closes your pores, kick-starts your metabolism and makes your hair shiny. The fact that I've continued this into the winter only speaks to my willpower.

I get out of the shower and pat my body and hair dry. It's important to take the time to do this. If you rub the towel over your body and hair roughly, it can cause your skin to loosen and hair to split. You want to be pretty enough that people look up to you, but not excessively. People who are attractive in a way that showcases the time and effort they've put into their appearance are not valued the same because other people see that as attainable and shallow. Inconspicuous beauty is power.

I hurry back down the hall, in case loitering will allow the canteen stink of cooked dinners to absorb into my fresh skin. Does George not mind living somewhere that smells like this? The first time I met him, whilst unpacking my few belongings into a free kitchen cupboard, I couldn't quite work him out. Well-ironed but casual clothes, attractive but seemingly unaware of it, smiley but nonchalant, friendly but also didn't seem bothered to make any particular type of impression. He asked me if I needed help, but after I feigned a no, he just told me to knock on his door if I changed my mind and left. The next time I saw him I was exhausted after a hard week at work and could barely get my face to smile. We had a brief but polite chat which set the pattern for every interaction we've had since. I know the basics about him – George Williams, twenty-seven, chef, lived here two years – and I think that's all I'll ever know. Sometimes, when I hear him laughing with a friend, I feel a pang of regret for the missed opportunity. But mainly I feel relief. It's like he's the only person I don't have to impress or win over and I'm grateful for the space we give each other. Anyway, as soon as I get the promotion, I'll be out of here. Onto the next rung.

Back in the safety of my room I light my neroli-and-jasmine candle. I read the label – 'refreshes and invigorates'.

I take a second to look out my window, onto the courtyard that it overlooks, and appreciate the world. Or try to. It offers me a few 'No Ball Games' signs which take a sarcastic tone in the context of this small square of overgrown, dead grass decorated with rubbish. The sky is obstructed by three grey walls. I decide instead to concentrate on the fact I live in London. Yes, people's rubbish might be at my feet, but everything else is at my fingertips.

I check my phone now. Send an email to Maggie about something that sounds vaguely important and useful. It's always good to show you're doing work before 8 a.m.

I flick through my podcasts and choose one to listen to whilst I get ready. Beauty should never come at the expense of knowledge – I want them both. I want everything. Today I choose one that recounts a true love story between two teenagers who met whilst living at a refugee camp.

While it plays I get out some cocoa butter and mix it with some jojoba oil in my hand until it reaches a lotion consistency. Today I moisturise my whole body, not just my legs. It hasn't seemed worth it until this point, but I'm beginning to think I should start because when someone touches my shoulders, my back, my stomach, I want it to be the softest skin they've ever touched.

What I've started doing recently after moisturising is spraying some of my perfume in front of me in the room and stepping into the mist. This means that some scent is actually on my skin rather than just my clothes. When creating an impression you want to dazzle all the senses.

On the podcast, they are describing how one of the teenagers didn't want to take an opportunity to flee the camp as it meant leaving her lover behind. I can't help but wonder what would happen if she got what she was fighting for? Would they become a boring cookie-cutter couple just like everyone else? Is lack of passion the price you pay for stability? There's a reason fairy tales always finish after the wedding. But we love to ignore the chapter after that.

Just before I leave for work I look in the mirror and say my affirmations. I read that by focusing your mind on a particular pathway, you're naturally more likely to end up walking down it. I'm not under some impression that you are able to will anything you want into existence simply by saying it, but I do believe that it's helpful to remind yourself to work for your happiness.

I'm in charge of my thoughts.

I will become the best version of myself.

I'm about to make my life incredible.

4

The buzzing from the living room tells me that George hasn't left yet. I glance at my watch for a few minutes. 8 p.m. is a lot later than normal, so I guess he's not going at all. I hold my face in my palms and try to suppress the feeling lurking behind my eyes. My stomach rumbles and my body walks out of the bedroom door and down the hall to the kitchen.

George is sitting on the sofa, laptop on lap, phone in hand, TV on. No signs of movement. But maybe a slight surprise on his face to see me join him in the room. We've barely ever been in here at the same time before. Mostly it's just polite nods as we pass each other in the hall. I turn straight into the kitchen part and bend down to open my cupboard.

It feels weird not to acknowledge each other so I say, 'You're not in work tonight?' I pretend to rummage around to create an impression that I'm going to have something more complex than a packet of couscous and some asparagus.

'Good evening to you too, Iris. How's it going?' I stand up and look over the counter. He's still facing the TV, so I take a second to look at him properly. He looks neat. He has short, curly, black hair which fades into shaved back and sides, warm brown skin and a cute little nose. His teeth look like the natural version of what celebrities pay for. I don't know if he's trying to say anything by wearing a plain white t-shirt and jeans.

'Yeah, good thanks. How have you been?'

'YUUUS.'

He kind of bobs up and down in his seat. The crowd on the TV celebrating with him.

'Good then?' I ask, taking the opportunity to walk over to the fridge and remove the packet of asparagus. Looking around the work surfaces I help myself to a tiny drop of what is definitely not my oil into what is definitely not my pan.

George remains fixated on the TV, briefly checks his other screens, and then stands up and walks over to the kitchen. 'You want dinner?'

I look down at my asparagus frying, struggling to think of what to say. I feel caught off guard. I want to say yes because I feel intrigued by him. But the thought of signing up to eating something I haven't chosen makes my palms hot. I remind myself that it's probably okay to deviate as I've eaten less than planned today.

'Yeah sure, that would actually be amazing, thanks.' I move back without even turning the hob off. I wonder if he's just being polite. He doesn't seem like he's flirting. I feel unusually awkward and I'm not sure how to act. I can't suddenly turn on my charming, public self because it would seem so fake now, after all the low-key interactions we've had. And anyway, do I even want to make him like me or do I want to just get through the evening? My thoughts are all over the place.

He grabs a bunch of stuff from the fridge.

'Need me to help?' I don't quite know what to do with my asparagus or myself so I just stay standing behind him looking at his arms, which are more toned than I thought.

He turns off the hob I was using. 'I think we're all good.'

I walk around to the sofa. The electric heater is on and I have to take off multiple layers even though I looked better in my sweater. I tell myself to try and relish this rare dynamic. Being in company without having to think about everything I say and do. But it's so strong in me, the instinct to control the situation, that I feel lost without the guidance. I pretend to watch what's on TV – some kind of football debrief – but worrying that he's going to ask me if I like football or something, I switch it on to silent. I'm left looking at the wall like I'm in a gallery. I can feel my shoulders tense up. But I guess from his laid-back and rhythmic chopping that only one of us finds the silence uncomfortable.

I try and sound relaxed, 'How come you're not at work then?'

'Were you wanting the room to yourself?'

I look over but he's not looking up, he's grinning down at the chopping board like he's addressed what's unsaid in the room. I guess he isn't going to chit-chat with someone who has clearly been avoiding him since the day they moved in. I lean back on the sofa deciding to stick with the silence.

'I was made redundant,' he says finally.

I look over again and this time he looks at me. My chest twinges imagining what he must be feeling right now and I struggle to find words. I search for what he's thinking in his expression but he has no intensity behind his eyes.

'Nah, actually, I don't think it counts as redundancy if they're not going to give you any money.' He laughs and drops a mix of Mediterranean vegetables into the asparagus pan and they hiss.

The news feels inexplicably upsetting to me but I try to sound sympathetic in a neutral way. 'Oh. . . So what are you going to do?'

'I dunno, probs some kind of spaghetti. What you reckon?' He flips the vegetables around in the air and puts a pan of water on to boil.

'Are you all right? Are they allowed to just cut you off like that?'

'I don't think they've got a choice what with going out of business. Not sure what that says about my cooking skills, but I guess you can be the judge of that.'

He pours in some chopped tomatoes, adds a dash of some things from his cupboard and then turns down the hob and leaves the sauce bubbling away. He looks up and the direct eye contact tells me we are now in a conversation. I can't think of anything to say in time because I'm wondering if I'm coming across strangely. I need to regain some control.

He jumps in with a, 'How are you then, Iris?'

I don't know if he means 'how are you?' or 'what brings you in here?' or even 'why do you never come in here?' but I just go, 'Yeah, good thanks.' I try to think of something else to add. What would I usually say in this situation?

'Work's good.'

I suddenly realise my mistake but he's already smiling and back to cutting up some fresh herbs.

'Nice, nice.'

'Oh, sorry that's really insensitive of me. I have no idea why I said that. It's not even that good to be honest.' But I immediately regret saying that. I want him to know that work is great. That I'm doing great. I regret not trying to make a good impression tonight.

He looks up confused, 'Oh, I didn't even make the connection. I was just thinking it's nice that things are going well for you. You always seem so busy, so I guess it's paying off.'

I look down and turn the ring around on my finger. My stomach contracts but not from hunger. I want to offer to help again but it would just seem insincere this late in the preparation. So I wait and after a few minutes watch him turn the hob off, taste the sauce, add some more seasoning, and drain the spaghetti. The smell of the room becomes herby and comforting. I look around at the combination of all his stuff scattered and feel the warmth of a used kitchen. For the first time I think this room looks like somebody's home. Somehow he's made this lifeless space remind me of a living room on Christmas day: that sense of there being nowhere else in the world other than this room right here, right now. I have a strange urge to say all that to him but I manage to stop myself.

He walks over and hands me a generous portion of tomatoey pasta and my stomach rumbles loudly. I blush and he plonks down next to me. 'I'll take that as a compliment.'

A few mouthfuls in, I'm already full. My stomach expands to make room for the pasta and I need to take a few breaths. I get the impression George wouldn't notice if I stopped eating, but something compels me to eat more. This is the first time anyone, other than my parents, has cooked for me and the realisation briefly emotionally overwhelms me. He's unmuted the TV and switched over to the news. The main stories have already finished and now there's a feature on the epidemic of loneliness in our elderly population and the impacts this has on their mental and physical health.

I eat more of my spaghetti, but I can't really taste it, and watch Ron tell us that he only realised it was Christmas Day when he got to his local supermarket and found it was closed. My throat feels smaller and suddenly it hurts to swallow. The last time Ron had spoken to another person, except cashiers at the shop, was months before, when his boiler broke. The same strands of pasta are being twirled around my fork again and again. I'm willing Ron to break down, start crying, call out for help, anything. But he doesn't, his soft voice carries on reciting the story as if he were recounting a weekend with the grandkids. I search for sadness or despair in his eyes, but all I can see is a dull optimism and I feel like I'm going to double over from the pain in my chest. I can see George putting his bowl on the table and picking up his phone. I feel the tightness in my chest give way and the tears start to fall. Then a sob.

He tries to put his phone down and it falls on the floor. 'Hey, what's up?'

I want to stop crying but I can't. I have no sense of control over myself which is terrifying. I don't know how this has happened.

George seems concerned, but he doesn't move any closer to me or say anything. Eventually the complete lack of expectation I feel from him to stop or explain myself is what helps to calm me down.

I finally manage a 'Sorry.'

'No need.' He assures me and relieves me of the bowl I'm clutching in my lap. He moves back over to the kitchen. I stop crying, mute the TV and lean back into the sofa, closing my eyes. I listen to what sounds like water running and then the click of the kettle and the slow rumble of it boiling. I almost feel like I'm nodding off when the bounce of someone sitting down next to me on the sofa brings me back to reality.

'Tea?' He asks with a lightness in his tone that I appreciate.

'Oh, no, thanks though,' I reply suddenly with a forced lightness in mine, scrambling for any sense of composure and self-sufficiency.

'They were both for me anyway.'

I look at the two steaming mugs on the table and decide it would be stupid to double down on this attempt to save face. 'Actually, I would die for a tea right now.'

'That won't be necessary.' He gestures towards the mug in front of me which I notice is sitting right next to a coaster.

A weak laugh comes out of me. 'Thank you. And thank you so much for dinner.' I smile, and it stays there as I lean forward and grab my tea. He nods and then finds his phone and returns to whatever he was doing.

'I guess that news story was. . . pretty bleak.' I don't know why I say it. The fact he doesn't ask me to open up somehow has the opposite effect on me. It's disconcerting. I want to explain this whole outburst but I don't even understand why it's happened myself. Tears roll out of my eyes again, but this time silently, on their best behaviour. I glance at George's face and it's as serious as I've ever seen it.

'Yeah, it is really sad. It's pretty nice that you feel it so strongly though. Well, maybe a tad strange but there's nothing wrong with that.' A suppressed smile appears on his face.

I can't help but let out a laugh and he looks pleased, like he's achieved something.

He leans forward to put his mug down and his arm brushes mine, which makes the hair stand up on the back of my neck.

I turn to him. 'What are you going to do?'

He looks up from his phone. 'Now?'

'No, I mean with your job.'

He looks into the distance like he's considering this for the first time. It's unsettling to me that he doesn't seemed panicked by this loss of direction and identity.

'Probably sit down here for a bit and then see what I feel like. Maybe sit over there.' He gestures to the worn-out armchair. 'Who knows. The world is my oyster.'

I look away. The only explanation is that he's pushing it down or pretending to be okay, so I decide not to press further.

He caves. 'I guess get another job. People gotta eat right?'

Both as a surprise and not, tears start falling from my eyes again. Humiliated, I try to press them away.

He puts his phone back down. 'He's gonna be fine! Now he's been on the tele you know all the Pats and Mavises will be ringing up his landline.'

Another laugh breaks up my crying.

'No it's just. . . so unfair. You work and work, cooking people the same fucking dishes with probably no recognition and then just like that, you're done. What was the point? All that time and energy wasted. I can't even imagine how disheartening that would be. You must feel completely stranded. Like it was all pointless.'

He's looking at me right in the eyes like he's trying to work something out. 'I can guarantee you, it's going to be all right.'

I know he's only reassuring me so I'll calm down but I manage to believe him, and somehow even take it as if it applies directly to me too. I stop crying and exhale. It's strange that this is the first time we've properly interacted and yet I've been more open to George tonight than I have to anyone else before.

'Sorry to add all this random stress to your already bad day.'

He stands up to take our mugs back to the kitchen. 'It's fine, don't worry yourself. It's not even a bad day to be honest. I've just been told not to come into work for the rest of my life!'

5

I put some lavender essential oil in my electric diffuser to create the best atmosphere for unwinding after work. The cushions on my bed are perfectly arranged, floor hoovered, surfaces cleaned. I've even stuck on the heating for an hour so I don't have to walk around with a dressing gown over the top of my clothes. George hasn't spoken to me since he made dinner over a week ago and I'm trying to work out if it's because he's busy or because I was acting insane. I have to squeeze my eyes shut to stop myself thinking about his shocked face. I take a second to pull myself together and redirect my thoughts to my relaxing evening activities.

I've got my small, black Moleskine notebook out to make a list of the things I want to do to relax. I write down: moisturising hair mask, sort out jewellery, start reading new book. But, as I'm writing the list, I notice that my nail varnish is slightly chipped. I put the notebook and pen neatly on my bed and get my manicure box.

Halfway through painting my right hand the bed starts vibrating. I reach over and get my phone. *Mum.*

'Hey.'

'Hi, sweetheart.'

I wait for her to say something more, but she doesn't, which annoys me. She can never just be straightforward.

'Hi, Mum.'

'Hello, love, it's lovely to hear your voice.'

She doesn't say anything else.

'Are you ringing for a chat?'

'Would that be such a crime?'

I laugh, but don't say anything.

'Dad says hello.'

'Is that what you've called to say?'

Her voice is clipped. 'If you didn't want to chat you shouldn't have answered your phone.'

'I'm sorry, I do want to chat.' And I do, in a way, but I already know how it will go.

'Your only remaining grandparent has passed away this afternoon.'

I take a second. 'Why have you said it like that?'

Her voice turns an octave higher. 'Oh, bloody hell, Iris. Someone has died and all you can do is be sarcastic.'

'That wasn't sarcasm.'

I can tell she's doing that thing where she's looking at my dad shouting towards him as if he's me. 'Do you want us to leave you alone? So you can get back to your work?'

I open my mouth to ask what's wrong with working but it's not the time for that old chestnut.

'I'm not doing work, it's 9 p.m. I'm sorry, Mum. That's really sad to hear. Is Dad okay?'

'Dad's right here.'

'Okay. . . well can I speak to him?'

I hear her thrust the phone over.

'Hi, sweetheart.'

'Hi, Dad, I'm so sorry about Nan. How are you doing? Was it out of the blue?'

'Yes, well, the visiting nurse told us a couple of days ago that she seemed to be going this way. She's just been having a restful couple of days before. . .'

'How come you didn't tell me a few days ago?'

'We didn't want to disturb you, love.'

I wonder if this is a sly dig but I stop myself from arguing about something I've chosen not to care about anymore.

'Well, how are you, Dad?'

'Yes, yes. We're okay. But we'd love it if you came back down, love.'

'Tonight?'

'Or as soon as you can. We'll be having a funeral for her on Friday morning.'

'Okay, that's fine, I can come on Thursday so I'll be there for Friday morning, and then I'll have to go back.'

'You can't stay the week then?'

And do what? Listen to how all Londoners are too busy and rude? Try to justify my life choices to people who think it was self-indulgent to go to university? Explain that working for a digital magazine isn't this crazily precarious career?

'I can't. I'll see you Thursday then. And I'm really sorry, Dad.'

'She loved you, you know, Iris.'

I roll my eyes. 'I know she did, Dad. Bye.' I hang up the phone before he can say, 'I love you too.'

I look down and see the nail varnish is in thick smears on my nails. I press down hard on them and smudge it all over my fingers and then wipe it on my duvet cover so it will stain. The room is thick with a nauseating lavender-scented mist. I go to rip out the meaningless list in my notebook but a metal rattling of a key in the front door makes me jump.

I'm tempted to go out but why would I want him to see me so unravelled again? I turn off the diffuser and get under the throw fully clothed. I pull one of the decorative cushions towards me to rest on. It's thick and my neck cranes up too much to lie on it so I throw it on the floor and lie with my head unsupported.

There's not even one thing about my life Nan could relate to and it makes me laugh. I remember being a child and having to stay round Nan and Grandad's house when Mum and Dad went away on an awful 'romantic break' to Deal or something. I would be crying in bed missing Mum, saying I wouldn't go to sleep until I saw her, and Nan would say to me, 'Be happy and a reason will come along.'

I had no idea what it meant, but I usually stopped crying, probably because I was creeped out and confused. I don't know if she still believed that when she was sitting in the same armchair day after day, presumably just waiting for them to pass. It's a nice idea but who is happy for no reason?

I whisper, 'Goodnight, Nan,' and one tear falls down my face onto the bed but I bite down hard on to my cheek to make sure that's it.

6

It's announced that the train is too long for the upcoming platform, something I had forgotten and am not prepared for. I go through the automatic doors and speed down the aisle and jump onto the platform. People milling around the concourse seem to be starting their day even though – I glance at my watch – it's past eleven. Some of them are queuing to buy a latte or whatever, probably arrived here early so they could treat themselves at the beginning of their 'day out to London'. The highlight of their month. I consider getting a coffee from The Engine Room to fill me up so I won't have to eat for a while, but I bet they only take cash and I know they would use whole milk.

I arrive on the high street that counts as the 'town centre' and I wonder what people will think about the fact I'm not at work. If my desk was empty for a week would people just think I was in a meeting every time they walked past it? Or am I a noticeable absence?

Walking into the town everything looks so still, even the buildings look still. And grey. Dull metallics speckled throughout the architecture reveal the council's failed attempts to modernise the town. I pull my coat tighter around me. It's colder here.

I don't want to go straight to my parents' so I decide to browse some of the shops for a bit instead. Unfortunately, for a town centre it doesn't have much to offer. There are a few enclosed streets referring to themselves as 'shopping arcades' but inside only two of the buildings are shops. The rest are dark windows displaying empty rooms. Some of them carry the memory of what once was with the shops' name still up in a bad font. There are a few independent 'gift' shops still hanging on somehow, that seem to provide the locals with wooden signs that have encouraging slogans written on them like: 'Don't Just Exist: Live'.

I go back to the main high street and walk towards a small Tesco to buy an apple. Everyone looks so depressed. Or do they? I can't tell.

Back outside and it's not even 12 p.m. yet. Although it looks like 7 p.m. thanks to the ceiling of cloud protecting everyone from any light. Time feels different here and I'm looking for somewhere else to waste it, but all I can see are banks and a disproportionate amount of phone shops considering there isn't much of anything else.

I go to a bench in front of the old church. I used to sit here with my best friend from school, whilst she kissed boys and I pretended not to notice. I almost laugh out loud thinking about how naïve I was back then, but I don't. Fourteen-year-old me didn't even consider there was anything else in the world other than this high street and these people. I felt invisible. I felt inferior to everyone. These people walking around in front of me. Their clothes look thin to me now. I notice a few people carrying designer handbags, and I can't help but think it's a shame if they're real because the rest of their clothes make them look like fakes anyway: the pretend denim of their jeans and the plastic sheen to their shoes.

I'm bored and tired and cold now so I walk home through the back streets where there is no one and nothing but loud air vents and rubbish bins.

I walk down the long street of Victorian houses to my parents' one right near the end. It's funny to think how much more these would go for if they were in London. Although if I said that to Mum she would say, 'Why would you spend all that money on a house like this just to live somewhere scary and dirty?'

Before I can knock at the door my uncle Steven opens it with a huge smile. 'I saw you coming up the path, how are you doing, love?' His face drops to a concerned expression and he gives me a tight hug, which makes me feel sick. Not because he's creepy, just because I don't want a tight hug with any middle-aged man that I hardly know.

I pull away as soon as possible. 'I'm okay, Steven, how are you? Is Lynn here too?'

'Yes, yes, we're all here.' He leads me into the living room like this is his house.

Dad's younger brother, Peter, and his wife Carol are in there with my parents and Steven's wife, Lynn. Everyone smiles as we walk in and then their faces drop to earnest frowns. They all speak and stand up at the same time which stresses me out. 'Please, guys! Sit down, it's okay.'

Carol and Lynn both sit down, but my parents and Peter carry on towards me. Dad gives me a kiss on the cheek and goes to sit back down in what looks like a new, small leather armchair.

Peter puts his hands on my shoulders like he's pushing me away. 'Hello, Iris, I'm so glad you've arrived now. It's not felt right without you here.' He pulls me in for a hug. I can't tell if there's some judgement in his tone.

'Are Joe and Emma here?'

'No, Joe is in Australia, as he's been for two years now. He's doing really well out there. The standard of living is, well,' he looks around the room, 'you wouldn't come back here, let's put it that way.'

'Amazing. I'm so glad he's not here. . . Because he seems to be having such a good time there.' I smile, readying myself to see his face drop, 'And Emma? Surely she must be here for Nan's funeral?'

'She would have loved to be but she can't make it.'

I go to push him for an answer as to why but realise I don't care. Today is about Nan, not arguing with Peter.

Mum puts her arm around me. Some quiet awkward talking resumes in the room and then she whispers in my ear, 'Let's get you out of here.'

She pulls me into the kitchen and pops back out to put my bag by the stairs. I sit down at the table.

'Sorry, sweetheart, it's all a bit intense in there, isn't it? I thought you might prefer it in here whilst you settle in.'

'Thanks.'

She starts boiling the kettle. 'Tea, yes?'

'Yes, please. Should I ask them if they want one?'

'Oh no, they've all had some.'

I can tell she wants to say something but is waiting for an appropriate time. She pours the boiled water in a mug and then turns around. 'It's all a bit tense in there, isn't it?'

'Is it? Why, what's happened?'

'Well, your uncle Peter is already talking about selling Nan's house, and you can imagine how upsetting that would be to Dad. Before the funeral too. And I've noticed he's mentioned splitting everything three ways, but it's been Dad this whole time, looking after Nan, going to visit every week, I don't even remember the last time Peter paid towards anything she needed.' She looks angry and I'm getting the impression it isn't Dad who's upset about this.

31

I can't help but feel frustrated at how hypocritical she is. Always telling me that there's more to life than money. Telling me that I don't need 'fancy' clothes or 'rip-off' make-up or a 'flashy' job. Telling me that I should just be happy with what I've got. And yet she's here leering at Nan's money from the sidelines.

She goes back to finishing the tea. 'Anyway, sorry, love. How have you been?'

'I've been good. Work is going really well. Actually, I think I might get pro—'

'I hope you're doing more than working! You need to live your life, girl!' She says in a slightly American accent.

I've never heard this version of the 'having a career is not valuable' talk before and it takes me a little by surprise. I want to ask her if she thinks 'living life' means doing the exact same thing in the exact same place for your whole life, like her, but I can't be bothered to get into it. 'Don't worry, I'm living my life too.'

She hands me a mug. 'Good girl.'

The lightbulb in my room has gone so I have to traipse back downstairs to find a new one. I walk past the living room and hear hushed voices talking. It's weird to think of Peter and Carol lying on our medium-sized sofa cushions trying to sleep. I wonder if they're bitching about my parents.

I try to be quiet creeping around the kitchen, but I suddenly worry that Carol will come out to get a glass of water in a nightie or something and I can't imagine anything worse right now. So I clatter around opening miscellaneous drawers and cupboards. And I'm now worried Mum and Dad will come down to see what's going on.

In the medicine cupboard I find a bulb. I run back past the living room and notice how strange it is that they haven't fully closed the door. I go and clean my teeth. Looking around the light blue bathroom I remember what it was like to be in here every day as a teenager. I was embarrassed Mum and Dad left their shampoo and shower gel around the side of the bath, and so I bought them a storage caddy for Christmas. They're still using it now, which hurts my chest. It's rusting a bit. I wish I could throw it away.

I can't be bothered to replace the bulb anymore, and clearly neither could they, so I just take my clothes off and get straight into bed. The sheets are cold and slightly musty like they're symbolising how long I haven't been in them.

My 'one remaining grandparent' has gone.

Is it better to bleed your life dry or die when it's a tragedy that you no longer exist? I can't work out if anyone would think it's a tragedy if I died tomorrow. I mentally flick through everyone I know, trying to find a person who feels deeply about me. Yes, people might *think* nice things, but does anyone *feel* anything? It dawns on me that no one at work really knows me, let alone cares about me. And I haven't even managed to form any kind of relationship with the person I live with. The other night it seemed like there was potential for something, but then I accidentally let go for one moment and it drove us further apart. I turn over and try to think of something else instead, but my mind keeps returning to the thought until it shuts off.

7

Three taps at my door wakes me up from dreaming about having sex with Dylan on my desk. I remember reading somewhere that people often get horny after someone they know has died because an evolutionary instinct to procreate kicks in but I didn't realise it made you desperate.

Mum knocks again and opens the door slightly. 'Wake up, sweetheart, we want to have breakfast together before we set off.' Why does she always have to do that rather than just shout through it? Privacy is an all or nothing concept. But she'd happily cross any boundary, even a closed door.

'Okay.'

I get showered and put on a nice black dress that is tighter than I would like it to be for an occasion like this. But really it doesn't matter if I look awful. There's no one to impress here. I put my hair in a bun and forget about make-up.

Downstairs I am horrified to find Peter and Carol still in pyjamas sitting at the kitchen table, being served scrambled eggs on toast by a fully washed and dressed Mum.

'Good morning, Iris. Nice to see you,' says Peter in what sounds like a 'You're finally here, are you?' tone. Mum speaks before I can process this. 'Scrambled or fried?'

34

'None for me thanks.' I can't move fully into the kitchen because then I would have to go and sit at the table. 'Where are Dad and Steven?'

'You must eat, love, you can't be having a rumbling stomach at the church.'

'Have they left already?'

'At least have a banana. I don't know the next time we'll be eating.'

Peter is eating with his mouth slightly open and the noise is excruciating. I need to get out of here immediately. I grab a banana and say directly to Mum, 'Where's Dad?'

'Steven and him have gone to sort some of Nan's things out. Peter has kindly arranged a quick sale of her house.' She does a quick, fake smile.

'I'm going to finish getting ready. Can you call me when we're about to leave?'

'Yes.' She hands me an apple as well.

I go and sit on my bed and try to think about Nan. Unfortunately, I can't think of that many good times we've had together. She wasn't exactly the most loving grandparent. But to be fair to her, maybe she was all out of love. She'd married the first man she met, who, according to Dad, never once told Nan he loved her. She raised six children, who all left home as soon as they could, and by the time they were gone, Grandad had died and she was alone. Nearly twenty-five years she spent sitting around doing nothing but waiting for the next person to come and visit her. A whole life surrounded by people who didn't really care.

It's chilly so I get under the cover and curl up. Recently 'visiting' Nan seemed to entail going to sit opposite her in her little front room, telling her about what I'd been up to, asking anything except what she'd been up to. I bet nobody even really knew her. I struggle to think what the point of her life was. But I guess she might have thought the same of mine. Maybe we've both missed the point.

When she was younger she wasn't the warmest 'Here's the biscuit tin' kind of grandparent, but at least she could be a host of some sort, make us a Horlicks or whatever. I remember the last time I went round to her bungalow, Mum and Dad were having a hushed argument in the kitchen about whether 'it's time'. We both sat there a bit awkwardly because we could hear everything they were saying. She looked at me and said, 'Everyone I know is dying.' I just shrugged and said, 'Same here, I suppose.' She burst out laughing into almost a cackle and then winked at me. I don't think I ever made her laugh before or after that.

'Iris, we're going in a minute!'

I get up, straighten out my dress and start walking downstairs. But then I start crying, a lot. So I sit down on a stair and try and compose myself, pressing my palms hard into my face. I hear someone walking into the hall so I quickly stand up, wipe my face, and walk the rest of the way down.

Mum strides right over to put her arm around me. 'Oh, love, I know it's hard.'

'I'm fine, Mum.'

She looks at my face. 'Oh, you've been crying, sweetie.' She gives me a hug. Her hair smells of 'luxury' supermarket conditioner.

'No, I haven't. Is the car here?'

'Yes, you have. Look, you're all blotchy.' She touches my face and then reaches in her bag pulling out a crumby old face powder. She tries to dab my face and flatten my fly-away hairs. I feel suffocated.

'No, Mum. Can we just go?' Luckily Peter and Carol join us in the hallway.

'We're waiting for your dad.' Peter joins in, looking at his watch.

'He'll be just a minute,' says Mum, looking at hers.

I notice that Carol is nodding to everything anyone says. Peter looks at his watch again. I glance in the hall mirror and notice my legs look a bit stubby in these black ballet flats, but then ask myself why I care.

'Let's wait in the car.' Peter says to Mum. Carol nods.

I walk out the front door. The sky feels low and grey and it's been raining so the air smells like wet pavement. The smell is nostalgic somehow.

Steven, Lynn, and Dad pull up in another car. The hearse is waiting in the middle of the road. The driver is frowning, presumably because he thinks that's the best way to convey his condolences. He's actually reasonably young, maybe thirty. Would he feel ashamed if he thought I was attractive? *She's trying to grieve and all you can do is check her out.* I smile at him and he frowns back.

The journey is more awkward than sad.

Peter says, 'It's nice to all be together for once, even if it is for something so tragic.'

He likes to think he's 'gotten away' from here, unlike Steven and Dad, because he's moved ten miles away to a slightly bigger town. And yet all he's done is create the exact same life over there. No one replies. Mum keeps tucking her dry but perfectly neat blonde hair behind her ears and then untucking it. Carol smiles at me and I look away. When we pull up to the church Mum says, 'Beautiful church,' even though she's seen it a million times. Dad and Steven haven't said a word since they got here. I get out the car and it's drizzling again. It feels wrong seeing the few people huddled around in their cagoules and puffer coats like it's a school trip. Someone sheltering themself with an envelope that has 'To the Ellises' written on it. All of them making their way towards us to say something generic.

The funeral is long and upsetting, but not because I'm sad she's dead. The priest conducting the service is clearly reading a blanket eulogy, saying she lived a rich and full life, loved her family, and will finally be reunited with her husband.

My grandad was not a nice man, so I hope for her sake that she is not reunited with him. And unfortunately for Nan, she did not lead a rich and full life. She was born, lived, and died right here, and mostly her time was taken up with other people's problems. It isn't surprising she was never happy. If your whole identity stems from who you are in relation to other people you will never become a whole person yourself. One thing he's right about is that she was a faithful servant to the Lord. The sad irony though is that the priest clearly has no idea who she is, even after all her years coming here. Maybe she never really knew who she was herself.

Mum glares at me for not going up for communion. Dad, next to me, looks thinner and older than last time I saw him and I repeat in my head, 'Nothing matters.'

I make sure not to turn around until everyone's left so I don't have to see how empty the church is.

We drive to the cemetery, again in silence except for Carol saying, 'Beautiful ceremony.' I get a sharp pain in my chest when I realise no one spoke except for the priest. I look at Dad, face swollen and puffy, looking out his window like a sullen teenager.

The 'wake' is at a tiny village hall near our house. They probably wanted to cut costs so they don't have to dip into the inheritance.

Steven and Dad stick together which confuses me. All their life they've lived a few streets away, but I still only associate seeing Steven with national holidays and now they're best friends. Maybe grief makes you realise what you really have.

I busy myself in the tiny 'kitchen' making finger sandwiches out of the few tubs of pre-made fillings. My great uncle walks in so I quickly reach into my little bag and pull out my phone to pretend-answer it. I hold up a finger as if to say 'One minute' to him and walk outside. The sky has cleared into an oppressively boundless white and I have to squint. I see a young couple walking past, they're holding hands even though she's wearing mittens. I hope they look at me so I can do a blank stare instead of a smile but they don't. I want to crouch on the ground and wait in that exact position until I freeze over.

I look at my phone, with no expectations, but see a message from Sara: 'Ran into the boys who work in the post room. HIL. AR.IOUS. one of them said they always think that I'm beautiful. was so funny. I'll tell you all on Monday. ciao'

I type out, 'Oh cool, sounds so funny. my grandmother died. see you Monday', have a little laugh and then delete it. Then I delete her message too and walk back inside, straight into the kitchen and eat four egg mayo triangle sandwiches. The bread is white and so soft it sticks to the roof of my mouth. I feel even more hungry and eat three cheese and pickle ones. The pre-grated cheddar is rubbery and flavourless. I remind myself that even though I'm having all these sandwiches, I've still only eaten one and three-quarters of a normal sized sandwich. And I haven't eaten anything else yet today. So if you spread that out over breakfast and lunch I've actually still eaten way less than the average person.

Someone taps me on the shoulder and it's Steven with Dad.

'Why do you two seem so secretive?'

Steven replies, 'We need to speak to you,' in the kind of tone someone uses before they tell you they're dying. Are they both dying?

'Okay. . . why are you saying it like that?'

'It's about Nan's will.'

Is there really going to be a family rift over what to most people must be a very insubstantial amount of money?

'Your Nan wasn't a material woman, and there isn't a lot of wealth to spread around, so if we did, it would become meaningless amounts.'

Oh my god, they're cutting Peter out.

Steven adds, 'Well, that's your Nan's explanation anyhow.'

I can't wait any longer and turn back briefly to take another egg sandwich, which is hardening now around the edges because it's been sitting out so long. I take a bite and try to chew discreetly to be polite. Dad crosses his arms to communicate he's going to wait until I've finished to carry on. I moodily put the half-eaten sandwich back on the platter.

'We've got a few items to sort out between us, rings and things, but Nan wants you. . . wanted you to have the financial. . . estate.'

I feel my cheeks go red, even though I don't feel embarrassed. 'Wait, can you explain that in normal words?'

'She left you all the money,' Steven says a bit loudly.

'Me?' Is this going to be the family rift? I get thousands of pounds and they get a ring?

'Yes, sweetheart. You. I did think that we could hold on to that money for you until you fall in love and need a deposit for your own house! But since you're "of age", you're entitled to it, well, now.'

I look in both of their eyes for any bitterness, but I don't actually think I see any. 'Wow. Okay. Do you mind me asking, how much is it?'

'Of course not, it's your money! There was a lot of debt to settle but I think it will be just over £26,000, once the sale of the house goes through. Peter's organising it. I can't remember the exact amount off the top of my head.'

Steven gives me a big sad-eyed smile to show me there's complicated feelings involved.

I'm worried I look disappointed so quickly say something. 'Does Mum know?'

'Of course she does. We're all very pleased for you. Don't be feeling any guilt now. She made the right decision, give the youth a helping hand, us old dodders don't need it.'

I can't think of what to say so I just look down.

'Let us know about whether you want us to save it for you. It's hard to have that much money sitting in your account and not spend it all on dresses!'

'You don't think I'm someone who knows the value of money? I haven't asked you for a penny since I turned seventeen.'

'And we're very proud of you, sweetheart, I'm only pulling your leg.'

'I think I'll just put the money in my savings account.'

'As you wish.' He gives me what seems like a genuine smile.

We both walk back into the main room and I can tell by the way Peter nods at me that he doesn't know. I see Steven and Dad head over his way, and so I give him a massive smile back.

I walk over to Mum who's talking to Carol and looking bored. 'Hey, Mum.'

She looks thrilled to see me. 'Hi, sweetheart, how are you?'

'I'm feeling really drained.'

She puts her arm around my shoulders. 'I was just telling Carol about why you have to head back so soon. Because of your high-flying job as a journalist.'

'I'm not a journalist, I just work for a magazine.'

Carol nods.

'Mum, I'm feeling really tired. Might have to head back.'

'Of course, you must be very tired. You should head back, get some rest.'

I give her a heavy-eyed smile and Carol a nod, which is returned, and then quickly walk out.

At home I find a tub of peanut butter in the kitchen cupboard and have nine level teaspoons of it and then go to the living room. Carol and Peter's things are still here, which means they'll have to come back. Maybe I should go back to London now and say it was all too much for me.

I go into the kitchen and fumble around in the medicine cabinet and find some codeine Mum was prescribed for back pain but was too scared to take. I take two 30 mg tablets, have another couple of heaped teaspoons of peanut butter and go upstairs to bed.

I'm lying here, half-asleep, trying to feel something about the money. I close my eyes and picture moving into my own flat. All I've dreamed about for so long but now the dream is more of a picture. And the picture is of me sitting in an empty flat waiting for the evening to end so I can get back to work. I curl into a ball and try not to think of Nan. I wish I could hold her hand and say one nice thing to her. But I know it's easy to wish you could do a nice thing that isn't possible.

Maybe the least I can do is use the money to make a positive change to my life. Blow it all making real memories and deep human connections. I could go travelling, making new friends around the world, getting with boys who wear shark tooth necklaces. I try to think about Dad suggesting I should save the money for when I 'fall in love'. It's not been something that's appealed to me so far. I read somewhere that when you fall in love you gain seven pounds because all you do is watch TV and eat, but maybe people don't care about that stuff anymore because they're so happy being in love. I hear the front door open and let myself fall asleep properly.

8

I wake up at 6.45 a.m. feeling surprisingly refreshed and alert. But as soon as I remember where I am and why and what lies ahead with who, all positivity drains from me.

I go downstairs and stand in the kitchen and realise I'm hungry. I eat, in large handfuls, a packet of chocolate chips I find in the baking cupboard. They taste dry and powdery and turn out to be two years out of date. I'm retching over the sink when I hear someone plodding down the stairs.

Sure enough, Dad comes in, in his pyjamas, and starts making toast in silence, which I appreciate. I wave away his offering of toast and then Mum comes down, fully washed and dressed. Her hair blow-dried into the little blonde bob she's had as long as I can remember. She's wearing a pastel pink t-shirt, which is classic for her, but slightly tighter than she usually wears, it's a bit too long and it's pulled down over the top of her chinos which gives a very unflattering effect. 'Hello, love! Good morning to you.'

'Morning.'

'You go make yourself comfy in the front room and I'll bring us a nice cup of tea.'

Dad says, 'I'll put the kettle on.'

But Mum walks straight over to do it herself. 'You have to get dressed before you have your cup I'm afraid.'

He goes to kiss her but she turns so it lands on her cheek instead. I don't understand how she lords their perfect relationship over me as an example of a successful life and yet they've clearly just settled for each other. Two people who think finding someone vaguely nice is enough of a reason to spend a life together. I can't bear to watch this interaction continue so I walk out and go into the front room. I inspect the new leather armchair. A closer look and quick smell tells me it's not actually leather, just light brown with a subtle 'mottled' effect. I sit down. It's firm, high off the ground and seems like it would squeak if I moved the wrong way. I practically take up the whole seat which confuses me because I'm much smaller than both of them.

Mum walks in and hands me a mug of what smells like Earl Grey and then sits down on the sofa holding hers. I've never seen Earl Grey in our house before.

'We got a new armchair! Dad always wanted his own leather armchair, didn't he?'

I agree even though I've never heard that in my life. The armchair is in line with the sofa so we have to turn in our seats to face each other and it irritates me.

'So now all that's over, tell me.' She holds her mug with both hands wrapped around it, 'How is everything in London going?'

I don't understand why she is suddenly pretending to care. 'Yeah, good thank you.' I try hard to make it sound genuine but there was a curtness to it that I couldn't hide.

'Now, forgetting work, tell me all about what you've been getting up to?'

45

I take a tiny pause to work a natural looking smile on to my face. 'Just what anyone gets up to really.'

She doesn't say anything, just looks at me waiting, and I hate that I feel the need to carry on. 'Just, going out, doing things, with people.'

'Oh, yes? What people? I never hear you mention names. Sometimes I worry you don't know anyone all that well.'

I have no idea what her motivation is here. She usually hates speaking about my life in London. But I don't want her to think I've got no answer, so I say the first thing that comes into my head. 'I had dinner with my flatmate the other day. George.'

'Oh, lovely. I didn't know you were friends.' She sits back in the chair slightly and crosses her legs. 'So, tell me about this George. Where's he from?'

'Urm, I don't think we've spoken about that. . . or I mean, we probably have but I can't remember.'

Her expression looks on the cusp of concerned so I blurt out, 'He's a chef.'

'Ooo, how trendy. What kind of food is it he cooks?'

I feel my cheeks heat up. 'I think. . .' I look up as if I'm trying to remember, 'just a bit of everything really.'

She looks down and pushes her mouth to one side like she's considering something and I hate it. We speak at the same time.

'Who's your closest friend in Lon—'

'How have you been?' I ask it again to ensure my question wins.

'Oh, you know.' She looks wistfully up at the ceiling and sighs. I consider making a joke about how in fact I don't know, that's why I asked, but luckily her face flicks back to joy. 'There's a new ice-cream shop, right at the top of town, where all the little foreign supermarket type shops are. It's quite up-and-coming there.

A few cafés are opening. But yes, they do this lovely "gelato" type ice-cream. Loads of flavours, not just the normal ones. I know it's still a bit chilly out but I couldn't help myself. Last time I got hazelnut chocolate and, what was it. . . raspberry cheesecake! It was very tasty.'

I should be happy at her expanding interests but I just feel very uneasy inside. I try to match her enthusiasm. 'It sounds delicious!'

'You really have to go. It's the best ice-cream I've ever had! I tried to drag Dad there but no luck.' She rolls her eyes.

I sip my tea and struggle to swallow it. 'Who did you go with?'

'Oh, I just went on my own after work. It's on my walk home, that's how I saw it.'

The pain that's been growing in my chest is becoming harder to push down and I'm worried I'll keel over or drop my tea or burst out crying, so I do my best enthusiastic face and stand up. 'We should definitely go there sometime. I'm just gonna go pack.'

I start walking out and she follows behind me.

'Oh, are you going today then?'

I call out while I'm walking quickly up the stairs. 'I actually think I'm going to have to.'

'Well you can at least stay for lunch. Peter, Steven and co are coming over. It would look very rude to leave before that.'

By the time I get downstairs again it's completely quiet. I assume someone has gone out but as I reach the kitchen I see Mum and Dad sitting at the kitchen table chopping carrots and potatoes in silence. They don't see me so I watch them for a second.

Mum says something I can't quite hear and then Dad replies, 'He means well. I just think it came as a bit of a surprise to him, that's all. He'll get over it.'

She doesn't say anything, just presses her lips together and looks at the potatoes. I want to run back upstairs but my body is frozen.

Dad speaks again, 'What's the difference between in-laws and outlaws?'

Mum looks up at him but her face is blank and she doesn't speak.

'Outlaws are wanted!'

He laughs, shaking his head, as if someone else told him the joke and she looks down again.

I burst in before it falls back to silence. 'Good one, Dad.'

He beams back at me. 'Here you take over this and I'll pop to the shop for a nice bottle of red.'

Two minutes later I'm chopping the carrots and hoping to be granted the same silence but I'm not so lucky.

'You must be very glad. About the money.'

'Well I'm not glad. Someone died.'

'Yes, it's very sad, of course. But she would want you to be happy about it.'

'Well, I think she would want me to be sad that she died more.' I don't want to be snappy but I already know what's coming.

'I was simply thinking that you could use the money to put a deposit down on a house back here, which is pretty incredible for someone of your—'

'I don't want to live back here though? I want to live in London. So. . .'

Mum stops peeling for a second and her voice goes slightly whiney. 'But you've got family here. You've got no one in London.'

'Well, first of all, that's not true, I have friends in London.'

'Close friends?'

'And secondly I work in London. You can't do what I do here.'

'But life isn't all about work though, or am I wrong? Tell me if it's wrong to think that family can be enough for some people—'

'What is life about then? Making roasts for people you don't even like?'

'I'm not even going to dignify that with a response.'

'Good.'

She stands up to empty the potato peels and carrot ends into the bin and I try desperately to think of a subject change but I'm so riled up I can't bring myself to ask her anything.

As soon as she returns to the table she resumes the conversation in her original, calm voice. 'How does someone so busy, like you, go about finding a husband? And don't get angry. I'm asking out of interest!'

I have to close my eyes and take a breath in. ' "Find a husband"? What do you even mean? Where did I lose him?'

'Oh, very clever. I just wish you would take a second to think about your priorities before it's too late.'

'I *have* assessed my priorities. They're just not the same as yours.'

'You didn't used to be like this though, so focused on things like work.'

'That's because I didn't even know it was an option. You never encouraged me to do anything except be mediocre. You wanted me to aimlessly drift through life until I became you.'

'What are you talking about "encouraged you"? We've been supportive—'

'You never cared about what marks I got in school or took me to any clubs or got me music lessons or told me about university or—'

Mum raises her voice now, 'I've told you before. Music lessons

49

are expensive and not worth the investment unless you're exceptionally musically talented.'

I can't take it anymore and so push back my chair, stand up and shout, 'How could I be talented *before* I'd had any lessons?' Before she can reply I walk out, run upstairs, and slam my bedroom door. It's disconcerting how easily I've reverted back to being a teenager. I lie on my bed staring at the ceiling thinking, manically again and again, how grateful I am to live *my* perfect life in London.

When Peter, Lynn, Steven and Carol arrive I return downstairs and pretend to be normal. Ready to get this over with.

I have to clean the dust off the dining room table because it hasn't been used since Christmas and I can't help thinking how fake this all is. The façade is so strong that we have a whole room dedicated to pretending we're a close family.

It doesn't take long for Peter to bring up the inheritance. 'What will you do with all that money, eh? Night clubs and clothes?'

I reply in an equally fake-jovial tone, 'I don't know why everyone keeps saying I'm going to spend it on clothes! I only wear them as much as you guys.'

Everyone laughs.

Steven starts nervously shrugging before he speaks, 'She's got her whole life ahead of her Pete, she'll need it for plenty of things.'

Peter's eyebrows move comically high up his forehead. 'Yes, and some of us worked very hard to get the things we have. Did you know it's ten times harder to build a life for yourself if you move out of your hometown?'

Dad chips in as if Peter hasn't said that a thousand times before, 'That's interesting.'

I raise my eyebrows to match his. 'Ten times, is it? That's a nice round number. Do you have the reference for that statistic?'

Mum snaps, 'Iris, please. You're being rude.'

'I'm just saying, Steven and Dad have had to buy a house just like Peter did.'

Peter lets out a flat, 'Ha!' and leans back in his chair. 'Life is more complicated than just buying a house. Which is something that young, whiny *Guardian* readers don't seem to understand.'

'I don't want a house.'

Dad points to the plate with his knife, 'Lovely beef.'

Peter, ignoring him, looks at me. 'You don't want a house. Okay. Right. Do tell – where are you and your family going to live then?'

'My family? Who said I want a family?'

Mum's face and hands drop. 'For heaven's sake, stop saying things you don't mean to try and get some kind of reaction. Of course you want a family.'

'Not "of course". I don't know. I don't think that far ahead. All I want is to be happy, and I haven't worked out what will do that yet.' I regret the wording but luckily Carol speaks up.

'It's selfish not to have children. The pope said.'

I can't help but stare at her for a second. 'You think Steven and Lynn are selfish?'

I can see Lynn going red and I wonder if it would have been better to leave them out of it.

Steven looks at me and speaks quietly. 'That is not what she meant.'

'Okay, well, sorry, Steven. But regardless it isn't selfish. Surely it would be more selfish to bring a child into the world when you don't feel capable of doing the best for them?'

Mum looks down at her plate and cuts into her beef with force, muttering, 'I think that sounds sad and strange.'

I can't help muttering back, 'I think caring whether other people have children or not is sad and strange.'

Mum glares at me. Peter leans back in his chair and tilts his head to the side.

'So no house, no kids. What are you planning to spend the money on then? Rent?' He turns to Lynn laughing and rolling his eyes. She nervously laughs along.

'Can we stop talking about the money? Nan has only just died.' I realise I've shouted a bit. I feel very uneasy. Confused even. Like I could burst out laughing. Do we really not care that much when some people die? Nothing more than a lukewarm sadness? I'm struggling to feel anything towards this 'life-changing' money when it's come from someone not existing anymore. If anything it's beginning to disgust me. How easily they can reduce a human life down to a bunch of numbers. And yet Mum thinks I prioritise my shallow career over family. I finish my carrots and then excuse myself.

I go into my old room and lay face down on the unmade bed and sob. Then I get up and get ready to leave as quickly as possible.

Mum and Dad say goodbye to me by the front door. She uses her quiet, serious voice again. 'I'm sorry if I offended you earlier but it's only because I'm concerned about you.'

I feel bad for a second but then it dawns on me that she'd never be concerned about anything real I'm struggling with because she doesn't even know me. Then again, is there anyone who knows me?

'You don't need to be concerned about me, Mum. I'm fine. I'm good.'

'I'm just worried you're a little. . . lonely.'

'I'm not lonely. I'm surrounded by literally millions of people.'

'Well, that's not quite the same. . .'

Suddenly Dad blurts out, 'I'm worried I'll wind up a lonely old man.'

We both turn to him, taken aback. 'Why?'

'Because he might attack me!'

I want to laugh because I don't want him to feel deflated but it's like I've been winded. Mum just rolls her eyes and nudges him. I vow to never have a relationship like that, two people together for the sake of it. I can't understand how she thinks she's got her priorities right. Her life is hard to watch.

I have brief, awkward hugs with them each and then run to the station.

9

I've gone to the new brunch place in West Hampstead. Sunday is the perfect day for self-care. To be grateful, mindful, peaceful. I haven't been able to get rid of the dull ache in my stomach since I got back to London yesterday. But today will help. I take a deep breath in and try to exhale away the last few days. The waitress asks me if I'm waiting for anyone. It catches me off guard, like she's just said something spiteful, but I resettle myself by smiling and saying, 'No. I'm on my own.' I don't actually think she's being rude. She just doesn't realise how common it is for people to go out by themselves. I want to tell her that it's not sad to do this. I'm not sad. But I'm not here to justify myself, I'm here to relax.

I pick up the Sylvia Plath book I've been meaning to read. My eyes can't seem to focus on the words and I end up reading the same sentence four times. But I'm not sure what else to do whilst I wait for my food – going on my phone isn't part of the plan – so I pretend to read it instead. I make sure my facial expression is still flattering even when it's idle so that the waitress can see I'm pretty enough to be here with someone else if I wanted to.

My mind completely zones out and a plate put down in front of me makes me jump. The waitress has a pitying expression that I'm beginning to resent. I smile and put my book down to show her that this whole meal is structured and purposeful. Mashed avocado and sliced cherry tomatoes on dark rye bread with an aioli sauce. Seasoned with cracked black pepper, pink Himalayan salt, and chili flakes. If you make the description of the seasoning as long as the food then you can charge an extra £3, apparently. The plate is a bright cobalt blue, and with the green rectangle of toast, the small red tomatoes, and the smear of yellow sauce, it looks like a Miro. Time for a little bit of each thing on the plate. It is tasty – I can taste all the flavours. Like a Hollywood ending, everything comes together, predictably, perfectly. If I concentrate I can taste each component individually. I focus my attention on the textures. I chew for longer, becoming more aware of the physical process and bodily sensations. There is something to be said for making yourself present.

I know it's an oxymoron, but you do *feel* numbness. And I begin to feel it in my shoulders, moving down my arms, where it collects in the palms of my hands. I place the heavy cutlery to one side and look slowly around to see if anyone has noticed that I've stopped eating. Does being motionless attract attention? Tables of people enraptured in their conversations assure me that it doesn't. A girl takes a picture of the rest of her friends and I wonder if she is secretly upset not to be in it. I struggle to remember the last photo taken of me. But that's irrelevant to my scheduled relaxation so I return to the plate.

I don't want to freeze again, but I'm not confident I can swallow the food in my mouth. The avocado tastes stringy and images of hairballs keep flashing into my mind. I force the food down in a swallow that hurts. Then I start to focus on cutting up the food on my plate, slowly, into small pieces. The toast is so soft now it falls apart. The juice from a tomato sits congealed next to its skin.

Unfortunately, it seems, however present my body is, however attuned my taste buds are, however much I focus my thoughts — I'm struggling to experience this moment. I feel like I'm accessing it second hand. And then, as I look around the café, I notice it's not just the food that I'm removed from. I look at everyone sitting in their groups, at the modern art that punctuates the walls, at a tree through the window. It's all far away now. The air in here smells sweet and heavy. I realise there must be hundreds of sounds making up the flat drone in my ears. It's like a switch has been flipped and I'm suddenly witnessing this all from a different dimension. Observing it from the past or the future. My skin feels like it's vibrating and my mind feels a thousand miles away.

The numbness turns into a wave of irritation that settles in my clenched jaw. It's like these complete strangers know me as much as anyone else does. I think of my lonely Nan sitting on her own in that chair, is me sitting here any different?

I realise I'm holding my knife and fork static over the plate, like there has been some small glitch. The food has become an indistinguishable mush. I push it around trying to create another piece of abstract art, but I feel myself retch and so put the knife and fork down neatly together in the middle of the plate. I try to focus on the fact that I've basically skipped a meal, but I struggle to remember why that matters. Why this book or this place or this day matters.

I pay without looking the waitress in the eye and keep my gaze down as I leave. My brain is bubbling and my new shoes are rubbing the skin off my heels and I can't remember what the point of next week is. I power walk back home and as the bakeries and supermarkets and bars and coffee shops and Victorian houses blur in my periphery I wonder if I'm actually ninety years old and dying, and this is just my shallow life flashing before my eyes.

10

The next week goes slowly. I can barely eat and make excuses when people ask if I'm going to the pub. I keep hoping to bump into George, but we barely cross paths and when we do there isn't much conversation. I don't know what made him want to spend time with me a few weeks ago, but it clearly hasn't lasted. I want to claw it back. Try again. Be less weird. Feel the comfort of his soothing presence.

One night I see a card has been delivered for him. 'Don't open until 25 March.' My mind flashes with images, him at the pub with the eclectic set of friends he has over sometimes, probably people he's known for years, them chanting 'Happy Birthday' and him looking bashful and confident at the same time. My stomach drops. I hear Mum: 'I'm worried you're a little lonely.' I roll my eyes just thinking about it and then press my nails into my temples to get the thought out. I remind myself that I'm capable of getting anyone to like me and George isn't an exception. Regardless of what Mum thinks, having close relationships with people in London is not impossible. And soon George and I will no longer be two people who simply orbit each other. I quickly put the card back on the floor to pretend I haven't seen it.

After work I pop into this cool restaurant that everyone has been talking about. It does Spanish small plates, natural wine and Leche Leche coffee. Inside looks very edgy: exposed plaster walls, checkerboard tile flooring, industrial lighting. I buy a £30 voucher which turns out to be a hand-written note on the back of a train ticket. On the tube home I have to press my lips together to stop grinning. But by the time I'm in bed that night the smile has gone and I can't lie still. Why does George make me so nervous but in the strangest way? It's not nerves like a fluttering in my stomach, it's nerves like worrying what does he actually think of me? I want him to like me but not for the usual fleeting thrill. I'm just desperate for him to want to hang out with me. I try to think of what I can do to feel more confident in myself but all the usual things I do feel silly and pointless somehow. Does he care what I wear or what job I do or how many friends I have or how much money I earn or how talented I am? I don't think so. But then what does he care about?

Friday comes around unbearably slowly but also way too fast. I've curled my hair, brushed it out, and curled it again. But in the end it looks weird to me so I put it in a ponytail and try on different smiles in the mirror. I hear George come through the door and my heart tightens. I make myself count to ninety and then walk into the kitchen, but he's not in there. I turn around to walk back to my room but now he's standing in the doorway.

'Nice hair.'

I quickly run my hands through my ponytail to disperse the curls. 'Oh, I was bored.'

'Can't picture you being bored,' he says with a sceptical smile.

'You picture me wrong then.' I move to the side to let him in, but he stays there. I try to sound casual but my voice just sounds high, 'What are you up to tonight?'

He folds his arms proudly. 'It's my birthday tomorrow.'

'Oh, no way. That's perfect.'

'Thanks very much. I like it too. Not too hot, not too cold.'

'No, sorry. I mean it's perfect timing. I have this voucher for a restaurant that I just remembered I need to use up today. It looks good. Do you fancy it?'

He raises his eyebrows. 'Do you really think I don't have plans on my birthday eve?'

I try not to look gutted and say my prepared answer. 'Oh, yeah of course, don't worry, I was gonna text my friend anyway.' I turn to walk back into the kitchen as he's still blocking the doorway, but he carries on speaking.

'I don't.'

I turn back. 'What?'

'I don't. . . have plans.'

I laugh, a release. 'Cool.'

He looks at my face like he's trying to work something out and then says, 'Right now?'

'I mean, if you're up for it.' I can feel my heart beat.

He says, 'I'll go get my glad rags on then,' and walks out.

I pop back to my room. My stomach hurts with nerves. I whisper into the mirror the reasons I want to do this.

It will establish us as proper friends.

1. I can show him I'm not weird.
2. I like him.

I shake my head. No, that's wrong.

1. I want *him* to like *me*.

I decide to change my top to a silky shirt and keep it unbuttoned quite low but do up my jacket so he won't notice straight away.

When we meet at the door it feels a little awkward, so I find myself filling the silence saying, 'You look very dapper,' which he does. Even though he's just wearing a white t-shirt and navy collared jacket, he looks better than other people in a way you can't quite identify. Like a celebrity. Fresher, cleaner somehow. Standing this close together I can feel how tall he is. I wonder if he likes it, me looking up at him. I try to do a kind of feminine innocent eyes but I feel silly and quickly change expression. He doesn't look at what I'm wearing or compliment me, but gestures for me to open the door. I feel a little disappointed and wonder if I should have left the jacket open.

Everything is as relaxed as things can be when you're outside with someone you've never been outside with before. But when we get to the restaurant, I can already tell from fifty metres away it's going to be full. People are clustered around the door holding drinks and there's a warm glow from inside that radiates energy onto the cold street.

When we open the door the woman says, 'It's a two hour wait,' without looking up.

I notice it's the same woman who sold me the voucher and panic. I turn away and say, 'Oh okay, thank you anyway.'

George just turns to me and tells me to hold on. I quickly try to think of what I could say if she tells him the truth.

'She's got a voucher that runs out today,' George says to the woman. Instinct takes over and I quickly turn to him, 'No it doesn't run out, I just needed to use it today. Because I'm seeing the person who gave it to me tomorrow and I wanted to tell them how it was.'

She looks frustrated and I can't get a read on whether she recognises me or not. I keep thinking, *No, surely not*, but then I instantly think, *Well, you recognise her so. . .* It takes a lot of effort for me not to crouch on the ground and put my head in my hands.

George smiles at me and turns back to her. 'She needs to use it today because she's seeing the person who gave it to her tomorrow and she wants to tell them how it was. Anything you can do?'

I can't take it anymore. I let out a nervous laugh, give the woman a quick sheepish 'Honestly don't worry', and walk out. It feels like I'm destined to look like a loser in front of him.

Outside I can't look at him. My mind is frazzled and I'm desperately trying to think of what to do now instead of imagining worst-case scenarios. But it's not working and it dawns on me that this was probably the last chance I had to convince him I was normal and fun.

'So, what's the plan, man?' His cheerful energy unfaltering as ever.

I glance up and down the street, looking at a completely dead steak house and an overly bright sushi restaurant and wonder what the journey home will be like. 'I didn't really have a backup plan so, yeah. Do you want to just go another time?'

'Let's try there.' He points to a worn-down looking restaurant that I didn't even notice. 'Delrio's.' I look at his face and try to work out if he's joking without him realising.

'I'm not joking. Come on.'

Inside about half of the tables are full, but the clientele is middle-aged couples, and they don't look like they're going to the theatre.

I can't work out what their lives are, why they're here, who they are. An Italian waiter, or owner, it's hard to tell because of his enthusiasm, leads us to a table in the middle of the room. It's quite dark, but not atmospheric and the menus are plastic. It's the opposite of what I wanted. I whisper to George, 'We can just go somewhere else if you want?' But the waiter returns with a pad.

'Can I bring you some drinks please?'

I quickly say, 'Just tap water for now.'

But George adds, 'And a bottle of house red, please.'

'Very good, sir.' The waiter walks away, and I look at George shocked.

'Don't worry. I'll get this.'

'Don't be silly. It's my treat of course. I just thought,' I try to find a light-hearted way to tell the truth, 'maybe you'd wanna try and find somewhere else? It's got to be hard to impress a chef and I'm not sure this place is gonna do it.'

'What makes you think that?'

'Well, it's just the tablecloths are clipped—'

'Here we are, sir.'

The waiter comes back over with the wine and then hangs around one or two metres away. George gets stuck into the menu and so I try to come to terms with the fact we're eating here. I remind myself that I can order anything on the menu because I've only eaten an apple today for the exact purpose of being able to relax about how much I eat here. I can suddenly feel how empty my stomach is and it's about to rumble so I pull it in as hard as I can to try to stop the noise. George doesn't say anything if he heard. Luckily the waiter strides over and asks if we're ready. I choose the least heavy thing on the menu, baked seabream, and George orders the steak and the spaghetti, adding, 'She'll have the ragu too.'

'What are you doing?' I ask when the waiter's gone.

'It's Italian. You have a "primi" and then "secondi". They split the main into two. Geniuses.'

I take my ponytail out to distract from the deep breath I have to take, thinking about all the calories. I use the opportunity to ask questions about him, just like I'd planned to.

'Go on then, how did you become so knowledgeable about food?'

'By being a chef.'

I raise my eyebrow. 'Okay, wise-guy, why did you become a chef?'

'Well, I suppose, when my dad left, it was just me, my mum, and my little sisters. And so one way I felt I could help was by cooking.'

'Oh, I'm sorry. That's a really nice reason though.'

'No need to be sorry. They're back together now anyway.'

'Wow, every child's dream.'

'I mean, they broke up when I was born, got back together, had my sisters, broke up again and then got back together *again* when I left home. So I mainly grew up with them apart.'

'Do you wish they'd stayed together the whole time?'

'Nah, I liked living with my mum and sisters. And I'm getting closer with my dad now.'

'Do you see them a lot then?'

'Not loads. I go back and go to church with them sometimes. None of us kids are religious, but Mum and Dad are, so it's nice for them.' He gets out his phone from his pocket and pulls up a picture of them. A tall, bald, serious-looking man with his arm around a tiny, ginger woman with a manic smile.

'Aw cute, did they meet at church then?'

'Yeah, he was in the choir and she joined it because she thought he was cute. They got married a month later if you can imagine that.' I do imagine it and I feel surprisingly jealous.

Our primi dishes arrive and I try to stay silent until he says what he thinks about the ragu.

'Wow, now if that doesn't melt in your mouth then. . .'

'Then what?'

He lowers his fork and thinks for a second. 'Then nothing. . . I was hoping you wouldn't call me out on that.'

I try to twirl the spaghetti around my fork carefully but it somehow flicks everywhere and all over my shirt. My heart drops. I know it's a stupid thing but it feels huge. I can't have one non-embarrassing interaction with him. I muster a little laugh to show I'm a chilled-out person and start to dab it away.

'Oh well. . .'

He shrugs. 'Good idea. Save some for later.'

I actually laugh for real then. He breaks into a wide smile.

The waiter comes over to collect our plates and drop off our next ones.

'How was everything, sir?'

George looks over to me, so the waiter turns and looks too.

'Really lovely thanks,' I say quickly before he looks at my half full plate.

'How about your parents?' George asks once the waiter's gone.

I take the opportunity to cut my food up so it looks like I've eaten it whilst I tell the pathetically boring story of them meeting at school, and then again years later at a friend's wedding. Settling down together less than a mile away from where they grew up. Suddenly a couple at the next table start shouting at each other in French. They stop when they notice us staring at them.

George smiles. '*Bonjour.*'

They burst out laughing and ask what sounds like a question in French. George replies instantly, '*Pardon, je ne parle pas français.*'

I whisper to him, 'Do you speak French?'

He looks at me. 'Clearly you don't.'

'*Ich spreche ein bisschen Deutsch.*' I offer.

The French couple laugh again and go back to chatting with each other amicably.

When the waiter comes over to take our plates George confirms we would like to see the dessert menu.

'Do you like desserts?' he asks me once we're holding the menus.

'Depends if they like me.'

He does an awkward smile and leans forward saying, 'I've heard them say you can be slightly bitter if not properly cooked.'

'Well, maybe they just need a more refined palate.'

'I'll be the judge of that.'

I want to carry on the light-hearted chat I came here for but can't help looking nervously at the menu. I feel stuffed with pasta, fish and wine but I want him to think I'm naturally this thin, not one of these girls who can't enjoy their food, so I say, 'Can we share one?'

'Sure, which one do you like the look of?'

'Ooo, I dunno, the lemon tart?' But I remember fruit desserts tend to have more sugar in them than chocolate ones. 'Or the tiramisu?'

'Have you had affogato before?'

'No. What is it?' I wonder if he likes teaching me things, like most men.

The waiter comes back over with his little pad. He looks at George, but then turns quickly to me. 'What can I get for you?'

'Oh, he's choosing.'

The waiter lets out a little laugh and turns back to George.

'Can we have one of each please?'

I look straight at George, confused, beginning to laugh, but he just looks at the waiter with a pleasant but serious expression. He swivels straight back at me to confirm George isn't joking.

But before I can reply, George hands him the menu. 'Two spoons is fine.'

The waiter laughs again, although seems a bit flustered as he leaves. 'As you wish.'

'Okay, so what was that?'

He chuckles. 'I've always wanted to do that. Don't worry, I'll pay for them.'

'I'm hardly going to be able to eat any of them.'

The waiter brings out the desserts on a huge black tray and tries to find room for them on our table whilst me and George start moving the salt and pepper and side plates and the vase of small plastic flowers to the edges of the table, trying to stay serious.

When he leaves we look at the table and George bursts out laughing. He can't stop and it's making me laugh too until my eyes are watering.

He quickly pulls himself together. 'Looks good to be fair.'

'Looks like it's for a party of twenty.'

I try to have tiny bites of everything, but looking at all the sugary, creamy, stodgy food I tense up wondering how much I'll have to eat. Luckily George leans over to the French couple. 'Would you like to join us?'

They look at our table and laugh too. '*Avoir les yeaux plus gros que le ventre.*'

George nods and gestures for them to move their table close to ours.

Half an hour later I realise that all you need to have a conversation with people who don't speak your language is two bottles of wine. George has them constantly in stitches with his GCSE French, and they show us beautiful photos of Provence on their phones. Eventually we work out that they are telling us to come visit them, the man gives George his business card and they leave. I feel like I haven't taken a deep breath in hours and my face hurts from smiling.

When I come back from the toilet, George has already paid for everything.

'Oh no, I wanted to pay! I dragged you out and it's your birthday.'

'I'm sorry, but you didn't realise what an indulgent date I was going to be, so it's only fair.'

The word 'date' trips me up for a second but he doesn't seem embarrassed. He just looks me in the eyes and says, 'You get the desserts next time.'

'All right, it's a deal. I'll start applying for loans tomorrow.'

He laughs and I want to enjoy the positive end of the night but instead I feel unsatisfied. It seems like this awkward version of myself is becoming set in stone. Yes, I want our relationship to grow but I don't want him to build a connection with this person who I'm embarrassed to be. But I push the concern away for now and try to enjoy the warmth in my cheeks instead.

On the way home we draft out loud an email to the French couple detailing our dessert requirements. I list every single dessert I can think of until I start to run out and have to come up with increasingly more random ones. 'That cornflake tart thing you sometimes got at school and urm, a couple of those '90s box-cupcakes with paper pictures on them? And urm, Nesquik straws? Is that still a thing?' We're drunk enough that this is hilarious to us. George doesn't stop saying, 'ahh, oui' to everything. The joke goes through funny, to not funny anymore, to even funnier.

As we walk up to our building, I realise how desperate I am for the night to carry on. For us to be coming back to some kind of home that we share together. But I realise that was a silly thought, this is just somewhere I live. Surrounded by millions of people but completely alone. The thought of returning to my empty room for an empty weekend makes my breathing become shallow.

In bed I curl up as small as possible. Work looms in the distance. I struggle to picture it, being there, talking to all those people. Why does the idea of being myself seem so exhausting these days? Is it because I'm not myself anymore? I don't even know what that means.

I calm down thinking about how I'm only going to have fruits, vegetables, and black coffee tomorrow.

11

Everyone is talking except me.

'Sometimes I look at the person I'm speaking to and I think, what would it be like to kiss you.'

'Yeah, I get that!'

'No, but really, anyone, like even today this old male client with like, a five o'clock shadow and a wedding ring and I'm just sitting there thinking about kissing him.'

'As in like, what it would be like to kiss him, or like, what would happen if you kissed him?'

'That is so funny.'

'Does anyone want another one?'

'I guess it's more like, I'm just thinking, "what would it be like to kiss you right now. Like, what would that be *like*".'

'Yeah, but I mean, are you talking about the actual feeling or like the consequence?'

Someone taps me on my shoulder but as I turn round no one's there. I look the other way and this guy Alex from Finance is walking past me.

'You on a wild one tonight, Iris?' He winks at me and walks off. I barely know him and try to think why he might have said that but Sara comes back outside with some slimline vodka tonics, even though she knows I hate them, and jabs me in the waist with her elbow. She leans in closer.

'Alfie just texted me and said he's having people round his tonight. We can ditch everyone here later and go to Clapham.'

'Alfie?'

She still smells strongly of perfume at the end of the day because she can afford 'parfum' rather than 'eau de toilette'.

'You know Alfie. . . We've been to his before.'

I can't manage an expression. She looks a bit exasperated and leans in closer. 'He fingered you in his bathroom last month, babe.'

I want to say, 'Yes, of course I remember, Sara. The whole time I was thinking about you and the person who I actually liked. The person you knew I liked. And what you two were doing. And why he chose you. And why you would do that to me. And so, I was not thinking about "Alfie".' But I don't. I just look down at the cobblestones and wonder if they're hundreds of years old or if the pub put them down. She follows my gaze. 'Don't worry, I've got you.' She reaches into her bag and pulls out a mini tub of expensive looking moisturiser and hands it to me. I look at her confused.

'It's really common to have dry legs, don't worry about it.'

I stare at the tub and nearly burst out laughing but not because anything's funny.

'Thank you.' I start walking my body into the pub and Sara calls out, 'Get us another round!'

The colder, damp air of indoors makes a shiver run through me. I put my full drink down on an empty table and walk straight to the bathroom. One cubicle with a little gold lock that barely works. I sit on the toilet and look at my legs. Not dry. Smooth and moisturised. I feel a sting of disappointment. An unexpected part of me hoped they were dry, wanted this to be an act of kindness, but I shouldn't be surprised. I try to pull myself together. *This is just our dynamic and you've never struggled with it before.* I open the pot and dig my fingers into the expensive cream, take out a big scoop and wipe it on some toilet paper and throw it in the bin. I finish up, wash my hands and look in the mirror. My eyes look bigger and my nose looks smaller when I tilt my head slightly down and I remind myself I'd resolved to do this more.

But as I join the horizontal bar queue I get distracted picturing myself sitting on the ground in the corner of the room. Refusing to speak if anyone came over to check that I was okay. How I'd just sit and sit and sit until everyone left and I was locked inside here alone.

A man leans towards me from behind the bar to indicate it's my time to order. 'I'll have two gin and tonics please. One with slimline tonic, one with normal.'

Sara is standing at the other end of the group now. Fine gold chains dance around her collarbone as she speaks. As usual, she's only wearing black and white, and thanks to a warm spring day she's chosen a white off-the-shoulder top and a black smart skirt. Black leather flat shoes don't even make her legs look stumpy. I remind myself only boring things can be timeless and stride over to hand her a drink. But at the last minute I change my mind and decide to give her the slimline one. I feel relief in my chest. Mum asked about who my closest friend was and I guess the only possible answer is Sara. I haven't admitted it to myself because I feel embarrassed at the thought. We're not close. In fact I think we're purposefully distant from each other. Restrained and transactional.

'Thanks, babes.'

'You're welcome.'

I quickly hand back her moisturiser and walk over to the people I was with before.

'Hey, Iris, you going *out* out tonight?'

'Ha, yeah maybe.' I bury my gaze in my drink so no one will ask me anything else. Luckily, the copywriters are happy enough to fill the space with themselves.

'Yeah. . . so, anyway you were telling me about your multi-media play?'

'Yeah, yeah that's right. I haven't been working on it for very long, but it's something I've been meaning to get on for a while. So, it feels a long time coming. It feels like it's been in the works for a long time.'

'How do you even go about setting something like that up? I can barely organise my own dinner.'

'Yeah so, I mean, it's my job, isn't it? That's what I do. When you love something you just know how to do it. I guess that's why artists call their work their "babies", like "Oh, this is my child", y'know, like when people say that it's because they just knew exactly what to do, like when you have a baby. It's like an instinct in you.'

My eyes drift back and forth between them and I have to press my lips together to hide a smile. It's hilarious to me, the characters people pretend to be. I can't bring myself to play along with it. But the trouble with this keeping quiet strategy is it makes me drink more quickly, and so a few minutes later I'm stirring a bunch of ice around with my straw. I can't work out why I feel so different than usual but it's almost like I'm watching the scene suspended above myself. Like I've lost my instinct to navigate situations and can't remember why I should care about any of this.

I wonder if I should go and get another drink, but I force myself to run through some alternative options in my head. I could go home now, and then I would be able to get up early and start a new hobby or something. Running or learning a language. But the thought is ridiculous. Do I really care about any of that? I wonder if I could hang out with George instead. But we haven't really spoken much since the meal. Which doesn't surprise me because I'm always a mess around him. All I know is that I'd significantly rather be sitting next to him in silence than be standing here in silence. I don't understand what's different about George than these people but I feel it in my throbbing temples. When I'm with him I feel attached, anchored to the world. But right now I feel like I'm floating away and nobody is noticing.

I walk away from the group, back towards Sara, without saying anything, but I doubt they even notice. I stop. Watching her, shimmering with vitality, I realise I'd feel more alone staying here with her than being on my own. I think I might carry on walking, all the way to the station, holding my glass, looking down at the pavement, but I don't.

I stand at the edge, where the cobbles meet the smooth pavement, looking at everyone. Standing, drinking, talking. Because that's what they want to do? Because that's what they think they should do? Because what else are they going to do? Are they really saying anything though? Or are they just regurgitating their personalised scripts? Playing their part. Again, and again, and again.

What would happen if everyone just said what they were thinking? I can see it all going on, behind their flickering eyes. A flash of thought about the food they have waiting at home. A look of desire for someone. A momentary daydream for another life, with better friends. A memory of the night before, touching someone's naked chest in bed. A sudden feeling of pointlessness and relief as they remember that we're all going to be dead one day.

I feel a pinch on my shoulders and gasp.

I turn around and it's Alex from Finance again, with his tight check trousers, loafers, and wide stance. I don't know why he's talking to me. 'Woah. You all right over here?'

'Yeah. Sorry. I'm fine, you just scared me.'

'What are you doing over here on your own?'

'Oh, I was just waiting for someone but—'

'You look good today, Iris.'

'Oh, thanks. I think I just look the same as—'

'Let's go get a cheeky drink someplace else, eh?'

I wait for the voice in my head to guide me but it's gone. I take it as a sign to leave. 'Actually, I'm probably going to head off soon.' I flash a polite smile trying to end the conversation.

'You haven't finished your drink. . .'

I look down at my warm, flat drink. 'Oh, I don't really want this,' I say with a complete lack of conviction because how can I decide what to do when I don't want to do anything?

'Don't be like that, Iris. Drink up!' He clinks my glass. I do what he tells me.

As Alex grabs my thigh in the taxi, I feel far away. I can't remember who I'm supposed to be. But it's okay because it's not really me sitting here. It's a girl I'm watching from the safety of behind a translucent screen and by the look of it she doesn't have to say or do anything because she's not the one in control.

I lie on the floor naked and think, that was fun, sex is fun. I'm trying to stay present. I'm telling myself to think positive thoughts and concentrate on the good things. List things that I like about the situation. But I realise I'm not actually doing that. I'm just thinking that I should think positive things, and then thinking about why I should think about positive things. Instead I force myself to smile. It feels like it looks weird and I'm worried Alex might notice and get freaked out, but he just says, 'That was good eh?'

I think about looking him directly in the eye and saying 'No' which makes my smile relax into a real one.

My heart flutters uncomfortably in my chest. I wonder why this felt so different to Ish. It's not like I preferred him. I don't like either of them. And yet with Ish there was a certain buzz, whereas right now I feel sick and sticky and stupid. I watch Alex pulling on his boxers and scratching his armpit and suddenly see the difference. I didn't choose him and I'm not even sure if he chose me. Does he even like anything about me or was I just there? I don't really care what Alex thinks about me and yet, I can't help but feel a gnawing hollowness. How was I supposed to enjoy something that I didn't even feel a part of?

I wait until he goes to the bathroom, then throw my dress on and sneak out trying to squint my eyes so as not to see his belongings. The thought of knowing anything about who he is repulses me. The less I know the less I can regret.

The early morning April air is shockingly colder than last night. I rub my arms to warm up but then realise I don't care. In fact I feel grateful for the pain of the wind slapping my face, shocking me out of the mental hole I feel myself spiralling into.

Inside the warmth of the tube my eyelids grow heavy and I think of George. I feel desperate to see the little smile that reluctantly appears on his face when he says something funny. I wish he liked me more. I wish he seemed to have the pull towards me that I do towards him. But maybe it's a nice thing that there aren't unspoken motives and desires behind our interactions. I would rather be friends than have a short-lived fling with him. I try to focus on that but the thought of Alex's hands on my body pushes its way into my mind and my gut.

12

Saturday passes with little movement. I have skipped two meals now so that means I can eat whatever I want for the third one. I don't eat anything for the third one though.

On Sunday I wake up early and shower immediately. This day will not be wasted. But, after my routine, I sit on the edge of my bed and it feels like I know something desperately bad that no one else knows, I just don't know what. I'm not sure I will be able to move. But of course I can move. I get up and light my candle. I look at the label. 'Refreshes and invigorates'. I hold my hand over the flame until I think it will cause a blister. A knock on my door makes me jump.

'It's George.'

I freeze for a second but then speak without opening the door, 'I should hope so.' I stand there clutching the wrist of my throbbing hand. Waiting.

'Well. . .?'

'Well what?'

'I'm going south of the river today.'

I open my door. 'Very impressive.'

'What are you doing?'

I try to seem distant. Restore any semblance of mystery. 'I haven't decided yet.'

'Do you want to come?'

I try to swallow my smile. 'What are you doing "south of the river"?'

'Going to get a hoover.'

'We have a hoover.'

'Going to get a better hoover.'

He has his hands pushed into the pockets of his black zip-up hoodie. He looks good. He's that kind of attractive where anyone could fancy him no matter what their type is. But that's not why I feel like the day has opened up brightly in front of me.

'I'm not sure. I was supposed to see some friends.'

'You said you hadn't decided yet?'

'I haven't.'

'So decide to come with me.'

I've started to notice he always itches his cheekbone when he's being forward. There's something so charming about him. I don't know how far to push the 'I have other options' thing without him walking away because it's almost impossible to gauge his incentives. It doesn't matter though because he speaks again.

'I thought we could do something else too. Not just the hoover thing.' He shrugs as if to say, the choice is yours.

'And what did you want to do?' I say folding my arms and leaning on the door frame. I don't know what it is but whenever I try to act aloof around him I end up behaving like a corny sitcom character.

He gets his phone out of his jeans and starts typing on it. I leave him to type and go get my bag and coat. Glancing in the mirror I'm glad I wore a short skirt and black sheer tights. Today I will be my best self. No crying or spilling food, just composed and alluring.

He looks up, 'Tate Modern?'

I'm already standing in front of him ready to go.

As we walk into the Tate I say, 'Do you even like art?'

'There's that weird painting of waves in our hallway.'

'Yeah, so do you like that?'

'It really brings what you could call a *je ne sais quoi* to the space,' he says very seriously but clearly joking.

I act normal, encouraging him to continue this character. 'It's not a painting of waves though. . . It's of clouds, in the sky. And it's a photo?'

He shakes his head in a mockingly condescending way. 'No, you see, that's what an amateur would think. In the art world there isn't such a thing as "paintings" or "photos". It's simply either "art" or "something that Banksy did". Let's get you more acquainted with the medium, shall we?'

I see him checking whether I'm laughing, which I am. I feel myself start to thaw. Suddenly it dawns on me that he's asked me here on a date and I feel a warm glow wash over me. I hadn't let myself hope for it but now it's happened I realise how desperate I was for it. But then I catch myself, is it a date or is it genuinely a trip to get a hoover?

It's quite busy and I start mindlessly ambling around the room, painting by painting, as I have done in every art gallery I've ever been to. Whenever I get to a new one George joins me and stands very close to it, thumb and forefinger resting on his chin, nodding. It's so silly I try not to laugh, but I can't help it. I walk towards a new painting so I can glance behind to see if he's looking at my legs but see that he's not. He barely even looks at me. I can tell he's just excited to do the exact same nodding thing. I feel frustrated and assume his type must be vastly different to me.

In another, emptier, room, he asks me to take a photo of him with a canvas that is entirely blue. I raise my eyebrow, but I like the idea of having a photo of him on my phone, so I get it out. He stands in front of it and points with both hands, looking directly at the camera with a subtle smile. I take the photo and can't help laughing sensing the people around us looking amused by the situation. He thanks me and we move on to the next painting. After a second he taps me on the shoulder and quietly in my ear says, 'Would you mind taking a photo of me with this painting?' It's a plain olive-green canvas.

'Of course,' I say and step back trying to keep a serious expression. This time he holds his hands out flat, to make it look like he's supporting the painting.

'I've got it. Perfect,' I say, crouching down and taking a photo where his hands are completely covering the centre of the picture instead. He does the same forced smile a tourist might do. We both laugh looking at the photo, and his expression is the most illuminated I've seen it. I say I want to get it framed but all of this has been increasingly loud in this very quiet room, and I notice the employee standing by the door looking at us disapprovingly. I feel embarrassed and pull him out of the room, enjoying the excuse to touch him. He tells me I should get a photo too, but I coyly refuse whilst simultaneously trying to remember which is my good side for when he insists. But he doesn't insist and I hate that I always misread him. I almost always get it wrong. His face drops and he shrugs and says we should probably head off. I realise this must mean he doesn't want a photo of me on his phone.

As we're walking out I say, 'Actually, I would like a photo,' and make him take one of me admiring a radiator like it was art, and then another one standing on the stairs holding on to the banister like I'm coming downstairs ready for prom. After each one he stands looking at the photo laughing with comedic approval and it feels better than any compliment ever has.

Outside my face tingles from laughing. He starts leading us to Blackfriars Station.

'I thought we were coming here to get a hoover?'

'Yeah, but I checked in the Tate gift shop and they said they'd run out.'

He tells me his cousin who lives in Croydon has a spare one. I ask him why we need a new one. He says I would know the answer to that if I ever hoovered. I want to tell him I hoover my room every Sunday and have never noticed a problem with it but feel guilty for not doing the whole flat. So instead I ask him whether this is a ploy to spend time with me or if he actually just wanted help carrying a hoover. He asks me to show him my biceps. I tense one and he studies it and then says it was just a ploy to spend time with me.

On the train I realise I enjoy sitting next to him because it's the closest we ever get. He smells clean, but plain like a bar of soap rather than shower gel. I look at both his hands drumming on his legs and wish I could reach out and hold one. Or that he would touch me in some way, but I know he won't and he doesn't.

We eventually arrive at a semi-detached '70s style house with pebbledash walls. His cousin, Eddy, opens the door and enthusiastically greets us with big hugs. He's ten years older than George and married with four children. Inside the house is clean but everything looks a bit old and run down. A couple of the kids practically sprint over to George and hug his legs. He crouches down and asks them various questions, making fun of them a little. Each time he does they screech with delight. I feel lucky to know someone who can make people happy so effortlessly.

Eventually Eddy leads us into the kitchen and makes us a plastic cup of squash and gives us a packet of iced gems each. Me and George glance at each other smiling. Eddy asks me so many questions about myself I barely have the space to ask him any back and worry I'm coming across as rude.

He asks questions like, 'You do a lot of vacuuming then, George?' and George just shrugs and says, 'It's how I like to wind down,' in such a serious tone that his cousin takes it at face value. I can tell George is trying to make me laugh so I force myself to say something he might find funny too, 'Yeah, George really struggles unless he can get a couple of hours in every evening. I've seen him spill a packet of rice on purpose when he thought I wasn't looking.' I do a concerned shrug.

Eddy looks at me and then back at George replying, 'Whatever floats your boat, man.'

George puts at least five iced gems in his mouth at the same time and Eddy tells him to take it easy. George points at me and says in a muffled voice, 'She doesn't let me have sugar.'

Eddy's eyes get wide, seemingly taking everything seriously, and he says he's not going to get involved.

I look at George and try not to laugh when I say, 'You know why. We've discussed this.'

'Remind me one more time?' He leans back in his chair, testing me almost.

'Because one granule always leads to a whole bag.'

'And what's wrong with having a whole entire bag of sugar to yourself once in a while?' He dryly emphasises each word and it's pretty funny. I try to match it.

'Because it starts with "a whole entire bag of sugar to yourself once in a while" and it ends with you at 3 a.m. begging people for "just one sachet of Splenda".'

81

George chokes on his squash and Eddy puts his forehead into his hand.

A moment later after George has excused himself my mind starts to swirl with feelings of guilt. I'm in this kind person's house and I'm making them feel unsettled just for the sake of a laugh. Eddy has started doing the dishes but I try to speak loudly so he'll hear me first time.

'Sorry, I was just joking about that by the way. It was just a silly thing.'

He turns around to face me and his confused frown makes me feel even worse. 'About the sugar?' He pulls his head back and raises his eyebrows.

'Yeah, was just a silly joke. Sorry. Can I help dry?' I say standing up and suddenly I see George watching me from the doorway, crossing his arms and smiling at me. We both walk towards Eddy.

Eddy drives us home with our new old hoover in the boot. I sit in the back and listen to George say strange things for thirty minutes without Eddy catching on.

'What you been cooking then, G?'

'Oh you know, mainly food.'

Eddy looks at me in the rear-view mirror and rolls his eyes. 'You know what he's been cooking, Iris?'

'Urm, I think it's usually raw things.'

George smiles at me, which is what I wanted, but I still don't want Eddy to think I'm rude so I add, 'Stuff like Moroccan salad bowls.'

Eddy shakes his head. 'I don't know much about food but I know making salad ain't cooking.'

We all laugh. George's laugh is so lovely, it's distinctive and high pitched, and I love the way he rubs his eyes with the back of his hands afterwards. There's a gap in the conversation and I take the chance to tell Eddy about the delicious vegetable spaghetti George made me. I catch George looking at me through the mirror and expect him to look away but he doesn't. He just turns his smile up even more.

As we near our flat the dread of the day ending and the new week beginning starts to build inside of me and I find myself wondering if I should just call in sick and stay home, be with George, stay as happy as I am right now. I get out the car and breathe in the faux freshness of the evening London air and watch them hug goodbye over the gearstick and then George hand Eddy four £20 notes for the hoover.

I see Eddy protest saying something like, 'Don't be an idiot.'

But then George insists, putting the money down in between them and getting out saying, 'Buy something nice for the kids.'

Eddy leans out, 'I told you I don't want charity.'

'It's not charity.' George points to the hoover. The day makes a little more sense to me now. I was there for company, not the main purpose of the day.

I feel jealous watching their closeness. Effortless, genuine connection passes back and forth between them. I can't think of the last time I've had an interaction like that. I think of Friday night and my stomach contracts.

★

Me and George stand at the bottom of the concrete stairs looking at this hoover which I can now see is bigger and older than the one we already have.

I make a big deal of carrying it, asking for a few breaks. When we get inside I notice how old the hoover actually is.

'I know I'm no expert but this is definitely less good than our current one. Why did we go all the way there for this?'

He shrugs and says, 'I wanted to spend the day with you and this was the best I could come up with, remember?'

His forwardness takes me by surprise so I try to smile in a way which makes it unclear whether I took that as a compliment or joke. I decide to keep things light as that seems to be his style.

'Going to Croydon to pick up an old hoover that will now clutter up our flat is the best you could come up with? What was the worst?'

He laughs, perfectly comfortable, and confident as always. 'Okay, this was the only thing I could come up with.'

'I saw you give Eddy some money for it, and you paid for the meal the other night. I'm worried you're being too generous for someone who hasn't got a job. Let me transfer you some money.'

'No, no.' He puts his hand on my arm to stop me getting my phone out and it makes me want to close my eyes.

'What do you think a rainy-day fund is for?'

'Urm, like rain-based emergencies and not being able to pay rent?'

He looks into the distance and nods his head as if he was thinking about this for the first time.

'Stop it.' I nudge him.

'You don't need to worry about me. I've been saving since I was fifteen. I could buy you desserts every weekend for at *least* three weekends if I wanted.'

'How come we hang out when it's the weekend and then during the week we barely speak?' It always surprises me how honest I am around him.

He looks confused. 'You're at work and then go straight to your room when you get back. And when I do see you in the kitchen or whatever, you can barely look me in the eyes. I don't usually want to disturb you but today I thought I'd give it a shot.'

Suddenly I think of all the hours after work I spend lying in bed, paralysed, my head throbbing but not with a headache, the knot in my chest tightening.

The skin of my face is starting to prickle but I try to look unconcerned. 'Oh yeah, true, I forget how tired I am after work.'

'Well, if you're ever in need of a nice hot meal, just come to me.'

'Oh, thanks—'

'I've got a whole drawer of takeaway menus.'

I exhale a little laugh, my energy waning now.

He continues, 'Which. . . you won't be needing to use after I cook you up a delicious meal!'

I poke him with the end of the hoover.

After we've thrown it in our storage cupboard – where it now sits on top of a thousand plastic shopping bags, our old but clearly better hoover, and previous residents' possessions that have obviously been stuffed and left in there over the years – we stand there looking at it.

Then we turn to each other and I feel him move imperceptibly closer towards me. I instinctively mentally prepare myself for the night to progress into something sexual even though the idea of touching someone suddenly makes my skin feel dirty. George looks at me for a moment longer and then turns and walks to his bedroom with his back to me. He lifts his hand up in the air without turning round and says, 'Night!'

Even though I'm relieved, I feel rejected and murmur, 'You're welcome.'

But not quietly enough because he spins around just as he reaches his door and says, 'Thanks for your help today.'

I lift my hand up in a semi-wave. 'Any time.'

I can't help but stand and cringe for a moment thinking about the person I was today. I always go in with such clear intentions to be intriguing and charismatic but end up being silly and unaware of what I'm doing.

I clean my teeth and then stand in my bedroom's doorway reluctant to go in. It feels eerie, like it carries something bad about yesterday and something bad about tomorrow in its air. I enter and then quickly sit on the floor, back against my bed, not wanting to get in it. I slowly fall onto the floor and curl up into a ball, my hand starts throbbing again from the burn, even though I haven't felt it since this morning. I haven't felt anything bad since this morning, until now. Something is changing inside me. I lie there with a blank mind until 1 a.m., when I finally climb into bed.

13

The office is still mostly empty except for a few of the management team. I nod at them and they nod back a 'Well done for being here before anyone else'. I sit down and I can't help closing my eyes for a second trying to wash out the thought of how meaningless the act of setting my alarm an hour earlier to get me a nod of approval is. I'm worried I'm going to burst out laughing, but I swallow it and open my eyes and my laptop.

The tinted glass windows help me forget what time it is, and I write some nicely formatted bullshit that I'll send over to Maggie later. Or perhaps I'll send it to Ish and then copy Maggie in. I listen to my coloured nails tapping the keys. My fingers look so nice and slender.

The office fills up and I suddenly realise it's closer to lunch than breakfast but I'm still not hungry. The day is going well, I have smiled at so many people. I guess maybe this is what it's like to feel at home somewhere.

Sara swans over to my desk and perches on the side of the table.

'Wanna go for a cig?'

Tempting as it is, I want to cut down to only social smoking because I don't want to get wrinkles around my mouth. 'I've just been for one, sorry.'

There's no point in worrying that she would've noticed I haven't left the office all morning, because that would involve her thinking about someone other than herself. I've started to wonder if she even likes me at all or if she just sees me as another accessory. She shrugs and pops off the desk. As she walks away I look at her skinny legs in her tight black jeans and wonder if other people think they're perfect or too thin. Who wore it better – me or Sara – gets ready to play out in my head as usual but I can't remember what I look like or why I care. I glance around the office and everyone looks far away. I don't know these people, I realise. I didn't choose them. I'm not part of this.

A pop-up reminds me of my performance review this afternoon and I stare at the notification until my eyes blur. I'm unsettled by the fact that I forgot something I've been thinking about for so long. I feel my palms get damp but it's not nerves. Maybe it's excitement.

In the Red meeting room, Ish and Deborah, a member of the management team, sit on one side of a table. I smile at them both and sit down, cross my legs and lean back in the chair. This is not an interview after all and we should all be aware of that.

'Good afternoon, Deborah, Ish.' I flash Ish a look to remind him of our secret new status as equals. If Deborah notices then she will probably just assume it's a closeness from us working together so often, which wouldn't be a bad thing.

'Good afternoon, Iris.' Deborah laughs, probably at my blasé attitude, but she knows what women have to be like to get ahead in this world.

Ish, less comfortable than usual says, 'Let's get started, shall we?' I notice he keeps looking down at his notebook.

'I'm ready if you are,' I answer, looking at Deborah. She laughs again. I can't tell if I'm being confident or if my inhibitions are gone.

Ish is pushing his glass of water back and forth between his thumb and forefinger. But it's his ring finger that catches my attention. He looks at me, 'How do you feel this last year has gone?'

I take a minute to think even though I know what I'm going to say. I've gone through it in my head so many times.

'You know what, I honestly think it couldn't have gone better. I've learnt so much from the people around me and being immersed in this fast-paced environment. It's crazy how I've gone from booking rooms for meetings to organising and leading them; owning my own small-scale projects, delegating to interns, interacting with clients. And my highlight has definitely been working alongside Maggie on the Desperados feature, right from the initial briefing all the way through to the end product, which was all the amazing work we saw in the Monthly Meeting last week. Anyway, I'm really happy with how things have gone.' I reveal my teeth in a broad smile but I think it looks strange. I can't make myself be normal somehow.

Ish continues, 'That's good to hear, Iris.'

I bet he can smell my perfume. Scent is the strongest trigger of memory. I try to focus on that, let it give me confidence.

'We agree that you've made a quick progression and stepped up to the mark on everything that has been thrown at you.' He leans back with his notebook, ready to take me through my feedback.

When they tell me I've got the promotion I realise I am the youngest manager in the office. Just over one year and I've been promoted.

My heart is speeding up and I feel my face flushing, but it's fine because they won't mind if I'm a little excited, it shows my human side. And it must be the excitement having an effect on me because I can't feel myself or concentrate on what I'm doing or saying. There's a lot of shaking hands and 'Moving forwards. . .' And then things do move forwards, out of the meeting room and into the corridor and smiles, back on their phones checking in with reality, and then walking away into it, me still standing in the doorway of the Red room.

I don't know who to tell first.

I don't know who to tell at all.

I thought I had walked back to my desk but now I'm standing by the glass doors, and I'm going down in the lift and I'm leaving the building. Get some air. Get some space and time to process my achievement. I sit down on a concrete block outside the building. It's freezing against my bare legs, growing too cold for the skin and I should move off it, but I don't. When it stops hurting, I stand up and start walking.

After a certain amount of time, I come across a small courtyard in the middle of some residential flats. There's a square of plants and I'm walking towards it and then into the middle and then I sit down on the earth. Rocking slowly from side to side feels like the right thing to do, so I do that for a bit, and then stand up and start walking again. I can feel there's mud on my skirt, but I don't brush it off.

I can't work out if people can see what is happening to me, but I keep my head down and I don't think much about what I'm doing, or about anything at all. Crossing the river, I have to close my eyes sometimes, but once I'm over the bridge I'm safe. Though I'm not sure from what.

Then. Past glass offices with silhouettes of people sitting at rows of desks. Past the flat exteriors of the classic Victorian houses that I never see anyone leaving or entering. Past semi-empty city bars with men in suits sitting awkwardly on stools.

I'm trying to keep my head down, but it's hard and I'm getting tired. My legs and my eyelids are so tired. The streets are getting busier and the garish shops are getting more frequent and I think I'm going to have to sit down on the pavement, but I don't. I get on the tube. It's not busy, but for some reason I have lost the reflex to look away when anyone looks at me, and there's no doubt now that people can tell something is wrong.

Then it's my stop. I stand up and get off and I don't know how I'm going to manage this last part of the journey.

But then I'm there, in front of my door, looking for the spare key.

I walk through the front door, but I leave it open because closing it feels too normal. I don't walk any further.

Can you go to hospital for leaving your job right after you get promoted?

'Hey!' from the kitchen. Neither of us have ever greeted each other before. Have we become friends now?

I can only see in details. Chipped paint on the wall. Stain on the carpet. A safety pin by the skirting board. What happens if you just walk into a hospital and sit on the floor?

George appears in the kitchen door frame but I don't look up at him. He is wearing slippers that seem slightly too small for him. My brain is white noise.

'I'm making a tea. Want one?' But his eyes have already clocked that this is not the right question. I return to his slippers. I can't tell if they're too small or if he's just not putting his feet all the way in.

The moment has passed for him to ask what's up so now we're standing in silence, and I'm looking at his slippers which have faces printed on them. A yellow circle face that's smiling on one and sticking its tongue out on the other.

No doubt he is looking at me. I'm standing with my shoulders pretty hunched and I'm actually leaning slightly to one side like there's a magnetic pull from the wall. I must look very strange. But I don't care, I feel nothing now. The seconds pass through awkward back into normal.

He walks past me, closes the front door and then walks back to where he was to lean against the wall. His slippers look cheap. They have those thin soles like the ones you get in hotels. I can hear George start to laugh awkwardly. I feel outraged like he's laughing having walked in on me naked. I look up furious and lock eyes with him and he looks guilty. I have no idea why, but I start to laugh. I manage to stifle it for a second, but I start again. I slump to the ground and with an almost indistinguishable change in sound, I switch from laughing to crying and press my head into my knees. George walks over and I feel him sit down next to me.

'I don't think I've ever sat here before.'

He smells like garlic and it's making me feel sick.

'You smell like garlic and it's making me feel sick.'

He stands up, walks back to near the kitchen door and sits down there.

'You know what wouldn't make you feel sick? My homemade garlic bread.'

'It would make me feel sick.'

'It would not make you feel sick. I can tell you that for free.'

'It would.'

'I'm sorry, I couldn't quite catch that because you're speaking into your knees. Did you say you want some? Because I'm glad you finally agree that my homemade fresh garlic bread wouldn't make you feel sick. Really glad to hear that.'

I want to start crying again to show him how inappropriate he's being considering how I feel, but the sadness seems to have subsided slightly for now. I take my head off my knees.

'Do you want some then?'

I don't say anything.

'I'll go get some.'

'It will make me feel sick.'

He brings the garlic bread in and sits down right next to me again. He puts the plate to the other side of him and then his arm around my shoulders, which I didn't know until now was exactly what I wanted him to do. It strikes me that there's only one thing left in this world I like and it's having his body next to mine. I lean my head on his shoulder and a few tears come out of my eyes. I kind of move my head a little so one could potentially fall on his skin instead of his t-shirt, but even if one does, he doesn't have a reaction to it.

'Can I have the garlic bread?'

He reaches over and passes it to me with his other arm. I take my head off his shoulder and eat the whole thing pretty quickly. I don't know if I regret it or not. I want to tell him he's my best friend but I'm not sure that's what I feel. I think about lying down, but instead I turn around and kiss him. It's not a one-way thing, he's kissing me too. It's a bit awkward because his arm is around me and that feels too intimate and I have no idea where to put my hands so they're just in my lap. But instead of readjusting, I just lie down on the floor and he does too. Only the tops of our arms touch and that's the perfect amount. I get a flash of fear – what would I do if he wasn't here right now? I think about life without him and go cold. But that's not possible, we live together, we're stuck together.

14

I wake up at 5.15 a.m. and withdraw my nails from the flesh of my palms. I turn on to my back. The room is so dark that my eyes can drift around without focusing on anything. I picture getting into work before anyone else, hearing them coming through the glass doors, one by one, noticing my head sticking out like a turret from the bank of empty desks, but I don't look up as they walk past, I'm busy working, the empty mug by my side indicating I have been doing so for a while. Proving my worth. It all feels so abstract suddenly. Surreal, almost.

I think about how beneficial this extra time could be. It would be a good opportunity to start reading some of the non-fiction books I bought and catch up on the news and do a few stomach-toning exercises. I turn on to my side and squeeze my eyelids shut.

My alarm goes off at 6.44 a.m. I relax my brow and open my eyes slowly as if I have been asleep. I swing my legs out the side of the bed and sit up. My movements feel forced and performance-like, but I'm not sure how to make them more natural. I keep squeezing my eyes together and think about how scrunching your face up like that is terrible for causing lines and wrinkles. My chest feels heavy. In the shower I sit down so I can focus all my energy on the force with which each drop hits my skin.

Shivering in my towel sitting on the edge of my bed a weird breathy laugh comes out of me. I can't think of what to do next. On what basis are you supposed to choose what to wear? I look at all my clothes and wonder why we incessantly buy new ones just because we're told to. My limbs feel like weights hanging off my body. I put on the softest thing I can find but it still feels wrong. I see the mirror at the other side of my room and know I can't look in it. Everything feels far away. My skin goes cold.

I'm lying on the hall floor again in the hope that George will come home and find me here. I don't know where he's gone, but I heard him leave whilst I was still getting ready for work. But then I didn't make it to work. I made it to the hall, all dressed up and ready to go. But I couldn't go. And so I thought, I better lie down and wait for George. He will be able to stop my mind tumbling out of reality. That was about an hour ago and my body hurts but I've made a commitment to lie here now. The more time that passes the more I know I can't get up.

Everyone at work will be worrying where I am. Or they might just assume I have a day off. But Maggie will know I should be there, so in time everyone will know. Will I get in trouble? I could say another grandmother died. I could say I tried to come in but when I got to my front door I had to lie down on the floor.

I try to list the good things in my life:

1. I'm successful at a job thousands of people dream of having.
2. I'm surrounded by opportunities to do new things and meet new people.
3. I can make myself look nice. I can make other people think I look nice.

Right. Three, that's a lot. Some people would struggle for one. And mine are pretty substantial things. Essentially they add up to mean I'm lucky to have this life, and yet I don't feel lucky – I don't feel anything. I decide to think of a fourth, but before I can, I hear George's key turning in the lock, and I suddenly feel embarrassed for lying here so I sit up.

He walks in carrying shopping bags, looking sweaty. He's wearing black Adidas shorts, bright white socks and trainers. He looks good. I wait for him to say something, but he doesn't. He just stands and looks at me for a second and then sits down next to me with his bags.

'We can't keep meeting like this.'

'I don't want to go to work.'

'No one wants to go to work until they can't go to work. *Then* you wanna work.'

I want to reply about how he doesn't know how nice my job and office and friends are, but I can already see where that conversation would lead and I don't have an answer.

He reaches over and pulls out a bottle of Mars milkshake from his shopping bag and holds it up.

'This is what happens when you don't have a job.'

'Morning milkshake? I'll quit right now then.' I feel bad for joking in case he's struggling for money.

He peels off the foil seal and hands it to me.

'I'm okay thanks.'

He takes a drink from it. It smells strongly of artificial chocolate flavour and I feel a desperation to have some.

'Can I—?'

He hands me the bottle without blinking an eye. I have to stop myself from drinking it all.

'Have it all. I've got twenty more in here anyway.' He points to the bags, which I can see just have normal shopping in them. I drink it all anyway.

I can feel my body relaxing and my voice sounds perfectly normal now. 'Why are you doing your shop so early?'

'It's a nice day out there so I went for a run and decided to buy some stuff on the way back.' He gestures at his clothes.

'Oh. I thought you were wearing that for fashion.'

'You can be fashionable when you run.'

I love the freckles, only slightly darker than his brown skin, that go over his cheeks and nose, each one of them looks like it was placed there on purpose.

'I hate running.'

He kisses me and then pulls back. He does a cheeky smile, which shows off his straight, white, perfect teeth. I want to stroke my finger along them. So I do, just to see what his reaction will be. There's a pause for a second and I start to regret it, but then he says, 'Well? What do they feel like?'

'Teeth.'

He lets out a massive sigh and slouches against the wall. 'Thank fuck for that.'

I'm feeling better and better, but the deeper part of me that is aware of existing beyond this moment is feeling worse and worse.

He looks at me like he's studying my face.

'Why don't you go to work and when you're back you can have some delicious food? I'm making slow-cooked beef stew. It's so good. Caramelised meat, bit of cinnamon, bit of my special sauce. Perfection. My dad taught me this one, it's great comfort food.' He looks genuinely excited, which confuses me. Who is that excited for food they cook themselves?

'I don't want to go to work.'

'Just get through the day and I'll make sure you have an okay evening.'

I don't know why, but I practically shout, 'I can't "just get through the day" if all the days are the same.'

'Okay.' He pushes himself to stand up. 'Get through a different type of day then.' He holds his hand out to me. I just look up at him. He nods to his hand. 'This isn't me waving at you.'

I take his hand and he pulls me up. He picks up his shopping bags in one hand, then holds mine with the other and leads me into the kitchen. 'Right, you sit down. I'll make us some eggs. We could both do with a bit of protein.'

I've never met someone who is so present and as soon as I'm in his company I begin to forget about the past and the future. If I can just continue to live in each exact second, not the second before or the second after, I think I can manage to get by.

I sit down on the sofa. He's hypnotising to watch and I have no inhibitions anymore so I stare at him preparing the food. I decide his attractiveness comes from the perfect symmetry of his face and the precise but unostentatious way he goes about things.

Before I know it, he brings over a plate of beautifully orange scrambled eggs on toast and we eat in silence. When we've finished he leans over and puts our plates on the coffee table. 'You know what? I fucking hate that this place doesn't have a table.'

'There's no room for a table.'

'A table is more important than a sofa.'

'I don't want to go back to work ever.'

He looks at me, I'm on the verge of crying, but he gives me a massive grin. 'You love your job. You're always at it anyway. Why don't you take a break, take some holiday to get rested, and then try again?'

'No.' I stand up furiously. I've never been like this with someone before. 'You don't understand. I don't want to work there anymore.'

He looks up at me, shocked like a schoolboy.

'I got promoted yesterday.'

'Wow. Okay well, congratula—' But he trails off looking at my frenzied expression. I can tell he doesn't know what to say so I speak instead.

'I wanted that promotion so bad.' I press all my fingers into my face. I can feel them shaking. 'So badly.' I try to look up but I can't get my eyes to stay on anything other than the floor. 'But now I've got it I don't care. I don't care about literally anything.' I'm letting it spill out almost frantically now. 'Honestly, it's like everything sickens me. All the vapid, meaningless crap that people care about, that *I* cared about, is repulsive to me now. It's like everyone engrosses themselves in the most trivial shit possible just so they're distracted from some kind of deep, terrible reality. And I don't want to be near it anymore – all these delusional people pretending that things are fine.' I sound loud, angry, scary even. But when I look at him and see his alarmed expression my heart breaks open. I stare at him, tears streaming out my eyes now. 'What am I going to do?'

He stands up and hugs me. 'It's okay. I'll help you. It's okay.' He strokes the back of my head until I stop crying. 'You're not alone. I'm here.'

Eventually I pull away to look up at him. 'I can still pay rent. I've got savings. Maybe there's something else I can do.'

'Don't worry about that for now. Sit back down. I'll make some stew.'

After some time sitting on the sofa whilst George cooks, I get a strong and certain feeling that I can't live any more seconds. It's a miracle I make it through every second that passes. Time is too long. I need to get out of here, but I can't speak, so I quickly walk out without glancing at George.

Six hours have passed. All of them spent lying on my bed. I don't know if I've been thinking.

I look at the chest of drawers that are in my eyeline. Directly against the wall opposite. There's a small gap between the drawers and the wall, like there are with most drawers, and I feel like I should get up and squeeze myself into the gap. Obviously I wouldn't be able to because the gap is only about 10 cm wide, but it feels like the right thing to do. By 'the right thing to do', I'm not actually considering it, I don't think. But the thought calms me slightly. Or maybe even excites me, to think of doing something that weird, an action that perfectly matches and reflects how I feel. Then I actually consider squeezing myself in there, for real, and how, because I wouldn't fit, my body would push the drawers forward, and because all this would have to happen quite forcefully, everything would fall off the top of the drawers and make a noise when it hits the ground, and that would also reflect in some way how I feel.

I turn around in the bed so I'm facing the wall instead. Obviously I was never going to do that. It was obvious I wasn't going to do that. It was just my brain manifesting this feeling I have in my chest, in my heart, in my hands.

I feel like I should be inside the mattress – I think about cutting open the mattress and getting inside, and being inside the mattress. But I don't picture it visually. I just mentally think about the concept of doing that. Without having to picture it in images. The whole thought is just in my brain at once. And I keep thinking it. Sometimes I think 'I should be inside the mattress.'

And sometimes the thought is slightly longer than that: about the process of slicing the mattress with a knife and climbing inside – but not with pictures.

I think about work tomorrow and how people there know me and the crushing pressure to continue to be the person they know. Someone who I'm not sure I can be anymore.

I know so certainly now that I need to hand in my notice. To go somewhere I can be invisible. Where I can say nothing and be no one and go nowhere. I draft a simple email to Ish. *Thank you for the opportunity but I'll have to decline. . .*

15

Living out my three weeks' notice feels unbearably long and yet I don't like to focus on the end. I find myself relying on food to fill the gnawing void. Meals punctuate the day and so I make them something I can look forward to. There's no reason to stop myself eating anymore. And if anything, now nothing matters to me, food is the perfect thing to focus my mind on instead of the relentless, intolerable passing of time.

When I wake up, the first thing I think about is a warm bowl of porridge, drizzled in honey. I make this for myself as soon as I get into work and try to eat it as slowly as I can. Usually I can make it last ten minutes. Between breakfast and lunch I drink milky coffee to stave off any hunger. Then, at lunch, I buy a ham or tuna baguette at Nibs and try to eat it with people I hardly know so I don't have to confront the idea that people, like Sara, are continuing their lives exactly as they were before. Continuing on their upward trajectories whilst I trail off and stagnate. Just because I've opted out doesn't mean I'm not terrified of the nothingness I have waiting for me.

I only have twenty-minute lunch breaks because then I go and buy an extra snack and take it to eat at my desk. I'm still starving though, and anxious to settle my hunger, so I always opt for something stodgy, like crisps or a couple of the small packets of crackers they sell to go with the soup. Whilst all my other senses become numb, taste grows in strength and ceaselessly demands to be stimulated. I try to sit at my desk for as long as I can, and then when I can't bear it any longer, I move to the 'break-out area', a place supposedly to help people come up with ideas, but in reality just a place with bright-coloured comfy chairs that no one uses.

I spend my afternoons doing things I don't care about but that pass the time quickly, like reading about celebrity gossip online. Mid-afternoon my mind can sometimes feel like it's caving in on itself, when in an abrupt flash I remember what I've done and what future awaits me. So to distract myself I pop out of the building for a cigarette and then to the newsagents down the road. I never buy food in bulk because part of the excitement is walking around the shop or café and choosing whatever I'm craving. Sometimes I even make several trips to the shop to buy treats. I get anything: biscuits, flapjacks, scotch eggs, sausage rolls, pastries, sandwiches, muffins, bread sticks, cakes, hot chocolates from the little machine at the back. Changing hunger into fullness is the only satisfaction I am able to feel these days, and so I can't stop myself. The sun is out more often now and the feel of it warming my cheeks is like an assault, so once I've gotten my food I keep my head down and run back inside. By the time I've finished eating and browsing the internet, I only have about an hour of work left.

Sometimes I'll get Maya to send over some work I gave her or guiltily throw something together myself and then email it to Maggie or whoever. People smile at me like I have a terminal illness. As soon as it's acceptable to leave – at 6 p.m. – I pack up and sneak straight out of the office.

By this point I'm full of food and regret, so make a promise to myself to immediately break this unhealthy routine. But by the time

I reach the supermarket near my flat I remember there's no reason to be healthy anymore. I feel weak and nauseous, and the thought of feeling hungry scares me into buying some more food, just in case. But the idea of eating vegetables fills me with disgust, they all seem so soft and strong in flavour. The only thing I can manage is something like a plain bread roll. I get back to my flat, collapse on my bed, and eat the whole roll straight away.

I wake up at 11 p.m. to the darkness pouring through my window. Confused, I pull myself out of bed, stumble down the hall into the kitchen for a glass of milk, clean my teeth in the bathroom on the way back to bed, and then immediately fall back into a deep sleep.

My eyes feel puffy today so I try to keep my gaze down, but something catches my eye. From across the room I see someone standing, bent down, looking at an editor's screen. I don't know who he is, but I like his hair. It's dark and cut into an unassuming style. Short sides and a flop of slightly longer on top. I imagine he doesn't spend a lot of time deciding on what style to go for and that's one of the reasons I like it. He's talking to some producers and they're laughing at about 70% of the things he's saying. He laughs with them, sometimes. I don't know if he has amazing bone structure or if he's just a bit too thin. When he laughs his sharp features all crumple up. I've never seen such an attractive laugh. He walks away somewhere.

I go and buy myself a coffee from Nibs and sit down with my laptop on one of the comfy chairs near the entrance doors. I choose a big leather chair which has high and deep sides to it. Walking past, you probably wouldn't notice me sitting there.

I wonder if the guy is new. The thought of never seeing him

again seems hilariously unbearable to me. I go over everything I know. He had dark hair that flopped over his forehead a bit every time he laughed. All his features seemed to end in points, there was not one soft line on his whole face. And even though he was laughing most of the time I was looking at him, I thought he seemed serious. The only other thing I can remember is that he was wearing a checked shirt that seemed too big for him.

Just then, slinging a backpack over one of his shoulders, he walks right past me and out the glass entrance doors. I peer forward so the sides of the chair aren't obstructing my view. He presses the button for the lift, moves some headphones from around his neck to over his ears and steps through the opening doors.

I check my laptop screen. 3.45 p.m. He's leaving already. I guess he must have been a freelancer. I can see him, setting off on his way to meet a group of friends at one of their flats, or a bar, and then staying late until it's just him and maybe the girl he's seeing, who is probably an artist, even though she could easily be a model. His name is probably something like Finn.

It's my last day and people are taking a two-hour lunch in the park near the office because it's Friday, bizarrely hot for May, and everyone is hungover. I'm sitting in a circle made up of about twenty-five people. It feels like school. That contradictory feeling of being part of a group and yet completely alone. I don't know these people, I didn't choose them, it feels so fake to me now, this pretence that we're all friends. We spend so much time together but do we actually know each other? Or are we just fuss-free, feel-good, pre-prepared, bite-size pieces of our real selves? I'm unable to pretend to be a palatable person anymore.

My thoughts are much broader now, theoretical almost, not

focused on the small things that are in front of me. Things that used to make me happy seem inane. It's impossible for me to focus on anyone's individual performance and so I concentrate on the general buzz of the park. I don't want to seem rude or awkward though, people think I've become weird enough as it is, so I keep closing my eyes and tilting my head back to make it seem like I'm caught up with sunbathing. Though I have begun to suspect my participation isn't really expected anymore. Someone says 'At 7:30 tomorrow' and I feel so dizzy at the thought that I will still be alive then that I don't hear the rest of the sentence.

Then I see him sit down, staring blankly into space. His body is so still compared to the vibrating park around him, he seems to be in slow motion. He's had a haircut.

Adrenaline then decides to prepare me for something, so I hold my breath to slow my heartbeat. I can't help but look at him.

Ten minutes later he gets up and starts to walk away, but then turns and changes direction, straight towards me. Only then do I tune into Sara's buttery voice calling out beside me, 'Paddy! Paddy! Come here a sec.'

'Hi, guys.' He includes me in his greeting because I was accidentally staring at him as he walked over. I smile and look down at the grass trying to show my indifference at being involved in the conversation, but I think I just end up looking coy.

'It's *so* nice out today, isn't it? Haven't managed to drag myself back inside. You met Iris yet?' Of course Sara knows him. He's probably in love with her. It breaks my heart somehow.

'No, I haven't. I'm Patrick.'

I shake his hand. Patrick. My mind can't work out what to do.

'Cool. Well, either of you going back to the office?' He looks at me. I have never seen less desire behind what sounds like a direct proposition. I'm surprised that I care, it's the first strong feeling I've had in weeks.

I stand up. 'Yeah, I'm coming.' I don't know if it's a relief or not, but Sara declines and waves us away to soak up some more sun. We start walking and I'm not sure I will be able to operate in real time, so I don't speak.

'We're getting to that time of year again which isn't great for people who seem to have solely invested in long-sleeved shirts. I need to buy some t-shirts.'

I try to be funny. 'Well, I'm afraid I don't have anything in right now.'

'Oh, okay. Well, that's fine, don't worry. Just let me know when you're stocked up.'

'Well, I know there's no t-shirts but I've got all the other letters in, R-shirts and S-shirts if that might interest you? They're very popular. A lot of people's first choice in fact.'

'R-shirts, is it? Are they the ones that only have one sleeve?'

'Yeah you know it, and S-shirts are the ones which cover both shoulders, but only half your waist.'

'Yeah? That could be quite decent in this weather actually. I often find one side of my waist getting boiling. I'll let you know.'

We are approaching the door of the office, but I don't want to ride up in the lift with him and a bunch of other people.

'Cool, well, you better let me know quick cause the sequin V-shirts have already sold out. See ya.' I feel him turn his head towards me, possibly with a confused look on his face, but I don't see. I'm already starting to walk away.

I go behind the office and sit on the floor of a shady bay meant for bins with my back against the cool brick wall. My nose feels burnt. It's unsettling what that interaction did to me. How it made me feel something again. For a second I was a version of myself I thought had died. A person who wanted things. It felt like a spark had been re-lit in my mind and body. An energy propelling me towards something. I didn't know you could miss wanting to impress someone, but it turns out I did. It flashes into my head that I shouldn't have quit, shouldn't have stuffed myself with food, shouldn't have given up a life that would have linked me to him.

I picture short-haired Patrick crying whilst I tell him that unfortunately I don't feel the same way as him. I close my eyes and see his blue ones reluctantly releasing tears whilst I shrug and walk away. Even the thought of it lifts me. Being wanted by someone who made me feel like that. Being better than them.

Monday comes back around eventually. My alarm goes off at 6.44 a.m. I turn it off and deactivate it. I lie back down on my side and I can feel the springs digging into my cheekbones and knee. The thought of doing nothing until the end of the day is unbearable. But this is only the first day of the rest of my life. I shut my eyes tight as if it will somehow prevent my brain from fully understanding the bleakness of the situation. The irony, which I try to comfort myself with, is that there is nothing in this world that I could physically bring myself to do right now.

I remove the watch from my wrist, get up to close the curtains to make sure no light is seeping through. Even seeing inanimate objects in the periphery of my vision feels like a reminder of the world I'm no longer a part of. I pull my duvet off the bed, drag it to my desk chair, which I move to face the wall and sit with the cover over my head. What a sadly predictable way I have of living with these emotions. How self-indulgent, adolescent, pathetic. I whisper to myself out loud, to concentrate the mind.

'Do you really need to be here, under the duvet with the lights off? Or are you just trying to be "extreme" to prove something to yourself? To prove you're not just a failure, but someone who's in an "extreme" situation. At a breaking point.'

I take the duvet off. It was hot under there and I shouldn't care but I do. I go back to lay on the bed.

'I am not alive. I am not alive. I am not alive. I am not alive. I am not alive. I am not alive. I am not alive. I am not alive. I am not alive.'

16

At first I stay in my room. Even when I venture out, to grab some crisps or go to the bathroom, I make sure to stare at the ground and avoid mirrors, I don't want to be reminded that the world exists. George knocks, but I tell him to leave me alone. I watch the sun rise and fall and rise and fall and rise and fall. Weeks pass like this. Where I count down the hours of the day lying in bed. But I know that soon it will be night and I'll have to carry on lying down even though I'm not tired because I've been sleeping all day. Only in those few hours that it's dark do I get up and live freely in the room.

Sometimes I do something funny like put a whole face of make-up on and then get into bed and go to sleep. It was funny but it did concern me how bad I looked even with my normal make-up on. It looked unnatural, like a child wearing make-up. But it's easy to tell myself it doesn't matter. Sometimes I look out my window into the dark courtyard or up at the sky and think about how many losers have done things like this.

Sometimes I wake up with a certain uncomfortable energy. A nagging feeling that surely I should feel some kind of relief now. Why did I leave everything behind just to lie here and feel even worse? What did I expect? I rack my brains, looking for plans or ideas I must have had to make this decision, but I can't find anything.

I open my laptop and search for jobs that people with my experience could get but all roads seem to lead to Account Manager and Junior Copywriter and Content Executive and. . . I find my eyes losing focus on the screen as I dizzily think about all these places I could go and work where everything would be exactly the same as before. My throat aches. How can being completely free feel so claustrophobic? I know I can't do nothing forever but I also don't think I will be able to do anything ever. The thought of the future, even a day ahead of today, makes me forget how to breathe. Eventually the laptop runs out of battery and I just stare at my silhouette on the black screen.

If I ever open the window the sharp familiar smell of outside gives me a feeling of horror that I've never experienced until now. Sometimes I wish I was dead so strongly I can feel it radiating out of my wrists. The thought of killing myself seems unrealistic, but is there another way to suddenly not exist anymore? I think about taking a handful of pills. I remember reading somewhere that there's no method of suicide that isn't painful. What would it feel like, sitting there after I'd taken the pills, waiting for what's on the horizon? You can't regret killing yourself, that's the beauty of it. I laugh in my head. I know deep down I won't do that though, so why am I thinking about it?

Eventually I always fall asleep again. Often I wake up and my face is wet. I can't help but wonder how I can cry and cry and cry when I care about nothing and no one. 'What are you upset about?' I say to the mirror. 'Nothing,' she says back.

And then one day a knock on my door startles me. They're few and far between now. I stay completely still like there's any way he might think I'm out. I don't want him to come in but my heart hurts at the thought of him walking away. I think I hear him turn around but then my door opens a crack. He doesn't come in.

'Hello? Is anyone in?'

I don't know what to do. It probably smells weird in here, but the brutal truth is I'm terrified this will be his last attempt. 'Yeah.'

'Can I. . . enter?'

'Okay.'

It's only once he's walked in that I realise how strange I look. My head poking out of the covers, wide tired eyes, greasy hair, red-cheeked with warmth. I don't think I see his face recoil or catch him looking around the room in disgust. But he stays by the door. Does he find it uncomfortable, how much I've changed?

'What's going on?'

'With what?' I sit up but keep myself covered because I'm only wearing a thin t-shirt.

'With. . . you?'

'What do you mean?' I'm half-heartedly trying to be the normal, chatty girl he got to know. But my flat expression is giving me away.

He stares into space like he's thinking what to do. 'Why don't we go for a walk?'

I let myself go into autopilot. 'Okay.'

'Why don't you get a shower?'

'Okay.'

'Then meet me in the living room.'

'Okay.'

He smiles kindly and walks out.

I wait a second before going into the bathroom.

By the time I've washed and dressed I feel exhausted and lay back down on the bed, but a few seconds later I get another knock at the door.

'You ready? There's no dress code for this walk.'

'I don't know if I'm too tired to go.'

He walks in and over to me. 'You can sleep when you're dead.' He holds his hand out to me, so I take it and let him pull me up.

'Maybe I'll become dead now then.'

'Okay, I take it back, you can sleep later on, alive. But you have to come for a walk first.'

A comfortable intimacy in our relationship has developed surprisingly fast. It seems to have stemmed from a mixture of an intrinsic frankness between us and a general lack of inhibition from me. I can't help but relish the feeling that somebody knows me. It overrides any shame.

I put a jacket on because my mind can't comprehend it's nearly summer. We leave the house.

When we're out of the building he takes my hand and squeezes it. It takes me by surprise. My whole arm tingles and for a second I'm a teenager holding her crush's hand, I feel momentarily happy. But then it passes and I feel even worse. Temporary, fleeting happiness is worse than no happiness at all. The jarring desperation in my stomach to hold on to the positive feeling is torturous compared to the stable serenity of consistently wanting to die.

George leads me to the main road and then around some of the back roads and then back on to the main road and then home. He doesn't say much, and I want to be silent too, but I can't help saying things that come into my mind. Even stupid things like, 'I went to that café once and forgot to pay and so now I can never go back.' He laughs and I regret it because maybe he will think I was exaggerating everything I was feeling. That I'm fine now. But it's not that, he just makes me feel, for a second, like everything doesn't exist except this one frivolous moment.

Dread crushes me as soon as I see our building. My life has

changed so much I barely recognise it as my own. Sometimes it's terrifying, the feeling of moving further and further away from who I am even though I know I can't be that other version of myself anymore. I wish this walk was the end of my life. A calm and anticlimactic end. Me, walking around looking at the area I loved so much but from a distance, uninvolved with the action, a spectator. But we get to the front door and these aren't the last moments of my life, and all that is waiting for me is a bed and endless days of lying down on it. My face aches with a sense of foreboding.

I stand stupefied in the hall staring at my bedroom, and George looks between me and my door.

'Don't go in there yet. I'm going to make a cheese toastie. Two cheese toasties in fact.'

'I don't want anything to eat. I don't feel hungry.' I feel numb and dead.

'Well, come watch me eat mine then.'

I walk into the kitchen with him before I can think about it too much. I sit down. He goes over to the kitchen. My eyes feel glazed over and my body slack and my mind hollow. I wonder if looking at me freaks him out. We are silent.

He brings over two toasties. They smell strongly of warm cheese and Worcestershire Sauce. I salivate. As soon as he puts it down on the coffee table, I pick it up again and eat it quickly. I feel the food turning over in my mouth and my jaw opening and closing trying to break it up, but I can't do it properly and always end up swallowing big chunks and it hurts.

I didn't want to eat it. I feel so stupid for eating all of that food when I want to die. But I couldn't help myself, like a rat pushing a button. It's the only sensory stimulation I've had in so long my mind couldn't resist it.

I can't stand the silence after we've finished eating. I just want to lie in bed and count down from a hundred again and again. 'I'm going back to my room.'

'That might not be the best idea.'

I can't bear to look at him. 'I need to get into bed.'

'But it's—'

'You don't understand.' I've never been this blunt to anyone before. It's almost thrilling to be this blunt to someone. To be insensitive and not worry what they will think of you.

'I know I don't. Sorry.'

My head is in my hands to disguise my fast breathing. 'I'm sorry.'

'Couldn't you at least stay in my bed? I won't go in there with you, obviously. I just mean until it's night, maybe it would be nice for a change of scenery. It's really comfy in there, I swear the person who lived here before me left like, a luxury mattress or something. And if you want company I can just sit on the floor and read, or if you don't, I can just stay and watch something in here.'

So that's where I go, and that's where I stay.

At first it's just for a few hours a day, until I feel the need to go back to my room and scream into a pillow or lightly press a pin into the tops of all my fingers. But before long George will be knocking at my door again, calling me into the kitchen for food or telling me it's time for my 'day bed'. Sometimes I find it funny. I begin to expand my small world to include his space as well.

His room is a bit bigger than mine, but not by much. His bed is pressed up against the wall too, and he only has one set of drawers like me, but there is more floor space. I ask him if he painted it this light blue and he looks around and says, 'Oh, I never noticed it was blue.'

Every day he sits on the floor and gets out a spy novel that he says his uncle bought him for Christmas. I ask if he's enjoying it and he says no. I ask him why he's reading it and he says, 'Because my uncle bought it for me for Christmas.' I ask if his uncle will check if he's read it, and he says no.

Sometimes he finds me funny too, he brings out the silliness in me. If I'm feeling a little energised I'll make him do something like learn all the lyrics to Mulan's 'I'll Make A Man Out Of You' with me and then act out the kick-jump at the end.

Sometimes we kiss. He never kisses me first, but I know it's because he doesn't want to make me uncomfortable. He lies next to me when I'm crying, sobbing, and hugs me tight or kisses my head or holds my hand, but never says anything.

When we finally have sex he's more confident than I expected, although I don't know why I expected otherwise. At first I ready myself to bend over physically and mentally, in whatever way he prefers. But then I stop thinking. He manages to fill my mind with the things he does, the things he asks for, the things being felt, to such an extent that I am able to let go. And that is why he is able to do what no other man has done. I consider telling him but decide not to.

Weeks, who knows how many, have passed now and the job searches have become less frequent. George tentatively asks me if I need help. I stuff my face into a pillow and make a loud sound then turn on to my back and pull hard on the roots of my hair with both hands. The truth is I don't think I can work. Often I can't even get out of bed. I can barely speak or eat or move. You can't go into an office when smiling makes you want to die so much you can barely breathe. I whisper my reply.

'I know people have to work. I know that. Don't you think I know that? But—' I can't finish my sentence. I don't feel like a lazy person but I also feel like getting through the day alive is the only task I can concentrate on. Or maybe it's that deep down I know I can just use the inheritance money.

I calmy add, 'It's fine. I've got money.'

'Don't you want to save that?'

Save? For what? A future? The thought makes my temples throb and my stomach turn.

'No.'

The conversation is over. I roll on to my side and let myself drift off.

Later that day I transfer the rest of my savings into my main account and the number on the screen seems like a countdown rather than a balance.

Then George gets a call. He gets a job. 'The job'. An even better one at a small tapas restaurant/bar where there is always a queue. Or so he tells me. I ask him not to tell me things like that, but there's no stopping the outside world coming in now. Stories and smells and names of months passing me by. The heat of summer can't be shut out anymore and it mocks me. Asks me if I'm surprised that so much time has passed since all I've done with it is lie down.

George is part of all this that I'm separate from. So I stop going into his room as much and start sleeping in my bed. Time drags on but the days pass as if they're hours. But then he comes into my room one night after work and kneels on the floor next to my bed and presses his face into my arm and speaks into it which makes his voice muffled.

'I don't like coming home to an empty bed anymore.'

I thought I would've wanted to make him work for it a bit, but

I don't. I just stand up and walk with him back to his room. As soon as we're in there he looks at me worried. 'Or we can sleep in your room? I don't know why it's always been you having to come in here. I didn't mean for it to be that way.'

'No let's stay in here.'

George takes his backpack off.

I give him a long kiss and say, 'You're my happiness.'

He looks at me, concerned, and it seems like he's about to say something, but he just kisses me again.

17

Gradually a restlessness grows inside me alongside the alienation. They compete but neither win. I can't re-join what I left; it still repels me, but I can't lie down any longer. And so I'm left to use up this new energy without leaving the peripheries. I try going out more, on my own. When George has an early shift. I choose seemingly easy things – food shopping, wandering the streets, buying cheap coffees, sitting in parks – but it feels like I'm walking through jelly. Every movement is slow and tiresome and my surroundings seem fuzzy and muffled. I trudge home and then fall on the bed. The muscles in my face lax whilst water flows silently out my eyes. There is no respite from the feeling.

I don't need anything from the shop, but it's the only place I could think of to go today, so now I'm walking around it aimlessly and I have to squint. Apparently there are no windows in supermarkets because they don't want you to know how long you've spent in there, so they have the lights really bright instead. It's worked because I don't know how long it's been, but it's not really benefiting them because I haven't even picked up one thing. Everyone is snaking around the aisles trying to find what they need but accidentally finding things that they want.

I think about getting some canned soup because maybe that is something I would want one day, and there's also no pressure to have it straight away. But I'm standing here looking at the soups and I feel dizzy like I'm going to fall over. Actually, I don't feel like I'm going to fall over, it just feels like I should feel that. Because it's overwhelming, all the soups, so many of the same type, so many different types, different packaging that people have sat around a table to design, to try and make it so I will stand here and pick up *their* can, but all of the companies have done that, so now we're back to square one.

I feel like people will notice me standing here staring at the soup, but they don't, they don't even slightly notice. Maybe it's because the behaviour isn't even that unusual. This is how long it takes everyone to choose their soup.

I walk away from the soup and look at the people, slightly frowning, scanning the shelves as they walk up and down. I buy an apple because I can't think of anything else.

I reach the corner of my road sooner than I had expected and even the idea of seeing my building is too depressing, so I just stand looking forward at another grey wide building over the road, that looks exactly like the one I live in.

I am standing strangely upright now that I've stopped, but I'm not sure why. I could walk around the block again, but my whole body feels empty. I scrunch my face up really tight then I quickly sit down on the floor, cross-legged. Someone walks right past, but they don't even look at me because they're probably thinking about what they're going to have for dinner or also wondering what's the point in eating dinner again like they did yesterday and the day before. I get up and walk home, but I don't bother taking the apple with me. The loud array of sounds made by people enjoying their summer makes my body and mind clench. I'm so removed from all that now. From everything. Is that a relief or a loss?

I wake up in my room fully clothed.

I sit up and feel the rolls of fat over my trousers so I take them off and sit down on the floor in front of the mirror. I take my t-shirt off and lean forward to see my stomach all bunched up in front of me. I brush the hair on my legs in the opposite direction to how it grows. My bun is so tangled I struggle to pull the bobble out. My hair's greasy and dry at the same time.

I look at myself dead in the eyes and stare. Maybe I will see something. Find out something. Maybe she will move. *You are the only person you will know for your whole life,* I tell myself. *You are all you have.*

George knocks and peeps round slightly before walking in. I turn back and focus on my eyes in the mirror. He sits down next to me. My head drops down like my neck can no longer hold the weight of it.

'Why do I look like this?'

'You look nice.' He strokes up and down on my compressed stomach.

'I do not look nice.'

'I think you do.'

'Well, I don't like that you think I do. Why do you have to be so fucking positive all the time?'

I see a flicker of hurt but he almost instantaneously transforms it into a smile and then, realising what he's done, transforms it into a serious face. Even his serious face has a touch of smile. I rub my teeth together. I hate him. I'm with the nicest man in the world and I would be an idiot to leave him. For what? What could possibly be better than this? And yet this. This is what's killing me.

★

A few days later I wake up at 5 a.m. with a racing heart. I look at George, his breath so slow it seems like it could stop, and I desperately want to wake him. Ask if he's okay. Confess my love for him. But I don't. Instead I slip out of bed and go sit on the sofa. Jigging my knees up and down trying to get my thoughts to settle on something. I decide today will be different.

When it approaches 6 a.m. I throw on some clothes and sneak out of the house and to the corner shop down the road. I buy two bananas and peanut butter and yoghurt. Back in the house I see it is still way before 7 a.m. so I tidy the kitchen first. Then I start searching for a blender so I can make a smoothie. After a superficial peer into the back of each cupboard I start to get frustrated. I take a deep breath and tell myself to calm down. I see there is stuff stacked over the cabinets and realise it must be up there, but there's no seat to drag over to stand on and I'm not even close to being able to reach. I pull myself onto the worktop and stand up, steadying myself by holding on to the cabinets. Then, slowly start taking things off and crouching to put them down on the side. Yellowing tupperware, unopened letters, old faded bottles of soda water, and then I see a glass jug which looks like it could be the top to a blender. I pick it up and a huge spider crawls out from underneath. I have no idea what happens but I end up on the floor, with glass shattered around me, screaming and violently swiping my body all over.

George strides in eyes wide with concern, 'What the hell is going on? Are you okay?'

'Are you serious?' I shout. 'I'm in agony, surrounded by glass at the crack of dawn, screaming, so I'm obviously not okay!'

He puts on his slippers and walks over as little glass as possible to come and pick me up, carrying me over to the safe carpet. As he puts me down I nuzzle into his neck and say, 'I'm sorry, it's just

I was up early and decided it would be a fun thing to wake you up with a peanut butter banana smoothie and then we could go for a run and it could be your special day.' I sit down on the sofa and he walks back to the kitchen to get out a dustpan and brush from under the sink. I feel exhausted already but force myself to sit up straight.

He glances up at me. 'You want to go on a run?'

'No. But you like running and I wanted it to be your special day. I just said that.'

'My special day?'

It's almost offensive how good he looks, even crouching down sweeping up glass half naked.

'It's just a day that's all about you.'

'Oh okay, so it's usually always your special day then?' He warily looks up at me to check I've taken it lightly and is thrilled when he sees I'm still smiling.

'Yeah, the rest of the week it's mine, but today it's yours. So make the most of it.'

'Ah, I see.' He puts the last of the glass into the bin. 'For my special day I'd like to wake up at 7 a.m. to screaming and then come and clean up broken glass in my boxers while you chillax on the sofa. That all right?'

I walk over to him and kiss him on his arm. 'I'm sorry. I'm sorry. Your special day starts now. Special day starts now.' I pull away to look at him. 'Please can you find the blender so I can make you a smoothie.'

'We don't have a blender.' He puts his hands on my shoulders. 'Don't worry, I can make peanut butter on toast with sliced bananas. And honey if you're feeling sweet.'

I rest my head on his chest and mumble, 'I'm always feeling sweet.'

I think about how easily I could let this overwhelm me and slip under. How I desperately want to crawl back to bed. But I remind myself how much I want to give George even a fraction of what he gives me, and this is my chance to do that. I used to be an extremely capable person and I can be again. 'Right let's just go on the run now then, we can eat when we get back.'

I'm standing out on the street in the tiny shorts I used to wear for P.E., rubbing my upper arms up and down because even though it's not cold I've got goosebumps from the early morning air.

'Ready?' he says setting up his phone to track our route and time.

'I'm not sure. I haven't run in years.'

'It's just like riding a bike.'

'In the way that you're moving along a street quicker than usual?'

'Exactly. Come on.' He starts jogging, and I feel irritated that he didn't wait for me to go first. But I start running and tell myself it's a weird thing to be angry about.

He leads us down side streets and through residential areas I've never been to. About fifteen minutes into the run I feel like I'm radiating heat and that all my bones and muscles are about to give way. George is chatting away like we're on a morning stroll and I start feeling frustrated that he expects me to answer casual questions when I'm struggling to breathe.

I say, 'Can we stop now,' and then stop suddenly, so he has to take a couple of steps back towards me.

'Yeah sure.'

We walk home hand in hand without mentioning why we stopped, and I feel a burning shame that I make sure doesn't develop into anger.

I have a shower and stand there pressing my thumbs hard into my temples, letting the water pour so powerfully over my face that I feel like I'm drowning. There's a deep, dark feeling inside me that I try to turn away from. Knowledge that George deserves better, someone who doesn't try endlessly to test him, to chip away at the boyish pleasure he gets from the world. I almost feel like I won't be able to go on with the day, but I remind myself I'm once again making everything about me. I push it all down and then get out the shower.

Back in the kitchen, George hands me my peanut butter and banana on toast.

'Should still be hot. I waited until I heard you get out the shower.'

'Thank you,' I say without any appreciation apparent in my tone.

We sit down on the sofa and eat and watch a stupid programme about renovating houses. He takes the empty plates over to the sink, washes them and says he's off for a shower. I can't help wallowing for a second in my failure. But then I snap out of it and leave the flat to pick up some things from a few shops on the high street. When I'm back I tell him to look away whilst I unpack. I feel a bit relieved, like I can breathe, smile, talk.

For the rest of the day we play scrabble, watch this crime thriller that he's already seen a million times, and spend some time cleaning out the cupboards of old pans. I tell myself it's the perfect balance of giving him a great day without it feeling too forced. As it nears dinner I start to feel excited or anxious or both. He asks me what we're having, and I walk over to the kitchen and find a packet I put in a drawer.

'Sushi!' I hold up some rolling mats.

'No way. Awesome.' He gets up to come inspect all the things I've bought. 'How much was all this?'

'Don't worry about it.'

'But—'

'Please let's not. I've got it.'

He kisses me and retreats to the sofa to watch some football highlights.

As I'm cutting up strips of cucumber, carrot, salmon, I realise that in my head I pictured us rolling them up together, and I didn't even consider that we still don't have a table.

I look at the knife and remember someone telling me at school that if you want to die you should cut your wrists 'down the stream not across the river'.

I look away and try to think what George would do to solve this problem so I don't have to burden him. It hurts me to feel how incompetent I've become – how much I rely on him. Like I'm only half-alive and he's constantly dragging me onwards in the hope that one day I'll get up. If I feel exhausted I can't imagine what he feels like.

After preparing the rest of the food I put them in separate bowls and move them onto the coffee table murmuring, 'I think we're gonna have to roll them on our laps.'

'Yeah, that's fine,' he says clearing away our mugs and moving some books onto the floor.

We sit there with our plates and rolling mats on our laps. I already know it's going to go wrong but I try to tell myself that's just negative thinking. I make a line of rice and cucumber and salmon at the bottom edge of the seaweed and start to roll. It goes awfully, the rice is too wet and the seaweed is too baggy around the filling. I reluctantly glance over at George's and realise I've done it completely wrong. He's pressed the rice all over and done a line of vegetables in the middle. I try to cut mine into circles but all the filling squashes out and it looks wet and plain and disgusting. I watch out of the side of my eye to see him slice his. It's significantly better than mine but when he dips one into the soy sauce rice falls out. It's like I've regressed, the incompetency has become crushing. George is effortlessly capable and next to him I will always be a tragic failure. The shame makes my skin hot and tender. It feels like I'm only breathing in.

I get up, say something about having a headache and storm into the bedroom, flop face first on to the bed and let my sharp breaths turn into crying. I feel pathetic, like a parasite. I don't add anything to this world. My mind stings with the memory of what I used to be: so competent, so useful, so desirable. Don't think about it. Keep a blank mind. Think of nothing. Be nothing.

Next thing I know I'm waking up to George knocking on the open door. He's holding a mug but doesn't come in any further, just leans against the wall. A minute or so passes in silence but I will not speak first.

'How are you feeling?'

'Fine.'

'Any better?'

'About what?'

'Anything.'

'That's a broad question.'

'I brought you a tea, but it's lukewarm now.'

I don't say anything, hating how he never probes further to find out what I'm really feeling. I let it drop. 'Well you didn't bring it far enough.'

He brings it to the bed and dramatically leans over with one hand behind his back like a French waiter and puts it down on the table. 'Anything else, *Mademoiselle*?'

I stay lying down. 'Urm, yes actually, as a weak, feeble lady who had a touch of hysteria earlier, I might need a little help drinking it.'

'Of course, I should have offered, *je suis désolé, Mademoiselle.*'

He sits on the edge of the bed and picks up the cup and puts it slowly to my mouth, I lift my head up as far as it can go whilst I'm still lying down and try to drink from it but after a couple of sips I need to breathe and as I put my head down to take a breath he keeps pouring, but very slowly and it's going all over my face. I'm laughing but asking him to stop.

He stops, 'I'm sorry, *Mademoiselle.* It won't happen again.' And then he starts pouring it again and it's going all over the sheets and I'm laughing, but push the cup away .

'Hey, I actually want some of that.' I sit up and wipe my face with my arm and take the cup from him. He's smiling at me and I'm smiling at him. He kisses my shoulder. I drink what's left of the cold tea.

'I finished off all the sushi. Hope you don't mind.'

'How was it?'

'Yeah, was good. In fact, something a bit fishy about how good it was.'

'To be honest I wish I'd just made cereal. Don't know if I was in the right mood for squashing all my food into little balls before I eat it.'

'Yeah, you're just going to do that in your mouth anyway, seems a bit unnecessary to do it twice.'

I put the cup down on the side and feel the cover. 'It's soaking.'

'No need to be embarrassed. We've all been there.'

Laughing, I get out and sit up next to him on the edge of the bed, resting my head on his shoulder.

A few moments pass and then he moves his shoulder so he can look at me. 'Thanks for my special day.'

'You don't need to thank me. You didn't have a special day.'

'Yes, I did.'

'No, you didn't. You woke up weirdly early to a horrible chore. Went on a rubbish run. Made me breakfast. Lost at scrabble. And then had a disgusting dinner on your own and now it's evening.'

'It wasn't a rubbish run, dinner was delicious and I let you win at scrabble,' he says jokingly.

'You don't need to say that. I'd rather you didn't say stuff like that. Obviously today would have been better if you had a fit, happy girlfriend who could go on a nice run and who could do simple tasks without becoming overwhelmed and irritable.' We've never used the word 'girlfriend' or 'boyfriend' before. It feels strange and weighty. I don't know why I said it.

'The main reason today *was* good is because *you're* my girlfriend. . . and because I've seemingly just been upgraded from flatmate.' It feels a relief to say what we've known for a while now, to link ourselves together. But in the same way it feels a relief to land at the airport at the end of a good holiday – grateful for the comfort of home but aware that a certain bliss has ended.

'Well, I'm not a good girlfriend. I can't make you happy.'

'You don't need to. I'm already happy.'

I feel my mind pull back at this comment, searching for a hidden meaning. I go to tell him that the main reason I'm with him is because he makes me happy, but I don't know where that conversation would take us.

I hear him swallow and he continues. 'Have you ever,' he freezes staring into air for a second and then restarts, 'have you ever wondered why you're not. . . happy?'

The question feels cruel. Is he insinuating I'm being lazy? That I'm not constantly exploring this persistent feeling of detachment? I want to scream at him that of course I have, I've spent hundreds of hours wondering, wishing, negotiating, ruminating, reckoning, mourning. I've gone over everything. I rest my forehead on my fingers and let the hurt come out in irritation.

'Yes. I'm aware. I don't try hard enough to find whatever it is that will make me happy. I just sit around and rely on you—'

'No, that's not what I'm saying at all. The whole point is that some people can't make themselves happy just by "trying harder"—'

'Let's just drop it.' I can't be bothered to try to explain something to him that he doesn't understand. I shrug and do a bad impression of a happy smile which he'll undoubtedly take at face value. 'Since it's your special day I'll re-make the bed. You can go chill out for a bit.'

But he doesn't leave, he just kisses all over my face and then my neck and then my mouth. I stop and hug him in as tight as I can. Then I pull back and his shocked, happy expression physically hurts me.

Lying in bed later, as I can hear him drifting off, I say, 'Would you still love me if I got ugly?' I feel like I'm testing something but I'm not sure what yet.

'Huh?' he says, stirring sleepily.

'I just wondered if you would want to be with me if I became extremely unattractive.'

'It's impossible for you to be extremely unattractive. And besides, I'm not with you for some fixed idea of what you look like.'

'But it's possible for me to look like someone you wouldn't have got into a relationship with originally, so why would you stay with me? Just duty. I'd hate if you were with me for duty.'

He finds my hand and squeezes it. 'The reasons I want to be with you aren't conditional.'

A few minutes pass and just as I can feel him start to twitch I say, 'Would you still like me if I became fifty?'

'You will become fifty, if you're lucky. And I will still like you then. Now I'm going to turn away from you, but don't take that as a sign I don't want to be with you. Take it as a sign I'm going to sleep.'

How do I feel being with someone who has said they still want to be with me when I'm middle-aged, but hasn't said that they love me? He feels obligated to be with me before he even loves me. I wonder, is it possible to be liked so unconditionally that you stop feeling you're a person who is liked for anything in particular? I stare at the ceiling not understanding how I feel until my eyes hurt. I can't imagine feeling like this for the next thirty years. I can see it now, my whole life spent like this, being nothing other than a sedentary pet of someone else who is actually living their life. But why would I ever leave him? The perfect boyfriend: caring, safe, likes me no matter what. Well I guess 'no matter what' is the only way someone could like me because I have no motivation or desire to do or be anything worthwhile. The duvet feels increasingly heavy on my chest, and I'm worried it will stop my breathing. But as soon as I close my eyes I fall asleep.

18

The next day I wake up alone in our room and look at the clock on the bedside table. It's 1 p.m. There's a note next to the clock. 'Have some water :)' And a glass of water next to the note. I have a sip, but it tastes like metal so I pour it on the floor listening to the quiet sound it makes. The blind is open and piercing sunshine is blaring through the window, so I get up and lower it until the room becomes a smouldering cave instead. An accomplishment. It feels like I have weights for limbs.

I am lying on the edge of the bed, right on the edge, over the duvet, in the foetal position, facing outwards towards the door. Something feels different.

I hear George get back from work. He walks in, and I think he stands there for a second, looking at me, taking in this amateur dramatics show I am putting on for him, or for myself, I don't know which it is. The bed bumps up and down, it feels like he is walking on his knees up the bed. He flops down behind me, puts his arm so that it sits exactly over mine and then lifts up one of my hands, and unrolls the fingers of the hand underneath. I painted my nails earlier as a futile attempt to feel something good about myself. I wonder what he will say about it.

'Your hands are so dainty.'

He strokes my fingers with one of his fingers. He turns my hand over. 'You have such small hands.'

He turns my hand back over. 'Your nails look nice. Very red. Did you do this today? I tell you what would look good with this – a red lipstick. Though, lipstick is weird if you think about it. It's right around the bit where you eat and stuff. It always gets on everything like cups and glasses. That's the good thing about nails. It doesn't come off if you kiss it. . . Well, at least I think not. Let's check.'

He brings one of my hands to his lips and kisses my nails one by one.

'Yep. Pretty good. Nails are good.'

He lowers my hand down and softly massages different fingers.

'What are nails even for? I mean, I know they're for peeling oranges and things, but what else are they for? Fascinating if you think about it. . . Do you think I'll ever decorate my nails? Let's get you a bit more comfortable in here, shall we.'

He opens the window but then re-closes the blind. As he lays back down he puts his head on top of mine replacing the sound of his unanswered questions with the uncomfortably loud muffling sound of his face on my ear. Then he moves his head back onto the pillow.

'That's better, isn't it?'

He moves slightly away from me and lifts up the back of my t-shirt and starts tracing his finger around my back. Then he uses his whole hand, flat, like a whiteboard eraser to wipe the back clean.

'Okay, what shape am I drawing?'

He draws a triangle.

'Let me try again.'

He wipes the board clean. He draws a triangle.

'Any ideas? I'll give you a clue. The first part of its name also describes how many sides it has.'

He draws a triangle.

'It is a tough one. I'll give you another clue. The second part of its name is a word that describes the area between two lines.'

He draws a triangle.

'The first part of the word shares the same first part of the word as a type of bike with the same number of wheels as this has sides. Any ideas?'

He draws a triangle.

'The first letter is the same sound as the name of a delicious hot drink.'

He wipes the board and hugs me.

'I love you and I'm going to make sure you get better. I'm going to help you get better,' he whispers in my ear. But it's not the first time he's said that and now it just makes me feel worse. I can hear by his barely audible sigh that it does for him too. We both know I'm not going to 'get better'. And so the question has changed from 'how can she be helped?' to 'what do you do with someone who can't be helped?' Something needs to end or start or change or implode because this pretence that a transformation is just around the corner is wearing thin.

He tells me he loves me again and my lack of response hangs heavy in the air this time. But what does it say about him, loving a person like me? Does he not see that he deserves someone who appreciates and reciprocates his care and compassion? I want to tell him that I love him too. I know I do because love makes you realise that nothing else matters. And since meeting him the meaningless-ness of everything that I've spent my life doing has started leaking into my brain like a bright light that you can see even when you close your eyes. Love is debilitating. Love is demotivating. Love is desensitising. It's hard to daydream about someone you already clean your teeth with. It's hard to find a reason to paint your nails when someone loves you for who you are.

There's a reason fairy tales always finish after the wedding. Eating dinner with someone for fifty years isn't romantic, it's drip torture.

No it's not. It's self-harm.

Love is boring, but hard to give up, like breathing.

I need something new to think about.

19

A loud beeping wakes me begrudgingly out of a deep sleep. It takes me five minutes to turn it off even though the noise is piercing. I gradually remember myself last night, agitatedly setting an alarm for the first time in months. 9 a.m. The sound reminds me of work and for a second I can't remember why I ever left. My body panics, I sit up. Have I made a huge mistake? Maybe I was just worn out and now I've woken from a deep slumber ready to return to life? But then the agonising nameless pain in my mind returns and I remember there's a reason I don't have an alarm anymore. It was a stupid idea.

I detach mind from body and zombie myself out of bed. The long day ahead screams at me and I press hard on my ears to block out the sound. I catch sight of myself in the mirror. I haven't eaten much for about five days now and it's a relief to see the bones return to the surface of my skin. I focus on it, on why that used to matter.

George is at work, so I can walk around and do what I want without him reading into me just standing up as feeling 'better'. But then I feel bad, what's wrong with him wanting me to feel good? I decide to do something nice for him. Something he wouldn't expect. Maybe I'll bake. He'd be proud that I'd actually done something, and maybe I could even make myself eat it. George would love that and it could be fun. There would be a point to my day, which is so infrequent now that it's hard to think of a reason why I bother waking up.

I walk into the living room and log on to his laptop. I'm browsing the recipes and looking at the reviews for this lemon cake when I see a comment.

Love this! I have Type 2 diabetes now and live on my own, so I make this for my neighbours and they love it! Sue.

Suddenly it feels like someone has stabbed me in the chest. I can't be bothered to think through all the reasons why, but I can't help doubling over in pain and then lying curled up on the floor. Sobbing. The picture flashes into my head of Sue sitting on her own at her table, with three empty seats, and she's looking at the cake, smiling and checking her watch because she can't wait for her neighbours to get home. I'm worried about when she returns home from handing it over and she has to sit at the table again. My heart aches for her. I clench my teeth hard until the picture goes away.

It's only a few minutes later when I get up and close the laptop, making sure to erase any trace of my browsing before I do. I decide to take a long shower. Desperate to feel like a real person in the world. I shave all the hair off my body. I scrub every inch of my body. I turn the shower to cold and stand there until I can't feel my body.

When I step out the bath I feel so dizzy my eyes stop working for a second, but I go straight to the kitchen and drink three glasses of water, keeping myself up by holding on to the counter.

I go back to my old room and it's so clean and fresh compared to George's room which has absorbed all the smell of my decaying mind and body. I text Sara asking if she's around and she says she's exceedingly happy to hear from me at long last and that I absolutely have to come to the pub tonight.

I get ready, trying to look the best that I can. Attempting to find joy somewhere in my old routine, but I have no patience for the details. I don't remember what steps to do in what order, but I do remember exactly how it felt. The pleasure, the satisfaction of seeing it all come together, I feel hungry for that. I walk over to the chest of drawers and look at what's lined up on top of it. Products to hide the bad things and emphasise the good things. That's the game and I was good at it. Maybe it's the only thing I was ever good at. Because didn't everything positive come off the back of the image I'd created for myself? Maybe I was a fool to give it all up. I pick up each product one by one. I let them guide me.

Make-up looks surprisingly normal on my face as if I had never stopped wearing it. It potentially looks even better now that my skin has had some time to breathe. My eyelashes are probably stronger and the majority of my hair is in amazing condition. Months of nourishment from the intensive hair treatment called natural head oil. I get my nail scissors and cut, or rather saw off about an inch of split ends. A little skirt and a lot of jewellery and I almost feel like who I used to be, who I want to be again. I spray my perfume and the scent is like a portal into a different time. There's a hysterical desperation in me to be happy again. I can see now that it's in my control. My body feels tight with tension and my heart is racing. But not like it usually does. If I don't concentrate it might even feel quite nice.

20

Her clothes fall off her body perfectly like she's a mannequin. Not too tight, not too baggy. Sophisticated and put together, effortless. I'm standing at the bar with Sara. Over the last couple of months the thought of her has been repellent to me. It felt like I'd seen her for the first time for what she was. Shallow, insincere, conceited. Someone so self-centred she can barely see the person in front of her. Every conversation, every interaction, being used to her advantage. And if there was nothing in it for her? She's not interested. The disgust was so strong because when I thought about it, did I not used to be exactly the same?

But something has changed. I feel kind of drawn to her again. A choice presented itself to me: return or die? It seems laughable, surely life isn't so black and white? And yet I can't see another way of being. It feels so all or nothing. I can't be a George, seemingly fulfilled with being alive and well. For me, being alive is a chore. Something constantly needing attention and distraction. But I've been feeling restless, left alone with this endless misery. There is only so much a person can bear before they need a way out and I could only think of two. So I'm back here, entertaining my mind away from the pain.

Sara is telling me she's just put a deposit down on a flat in

Hammersmith. I internally roll my eyes but tell her it's an amazing achievement and that she's so lucky her dad could give her the deposit. She says she loves being so independent, but she's glad I have George to rely on. I tell her I've been using the time to work out what I want to do with my life, and she tells me that being a manager is hard but rewarding. I zone out as she tells me that a Cambridge rower broke up with his girlfriend for her. I stand here, nodding and smiling, picturing walking out the door without saying goodbye. I ask for a soda water because I don't want to spend money, but she orders us gin and tonics and pays. As we walk back she starts talking loudly to another girl at our table even though we're still three metres away.

At the table I say the things people want me to say and smile, remembering to crinkle my eyes. Studies show you can subconsciously tell if a smile is genuine because the person will get creases around their eyes. So I make my eyes crease. Yes, I can still see how performative and pointless this all is but fake happiness is better than despair. I understand now this is the closest I can get to life satisfaction.

I go out for a cigarette with Sara. I want to lean against a brick wall and enjoy a moment with my friend, or whatever she is. The warm air touches my face. I look out at everyone else smoking and drinking, enjoying themselves and I start to feel invigorated. I feel desperate to be part of it all. It seems just out of my reach. But I still think George is wrong, people can always make themselves happy they just need a reason to try.

Patrick walks out the back door into the garden. I didn't let myself hope for this to happen. Or maybe I did. Or maybe just the perfect amount, not to hope for it, but to prepare for it. He's looking around but hasn't seen us and so he turns to walk back in.

Sara is facing towards me talking about the pros and cons of holiday homes, so I interrupt, 'Patrick!'

He turns and raises his eyebrows like he's found who he was looking for.

'Paddy!' Sara turns and runs towards him like he's a soldier who's returned from war and escorts him back to where we're standing. A wave of jealousy goes through me seeing their closeness. And my mind involuntarily scrolls through all the reasons he would prefer her to me.

'All right, Iris, how's it going?' My heart jumps at him saying my name.

'Yeah, not bad. Want a cigarette?' I hold out my packet.

He gets tobacco out of his pocket and lifts it up as if to say, 'No, thanks.'

Sara starts telling him about some things he 'won't believe' happened in her day. He concentrates on rolling his cigarette as if no one is speaking to him but as soon as he's finished, he pops it in his mouth and turns to her smiling and ready to engage. His pupils are dilated in the dark so there is just a ring of the bright blue. Once he's lit his cigarette he pushes his hair back on the top of his head. I haven't seen him in so long I forgot how intimidatingly good-looking he is. I struggle not to stare at him, but I also struggle not to look away anytime I feel his eyes on me.

Sara says something about how women who take pregnancy leave should 'potentially' have less senior positions. Patrick looks at me and laughs. I notice his front two teeth turn in marginally. It suits him. Every detail about him, conventionally attractive or not, seems perfect in the context of his character. Serious and self-possessed to the extent where he makes those around him teem with nervous energy. But also withdrawn and with an air of indifference to himself and those around him. The conversation lulls as neither of us respond to her but he restarts. 'I don't notice you at work anymore.'

Sara replies for me. 'She doesn't work there anymore. Left me on my own ages ago, didn't you, babe?' She nudges me.

I keep my focus on him. 'I didn't know you actually worked there.'

He smiles and I notice he has a really defined dimple on one side. 'Did you think I just hung out there to make friends?'

'No, I just didn't see you often.'

'You weren't looking in the right places then.'

Sara's eyes are heavily lined with black pencil. Hopefully he can see mine don't need enhancing that much. I maintain eye contact with him even when Sara says, 'He freelances, but we keep finding work for him because we can't get enough.' He turns and looks at her, and I notice his hair has grown slightly over the top of his ear.

'I better go get a drink then.' He drops his cigarette, only half smoked, puts it out with his foot, and starts to walk inside. Sara follows him in saying, 'Are you trying to quit? I've been quitting for two years now!'

I stay outside and lean my head back against the wall and close my eyes for a second. The sound of everyone around me speaking makes my heart beat faster but for once it doesn't feel bad. My mind fills with ideas and feelings and wishes and instincts. I feel a glimmer of who I used to be. I can feel myself aware of every movement and decision I'm making. Navigating each moment with one goal in mind.

Inside Sara is sitting next to Patrick, but there is a space on his other side, so I sit down there. Sara is speaking at a group of people including Patrick. I'm aware that I have no one to talk to so I'm about to stand up when he turns around and says, 'So tell me, Iris, what do you do with your time now?'

The one question I didn't want him to ask, but an inevitable one. I press play on my recorded answer. 'Mainly trying to find something to do that doesn't make me want to kill myself.' I laugh and he smiles but not with his eyes.

A tiny moment passes and he hasn't said anything, so I can't help but fill the gap. 'I don't want to waste my life doing something I hate. Not that I'm judging what you do. . . It's just that it didn't suit me. But I don't think everyone who does stuff like that is wasting their life. . .'

He has almond shaped eyes that slope up at the sides. The crease of his eyelid a perfect line following the same shape.

'I think that's pretty brave.' He's looking down like he's thinking but carries on, 'Most people don't do that until they're, what, forty? To be honest, most people don't do that ever.' He looks me right in the eyes and he's not smiling, but I can't help myself. I didn't think he would react so empathetically. I'm just about to speak, but then he says, 'And then they're unfulfilled by what they do with nine hours of the day, five days a week, so they become disillusioned with their lives and end up desperately trying to distract themselves with Friday night TV and trips out to the local reasonably priced Italian restaurant.'

I worry I'm bringing the mood down so shrug and respond lightly, 'Yeah, or maybe I'm just being pretentious.'

His face stays serious. 'I don't think so.'

'Thanks. Well, I hope it works out and I don't just become a different type of forty-year-old who endlessly talks about opportunities they chose to pass up that "could've made them rich and successful" whilst sitting in the kitchen drinking £5 wine at 4 p.m.'

He nods and sharply exhales out his nose as if he's amused. I can't handle the pause again so I continue. 'Do you like your job? What is it again? I don't think I actually ever knew.'

'It's just film editing. Freelance, so there's always a small possibility I could get something cool. I like doing NFP stuff, but mostly it's just a job that allows me to fund my own shit.'

'And what's that? Film stuff?'

'Yeah. I'm trying to make sure I'm always doing something for myself, or – as you say – you end up just helping someone else realise *their* dreams, which I'm happy to do, but we should all get a chance.'

He reaches for his beer and takes a long sip. He has three faint moles making a line down his left cheekbone.

'Do you make films about anything in particular?'

'Not really.' He rubs his thumb over the other hand's bitten-down nails and looks at them. 'At the moment I'm working on one exploring male friendships. Just a vignette about how something can look restrained and insignificant on the surface, but can actually be very deep and indispensable.' He looks up. 'I like looking at unassuming things.'

It surprises me how sensitive he is. I look at him, but this time I don't speak. He can fill the space. But he doesn't, he just smiles back and then picks up his drink and finishes it. So I pick mine up and finish it too. He stands up and moves around his chair, picking up his jacket like he's going to leave, but then turns around. 'You coming for a smoke?' And then he immediately turns and walks out.

I sit there for a moment, Sara glances round behind her, but someone is speaking to her, so she has to turn back. Is she frustrated? I look at all the people at the table talking and laughing. I can feel the alcohol in my body. I'm tingling.

I stand up and walk outside. As I'm walking out I catch my reflection in the glass, my hair looks messy, but in a good way and my face looks thin.

I stand just outside the door for a second and look at Patrick leaning on the wall where I was. He's looking down at his worn brown brogues and smoking. His hair has flopped over his forehead. I walk over to him, and he looks up and pushes his hair back. I get a cigarette out and he passes me a lighter. I light it and lean against the wall next to him. He holds up his cigarette. 'I'm nearly done.'

'That's cool.' I don't seem bothered. I know he wants to stay.

He stubs it out and walks over to a table to put it in an ashtray. His legs look long in his black jeans even though he must only be about 5'10. I think the girl at the table looks him up and down.

He comes back over. 'Better roll another then.' We stand in silence for a moment. His jaw makes an L-shape from the side.

He asks me what music I like, and I ask him about his favourite films, and we talk about people who say it was in their blood to be an artist and if they actually just want fame and money. We're not smoking anymore and we're slightly closer together. His eyes are so intense and flit between furrowed with concentration and scrunched up with laughter. He tells me that he lives with a friend that he's known since he was a child and explains the reasons why he likes and respects him. He sounds so proud when he talks about him, like a parent. The only time he looks away from me is when he's talking about something passionately. He asks who I live with, and I tell him that none of my friends moved to London, so I had to get a flat share. My chest feels tight but not in a bad way. His eyelashes are so dark he almost looks like he's wearing liner. I'm telling him why I love London, and I speak for a while but when I finish he doesn't reply.

I say, 'Are you going to kiss me then?' half joking, but he doesn't do it or laugh. He just turns around so his back is flat on the wall and looks down and then pushes his hair back, but it just falls down again. I feel my face going red and my heart beating faster and the fuzziness behind my eyes suddenly leaves. I don't think I misread him. It certainly seems like it now, but I still don't think so. I'll just go inside, I'm sure I can talk to someone else who wants to kiss me. He probably already likes someone else. Petite, tanned, brunette with big beautiful brown eyes and wavy hair.

'Stuff like this is complicated for me, okay.' He speaks in a tone I've not heard before. Slightly angry, more authentic, like it's coming from somewhere deeper in him.

'Yeah, sorry, I get it.' But I don't understand. I feel bad, I want to apologise, but I don't think it's appropriate, so I just keep silent. He looks up and pushes his hair back. His nails are bitten right down.

'It doesn't matter why, but just trust me. It's not straightforward.' His face is serious and although his words are vulnerable, his tone isn't.

I break eye contact again and say, 'I'm sorry.'

His voice relaxes, 'It's okay.' He touches my hand and I get goosebumps, but it also feels like an anticlimax. He lets go. 'Do you want to get another drink?'

I relax. 'Yeah, I do.'

He has two more drinks and I have one. For the first time he is speaking more than me. We both find the same things annoying and it's invigorating to speak freely about them. The meaningless small talk at work, music being played out loud on trains, old people pretending to be young, team building exercises. Sara pulls him to the side 'for a minute' and I finish my drink listening to the rest of the group talk about whether they're cat or dog people. I stand up to leave but my desire to cement some kind of relationship with Patrick overrides any awkwardness. I ask him if he wants to go and smoke again even though I really don't want another one. He says, 'Yeah, can do,' and I feel embarrassed.

As we stand there my confidence that he likes me wanes even further. He looks me in the eyes less and the conversation falls flat because after we finish smoking he has to text someone whilst I just stand there looking like an idiot. I want to ask if it's a girl but obviously I can't. I take a breath in and in the most easy-going voice I can manage say, 'Anyway, I think I'm going to head off.'

He looks at me and nods and gets back to texting. I leave through the beer garden so I don't have to say goodbye to Sara. I feel both gutted and relieved. I feel like it's been confirmed that I'm not good enough for someone like him. I'm just another forgettable person. But I also feel relieved that I didn't do anything I'd regret. I can't wait for tomorrow when me and George can make eggs and laugh, and I can hug him from behind as he cooks, and there won't be anything unsaid hanging over us, we'll both genuinely be having a nice time. Suddenly I remember, 'Are you going to kiss me then?' The guilt hits me. Deep down I've always suspected I didn't deserve George and it feels liberating to know now for sure.

At home I stand for a while next to our bed, digging my nails into my scalp. Watching George asleep on his back, dreaming about something nice I assume. I take my clothes off and leave them on the floor and climb in next to him. I rest my head on his chest, but he only stirs. I consider making more movements so he wakes up, but before I do he speaks without opening his eyes. 'Don't forget to clean your teeth.' I kiss him on the cheek and go to the bathroom, but I only give them a quick once over before running back into bed. I lay back on his chest and then tilt my head up and whisper, 'I love you.' He wiggles his arm up and around me and gives me a squeeze. 'I love you too.'

21

My phone is vibrating on the table. I lean over — *Sara*. It rings off. George must have left for work without waking me up. I replay the scene at the pub again and again. Did I completely misread his signals? He seemed keen to talk to me and then it just stopped. It dawns on me when he changed. It was after he spoke to Sara.

Sara again. I answer this time, 'Hello, who's this?'

'It's your mother. Who do you think it is! How are you? Did you go back with Paddy? What happened there! Can you talk about it right now?' Half of her questions are exclamations.

The sound of his name gives me butterflies like I'm a teenager. I don't want Sara to know he rejected me because I know how good that will make her feel. And I also don't want her to know that there was something to 'reject' because it's risky to show her how much I want something. 'Nah, I didn't.'

I sit up and move my legs out the bed. I stick them out and look at them. For a second they don't feel like mine but I focus on how smooth and even they are.

For someone who works so hard to sound interested in my life, she struggles to sustain a conversation about it for more than one minute. 'Okay, well an insanely good-looking burger place has opened at the end of my road and I'm going crazy sitting in this flat alone. Come and let's go?'

I wonder if I actually want to go but then I see the alternative. Lying here, thinking about George, about Patrick, about the pointlessness of it all. And, besides, maybe I can find out what she said to him.

I wash my hair, put on some basic make-up and a plain outfit. I don't want her to think I was trying especially hard at the pub yesterday, but I also don't want her to notice my appearance improving. As soon as she knows I like Patrick she will need him to choose her. She's done it before and she'd do it again.

I turn the corner and Sara is standing there waving animatedly. She is wearing a tiny black strap dress. It's not tight or revealing, but her long, tanned, pole legs are sticking out the bottom and holding her up above everyone else. I can't help but think it must be a good thing I'm noticing details like this again. She gives me a big emotionless hug and then holds me by my shoulders. 'You look stunning, babe. Come on, let's get burgers, I'm starved.'

She orders some kind of rich burger with a side of fries. I don't know if that means she's not going to eat for the rest of the day or throw this up afterwards, but I can't be bothered to pretend with her today, so I order a salad. She doesn't say anything. She beams at me but there is nothing behind her eyes. 'So! Tell me then!'

I don't feel the pressure to return her enthusiasm today. I have information she wants therefore I have the power. 'Tell you what?'

'You and Paddy! I saw you guys in the smoking area for ages. I didn't want to bother you, of course. What went on?'

The waitress brings our tap water over and Sara orders a bottle of Pinot Grigio and beams at me again. 'Well, if you're not going to speak on your own!'

I don't have much of the wine, but she does, and very quickly. It's not hard to avoid the subject because she is more than happy to talk about how she had the *craziest, funniest* night where she got blackout drunk and woke up somewhere she didn't recognise, and how she's been burying herself in work. I notice the foundation cracking around the side of her nose and the skin she's picked around her nails. She isn't perfect, and at first it feels good to think about my smooth skin that doesn't need make-up. But then it makes me feel pathetic that after all this time I still can't help seeing myself in relation to her. I try to tell myself that's not who I am now. That I want George and our simple life. But an image of me lying, comatose, in George's bed flashes into my mind. I swallow it away.

She is talking about her first car and how it was so cheap she can't believe she used to drive that around and how she can't imagine not having a car now and she doesn't know how I do it. I feel like stabbing myself in the brain, and I keep picturing it, but like a cartoon. I want to stand up and leave, but I remind myself it's nice to waste time not thinking about him and picturing every moment of last night.

At the end of the meal Sara is drunk and suddenly remembers why she came here.

'What's going on with you and Paddy then?'

'What do you mean?'

'I saw you two talking at the pub. Don't play innocent with me, lady.'

I try to do a simple smile, but it comes out more 'hopeless romantic' than I would've liked.

'Yeah, we did for a while. He's nice.'

'Yeah, well, he thinks you are too!'

I don't say anything, but I can feel my cheeks warm.

'He wanted me to give you his number, babe.' She's smiling and looks genuinely happy, and I wonder if maybe she's had my back this whole time, if she'd been calling him over to be near her at the pub because she could tell I liked him and hoped this would happen. For a moment I feel an intense loneliness, picturing a friendship like this. A friendship I've never had. But I push it down. There are better things to think about. My face relaxes into a smile and it doesn't matter to me what it looks like now. She leans forward and taps my arm. 'You were "just talking", huh? You seem awfully happy about that.'

A pause hangs in the air whilst I decide whether to try something new and open up to her about George, but she reads my mind.

'I told him you're ending things with your boyf, yeah?'

My body tenses up. 'You told him about George?' I look down at my salad to avoid seeing any judgement.

'Yeah, I mean, I saw you chatting and I thought it was the right thing to do. He deserves to know. But I said things were probably over with you guys. Right?'

'Yeah. The thing is. . .' I consider telling her about how George is perfect, and that I don't know what's wrong with me, and that the thought of losing him sends a shock of pain through my body, and that I have no idea why I'm doing this, but her wide gossip-y eyes change my mind. I don't trust her motives.

'The thing is what?'

'I don't think I can move out yet. So it's a little awkward. But I'm sure it will work itself out.'

She drinks all the wine, eats half her burger and we split the bill. Then she gives me his number and slurs, 'He's a good guy. It's hard to find a good guy who's not desperate. I'm always going for these men I *think* I respect, even though they give me no good reason to respect them, and then. . . well. . . anyway. . .' She trails off and I look at her sunken face wondering if I should ask her if she's okay, but I remind myself she has everything and anyone she wants. I give her a tight hug. 'We should do this more often!'

She looks like she's about to burst. 'Of course we bloody should, I need some serious girl time.'

On the way home I picture all the different ways he might have asked her to give me his number. If he went out of his way to say it or if it just came up in conversation. I wonder how rare this kind of behaviour is from him. I think about his laugh and his serious face and what it would be like to kiss him.

I realise I'll have to message him first because I have his number, so I wait a week. And in that week I feel myself return. I shower every day, I eat fruit and vegetables, I go on long walks and dream about Patrick, smiling outwardly at the things I picture us doing together. When I look at myself in the mirror, I know things are going well. I am becoming the best version of myself again. I don't want to lose that.

George is smiling at me more; says I seem brighter. One day I put on make-up and I ask him if he thinks I look nice, he says I always look nice, I roll my eyes and walk into my room. I feel myself being cold to him but it's only because being nice to him feels dirty and cruel.

I message Patrick, 'This is my number btw (iris)(from work and the pub).' He replies straight away asking how I got his number. I reply that Sara gave it to me and he says he was joking and that he's had his phone on loud since he told her to give it to me which meant he got some funny looks at the funeral he went to. I apologise and say I should have messaged him sooner. He says don't be sorry all that matters is that I eventually did because that's what they (the deceased) would have wanted anyway. I ask him if he's at least got a good text tone and he says not yet but he's trying to save up for a Crazy Frog one he saw on an advert. I don't reply because I have to eat dinner but when I next check he's messaged again saying he's sorry about how abruptly it ended at the pub the other week. I tell him there's nothing to be sorry about and he asks if he can earn my forgiveness by taking me out for an alcoholic beverage of my choice. I say, of my choice? Are you sure? Because my choice is usually a mid-range bottle of champagne. He says, okay an alcoholic beverage of my choice up to the value of seven Great British Pounds.

We speak all day every day for a week about everything and nothing. Every time my phone lights up my body and mind feel bright and electric. I barely lie in bed or think about dying. In fact, I don't think about anything else.

22

Patrick is late. I'm waiting outside Moorgate Station, leaning against the wall so I'm not facing the entrance when he walks out. Not only is that less awkward because you don't have to maintain eye contact for the whole time they're walking towards you, but also he'll be able to look at me for a while without having to pretend not to. I think about looking at my phone, but I decide staring into space seems more intriguing. The melting-yolk August sun is still harsh in my eyes and the air is hot in my throat.

He is ten minutes late when he comes out. We hug like we're fifteen-year-olds. The atmosphere is slightly more uncomfortable than I thought it would be. He says, 'I thought here would be a good shout. I know this sick place,' and walks off.

His hair has grown out a little around the nape of his neck. He's wearing a short sleeve shirt and his pale thin arms poke out the baggy sleeves. He looks effortlessly cool. I wonder if he thinks I've tried too hard. My eye make-up is heavier than usual, my top is small and my skirt is short. I reassure myself that next time I will dress better. No one has spoken but he seems too preoccupied with leading us there. How can I show that I'm not awkward?

'I like your shirt.'

'Thanks.' His thanks has barely any tone. Things are going to fall into another lull, and I'm desperate for that not to happen so I blurt out, 'You're very welcome,' and then quickly move on, 'What have you been up to?' My body is tight with tension. I start to worry that this whole thing will be awkward and that he is disappointed with my looks and personality.

He stops suddenly, but I keep walking for a few steps before I see he's not next to me and turn around. He still isn't smiling. 'This is it.' He's pointing to an entrance of what looks like a multi-storey carpark. I don't want to laugh in case he's not joking. And it's lucky I didn't because he walks into the concrete building.

We go up a number of flights of stairs, me trailing behind him, until we come out onto the roof. There are lights strung up everywhere, little stands selling different types of drinks and food, people talking in groups or pairs, holding plastic cups of alcohol with slices of citrus fruits. People posing for photos of where they are rather than who they're with. I shake off that thought and instead focus on the fact I'm included in this crowd. I'm on a fun date, on a rooftop, whilst the sun sets, with a strikingly attractive guy.

We stand in the corner and I'm glad we're not sitting because it's easier to get close like this. As Patrick goes to get us some drinks I take a deep breath in as if I could take in the entire atmosphere – sounds, lights, smells, heat – just by inhaling. It occurs to me that I might want to do things with Patrick simply because I've done less things with him than George. I can't help but feel it's refreshing to see the world through a new pair of eyes, to see myself through them too. But is that a good enough reason?

Patrick brings back a trendy pink drink for me and a beer for himself. His body language immediately relaxes like he can finally start to talk. He looks right at me, smiles, just slightly, and says I look 'really good' and that I have 'incredible eyes'.

I don't love the bashful smile that grows on my face but I can't help it. I actually feel giddy. This is why I'm here. We speak about our days for a minute or two, but I don't want this to be boring.

Something about him makes me want to open up so I tell him I think everyone here is pretentious and he agrees. He says he feels uncomfortable in these situations, even though he pretends not to, and that he's spent a long time learning how to do that. I say maybe everyone is pretending. He looks away while he tells me that he thinks most people are to some extent, but as a child he didn't have a role model – his mum left when he was young and his relationship with his dad was close, but too intense – so he learnt everything by copying other people's behaviours. He says he's so used to pretending to enjoy himself that he finds it hard sometimes to work out if he really is or not. I tell him I know exactly what he means. I can't help nodding at everything he says. I'm surprised about how affirming it feels talking to someone who knows how hard the simplest things can be.

He asks me questions about my vanilla life and listens intently to everything I say as if it's actually interesting.

When there's a break in the conversation he glides his finger over the piercings in my ear and says, 'These are class.' My body tingles.

'Thank you.' I love that he notices little details. 'These are "class".' I run my finger in the hollows underneath his cheekbones.

He touches his face confused, 'My cheeks?'

'Your cheekbones.'

'You like my skull?'

'I like your face.'

He briefly smiles and I take the pause to change the conversation. 'The other night in the pub garden, when you said that these things were complicated, what did you mean?'

He pushes his hair back. 'Look, I don't really want to get into the reasons why but when it comes to dating, I'm really. . . urm. Picky, I guess.'

'Oh, right. What are you picky about?' I'm suddenly ultra-aware of all my assets and flaws.

'I just know what I like and I won't settle for less.' He does a little smirk. I'm tempted to press for more, to hold myself up to his ideal, but I decide to drop it, not wanting to dwell on the other girls who make this list.

'Oh, right.'

'I don't mind being on my own and so I don't fall into relationships for the sake of it. The last time I told someone I loved them was three years ago.'

I will my face not to show that hurt to hear. 'Yeah. . . I guess that is long.' I calm myself down with the thought that soon I will replace that person entirely.

He looks me right in the eyes and says we should get out of here.

As we walk down the stairs to leave he puts his arm around my waist to guide me out the way of someone trying to get past and the excitement of everything to come with him is so overwhelming. I can't help but stare at his dimple as he smiles politely at the person walking by us.

We are walking back to his but he stops briefly every now and again to look me in the eye when he's saying something passionately. 'I'm glad we met even though you left.'

'Well, actually, we met when we both still worked there, and I've been wanting to re-meet you ever since.'

He laughs with a little confused frown and starts to walk again, but I can't help standing still and squeezing my eyes closed for a second. As soon as he knows I like him this much he won't like me anymore. I feel as if I'm losing control.

He turns around. 'Aren't you coming?'

I stand still. 'Maybe I shouldn't come.'

He frowns. 'Why?'

'I don't know. I just thought maybe I shouldn't. . .' I trail off.

He hasn't walked towards me and I haven't walked towards him so we're slightly raising our voices.

'So you don't want to come?' I can tell by the tone of his voice that this is the final question and I guess if I say no then it will be the *final* final question.

'Yeah, I do.'

He smiles and walks over and puts his hand lightly on the top of my back. 'Come on then, let's go.'

I'm at his flat looking around his room as much as I can without making it obvious. It's not tidy, but it's not messy. There's a small picture of a footballer BluTacked on a random part of the wall like a child would have, a small pile of unopened post on his floor near the door, a towel on his unmade bed, the window is fully open, but it's small and still really hot in here, there's a football and a couple of tennis balls on the floor at the back of the room. Other than that, the room is pretty empty and has a fresh smell, maybe citrusy.

He's emptying his pockets of keys, wallet, tobacco onto the bed, and I'm talking fast about East London and how it has a different feel to the north. He asks me if I still live in Kilburn and I say yes but he walks over and kisses me so I don't have to elaborate. He puts his hands on my waist and pulls me really close. My head feels like it's going to explode. I love kissing him. I love his hands on me. He starts taking off my clothes, but I don't know whether to wait to take his off because it might be hard to do it at the same time, but soon mine are on the floor and he's taking his off and I'm wondering if he thinks it's weird that I didn't do it for him.

He reaches for a condom in his chest of drawers, and I see the packet is already open and it gives me a twinge in my stomach, and I feel like getting up and leaving without saying anything, but instead I put my energy into making it seem like I'm having a good time. But I don't need to pretend for long. The way he looks at me, my body, my eyes. I feel desired. And it's exhilarating being chosen by him. I tingle with pleasure but it isn't from his touch. It's the sensation of liking myself. My life, for the briefest moment, is validated because this person I'm obsessed with is enjoying my existence.

I can tell he's concerned I won't get there but I can't get out of my head enough to let go. Luckily, I know how to act in this situation, to work out how and who he wants me to be. One of my greatest talents, after all, was making men feel relaxed and confident enough to enjoy themselves.

We're both lying on our backs a few inches apart. He turns his head towards me, so I turn mine towards him. I wonder what he thinks of me compared to everyone else he's slept with. I want to be the best.

'Cigarette?'

I try to keep my expression neutral. 'Yeah, all right.'

He bounces up and puts his boxers on and picks up his smoking things off the floor, sits on the edge of the bed and starts rolling a cigarette. It feels exposing to be lying down, naked, whilst he's sitting up, partially clothed, so I get up and hop around finding my clothes from the bed and floor. When I've finished dressing, he's finished rolling, so he goes and puts on his jeans and a fresh t-shirt.

We go to the tiny lift down the hall and then walk outside.

I break the silence. 'It's strange to think of all the people in there, sleeping, the hours passing by until they wake up and spend their only totally free day and night doing something to make them feel like the last five days were worth it.'

He blows smoke out to reply. 'Most of them probably know it's not worth it, at least deep down.'

'But they have to believe it or they wouldn't be able to carry on. This isn't about getting through a week, it's about getting through a life.'

His hair has become tufty on top, and his lips are chapped and I wonder how long he will like me. How much he likes me now. How many times he's had conversations like this, with girls he's rolled a cigarette for, working out if they're good enough for him.

'Maybe it's not only weekends that make people feel happy.'

I feel my voice turn a shade too serious. 'What then? A night at the bar on a Thursday with their friends where they get drunk to forget about things? And then end up saying things they'll want to get drunk to forget about next week? Or a meal that they buy from Itsu on a Tuesday which is slightly nicer than the ones they prepare for themselves?' I cut myself off before it becomes a rant.

He shrugs. 'I mean more like, seeing a person you like? People?'

Is he flirting? I pretend that I don't notice any subtext to what he's said.

'Do you think connections with people are more valuable than the other superficial things?'

'Yeah, I think I do.'

'How come?'

'You can't stay with someone for fifty years just as a distraction for how shit everything is.'

I put my cigarette out and walk over to a bin and then lead the way back in. We travel back up in silence again. The plastic 'mirror' on the wall of the lift shows only a Cubist version of my face, but I can still tell I look awful.

While he opens his door I start speaking again. 'I think being with someone for fifty years is the ultimate distraction, why else would you do it?' He shrugs and goes to brush his teeth. When he comes back in he sits down on the bed with a huff. I feel awkward like I'm intruding. I want to ask if he'd rather I leave, but I know that's the more embarrassing thing to do.

'The bathroom is the one at the end of the hall by the way.' I turn to look at him. 'I think your make-up looks cool a bit smudged like that.' He points at my face. I love how his compliments are so specific. It makes me feel seen in a whole new way.

'Thanks.'

I get my toothbrush from my bag, feeling myself blush a bit. I walk out. It makes me feel out of control that I've had to bring a toothbrush with me. I hate that it shows that I was expecting to come here, and it wasn't an impulsive choice based on our interactions tonight.

When I walk back in, he's lying flat on his back with his eyes closed. His lack of bedside table means no bedside lamp, so I don't know whether to switch the main light off before getting into bed. I decide it would be worse to get into bed and lie in silence and then have to get up again and turn it off. So I do it now, take off my skirt and top and cautiously walk to the bed in the dark.

'Let me guide you with my voice.' His voice says and then a cute laugh comes from the darkness, and my head pulses with how much I like him. I get into bed and face away from him and drift in and out of a light sleep until the sun comes through his blindless window at about 6 a.m.

I wake up with a start. I can hear my heart thudding. I turn on to my side and curl into a ball but the sound is still there. My mind is whirring. It doesn't even finish a thought before it moves on to the next. I think about the fact my parents will one day be dead and I will be completely alone in the world. I think about how I don't know if I've ever truly felt joy. I think about George, home alone, trying to persuade himself that the reason I haven't come back isn't to do with the person I've been texting all week. I think about all the upcoming years I somehow have to use up doing things and being someone. I squeeze my hands into fists and tell myself to concentrate on last night. I turn to look at Patrick and his beauty calms me down slightly but my skin still prickles. The heaviness growing in my shoulders tells me I need to leave before something bad happens and he sees me like this.

I slowly slip out of bed trying to be as quiet as possible, but I feel like the slow movements actually end up making the whole thing louder. I pull on my skirt and top which looks even more try-hard than last night. He stirs and turns on to his back, his arms behind his head, but doesn't open his eyes.

'You off?'

I sit on the edge of the bed. I can feel the warmth from him, and I'm so tempted to get in and hug him and put my head on his chest and fall asleep, but I don't.

'Yeah, I think so.'

His voice is hoarse. 'All right, cool.'

Cool? My heart twists. I think about spending the rest of the weekend with George.

'What you up to this weekend then?' I know it sounds weird as soon as I've said it but my brain isn't working.

'Think I'm going out tonight.'

He doesn't ask me back, just turns over. His shoulder blade is sharp and white except for one mole on the top. I want to lean over and kiss it. I wait for a second to see if he'll say goodbye or that he'll text me later but he doesn't.

I stand up and wait for a second, squeezing my bottom lip in between my fingers. Wondering if this is what he does with girls; tests them to see if they meet his standards and then if they don't never speaks to them again. I walk out letting his heavy door slam behind me. I clench and unclench my jaw and try to keep my breathing reasonably slow.

When I get outside, I breathe in the early morning air which has that particular fresh smell I only associate with the excitement of going to the airport or the regret of leaving a random location after a night of no sleep. I feel like I should crouch down and press my head into my hands. But I pause and lift my head slightly to feel the sun on my face instead and breathe in the unusually crisp air reminding myself I don't need him and I don't want him. I want someone who will stroke my hair and hold my hand while I fall asleep. I want someone who is kind and thoughtful. I want George. I've made a huge mistake but at least I know that now. It's over. Maybe I can rectify things.

23

I don't try to be quiet when I open the front door, but I think it ends up seeming like I'm trying *not* to be quiet. I can hear him in the kitchen rattling around, though I can't smell anything cooking. The fact he doesn't shout 'Hi!' makes my chest tighten. It's not usual behaviour, but then I remember this isn't a usual situation.

My body is pulsing with adrenaline. I walk straight into our bedroom and start taking off my clothes which smell of cigarettes, alcohol, and probably another guy. I think a shower might be too obvious, so I throw on some shorts and a grey t-shirt of George's that's lying on the made bed. I go to the mirror over the chest of drawers, which is always too far away for me to see my face in detail, but right now I'm happy with the distance. My eyelids are purple, and my skin is blotchy. I picture screaming at myself 'Who gives a shit' and then smashing the mirror.

I grab the toothbrush from my bag and go to leave the bedroom, but George is just about to come in. My chest tightens again, and the atmosphere feels so tense but I can't help doing an awkward smile. He steps to the side. 'After you.' He gestures with his hands out towards the hall like a bell boy. I want to drop to my knees, hug his calves, beg for forgiveness. But instead I walk into the space and off towards the bathroom.

I have to squeeze my eyes from the pain. I feel worse than ever. In the bathroom I shut the door and let my eyes lose focus. I try not to let myself hope for everything to be fine. But that's what I want. I want to rewind time. I want to never have met Patrick. I want me and George and our life together. Yes, Patrick gave me a buzz, a high, but it meant nothing. It was hollow. And I was weak and selfish for choosing that momentary relief over what I have with George.

I slide down the door like I think I'm in some kind of film, but it doesn't really work so I end up basically dropping down. I sit there for a few minutes looking at all our different products lined up around the thin rim of the bath. I see the Nivea Creme moisturiser which he uses for his face wash because 'it feels soft'. It's funny, and I laugh in a small exhale, but I think I've forced myself to do it.

I stand up, inhale deeply and open the mirrored cabinet to get the toothpaste but then see his toothbrush, lying there, next to nothing. I wonder if he even noticed. I feel a deep sadness, but also a calmness, I think. I realise I shouldn't try to save this. He deserves better. My heart burns but I try to console myself with the fact the constant underlying ache of not being worthy of his love is about to be over. I clean my teeth and put my toothbrush next to his and close the cupboard unnaturally slowly and purposefully.

I leave the bathroom and as I walk towards the bedroom I take my hair out of the bun and start running my fingers through it so I have something to do with my hands. He is sitting on the edge of the bed looking at something on his phone, but I don't look too much as I walk past the bed back towards the mirror. I continue with my hand-combing but I can feel them shaking so I stop. I can see him in the reflection, and he doesn't so much as look up for one second. I'm desperate for this to be over with but I don't know how to start it. I look at him through the mirror and say anything.

'Did you already have breakfast?'

He looks up, but not at me, not at my reflection. He does the expression of someone who has been fully engrossed in something and then suddenly realises they're not alone.

'Oh yeah, sorry, I just had cereal today.'

'I might make something.'

He's looking back down at his phone now. 'Go for it. I'm still full from the cereal though so don't worry about me.'

I turn to look at the real him. Suddenly I can't bear the idea of never seeing that face again. I need him. I need us. But he obviously knows something has happened and an instinct in me decides to take a risk.

'Thanks for asking me how my night was! Even a flatmate would've asked that!'

I can hear my heart beating and even though I know it's impossible, I'm worried he can too.

He looks at me, an unreadable face, so neutral, nothing bad in the eyes, but no warmth.

'How was your night?'

I don't let myself think and the words just fall out.

'It was okay. Pretty good actually, it was just one of those super late ones where you don't leave even though nobody really wants to be there anymore, but it's just no one suggests going home. We stayed out so long the night ended up being a bit shit really, like I was basically hungover before I left. We went back to Sara's because it was way closer and honestly at that point I just needed to lie down. I kind of woke up at one point and Sara was right in the middle of the bed and I was like, hanging off it, and also just had that feeling where I *really* wanted my own bed. You know when you just get that sudden pang to be back in your own bed, with like all your own things around you and not surrounded by someone else's smell? Like you can't fully relax properly unless you're in your own bed, which is why hotels are never as fun as you think they're going to be. Anyway yeah, so I just got up instead of going back to sleep and came back here rather than falling asleep again there.'

I gaze at him. Waiting to see if I passed the test. But he just smiles at me once I've finished.

'Yeah, I know what you mean.'

I want us to be okay, I want things to be normal, but I can't help wanting to see that he loves me and in the way that I love him; painfully, desperately. It hurts to see how little this has affected him.

My pain comes out as anger. 'Why are you being like this?'

George puts his phone in his pocket, looks down for a second, runs a hand over his hair and looks back up, but not at me.

He speaks calmly. 'Why are you doing this?'

He doesn't look angry, and he only looks a bit sad, like someone who's just missed the bus. My breathing is fast now. I press my thumbs and index fingers on my temples and close my eyes and take a deep breath and then I shout.

'Why don't you care about anything?'

He doesn't reply so I open my eyes and look at him to check his expression. He's looking at me now, still slightly sad. 'I do care, that's why I asked.'

My heart tears open with guilt. But it's the salt in the wound which makes me want to double over. This proof that his feelings for me don't run deep. Maybe he cares for me, yes, but he doesn't love me.

I suddenly feel so overwhelmed I don't know what to say or do. I feel like I want to crawl under the bed and shuffle right to the back, through any cobwebs or dust, and I wouldn't even care about them, I'd just get right up against the cold wall and lie there for as long as I wanted. There's a lot of stuff under the bed so I would have to get past it, but hopefully I could just push it away. Although I don't want to move things with my hands, I just want to push my body quickly and forcefully right to the back so I can be against the cold wall.

He is still looking at me, his facial expression I realise now is worry. I walk to the end of the bed, climb on and lie down next to the wall, facing the wall, nose pressed up against the wall. I close my eyes and try to work out how I feel. I think I feel terrible, I think I feel like there is no point in anything, even the things I thought there was a point in. All along I was just telling myself there was a point in things. In people. But there's not. I cling on to this emptiness as protection from the pain.

It doesn't feel like George has moved. I wonder what he feels right now. What is he thinking? It feels like so much has been said, but technically nothing has. How much does he know? Maybe it's not as much as I think. Maybe he's just upset I stayed out late without telling him. Or is his heart ripping open right now? What would his life be like without me? Unbearable. Painfully mundane, day after day, working, having a beer with people who only talk about football and food. Or not. Probably just carefree, peaceful, day after day without drama, socialising with happy people who appreciate him. My eyes keep rolling back because the feeling is too strong. I push my nose hard against the wall but it hurts and I'm worried about damaging the cartilage so I stop.

I feel him stand up from the bed, so I turn around. I desperately don't want him to leave, but he wasn't leaving, he's looking at me, so I quickly turn back around. I hear him climb onto the bed and he lies down next to me, pushes my hair up on the pillow and strokes my neck. I let out a huge breath, but my chest feels even tighter and I start crying. I could sob loudly but I don't. I stay silent. The tears are pouring out of my eyes and some of them fall on the blue wall beneath the crack of the bed. He either can't tell or doesn't react, but it doesn't matter either way because eventually I drift off to sleep and I can tell he does too.

When we wake up we pretend to be normal. I don't know why or how but it's like we woke up from a nightmare and now can get on with our evening. He makes roasted vegetables with orzo and mascarpone and I sit on the sofa. We don't speak much. I just watch his perfectly proportioned body move around the kitchen, his chestnut brown eyes focused on the worktop. The warmth of his company begins to melt me and for a second the regret of everything with Patrick is so crushing I feel as if I could choke. But I swallow it down with everything else. I have got the impossible. I've clawed my life back. Now enjoy it.

After dinner we stay on the sofa. He puts his legs over my thighs. The TV is on quietly, but we're not watching it. His eyes are closed and I'm giving his calves soft strokes.

'Do you ever get that thing where you look around and there are so many other people, like even just on one street, in one city, in one country, and they all have their own thoughts and problems and wishes?'

A little smile appears on his face, but he doesn't open his eyes. 'Yeah, I guess so.'

'And I just think, are we all thinking about the same thing?

Not the same thing but the same *things*, like, probably most people are just walking around thinking of someone they like, or how an interaction with someone they were with earlier went. Or just about something they want, and it will feel *so* important to them, but I'll never even know about it, their thoughts, no one ever will except them, and that's just how unimportant they actually are. It's all so pointless.'

He doesn't say anything, and when I look around he's still got the little smile, but his breathing is slower and he looks sleepier. I lean over and flick him softly on the forehead. 'I know my thoughts also mean nothing in the context of the planet, but it would still be nice if you listened to them.'

He still doesn't open his eyes, but now his smile gets big. 'I did listen.'

'Okay, what did I say then?'

'You said. . . uh. . .'

I push his legs off me and stand up and look down at him, his eyes are now open. 'Even if you find what I'm saying *so* boring, just actually listening to what I'm saying and dignifying it with any type of answer is the most basic level of politeness. Imagine if you did that to literally anyone else? It would be so rude. Even your own family would be like "what the fuck" or whatever. So why do I get such "special" treatment?'

I'm so far away from being a rational person these days I have no idea whether I'm being reasonable or not. But sometimes he makes me feel like I am no one in particular, just a person who he's ended up spending time with. I consider asking him why he loves me but an image of watching him trying to think of an answer pops into my head and I realise it would destroy me.

He sits up, shocked, and leans forward to touch my leg. 'I did listen. I was only joking. You were saying about how everyone has their own stuff going on and how it all means nothing. Honestly though, I'm so tired, and I'm not even sure what I would say to that at the best of times. I'm sorry.'

He looks up at me and his warm eyes are so pure like a puppy. Maybe they even look like they're filling with tears. My eyes ache with how much they've been crying, but I can't stop it happening again. I try to force out the words 'Let's just talk about it' but before I can he stands up and hugs me and holds my head against his chest and kisses the top of it. The sobbing eases up, but I have an aching pain in my heart and I don't know what to say to make it go away, but I don't need to because he says, 'Let's go to bed' and holds my hand and walks me to the bathroom and passes me my toothbrush and we clean our teeth together. Every now and again I start crying, but he just does an impression of me crying with a toothbrush in my mouth and laughs and I always laugh too. There's yet to be a time when he can't make me laugh.

In bed he faces away from the wall, and I spoon him. I feel like something terrible is going to happen. Like I'm out of options. The upcoming hours and days and weeks terrify me. The only reason I can sleep is because I physically cannot stay awake.

24

I have saved my relationship but not my mind. I'm overjoyed to be secure again with George but nothing has really changed. Either I'm lying in bed and not responding or I'm briefly sitting up to eat the meal he's cooked. Sometimes I look at him and feel such a surge of love I have to squeeze him tightly. But when I cry into his shoulder and beg him to tell me what to do and he whispers, 'Everything is going to be okay,' a fury rises in me. He knows it's not going to be okay, so I ask him why he keeps saying that. He offers suggestions instead, things I might do to feel better. But it feels like someone telling me that if I tried hard enough I could change eye colour. I know all I give to him is negativity, worry, disappointment, stress. But this pressure I feel from him, to be displaying some kind of upward trajectory in mood is frustrating and soul-destroying. So I shut myself away. Just like my nan I sit alone, waiting for the days to pass.

I hear nothing from Patrick. And it doesn't take long for me to stop checking my phone. I wear out the same trains of thoughts; about me not being good enough, not passing his tests, listing the reasons why I might have failed. But it's once there's nothing left to think about when the days become insufferable again. I miss the days of cataloguing my flaws, because suddenly there is no such thing as a flaw. Life slips into the abstract. I forget why people care about anything. I laugh at the concept of having trivial concerns and petty wishes because it all means nothing to me. Then I get a message.

Patrick is talking a lot, filling up most of the conversation actually, whilst I sit here, sipping the drink he bought me. He's talking about finding an authentic self.

'I gotta say, I don't think there is such a thing. People seem so sure of themselves.' He does an impression of someone being defensive *'That's just who I am.'* He rolls his eyes and continues, 'Like everything they are is a given or something. But it's like they can't see that they've just chosen to be that way. You're not *"you"*, you're just someone you've chosen to be.'

My mind is fizzing with how much I love speaking to him about these things, but on the outside I'm just nodding and smiling and not saying much.

I don't think he expected me to ignore him back and it became clear that something as simple as not speaking to someone for a while can make them desperate to speak to you. It was impossible to stay away from him when he decided, eventually, to reach out to me. And so we met and had an exhilarating time together. And I told myself that this was the last time, but then he didn't speak to me for days and I felt myself drawn back into the cycle. The relief it gives me to fill my brain up with him.

He finishes speaking. 'Anyway, that's just something I've been thinking about recently. Maybe none of that made sense.' He looks slightly embarrassed and pissed off at my lack of engagement. I reach over and briefly touch his hands, which are crossed on the table.

'I'm just going to get us some more drinks and then I'll respond to that.'

He almost seems out of breath and he's jigging his leg under the table.

'Yeah, okay.'

I have to appreciate every moment where I have the power because before I know it, it will be gone.

At the bar the guy serving me, who makes a ponytail and earring look cool, asks me how it's going and nods his head to the table where we're sitting.

'Well we're basically talking about whether you're born with a personality or if you create your own, so, I don't know. What do you think? As in do you think that means the date is going well. . . not do you think we're born with our personalities or not. Unless you happen to know? And then feel free to tell me that too.'

He laughs a lot, and I hope Patrick sees. Attraction comes from the desire to have what other people want.

With Patrick I'm living in the past and the future. I think in 'last times' and 'next times'. The next message, the next kiss, the next time I'll see his face. I pick apart and analyse every interaction we've had. When I'm with George I'm living in the present. I think in 'whys' and 'hows'. Why do I feel like this? How can I get through the day? I question the world around me, the concept of life. It's all so absurd and meaningless. I make myself ill trying to find a reason for this debilitating ache in my mind and body.

So instead, I let my mind teem with questions about Patrick: is he seeing anyone else, what does he like about me, where does he see this going? Things are perfect and yet it could all slip through my fingers at any moment. And that is the whole joy of it. Living like this helps me with the time spent in my bedroom. Without thoughts of Patrick, long hours elapse lying down, picturing the relief death would bring me and everyone who knows me, listening out for when George goes to work so I can leave my room, just like back in the old days.

I walk back with our drinks.

'Right, where were we?' I take my hair bobble from around my wrist and put my hair up quickly in a rough bun. 'I totally know what you're saying, although I almost wish that I didn't because I don't know what we're supposed to do with that information. Sometimes I think, if I was born and put on a concrete slab with nothing on it except me until I was like, twenty, and then released into this world. . . I think, how would I turn out? What I'm trying to say is that, am I just this person because of everything that's ever happened to me? Cause of the parents I had, and all my experiences till now? Like, basically, was it inevitable that I turned out like this? That everything I do isn't a "choice" I've made but just the next step in this relentless algorithm? And if so, what does that make me? Basically nothing more than this equation that I've had no say in. Which surely means there isn't some "calling" in life I need to figure out, because essentially, everything has already been decided for me. So there is no "point" in my life.'

I've not been looking at him and I feel like my face is flushed because saying all that out loud reminds me of the dark thoughts I try not to focus on when I'm with Patrick. They cry out for attention. But then I look back at him and he's smiling with the wide-eyed look of someone who is falling in love. I feel like I'm more alive than usual.

He doesn't reply for a second and then leans back on his chair, smiles and shakes his head a little.

'Since I've met you everyone else bores me, you know. I feel like you get it.'

I give no reaction except a small laugh and a shrug even though

I'm tingling by now. The less seriously I respond to these comments the more likely he is to keep taking it up a notch to see if he can get a reaction.

'Maybe you just know boring people.'

It's crazy to sit here looking at his perfect face, looking at mine. Looking at me like I'm better than anyone else he's ever met. When I can see Patrick's desire, it lets me believe in all kinds of things I dream up – like right now I'm thinking that any of his other girls wouldn't be able to hold a conversation about the kind of things we talk about. That they probably just talk about their jobs and ask generic meaningless questions like 'Do you have any tattoos?' I feel better than them. I feel like someone needs me.

'Shall we get out of here?' He gets his tobacco out and rolls us cigarettes and then stands up. 'Let's go.'

I've barely even touched my drink, but I don't think he's noticed. He looks at me in my short gingham dress. 'You're going to be cold at this hour, Iris.' He stops and rummages in his backpack and takes out a zip-up sports jacket. 'This is as best as I can do I'm afraid.'

I laugh and put it on, it's basically the same length as my dress so I leave it unzipped. We step outside into the evening light, there is rarely an evening darkness at this time of year.

'Let's see then.' He walks back a few steps to look at me. I think it probably actually looks quite good with my bare legs poking out the bottom.

'Let me guess, I look stunning?' I spin around.

He walks over to light my cigarette and then his. I'm just about to ask what we should do next, but he puts his arm around my shoulders and leads me away. 'You actually do. Always.'

I feel the perfect amount of warm in his jacket and under his arm, and I have to take a deep breath in because I feel so happy. I feel beautiful. I wonder if he's thinking about having sex with me. I can't understand why people don't like to be seen as objects when to be seen as an object is to be desired. This is why I keep coming back.

The sky is finally colourless. His open window letting in air that's no cooler than the room's. Its lack of blind has not become a problem yet. And so, we're lying half naked and facing each other, in this fleetingly dark, oppressively hot room. Sometimes he tucks my hair behind my ear and then I pretend to tuck his hair behind his, and we have a little laugh. Whenever he touches my skin I shiver. He tells me he likes my body and I wonder what he thinks is the perfect weight for a woman. I remind myself to start doing crunches again. This is exactly how I knew it would be: infatuation fills you with motivation and true love empties you of it.

When I wake up to the sun, we're lying in the exact same position so I doubt we have been in a deep sleep. I glance at the window. The light is shining mainly on the wall next to it. Even in the warmest of lights his skin is a cold white. His black hair has stayed pushed back and the roots seem a little greasy, but in a way which somehow still looks nice. Even in his sleep he seems in control of himself. His arms are stretched out in front of him, but have the limpness of sleep. I look at his thin arms and visible rib cage and his stomach which is so taut even when he's lying on his side. How can someone made of so little be so intimidating to me? I wonder if I could hold him down, but then I remember last night when he picked me up to carry me to the bed, and I guess he's stronger than he seems.

'Don't get up and leave this time.'

I jump a little and look at his now open eyes. 'How long have you been awake?'

He rubs his eyes like a cartoon character waking up. 'Why, what have you been doing to me?'

I want to touch him as in the mornings we tend to become sober people that did something because they were drunk.

I smooth his hair back over his forehead and say, 'Nothing to see here, I'm afraid.' I'm not sure what that really means or if he thinks me touching his hair is like me saying, 'I'm your girlfriend who sorts out your hair now', but before I can rectify it he turns on to his back and stretches his legs down and his arms back, though he's too close to the wall so his arms can't extend fully. He makes a little sound, which sounds like a fake yawn and rubs his eyes again.

'What time is it?'

I hate how I'm watching him and he's looking up, but I can't exactly turn on to my back now. I wish he would touch me.

'I'm not sure, maybe looks like early morning time.'

He crosses his forearms over his eyes. 'Is that how people told the time back in ye old past times?' He does a weird country-bumpkin type accent although I don't know why.

'Why, would ye look at that, it's nearly-early-morning-time, yer gonna be late fa' work. Won't get thur 'til slightly-later-mornin-time if ye don't get goin'.'

I'm smiling, but I don't find it funny. I just want him to look around so I keep quiet. He does. Just his head though, not his body. Is he going to touch me? I want him to change the subject back to me not leaving. He returns my smile and then turns back putting his forearms over his eyes again.

'You know how to get a man tipsy, don't you?'

I don't say anything and he turns his whole body around this time. He opens both his eyes really wide. '*What* did we do last night?'

I don't reply. His eyes return to normal. The lines of his eyelids are straight lines rather than round and it makes him look like a pixie. I want to tell him I love his eyelids. He moves my nose side to side.

'How are you this early morning then?'

'I'm okay. I do have to leave now though I'm afraid.' I immediately regret saying it but I had to. I felt myself slipping towards him. To leave myself open like that would be to lose.

The sky outside his window has already reached baby blue by the time I've gathered my few things and put on my dress. He hasn't even sat up to engage me in conversation. I was hoping he would see me walk around in my underwear for a bit as I don't think you can fully appreciate someone's body when you're tangled together having sex.

He sits up just as I'm ready. 'Where do you have to be to leave here at 6 a.m. on a Saturday?'

I let a second pass. I think there is a momentary non-verbal communication acknowledging the reality of George, the fact he's still my boyfriend and I live with him. Someone I haven't broken up with, but I'm cheating on. With him. But he just lies back down and puts his forearms over his eyes. He's so stunning it makes me want to cry. I hope one day he'll tell me he loves me and I won't say it back. For now my relationship with George is something I have over him. Something Patrick wants to get from me. But he can't have it without giving me more first: declaring his love for me, asking to be my boyfriend, telling me he's never felt like this before. Something, anything, to feel something, anything.

'I don't need to be somewhere that means I have to leave at 6 a.m.; I have to be somewhere that means I have to leave here at 6 a.m. to go home first.'

My body hurts and I'm clenching my jaw.

He grunts. 'Bye then.'

I open his bedroom door to leave and the desperation I feel for him to stop me is terrifying. He speaks. 'Are you not going to say goodbye then?'

I turn back into the room but stand holding the door open. My hope sickens me. I don't say anything.

'You genuinely aren't going to say goodbye?'

I feel a rush of relief. Patrick is upset that I'm leaving his room without saying goodbye. Take it in, absorb it for later. I sit down on the side of the bed. 'Sorry, I didn't even really think about it.' I could lean over and take his arms off his face and kiss him and tell him I want to see him as soon as possible, but why take the risk? His uncertainty is my power.

'Goodbye, Patrick. I honestly had a great time.' My voice is happy and confident. I get up and as soon as I do he takes his arms off his face, sits up and grabs my arm.

'Are you sure you have to go? Just stay here. You can shower here and we can chill out and do whatever. Watch a film or something or just like, sit outside until the sun cures all our mental and physical ailments.'

His eyes are practically sparkling. The lilac of the skin underneath them bringing out the bright pale blue. He's trying to look light-hearted, but his eyes are giving him away, they look so sincere. His hair isn't floppy, it's still pushed back and he looks so good it physically hurts, I desperately hope he doesn't know how attractive he is. I take a second to pretend to think about it, but I don't make it a really big deal otherwise it will seem fake. 'All right then.' I put my bag down on the floor.

I start to say something, but he pulls me towards him and lifts my dress over my head. He touches me, looking into my eyes, expectant, like if I didn't feel anything it would be a failing on my part. My body tenses worried he can tell that all I can focus on is the thoughts in my own head. I close my eyes and listen for the sound of pleasure in his breath. If I focus on that I can let go just enough to give him what he needs from me.

Lying on our sides we're staring into each other's eyes like sickening teenagers falling in love. We have made the heat hotter. He asked me to stay, and I want him to know that being nice is worth it. I don't find it hard to reward him.

'You have such bright blue eyes. Do people always tell you that?'

He leans over and gives me a kiss on the lips. 'Thank you. Yeah, people do say that sometimes.'

Why did I ask that? I want to close my eyes for a second but I can't. I remind myself that 'people' aren't the ones here. But I need him to tell me that.

I give him a kiss and when I lean back I play around with his hair a bit and he closes his eyes. I brush it down flat over his forehead. He opens one eye. 'How do I look?'

'Beautiful.'

I want to tell him I love him, but I know I don't love him. It just feels like I love him. And maybe that is the best kind of love. The fake kind. It's hard not to say it though. Maybe he thinks he loves me too. He doesn't, but maybe he's naïve enough to think he does. He touches the hair I've pulled down along my hairline.

'I like your hair. It looks nice when you have it in a thing like that.'

I smile and close my eyes so he can look at me as much as he wants. He starts running his fingers over my shoulders and arms and back up my neck. I don't love him, but I do feel something strong for him, and this, and us, even if it's not real. I wonder if it could be real with him. It's hard to remind myself that if I got it all, if it did become real, it wouldn't feel like this anymore. And then what would I be left with? More importantly, who is this person I would be left with? Do I like him more? A nagging feeling that I'm going to regret this chips away at me but I push it down and focus on the soft strokes.

I wake up again, and I can tell I've been properly asleep because my mouth is open, and I have no idea how long it's been, or what I've been doing. The room is bright now so he will be able to see my face in as much detail as a magnified mirror. Which is terrible news because Patrick is awake, showered and dressed in shorts, a short-sleeved shirt that's too big for him and white socks. He's sitting at the end of the bed, against the wall, with his legs stretched out so they would be over mine if I wasn't curled up. I touch my face and hair, which both feel puffy and my bun has half fallen out so it's hanging down the side of my face. I sit up against the headboard and try to pull the duvet over me but he's sitting on it so it doesn't move. I pick up a pillow and hug it instead. He's rolling a cigarette.

'I didn't want to wake you. You looked so tired.'

I don't say anything but can barely hide the fact I'm pissed off. I can't believe this is happening again. This distance, this unreadable coldness, I hate it and yet it's like I willed it into existence.

'You want one?' He holds up the finished product.

'No, thanks.' I'm going red with both embarrassment and anger, and I can't even get up and leave because I've already said I'd stay, and I can't keep changing my mind. I try to take deep breaths and think about what to do. I could just leave and never speak to him again.

He puts his cigarette behind his ear and I hate that even though he's acting like a pretentious teenager, he still looks cool. I remind myself he's *trying* to look cool and is no different to anyone else.

He shuffles forward on the bed and stands up. He doesn't seem to even notice that I haven't said anything. 'Oh, I forgot I said I'd see my mates today.'

He's not facing me when he says it, but I can tell it's not because he's ashamed, he's picking up things like the shirt he wore yesterday and a packet of gum and an old glass of water and putting them back in places I assume they're supposed to be. But when he does it, it doesn't seem like tidying. He puts on some scruffy trainers and stands up like he's ready to go. I wish I could look him in the eye and tell him I've faked every orgasm because he never focuses on anything but his own pleasure, even though he probably likes to think he does the opposite. But I don't need to tell him that, I just need to know it myself.

I stand up and pick my dress off the floor, the last thing messing up his room, and slip it over my head. For once, I think the most dignified thing I can do is be upset. I pick up my bag and open the door and I guess he's turned around now because he says, 'Wait, hold on where're you going?'

I don't even pause, I just say, 'Home' and walk straight out.

He's walking behind me, but I don't hold the front door open so it closes on him. I can hear him open it again. I don't know why he's following me in silence. It doesn't matter how good you look, you can't be attractive if you're a horrible person. I feel a deep relaxation in my body knowing I don't care anymore, there is nothing he can say or do, and I don't care if he does or doesn't say anything anyway. *You were just a game*, I tell him mentally, *maybe I lost it but you mean nothing to me.*

The corridor outside his flat smells like school or something nostalgic, and I smile thinking about what my sixteen-year-old self would think of all this. I look great, someone loves me, and someone else is following me down a hall. I think she would be happy with that.

I get to the elevator and press the button and lean against the wall to wait. He walks past me and then turns to face me.

'Where are you off to?'

'Home.' The word I can tell briefly hurts him to hear.

'Please don't go. I know I have to go and see my mates, but I want you to come and meet them. I want them to meet you.'

The lift arrives with a ping and if I wait here and listen to what he has to say, the doors will close and then I will lose the last shred of my dignity. It takes all of my strength to walk into the lift and I feel like I want to pull my hair so hard it might actually rip a clump out. But I just press 'G' and lean against the back, exhausted. I don't even bother looking in the terrible excuse of a mirror because at this point it doesn't matter what I look like. I'd rather be someone who doesn't care if they have knots in their hair anyway. What a better quality of life that would be.

'Iris.'

I hear an exasperated voice from outside the lift, which is taking comically long to close. But just as the clanky doors start to move he walks in, just like a film, except for the loud mechanical sound the lift makes as the doors stop closing and start re-opening. It still feels good though. I press 'G' again and the door closes with us both inside.

'Iris, please don't go and do whatever you're going to do. I thought we said we were gonna hang out today?' He's looking at my eyes like he's thinking they're beautiful. 'What do I have to do to get you to stay?' He touches my arm. 'Please.'

I stand there until the lift reaches the ground floor and then walk out. I'm too exhausted to even know what I think about anything. I haven't eaten in so long and it's going to feel good to go and eat what I want.

'Iris, please!' He grabs my arm from behind me so I turn around angrily.

'What?'

'I can't stand the idea of you being at yours with him today. Please spend the day with me. I want that more than anything. I want you.' It takes me by surprise that he mentions George so explicitly. I had an idea that he thought about it but I didn't know how much he cared. His eyes almost look circular with desperation, and I think his breathing is slightly quicker. This is what George doesn't give me. This. All of this. I've looked at mine and Patrick's relationship as if it's superficial, a means to an end, but it's suddenly clear to me that it's not silly to want this. I deserve someone who needs me as much as I need them. It feels a relief to admit that to myself.

I get a strong stabbing in my chest and nearly roll my eyes at how excessive my physical reactions are.

'I want to shower and change, and then I'll come see you later.'

He does an exhale of relief. Maybe we are falling in love. I wonder what he tells his friends about me. I can't help the endorphins that are released when I get these thoughts. He comes towards me and holds my head in his hands and kisses me on the mouth, but all I can think about is if he thinks my breath smells bad. I pull away and he tells me what park they're going to and I say, 'See you later then,' and walk straight out. I know what I need to do.

25

I walk up the grey stone stairs to the second floor as I've done so many times before. My shoulders are pink from walking in the sun. I sit on the top stair and imagine walking through the door and seeing George. I almost sputter out a nervous laugh thinking about what will happen in there. It's the first time for a while we've been home together in the day. I ready myself.

What if he's in there doing nothing? Sitting there, contemplating? I have never seen him doing nothing. The thought horrifies me. Would I care if I saw him with another girl, walking down the street, holding hands, going to get a pastry and read the newspaper?

I wouldn't cry. I wouldn't even care. But is that because I don't love him or because I believe in our love so strongly that even if he was with someone else, I know they could never have what we have? Because no one can take his place in my life either. Although it seems they are going to. I stand up and walk towards my door and I can't help thinking, one day I'll look back with regret for all these stupid, selfish decisions I'm making.

I open the door and close it behind me, but I don't feel like walking anymore so I just stop there and lean against the wall to take some of the weight off my feet. The dark coolness is a welcome relief, but it also makes the pain in my head worse. I hear a key in the lock and I think about running and hiding, but I don't know why. I'm starting to think I don't know why I feel or do anything anymore.

I turn around and George walks in, slightly dewy from the sun, carrying three shopping bags in one hand and the key in the other.

'Hey.' He sounds slightly out of breath. I wonder what's in the bags. Nothing has ever felt more inappropriate than to give him a kiss.

It's almost comical to think of how he is going to walk past without touching me, but also without making it uncomfortable that we're not touching. He closes the door behind him.

'You going out or coming in?' He stuffs his keys into his pocket and transfers one of the shopping bags into his empty hand. Maybe it feels so nice to be a good person that it doesn't matter if anyone treats you badly. He's never felt this deep, burning, self-hatred.

'You need any help with those?'

'Nah, it's all right cheers.'

He walks past me and then straight down the hall to the kitchen so I walk right behind him, dropping my bag on the floor. He starts unpacking what seems to be a normal shop. It feels like he's doing everything so fast and loudly, almost hysterically, but I know he isn't. It strikes me, suddenly, that he will keep this nice, content life where he plans and buys and unpacks and eats his weekly food. But I will lose it all. It was just something he had leant me, this normal, it was never mine. My voice is completely flat.

'Why are you being so normal?'

He immediately stops unpacking and turns to me. His face has dropped. There is the hurt he is feeling, and it's unbearable to see. I want to close my eyes and never see it again, but I won't do that to him. The least I can do is see what I've done.

'How do you want me to be?'

It's a good question. I shake my head and look down. It feels stupid to be in a little dress, in the middle of the day, in a boiling hot room, feeling so bad. I look around, everything is tidy. He is still looking at me.

I say, 'I don't know.' But with my eyes I try and tell him, 'Distraught? Furious? Relieved? Anything other than nothing?'

Eventually he replies in a very calm voice, 'Arguing is only useful if there's something you're trying to get from the situation.'

I want to scream, 'Why aren't you "trying to get" *me*? Why do you want me less than someone who barely knows me?'

But I know he'd have nothing to say. And the answer is probably just that. He wants me less because he knows me more. My eyes burn. Everything has changed forever, no matter what happens now. I walk away and into my old room. It's so messy. I notice how many of my things I've brought back in here now. Which means he's probably noticed how few of my things are in our room now. We've broken up and neither of us wants to be the person to say it. I close my eyes trying to work out why he won't just confront me but come up with no answer. Everything in this flat feels wrong now, I'm not the person who used to live in this room, or the person who lived in George's room. I'm no one. Nothing. And I have nowhere to go. I try to remind myself that this is what I want but I struggle to believe in Patrick's feelings when he's not in front of me. I get a towel and go into the bathroom.

In the shower I sway my head from side to side. The water falling over one ear, then the other, makes a lulling *vrmm, vrmm, vrmm* sound. It feels like the kind of thing people would do in this situation. Maybe now I know I'm a bad person I can just go out and enjoy my life, stop berating myself, since I can't seem to change anyway.

When I walk out of the bathroom I can immediately tell I'm in an empty flat. Why would crying feel so fake when my heart feels broken?

I won't wear a dress because I'll probably be sitting down on the ground at some point. I think about wearing a baggy t-shirt but I want his friends to see that I'm thin so I wear a tight one and some shorts. My phone buzzes.

London Fields. Near the big tree.

The overground is cancelled and it's seventy-five minutes away. I hope my journey doesn't come up in conversation because over an hour is a long time to travel to see someone. Although maybe at this point, who cares? What do I have to lose except the last thing keeping my mind together?

I look at the clusters of people in the park sitting in circles or kicking a ball around or lying on blankets or having a picnic or drinking prosecco. There is no way all these people can be happy, and yet here we all are, pretending to be as happy as we can so other people feel worse about their unhappiness. The thought crosses my mind that maybe all these people *are* happy, and it makes me feel sick.

I have walked by most of the trees when a sudden feeling winds me. As I look around now everyone seems further away, their movements exaggerated, the noise becomes one. It's unbearable to watch. I decide to go home, but then I realise I don't have a home anymore. Just a place where my things are stored. I feel like I'm swaying so I refocus my eyes on the park and see Patrick right on the other side.

The group of people he's with turn out to be both the kind that kicks a ball around and the kind that sits in a circle talking. Patrick is part of the game which seems to involve someone kicking a football to another person in the circle and so on. I can only see the side of him but I notice his slim, long-looking legs. You are my everything now, I think. I take a deep breath in and hold it there as if I can freeze time. I smile and remind myself I'm excited for this. He will introduce me to his friends and it will be the start of something new. The start of us being together, properly. I let my breath go like I'm blowing out a candle and walk over.

People start to look up at me like I'm coming over to ask for directions. I wish Patrick would turn his head this way. He's wearing dark brown sunglasses and he looks so good I can't understand why he has ever spoken to me. If he kisses me I can completely relax. He pushes his glasses onto his head and because it's so bright his pupils shrink and his eyes become sapphire blue. His ears are a little pink on the top.

'Iris! Can't believe you found us just by, "Meet us at the big tree".'

He doesn't seem to be initiating any kind of physical contact and I nearly go for a hug, but I bottle it at the last second.

'It wasn't actually that hard.'

'I didn't think you were coming. You took a while.'

It's hard to tell what he's thinking when I can't see his eyes.

'Uh, yeah, sorry. I was doing some stuff at home.'

'Oh. Right.'

I don't know if it's awkward or he's angry but there's a little pause before he speaks again.

'Help yourself to a drink if you like.' He points to a crate of bottles in the shade of the tree. He isn't 'playing' anymore, but he is yet to leave the circle of the game.

'Oh cool, thank you.' I walk over and run through my options; go back to the flat or stay and be as confident as he's challenging me to be. I glance over and he is back to kicking the ball. I feel a physical anger mixed with embarrassment, like when you get laughed at by a group of people at school.

I walk towards the group of guys sitting down and make sure to say loudly so I won't have to repeat myself, 'Does anyone have a bottle opener I could use?'

A guy with a cap, who I would guess by the peeled label on his bottle, the acne scars on his face, and his little smirk is 'the funny one in the group', says to me, 'I can do it with my teeth if you're willing to cover any potential dental bills?' He directs the joke to the circle.

One of the guys who is classically attractive in a way which makes me think he doesn't have a personality, gets his keys out and holds out a keyring to me. It's good because it means I have to walk right into the circle to get it and then with all the adrenaline in my body I make myself sit in one of the gaps. My back is facing Patrick and I have no idea why he thinks it's acceptable to ignore me. I'm sat next to Cap guy and he says, 'Uh not to be rude but, *who* are *you*?' He looks around the group with wide 'comical' eyes. People laugh, which surprises me, and I implore my face not to go red.

'I came for the bottle opener and stayed for the good times.' I cringe but another courtesy laugh comes from some of the group anyway.

'Nah, I'm actually here to see Patrick. He invited me. I'm surprised you can't tell.'

A guy with a blonde bun, wearing an unbuttoned Hawaiian

shirt and, what I assume are ironic, red heart shaped sunglasses says, 'I can believe that. Seems legit to me. Well, make yourself at home.'

'Thanks for having me.' I raise my bottle and thankfully four out of the five guys raise their bottles and mumble variations of Hi/Nice to meet you/Welcome etc. Cap guy is picking at the last bit of label on his bottle.

Attractive guy, who is tanned and broad, throws Hawaii some tobacco and rolling papers and then says to me, 'Are you the new bird who's been in our flat then?'

New? The way he phrased that makes me want to scream.

I say, 'My reputation proceeds me,' and then regret it.

Hawaii takes a long performative drag and then passes a joint along to Attractive guy who takes it without saying anything. I turn to Cap guy and say, 'How long can six people kick a ball back and forth?'

He turns to me, he has dark brown circle eyes which seem to contain a thousand emotions.

'It's the game that never ends. That's the beauty of it.'

I reckon I could make him fall in love with me in two hours.

He's actually quite attractive. The scars look good on him for some reason and his big anxious brown eyes are nice to look at. He's wearing black jeans and his trainers are very dirty, and I don't know why but it makes me really like him. I wish I had time to find out his deepest secrets and the thoughts he's never told anyone. I think I could get him to tell me.

He turns slightly more towards me. 'What's your name by the way, sorry?'

'Are we there already? Usually I don't get to "first name basis" until I'm three conversation topics deep.'

'Well, my name's Tom. I'm quite loose like that.'

'My name's Iris Ellis, but I guess you can call me Iris.' It actually baffles me that Patrick has not come over yet, but I remind myself I'm enjoying speaking to Tom so maybe I'll just sit here and talk to him all day.

I've been chatting to the group, but mainly Tom, for nearly an hour when I feel a pinch on my shoulders. I turn around.

'Hey,' Patrick says with a massive smile on his face.

'Hi,' I say with a small one on mine. He puts his hand out to pull me up and I clumsily stand trying not to drop my bottle. I wonder what everyone in the group thinks about me and Patrick. I wonder if there's a tiny part of Tom which is jealous.

Now I'm standing I can see the game of 'kick the ball' has ended which explains Patrick coming over to say hi.

'Come with me here a sec.' He walks over to the tree, so I follow.

He picks up a bottle of beer and breathes out. In the shade the pink parts of his face – nose, ears, cheeks – are more visible. He opens the bottle with a lighter from his pocket and lifts it towards me to cheers. I clink my bottle against his. He toasts, 'To passing the time until we die with comrades and cold ones.'

I smile to acknowledge the strange inside joke and add, 'And kicking balls.'

He walks further behind the tree, sits down with his back against it and taps the muddy ground next to him. He senses my consideration at his proposal and makes a big lean towards a pile of jackets to pull out his sports jacket.

'How about now?' He puts it over the dirt. I like that he doesn't care about it. Looking at each other feels too intense but looking forward feels too shy. It's ridiculous to think it was only a few hours ago we were having sex. He chooses to look forward while he speaks, 'I'm not made for the sun.'

I'm looking at him. 'Your nose is a little pink.'

He touches it. 'Oh this? No, that's on purpose. That's just a new thing I'm trying out.'

'Oh, yeah? The classic "blush on the tip of the nose" technique.'

He turns to look at me, his face is so close. 'It seems like you're into it too.' He touches the tip of my nose and looks at my face like he's inspecting it. 'Yes, I can see here you've tried to achieve the same effect but. . . you've actually failed quite badly.'

'Oh, really? How's that? Any tips for next time?'

'Yeah, I can see you've given it a good go, but I'm afraid your skin is still looking perfect.' He looks me in the eyes now and it feels like we should kiss, but I'm not going to do it and nor does he. In fact, he seems a little anxious and drinks a lot of his beer. I finish off the rest of mine. The silence isn't awkward because it feels like we're still communicating in some way. 'Thanks for inviting me here today.'

'It's all right. It's good that you've met my friends.'

'They're really nice. I like them.'

He finishes his beer and then takes stuff out his pocket to roll a cigarette.

'Get us a couple more,' he says gesturing towards the crate. 'Of those green ones.'

I get up and grab some beers and it feels so good to be out of the flat.

'I really like Tom, he's funny. Who's your best friend?'

I assume he'll say he doesn't have one, that he likes them all the same but, without a second thought he says, 'Simmo.'

'Who?'

'The guy in the bright shirt. Oscar Simms, known him all my life.'

I don't know how I can feel jealous of a male friend he's had his whole life but I do. Maybe I just wish I had an Oscar.

'And I live with Adam, so we're pretty close.'

'Who's Adam?' He points to Attractive guy who is actually laughing in an endearing shoulder-shaking way. He's showing off his muscles with a super tight t-shirt and I think it makes him look desperate for attention. I wonder what makes them friends.

'I'm gonna head back,' he says, still smiling. How can someone be so sadistic? I can't be bothered anymore. I'm tired and dizzy and have nothing left to lose.

'Are you being serious?'

'Yeah?' He looks confused, but his intense, beautiful face has no effect on me right now.

I drain my eyes of happiness. 'Okay then. It was nice to see you for a whole two minutes.'

He moves slightly closer and puts his hand on my arm.

'What's up?' I want to slap it away.

'If you don't know, then I can't be bothered to explain.'

'Please. It's been a proper good day.'

I can't hold in a laugh. 'Well, I'm glad to hear it. Maybe you could tell me about it sometime.'

'You're acting like I've humiliated you or something.'

'Well, yeah, it is a bit embarrassing coming all the way here to be ignored.'

'You didn't need to "come all the way here" if you didn't want to, y'know? You're not obligated to hang out with me.'

'I know I'm not. What's your point? You're upset I was late? I didn't even know there was a particular start time.'

'Why were you late?'

'What do you mean?'

'Fuck it. Whatever.' He gazes into the distance with a blank face.

'Aren't you leaving?'

Defensive changes to sad. 'I wanted you to come with me. Back to mine. Please. Come back with me?'

'Okay cool, what should we do? How about I'll sit in your room on my own and you go call your mum for an hour.'

A moment passes before he speaks. 'I haven't spoken to my mum in years. You know that.'

It's so frustrating that he also has something to be upset about now. It makes me want to say, 'Okay. You've won. What do you want from me? I'll do it. You have all of me now.' But I say, 'I'm sorry. I didn't mean it like that. I just said something stupid without thinking.'

'All I've been thinking about all day is that I can't wait to go home with you. I'm sorry if I didn't show you that.'

What else am I going to do? He is my only happiness now. I have nowhere to go and nothing to do. My stomach churns. 'I'll come if you buy me some chips.'

'Absolutely.'

We're sitting on the ground outside his flat's building with our backs against the wall. I'm eating lukewarm chips that I don't even really want. Sometimes he puts his hand on my leg and it feels more exhilarating than sex. I'm wearing his jacket and it's making me feel a bit too warm, but I like that I'm covered up and I like wearing it because it's his. We've been talking about how you only realise how many people exist when it's summer. The conversation has ended, but the silence feels nice, like we're comfortable with each other, like things have changed tone. Is there a better point in a relationship than when you're finally relaxing into their company but still have things to learn about each other?

He breaks it first. 'I really enjoyed today.'

'Don't start this again.' I laugh.

He moves away from the wall and faces me side on. 'I'm being serious. This was really important to me.'

I put the barely eaten chips down. 'How come?'

'I know for everyone else it's a big deal to introduce someone to their family, but that isn't really going to happen for me. I guess it will, in a way, but it won't mean much. My mates are my family, Iris. I know it sounds corny as fuck, but I've known some of them for my whole life and the rest for the best part of it.'

I don't say anything because I want him to say as much as possible. Every nugget of vulnerability he gives me feels like treasure. Because what is treasure if not something rare and elusive?

'It's not like I just bring any old girl along to meet them is what I'm trying to say.'

I want to feel all the good in what he's said, but all I can think of is any other girls that got this far. I want to know who I am compared to them.

'It's annoying because I didn't get a chance to speak to Simmo. Simmo? Oscar? What do I call him?'

'Yeah, Simmo, call him that. He wasn't on his best form today anyway. Think him and his girlfriend had an argument or summin.'

'I like Tom though. He's funny.' Will there be any flicker of jealousy? It's hard to tell.

'I've only known him for about a year. Good bloke though.' He says it in a way which seems to suggest the opposite.

'Thanks for introducing me to your family. I like you even more now.'

He grabs my hand and pulls me towards him and kisses me and my heart is beating so fast, and the way he puts his hands on my face makes me feel like this isn't a kiss leading to anything else, it's just a kiss in its own right, a kiss for love.

When he pulls away he looks at my hair and squeezes my bun. 'Love it when you have your hair in this kind of thing. It suits you.' The compliments still feel good but I'm hungry for more. Something bigger. I need to know this was all worth it. I need what he gave that other girl three years ago, I need his love.

We go back to his room and lie straight down, facing each other. He presses his hand against mine and then our fingers slip in between each other's. We link and unlink them, stroking down each other's palms.

We must have drifted off because I wake up in the same position. Patrick is doing that 'almost-snore' heavy breathing. I'm boiling and when I sit up to take the jacket off I see where his cheeks have caught the sun. I can't help but stare at him. What I love about feeling this way for someone is that the strangest things become captivating. The angle of his jaw, the smell of his neck, his straight thick eyebrows, the point of his nose, his prominent collarbone, the slight gravelly depth to his voice. I love these things with my senses.

My watch says almost 10:30 p.m. I shake him a little.

'Patrick, you've got to wake up, I think we need to be awake for at least an hour before we properly go to sleep. And anyway, we've got to clean our teeth and I wanna take the cover off this.' I kick the duvet at the end of the bed. 'So we can use it on its own instead and not boil.'

'Okay,' he says after a while in a sad voice with his eyes still closed. I take both his arms and try to pull him up, but he doesn't move and I'm scared of pulling harder in case his arms come out of their sockets, so I go for his shoulders, but his body is fully relaxed and he's too heavy so I have to let go.

'Can we quickly take this duvet cover off?'

'Of course we can.' He slowly opens his eyes and then turns to look at me and smiles. I smile. He crawls on his knees to the end of the bed, hops off, and kisses me on the nose. 'Come on then.'

We start on opposite sides undoing the poppers working towards the middle.

He looks at me. 'Is this really a two-person job?'

'Well, it's a two-person job in the sense that *two* people needed to be *off* the bed.' We both reach the middle.

'Is this the modern-day *Lady and the Tramp*?' I say, half expecting him to look at me confused, but he grabs my waist, pulls me towards him and kisses me.

He pushes me down onto the bed and leans down to kiss me, but then stops and pulls back to look at me. 'You're honestly so beautiful.'

His hair is flopping down and it makes him look pretty. I can't believe I get to kiss someone who looks like this. So I kiss him, and we have sex in the harmonised way that people who have already slept with each other multiple times do. But I can't help thinking how the desire I feel towards Patrick doesn't translate into sexual pleasure for me. And how, the exact thing that kills my desire for George – the trust that I can be completely myself and he would still love me – is what allows me to lose myself in the moment.

Afterwards, under the still-covered duvet, I lie on his chest listening to his heart rate gradually slow. We don't say anything and I run my fingers over his ribs. I like imagining him deciding whether or not to tell me he loves me. I'm impatient for it but also worry nothing good comes of getting what you want.

I wake up again to Patrick, who is stroking my neck and shoulders. My head hurts a little. I must have been asleep for a few hours because we're once again witnessing the few hours of true darkness coming to an end. I turn over and reach for the water on the floor, lifting myself up as little as possible to drink it.

'How do you look so nice when you sleep?'

I put the glass down and turn to him. 'I don't know, you tell me.'

He exhales loudly. 'I'm hot as fuck.'

'Yeah, you are.' I wink and hope he realises I'm joking. He tries to reach over me to get the water, but his arm barely gets to the edge of the bed so he just gives up and flops down over me. I reach down and get it for him and we both sit up against the headboard. He drinks the whole water in one go and then hands the glass back to me.

'Thanks. . . just let me know if there's anything else I can get for you, sir.' I put it down and when I sit back up he puts his arm around me, and then takes it back and holds my hand instead.

'Sorry for being a dick about my mum earlier.'

'It's okay—'

'No, it's not okay.' He turns to me. 'If I expect you to understand, why have I told you nothing?'

'You don't have to. . .' But I trail off because I want to know.

He moves his finger back and forth over the knuckles of the hand which is holding mine. 'My dad has schizophrenia, and my earliest memories are of him being very ill and my mum screaming at him and walking out and not coming back for days. I had no idea what was going on. Obviously.'

I try and keep very still so I don't disturb his flow.

'When I was about eight, the school contacted my parents and told them I was having problems and they were considering ringing childcare, so my mum took me away to live with her in this little flat on the high street. She used to go out a lot, and I don't have any brothers or sisters, so I was alone a lot. It was pretty bleak in that flat, I didn't really have any things cause she didn't bring much from our old house, so I just used to watch this clock that had a teddy bear on each side holding it up. No idea why that was the only thing in my room, but I literally just used to watch the hours go by like some fucking neglected child from a fairy tale or something.'

I start running my finger back and forth over his knuckles because he's stopped.

'She got this new boyfriend though, and then we moved into this massive house, way out of town. I thought it was so white, and like, bizarrely empty, but looking back I think it was just decorated and tidy.

'She did seem happy to be fair to her. She would make me go shopping with her to buy clothes or whatever, and would like, give me money to go and buy what I wanted. It was all right, I could have my mates over to this house, but she had to drive them back to theirs in the evening, and mainly she said no cause she needed "her evening glass of wine after a long day's work", which was this little joke. . . cause she didn't work anymore. And then one day after school she told me that I was going to have "a little sister or brother soon", and I remember thinking like, why didn't she just say she was pregnant, because I was twelve not five.

'But anyway, she had the baby and then told me my dad was

feeling "good now" and it would be better if I moved back in with him. I hadn't seen him in about five years at this point. She just dropped me off one day and I was crying and she said in this really soft voice that I'd thank her one day for letting me get to know my dad, and then she drove away.

'So after that I had to grow up proper fast, cause it turns out my dad was *not* well, and I had to look after him, just normal stuff, but I guess it's not "normal stuff" for like, a twelve-year-old to have to do. Cooking all our meals and tidying and shopping and stuff.

'But that was fine, I know loads of people have to do stuff like that. It was more the fear, never knowing if it was going to be a good day or a bad day. If he was going to lock me in a room all evening to "keep me safe" or stand there holding a kitchen knife for the whole evening or just like, sit down and watch TV.

'People came round to try and help, to "check in" on us. But usually I wasn't allowed to answer the door. And if I did, he would like, scream at me or sometimes other, worse stuff. Then the next day it would be all laughs and jokes about the night before. Even I would laugh about it, to be honest.

'I started to learn how to "play" my dad like, learn what I needed to say and do to cause the least trouble. Which basically meant enabling his mad rituals. Hiding from the outside world with him. Until it became *me* that was the enemy. I was interrogated, locked in my room, not allowed to go to school. . .'

He takes a breath and looks at me and kisses me lightly. I'm scared he'll stop speaking and I'll ruin it. I make sure to not say anything so we just sit in silence for a while. He looks back down.

'I started spending more and more time at my mates' houses, after school, even staying there quite a lot. They didn't know what was going on.' He stares at nothing for a second. 'Although now

I think about it, they probably had more of an idea than I realised.' He does a small laugh through his nose and inspects the nails of his free hand for a moment before he carries on. 'Obviously I had to pay the consequences for that when I eventually did go home, but it was worth it. Oh, and my mum was fully absent this whole time.'

His voice sounds different, a bit quieter and his hand is sweaty, and I just want to say, 'I love you.' But I don't. I say nothing.

He looks at me for a moment. 'Often it was Simmo's house I was at, by the way, he was an only child too so his mum liked having me there, cause it was "good for his development", i.e. she could go get drunk with her friends. I used to go to Adam's too. I don't want to say they're "like brothers" cause they're not. I didn't have anyone who was experiencing all the shit alongside me. Anyway.'

He exhales and continues. 'My dad was doing a lot worse, he never even left the house. So when I was like sixteen, I was spending most of my time fully caring for my dad, and then usually spending the weekends. . . taking a lot of drugs. I know that is so fucking cliché. I even knew it at the time, but I guess it's a cliché for a reason.'

He shrugs and I kiss his shoulder. My chest is so tight with empathy, and love, and desperation for him to tell me everything, desperation for him to love me.

'It was bleak. I was failing school. My mates didn't want to get fucked as much as me, for them it was just this fun rebellious thing to do on weekends, and then I guess they'd all secretly go do schoolwork during the week or something, even though nobody would admit it. I was. . .' He lets go of my hand and rests his over closed eyes. 'I started doing pills in my room, on my own. Not loads, but sometimes, if my dad locked me in there. So fucking embarrassing, I know. It's hard to explain it but it's like I couldn't bear to be in my own body and head anymore.' He looks up and pushes his hair back.

I feel like I could cry, I want to tell him I know that exact feeling, that I'm so sorry he's ever had to experience that, that I've never felt so connected to anyone. But this is not the time for me to speak.

'Obviously I failed all my exams. No one else did. I didn't give a shit though. All I really cared about was going out, getting fucked and doing things I regretted. I'd do anything for a thrill, to keep my mind distracted. And let's just say I wasn't so picky back then.' Even the thought of him being with someone all that time ago makes me feel sick. So much of my confidence rests on what he thinks of me compared to other people.

'Simmo actually took me in at this point. I had to pretend to his mum that I was going to college, but really I'd just kick about in town and then go home. I had no money and did fuck all and barely even ate, and I think Simmo was worried about me, so he sat me down and told me if I actually *went* to college, and like, did something practical, maybe it'd be all right. I was so bored of doing nothing constantly, so I thought, why the fuck not, and applied to do Film. I thought it would be a doss to watch films all day and you'd still get to say to people you're studying.

'You know what, I don't even know if my dad really noticed I'd gone, it's hard to tell. But anyway, I was good at the course and genuinely loved it and blah blah blah, I started making films on my own. I did this one about the local skaters, and it ended up being this pretty sick short film to be honest.' He does a little proud raise of his eyebrows.

'Basically, after a year or so, Simmo's mum asked me to leave. . . Well, she asked Simmo to ask me to leave, or "find somewhere I'd feel more comfortable". And having all that time away from my dad's, I'd realised how fucked up it was there, so I rang my mum, even though I hadn't spoken to her in like, five years, and she had

205

three other children by this point. But I just went straight in with telling her how I had nowhere to live.

'She told me I had two brothers and a sister and she couldn't believe I hadn't met them. I told her I had met one of her children. She sounded pissed off and said I was being insolent, I could almost see her pointing at the phone to Tony and rolling her eyes: "The Son that Went Wrong".

'I still went to live with them for a few months. They lived in an even bigger house by then. I didn't even really see my siblings or – "Toby, Noah and Poppy". They're not my brothers and sister really. It was funny to watch them all though. My mum, Tony and the kids. It hadn't occurred to me until then, the similarities between their family and my friends' families.

'How they all dipped into each other's lives seamlessly, helping out, supporting each other, just teaching each other how to navigate the world and like, be a good human. They don't even know they're doing it, cause it's so embedded in their mind, this way of doing things, there is not a second's thought to how different things could be. How different things *are* for some people.

'So you might say, "Okay, they live their lives and they don't think about why or what they're doing. That's just what everyone does, it's just ignorance." But they're not just ignorant. Everyone can see what's happening on the outside. They turn a blind eye. They're like cults – families. They have blinkered vision, they choose not to see anything outside the cult, and the more successful the cult, the more blinkered the vision becomes. When you're in a family you choose not to notice people who don't have one.'

I can't keep still anymore. I lightly stroke up and down the back of his neck and hope he doesn't find it patronising.

'Why is it that people have to seclude themselves like that.' His intonation makes it not a question. 'We all take it for granted, that it's normal. But it's only normal for people who have that life.' He's becoming almost monotonous in his tone. 'My mum told me she "wouldn't support laziness" and apparently studying doesn't count for shit. She was like, "Go and stand on your own two feet and you'll thank me one day".'

Suddenly there's the sound of the front door opening and people speaking in that 'we have to be quiet' way which is almost louder than normal speaking. It sounds like Adam and two or three other people. Girls, I think. I wonder if it's usually Patrick out there with them.

He's lifted his head like he's listening to them and I guess he's done speaking. His eyes are bloodshot, but it doesn't look like he's been crying. I'm not sure where to begin with what to say but then he carries on.

'Adam got a job over here, some well-paid financial services type deal. I dropped out of college right before the end, because who needs qualifications anyway.' He laughs, but not like someone finding something funny. 'Moved up here with Adam. Was just gonna get a job working in a bar, which looking back would've been a terrible shout, but I actually lucked out and got "scouted".' He does air-quotes, but I can tell he's proud. 'To make these music videos for this "best band competition" type programme thing.'

He moves his legs out from under mine and turns to look at me a bit more. He pushes his hair back and opens his eyes wide for a second like he's waking himself up from a trance.

'I haven't spoken to my mum since then, but Tony rang me a year ago to tell me I had a baby sister – Abigail. I said, "I can't wait to meet her" and we basically both just laughed. I do see my dad sometimes though.'

He looks so drained and his hair is a bit greasy and the burnt parts of his face make him look slightly less painfully attractive. Which is good because I don't think I've ever been so obsessed with someone and even contemplating the thought that he is too good to be with me is unbearable.

'I understand now it's not his fault. He's proper mental though. He's actually married, if you can believe it. He's this serious Pentecostal Christian now and apparently some birds are really into that. Pentecostal ones. . .' He smiles and I smile. 'I should probably see him more to be honest. . .'

'Honestly the fact you still see him at all is amazing!' I haven't heard my voice in so long and it sounds strangely high. I thought he might flinch at me speaking because I'm not convinced any of that was being directed at me, but he doesn't, he just looks at me.

'He's still my dad.' He shrugs but doesn't seem offended by what I said. I decide there isn't actually anything I should say to him. Who am I to comment on any of that?

'Thanks for telling me that. I think you're amazing.' This isn't the time to tell him I love him, this isn't about us. 'It's so special the way you and your friends support each other.'

He exhales deeply every now and again. I don't want any of my gestures or touches or comments to seem condescending, but I don't want to seem cold. 'Shall I get you some water?'

'Oh, yeah, cheers. It's well hot in here. I'm so dehydrated.'

Halfway towards the door I realise Adam and his girls are probably still out there, so I put my shorts back on. The only other thing I have is a strappy dress that I stuffed into my bag for tomorrow. Where do I even live now? I push the thought down and I creep through the hall and psych myself up to enter with an air of confidence, but the room is empty. The dim light coming through the windows and half full glasses scattered around the room give off that uncomfortable 'morning-after-the-night-before-regret' atmosphere.

How can Patrick be this normal nice guy after all that he's been through, and here I am, fresh out of my nuclear cult, and still struggling to get through the days. Even though I don't have a reason to feel like this I can't help but feel connected to his pain. It's refreshing to be with someone who understands what that feels like. If only I could give him a reason to feel this way about me but there's nothing to tell him about other than a life of privilege and success.

I look down and wonder if I squeezed this glass of water hard enough, would it shatter? How much glass would go into my skin? But then a hope wells inside of me, that I will be able to tell him about these dark things I think and feel, and despite the differences in our lives, he will understand me and we will support each other in a way I didn't know was possible until now.

When I get back to the room he's horizontal again, under the covers. 'Here's the water,' I say standing by the edge.

'Okay, cheers, can you put it down for now?' His voice sounds like he's trying not to sound flat. He hasn't opened his eyes. I take my shorts off and get in next to him. I stroke all of his hair down flat, so it's over his forehead, then push it back, and start again. His breathing is slow now.

'You're the only person I've told all that to really.'

My body has never sustained tension for this long. I nearly burst, thinking how much better this is than a declaration of love. A real connection.

His eyes are still closed but he carries on. I never want him to stop speaking. 'That's why it's nice for me to see you with all of my mates today, well, yesterday. I wasn't leaving you on your own, Iris, I was showing you a massive part of me.'

'I'm sorry. I'm so glad you told me all of that. I want to know everything about you; you're the most interesting person I've ever met.'

He puts his hand on my arm, without opening his eyes.

I continue. 'I don't want to do the thing where I tell you all about my life, like it's even in the same ballpark as the things you've gone through. You've made me think about a lot of things just by what you've said. I've had a very privileged life, just like the ones you've talked about. But I want to be open with you too.'

'I know it's not a competition. These are just our lives. I want to know about the one that's created you.'

'I really don't have much to say. . . my life has been pretty boring. Which I guess is why it's lucky. It's fucked up how little I've thought about that over the years. My parents are still together, no siblings, very stable family life, just the three of us. I'm not sure how normal this is for the "average person", but I've always felt a bit distant from them. Different from them. I'm from a small town; we've lived there my whole life. They're really happy people, but I haven't felt that connected to any of it. Sometimes I don't feel connected to anything.'

In case he thinks I'm drawing a parallel I make sure to add, 'I have no good reason to feel that way though.'

I turn on to my back, the pain in my chest is letting up. He starts drawing wavy lines with his finger on my arm.

'It's not that I was this outsider or anything. I'm probably making this sound bigger than it is. It's hard to explain.' I exhale. 'Maybe there is nothing to explain. The thing that's interesting to me is your close relationship with your friends. I don't know if this makes me sound like a loser, but I didn't feel like I had any close friends. It's not like I hung out on my own or anything. I was pretty well liked in school, not super popular, just like, friends with popular people I guess. But I didn't see what all the excitement or drama was about.

'I kind of felt like I was acting a bit, and then had to go home and do this whole different performance to my parents, nodding along to all their advice. But I was fine, I wasn't sad, it just felt a bit like I was. . . biding my time. It was good though cause when things went wrong, like someone fell out with me or a boy was mean, I just paused the act and distanced myself from it. None of it mattered that much, it all felt so. . . transient. Like, preparation for the real thing. And then I moved to London to begin. . . my life. But sometimes it feels like I'm still waiting. Like I can't shake off this feeling of being so detached from everything. I'm either laser focused on really insignificant things or I'm just blank, staring at a wall. And I'm so, I mean desperate is a strong word, but basically desperate to feel part of something. Something meaningful.' *Maybe that is what I have with you.*

I turn to him. His eyes are still closed. I pull my hair out from where I'm lying on it and push it behind me. It would feel so good to shave it all off, even for an hour or so.

'I don't know what I'm saying to be honest. I'm very aware this is just incoherent ramblings and not an equivalent story to what you told me. Sorry.' I feel bad for trying to make this about me. This isn't the time to talk about the trivial things I think and feel.

'Don't be sorry you haven't had a life like mine.'

'Yeah, I didn't mean it like that, of course. I'm trying not to make up a little story for the sake of conversation or anything. I just want you to know me.'

He opens his eyes. I know one truth I can give him: 'Your eyes are like cartoon eyes, cause they have that little sparkly "ding" bit.'

'Ding bit?'

'Yeah, like where it like pops with a sparkle. The eye doesn't pop. . . the little sparkle just pops up. . . you must know what I mean?'

'Yeah, I'm just messing, I know what you mean.'

'Anyway, they're like beautiful, sparkly, handsome prince eyes and I want to look at them all the time.'

'You can if you want. I might need to sleep sometimes though.'

I kiss him and he brings me right up close to him and kisses me again. 'I feel like I can tell you anything.'

'I love knowing about you. I feel less. . .' I go to say 'alone' but realise how cringey that sounds and change my mind.

'Less?'

'Sorry, I dunno what I was saying there. I meant, I feel like we're similar in a lot of ways. I can really relate to you.'

'Will you stay here tomorrow? I want you to.'

'I would love to.'

'That's good.' He smiles such a content smile and then gives me a little kiss. 'Go brush your teeth, we need to properly sleep now. I can barely keep my eyelids open and it's so bright outside. We need to get to sleep before it becomes a sauna in here.'

'Okay.' I get up. I'm not even dreading my reflection in the mirror because that hasn't mattered tonight. Although I do hope mascara isn't all over my face because you should never forget, you have to look nice for someone to tell you things like that.

26

It's not hard to avoid George almost entirely. I never leave the flat or come back to it when George is in. The thought of him hearing that kills me. I go to Patrick's just before he gets back from work and come home once I know he would have left. I design every meet up around this schedule which seems to grate on Patrick but hopefully just adds to my intrigue. If it becomes clear we are in the flat at the same time I cancel any plans and stay in my room. I use the alone time to re-perfect myself, but also to let out the person I've been pushing down whilst I was at Patrick's. I cry until I lose my breath, stare gormlessly into space, picture the bliss of being able to turn my existence off, lie down in an empty bath and press my fingernails into the flesh of my body. And then I snap myself out of it and wash my hair.

At Patrick's we usually just hug in bed, looking at each other, sometimes I have my head on his chest, sometimes we kiss. I find myself wondering what George would think if he saw this. But mainly I just focus on how happy I am, now that I have what I need. Someone who likes me for who I can be rather than loves me for who I am. Someone who fully understands me rather than simply caring for me. I know that last time I tried to open up to Patrick – tell him that I've felt some of those awful things he described – I did it all wrong, said the wrong things, at the wrong time. Next time will be different.

Patrick wants to have sex with me all the time, and the thought of that is the best part about it for me. I like it when Patrick takes a second to look at me. 'How is your body this good?' I kiss him hard. The bittersweet confirmation that barely eating is paying off. If I'm meeting his high standards then I must be good. He whispers, 'It turns me on to turn you on' and so I give him the satisfaction of thinking he's done that. I wonder about all the infatuated girls before me, doing the same thing, fuelling the idea that twenty minutes of penetration feels good. Why do I prefer having sex with someone who I have to fake orgasms with? Is it because I feel in control? These secret, pathetic, things I have over him.

I try not to think about the future too much because that is exactly what makes me feel bad but it's hard to see this as sustainable. I'm waiting for him to show me he's serious about us. And every time I see him I get more impatient to be upgraded. But things plateau. And then one day it stops. His messages stop coming and I hold back until I persuade myself I don't need to. *Remember the things he told you*, I tell myself, *you can put yourself out there.* And so I do, but nothing. No reply, no explanation. Just silence. I think of the new girl he must have met, the one he will fall hard for, the way he'll have realised when he met her that he wasn't being picky enough before. I feel so stupid for believing in us. A familiar sense of deep despair grows inside me and I try to turn away from it but it's wherever I look. A terrifying idea floats itself in front of my closed eyes and it calms me. But then it scares me. I get my phone out from where I put it under the bed, swallow my dignity and plead.

★

I make myself look incredible. I spend three hours getting ready but look like I've put no effort into my appearance. I hold my hand out to the mirror to congratulate myself but we settle on a high five. It takes all my energy not to wipe off the make-up, get naked and shave my head. I spray my perfume. Scent is the strongest trigger of memory, I remind myself. And it's true, because as soon as I've sprayed it I'm transported back to all the times I've gone somewhere, hoping to be thought of as someone who smells amazing, who looks amazing, who is amazing.

We arrange to meet in a pub garden near his flat. I arrive first and can feel my body retreating into itself at the sight of everyone around me, having loud, exuberant fun. I want to be sheltered from it, to pretend it doesn't exist, but I can't. Luckily, before I lose my breath, I see him striding towards me. I wonder whether to get up for a hug but he climbs into the picnic bench and breathes out.

'All right, Iris.'

It's easy to tune everything out when I can concentrate on the way he bites the sides of his nails when he's listening to me or the small line that appears between his pushed-together eyebrows when he's speaking about something serious.

The conversation is a little stilted but only because there's so much going unsaid. Eventually I ask if he wants to take a walk. And so we do. The sun is unrelenting and everyone around me seems worse than ever. My breath feels shallow.

'Is it me or is everyone particularly annoying today?'

He smiles at me for the first time today. 'Yeah, I know. What's that about?'

'I can't put my finger on why though.'

215

'It's like that laser-focused determination to get wasted. It's mobs of blokes walking around with their arms two inches out to the side like a crab.' He does an impression of how a gym-guy might walk.

I laugh.

'And all the girls tottering around holding them little bags overflowing with cans of gin.'

'I think I just hate seeing people having a good time but it's not because I'm jealous or anything. I can't exactly work out why. It's like it makes me sad to—'

'I've missed you.' He stops and turns towards me. 'I've missed you so fucking much but I had to stand my ground.'

'What do you mean? What ground?'

'I don't want you to live with that guy anymore.'

I don't say anything. I think part of me knew this was the problem all along but I can't let go. Living with George feels like the last thing I have to protect myself against anything he could do to hurt me. Even though it's not like George actually wants me anymore. But Patrick doesn't know that and if I give him this, he has everything. Has he given me enough for it to be equal?

He looks pissed off. 'Is it really that hard for you to move out of your ex's flat? Or do you want him there just in case you change your mind?'

'It's not his flat.' I won't explain without him giving me more. If you don't trust someone the only option you have is to test them.

'Are you being serious, Iris? After everything I've told you? Was this just some kind of joke to you? So you and your bloke can have this weird open relationship where you just go and fuck other people, but then get back together at the end of the day and curl up in front of a film?'

His voice is getting loud and I don't want him to change his opinion of me so I speak.

'Of course not.' I pull him on to a quieter road. 'You know it's not like that.'

'What is it like then, Iris?' He looks right at me, his straight eyebrows pushing inwards. I try to make my eyes emotionless enough for him to feel out of control. I tuck my hair behind my ears because I know he thinks I look nice like that. This is what I wanted after all, his desperation. If he needs me, then I matter, if he doesn't, then I don't. I think of George again, was him needing me not enough? No. He didn't need me. He didn't even want me.

I can see him swallow hard deciding whether to ask the question again or leave it and walk off. It's funny to see him this moody, I can't help but smile. It is my turn to hold the power.

'Forget it.' He strides off and I can tell it's not for effect. I trail behind him all the way to his flat.

I don't know if he's even aware I followed him until we get there and he turns sharply around. 'Are you coming in?'

His voice is so irritated I have to check, 'Do you *want* me to come in?'

'Can you not decide for yourself?'

He doesn't even wait for a reply just walks inside and leaves me to catch the door.

He doesn't stop me coming up to his flat.

I stay in the doorway of his bedroom wondering if I should leave.

'Shall I leave or. . . ?'

'I don't know, Iris. Why don't you tell me what *you* want? It's always me asking. I don't think you've ever asked me to do *anything*. How am I even supposed to know you want to be here? Maybe this whole time you were just doing stuff with me out of pity.'

'You know it's not out of pity.'

'No, I don't.' He has a tiny bit of froth by the side of his lip from saying that so passionately. I want to wipe it away but it's not the time.

He doesn't say anything, he just moves his gaze from one of my eyes to the other. He looks vulnerable. It makes me want to be.

I take a deep breath. 'You know it's not pity. I want to be here because I don't want to be there anymore. I just want to be here, with you, only you.'

He squints at me like he's trying to work out if I'm telling the truth and I almost laugh.

'Iris. I love you.'

Just like how my body reacts to everything these days, it feels like someone has stabbed me in the chest. It's funny how such a painful feeling can come from something so good. He pushes his hair back, full of energy now. It feels surreal that he said that to me. I try to feel elated but I can't. An uneasiness grows in me. A sense that something is over. In my head we shake hands and part ways. I worry that once you've said all the intense and risky things to each other then there is a sigh. A release of tension. A calmness. You are no longer 'coming up' from the drug. The excitement of the high has gone and you start to stabilise. There's less to think about and all you are left with is a warm body next to you in bed. It dawns on me that whenever someone says they love me it feels more like an ending than a beginning.

'I'm completely in love with you, Iris, and that's hard for me to say.' He's looking up at the ceiling like he can't believe what's happening. 'I've only said that to one other person.'

The same piercing feeling in my chest but this time it's not good. Why does he always have to say that? All I ever will be able to think about is the one other person he's said that to now. But it's something to draw me back in, and that's why I'm here, isn't it? To feel uncomfortable? To work towards something? To feel better than other people? To feel anything?

He sits on the bed and looks down, running his fingers through his hair again and again. Maybe I shouldn't say it back. Can you love two people if the love is different? Or is it just one love spread across two people? I still love George, but how is that the same word for what I'm feeling right now. I haven't said anything in a while, but I don't even think he minds. He seems to be completely in his own head.

I break the silence. 'Your voice is so nice.'

'Is it?' I don't hear any concern in his voice that I haven't said it back. To tell someone you love them and not care if they say it back – surely that is real love. I feel like my emotions are swinging wildly. As if I'm actually two different people fighting with each other. I try to step more firmly into one of their shoes.

'Well, it's hard to tell if it's nice or if I just think it's nice because I love you. I like it either way though.'

He looks up and raises his eyebrows. I sit next to him and hold his hand to say it better. 'I love you too. I think it all the time, pretty much every time you smile or push your hair back from your face.'

He looks really surprised. I feel like I shouldn't have said it, but maybe I don't need to be thinking like that anymore. Maybe this is the start of something I need to dive headfirst into. This thing I have dreamed of, worked for, focused on. But then I think of the promotion and the emptiness that followed. He leans in to kiss my neck and suddenly his hands on my skin are like an icy drink on a damaged tooth.

27

We both stir awake at the same time. He kisses me.

'Good morning,' he says in a husky voice.

'Good morning,' I say checking my watch. 'Oh, it's actually 1.15 p.m. How is that possible?'

'I guess time goes slowly when you're bored as hell. What shall we do today?' He turns onto his back and stretches, putting his hands behind his head.

I look at him lying there and I feel the day open up. With Patrick I feel weightless in an exhilarating, freeing way. The future feels bright and unknown. Almost tantalising. But I also feel untethered like I could float away at any moment. The bliss seems unsustainable. A fleeting and superficial burst of light. With George my future doesn't feel exciting and full of possibilities, it feels heavy and end-less, but is that just because he's stable and consistent? Is it because he anchors me to my reality which just happens to be heavy and endless? Am I making a huge mistake? I don't know. I'm exhausted and terrified. My throat clenches.

And then it happens. I can't speak. I can't make myself smile. The tops of my fingers go numb and I think about all the people out there who have to wake up and pretend to be okay and the thought is overpowering. I realise I need to be home, right now.

I want to sit in the corner of my room and cry and lie on the floor and sleep for twelve hours and then wake up and tell myself things are fine and eat something and look at all my clothes one by one and choose what I want to wear and work out who I'm able to be.

He rubs his eyes like a cartoon again. 'I need a coffee, a cig, and a shower. Not in that order. . . or maybe in that order?'

I need to say something. Anything. In a normal voice. 'You sound like you're in some kind of French film.'

'I don't think they drink Nescafé Gold in Paris.'

'Well then I don't want to go to Paris.' My voice sounds fine. Maybe I'm fine.

'A girl after my own heart.' He turns back over to look at me. 'Are you okay?'

'Yeah, why? Do I not seem okay?'

'I can tell when you're thinking things that you aren't saying.'

I feel myself unfurl. 'It's just. . . I don't have anything with me, and the idea of going back to change and then coming back again. It's so exhausting. And I don't even know where I live now. It's all so relentless and yet. . . empty. I don't even know. . . I guess, the truth is I'm finding it hard to get through the days. I'm struggling to remember what the "point" is in a day. Not. . . I mean. . . I like being with you, it's not that. It's just. . . it's like, I can't quite understand why things "matter". I like doing things, with you, so it's not that. It's just I don't know what the point—' I start crying and I have no idea how this is happening. But a growing part of me doesn't regret it, I want him to hold me and tell me he understands, remind me he knows what it's like to feel detached.

But he doesn't touch me or say anything and I can't stop crying and I hate him. It's easy for him to like me when he's the only one with problems. I stand up and breathe back the tears. I glance at him; he's looking at me like he's concerned and weirded out at the same time. 'Iris, I don't know what to. . .' He trails off.

I throw on my clothes, grab my things and walk out. He barely even moves a muscle, but I don't expect anything else. I feel like I'm breaking into pieces, and I need George to put me back together again. But I know I can't have that anymore.

The loud clunky lift reaches the floor and I get in. It's boiling but I notice I have goosebumps.

It makes me laugh that even walking through the streets, not caring about anything, barely caring about being alive, I'm still worried about getting wrinkles by spending this long in the sun without SPF on my face. I make myself laugh out loud; no one's around to see it but I want to do it anyway.

I walk down the steps at Liverpool Street quickly without holding on to the handrail. I keep picturing myself tripping up and falling over and hitting my head on the step and it splitting open, but as soon as it gets to this point in the thought, it starts from the beginning again. Over and over.

I look at everyone around me, they all look like they're on their way to a garden centre. Either that or on their way to work, deciding whether to end it all. Some people are wearing such bad and ill-fitting clothes, but also engagement rings and smiles. What does their partner like about them? What do they like about themselves? I know appearance isn't everything, but how can you care so little about how you look and still be happy? What kind of things do they think about? Would their boyfriends or girlfriends prefer them if they looked better, or do they like it that they don't care? If people could hear my thoughts, they would hate me. But I feel like there's something fundamental I don't understand about life. I want them all to explain it to me, to set me right, to let me in to their secret worlds.

I walk towards the flat and the inevitable adrenaline kicks in. I'm pretty sure George will be in there. My body has never known so much tension. I don't want him to see me like this. To see that I have tanned in the sun, been with someone else, slept in another bed. I desperately don't want him to see that. Or feel jealous or sad or bad about himself. It's hard to regret what I've done when I know he'll be better off without me. I want him to find someone who will make him happy forever. I want him to never doubt himself, even for a second. That is true love. Which is apparently something I don't want for myself.

I haven't drunk water or eaten in so long I have to sit down on the stairs up to the flat even though it's a twenty second walk away. My stomach feels so painful, like I've been winded. My tongue is bone dry. I laugh because George would hate me being this hungry. I close my eyes and feel like I'm swaying so much I could topple over, but when I open them I'm not swaying at all. I feel bony but I think it's in a bad way. I make a deal with myself – if he screams at me, sobs, tells me I broke his heart, I will get down on my knees and beg for him to take me back. If he doesn't then I will know for sure that he never wanted me anyway.

I pull myself up and walk to the door, very slowly, holding the concrete handrail tightly, find my keys and put them in the door like I'm being played at 0.5 speed. I think I'm doing it on purpose though.

I walk in the door and turn fully back to face it and close it slowly. But then I realise if George is in, it might look like I'm creeping, so I walk loudly, straight into the kitchen. He is in there, sitting on the sofa with the TV off. I have to swallow very hard to stop myself from crying. I can tell my eyes are bloodshot.

'What are you doing?' I don't sound okay. My voice is practically breaking.

'Not much.' His voice doesn't sound normal either.

'I am starving,' I say, walking into the kitchen. 'That's not a hint by the way.' I seem frenzied, I can feel my hands shaking.

'I know.' He's looking down. I've never seen him anything like this. I'm struggling to breathe normally. I look through the cupboards but I don't take anything in.

'Are you okay?' I don't know why I said it, but I have to know.

'I'm not great. I'll be fine though.' He sounds empty. I'm desperate to run over and hug him, but the thought of touching him at all feels so inappropriate now, like touching a stranger. How can that happen so quickly?

I see some bread on the side and my mind can't help but think how toast would be the perfect filling food.

'Can I have some of this bread, please?'

He looks up and smiles. 'It's your bread too.'

'Yeah, I guess. . . I thought, because you bought it. . .'

'Yeah, cause it's bad etiquette to eat your flatmate's food without asking?'

I could stop making the toast and concentrate on the conversation, but I actually feel like I'm going to collapse. I pop the bread down. There is a few seconds' silence.

'You should put some ham and cheese in that, I got some nice stuff from the deli. There's salad as well.'

I turn off my brain and my heart because they can't take anymore, and without the weight of them I can walk to the fridge to get the nice food he's suggested.

I stand waiting for my toast to pop up. He's leaning back on the sofa now but still looking at his lap.

'Oh, and don't forget to put mayo in it. It would be criminal to leave that out.'

My toast pops up, I jump a little and then freeze. It seems laughable to me to make a sandwich when the saddest thing that's ever happened to me is happening right now. Suddenly I feel dizzy and have to lean against the wall. My vision blurs. My breathing becomes shallow.

I can see him looking at me out my periphery.

'Do you want me to make it for you?'

'I'm not a child,' I snap back. I don't know why, but I just want to scream at him. I want to throw everything on the ground and ask why he's done this to me. Scream at him to get out. Cry on the floor as he leaves. But I know all he's done is support me, care for me, help me get to the end of days I didn't think I'd be able to. It's me who's done this to him. What have I done to him? My body aches with the guilt.

I sit on the floor and put my palms either side of me and try to calm my breathing. Was it so wrong to want to be with someone who hasn't seen me like this? I think of what I was like at Patrick's earlier and feel sick. I will all emotion to leave my body and pull myself up again.

I blink my eyes and look at him. He's raising his eyebrows at me with a little smirk, his eyes are sad, but I don't think they're hiding a deep sadness. How can he love me so much and only be like this? Is it possible?

I think about eating again. I stuff some crumbs of cheese into my mouth because I can't wait any longer. My stomach burns with emptiness. I take the toast out.

'If you're not a child then why is your toast so burnt?'

'It was your setting on the toaster. Not mine.'

'Never burns for me.' He shrugs. 'Can you make me one?'

I've just finished making mine. 'I'm honestly too hungry. Sorry.'

I don't know where to sit so I stand eating it. Trying to take small bites. But I'm barely chewing. It tastes like I've never had food before.

He stands up. 'Come sit here, I'm gonna make myself one anyway.'

I walk over, past him, like I've walked past him a million times in this room, except this time I want to close my eyes so tight I'll forget I'm even here. My core muscles don't support me very well, so I fall back on the sofa. I can see him look at me again. His expression is concerned. Always making myself the victim. I hate myself.

'I'll make you another one too.'

I want him to, but I don't know how I would say that, so I just sit here.

I listen to the sounds of him pottering around and my heart slows again. I don't know what comes over me but a few seconds later I say, 'And a tea, please,' lifting the corners of my mouth up cheekily. Even at a time like this he makes me feel relaxed, somehow.

'You'd be lucky,' he says, going to pick up the kettle. 'Don't worry. I'll move out soon. Just give me a few days.'

'You don't need to move out. I'll move out.'

'You have nowhere to go. Let alone store all your clothes.'

'Where would you go? Back to your parents?'

He shrugs and nods silently as he pours the boiling water into the mugs. I feel devastated watching him do something so kind and mundane after everything that's happened. It's as if he's saying, 'I care about you but I never really loved you.'

I manage to choke out, 'Why aren't you angry?'

'Because there's nothing I can do about it. So why be angry?

That's just another horrible thing to feel. I'd rather keep those to a minimum.'

'But surely you can't just choose not to feel pain?'

He can't look at me when he speaks. 'Maybe I'm more concerned for your pain than I am for my own.'

It's too hard to stop myself from crying, so I do, the tears are just running down my face silently, but there are a lot of them. He starts crying as well in the same way. It's too painful to look at him. But didn't I want this to happen? To see proof that there's depth in what he feels for me? I want to go over and hug him, to put my head on the tops of his feet and beg for him back, but I can't bring myself to move.

He takes a deep breath and wipes his face and finishes making the teas. I've never seen him cry before. It makes me feel uncomfortable and then that makes me feel even worse. I bite my cheek until it hurts, which is straight away, so I immediately stop. Clearly I don't hate myself that much.

He puts my tea and sandwich on the coffee table without saying anything and takes his into the bedroom. Some tears are still coming down my cheeks and I have to keep wiping my nose on my hand. Is it tears that I'm wiping away or is it my nose running? I never can tell, and I don't care but thinking about it stops me crying. I go into my old bedroom and lie on the bed. I don't deserve to lie under the sheet or on the pillow so I just curl up, but I don't feel comfortable enough to relax or fall asleep.

My room is stuffy and hot, so I get up and open the window, the small amount it can open. Maybe I should just force it open and throw myself out of it. Do they really think this flimsy device made to prevent it from fully opening would stop someone who had decided the days were no longer bearable?

Maybe I should go and lie down on the dirty concrete of the courtyard until someone notices me. What would they do with me? Ambulances aren't called for people having a rest on the floor. Maybe no one would come because no one would look out their window often enough to notice how long I'd been out there. Being realistic, at some point I would stand up and come in, which would be the saddest part of the whole thing. I get under the duvet in my dress and I feel unwell with the heat but I'm falling asleep and I like it.

When I wake up it's dark outside and I have to hold my head with the pain. It feels like knives have been stabbed into my eyes. It feels like the only way of curing the pain in my head would be if I took my eyeballs out. Does it really feel like that or do we just learn to describe pain in a few specific ways and not consider what the metaphor we are using would actually feel like?

I know George is not here anymore. I can just tell.

I have never felt such a deep sadness. Or is it even a deep sadness? I don't know what it is, but you can only feel emotions you have the language to express. It feels like everything has fallen away and I'm completely alone, the silence of the flat pulses in my brain. I roll on to my side and curl up into a ball, rocking myself back and forth. I start muttering to myself, none of it even makes sense, I don't know what I'm saying, it's just words, it's just to fill the silence, it's just to stop my mind plunging into darkness. I fall out of bed. I didn't need to fall out of bed, but that's what I wanted to do. My throat feels raw with emotional pain. I feel unhinged.

I go to the bathroom but blur my eyes because I don't want anything to remind me of George. I take some super strong painkillers because I can't be bothered to try the weaker ones. I walk to the kitchen. The lights in every room are off so I blur my eyes again because it hurts to see everything in darkness. I get a glass of cold water, still in the dark, and drink it so fast it pours all over my face and shoulders. I'm doing it on purpose though.

I fill up the glass again and walk to the bathroom. I turn the light off and the shower on. I peel my gross dress and underwear off and get in the shower with my glass of water. The hot water falls in the glass while I'm drinking it. That's what I wanted to happen though. I finish it and let it fill up with the hot water and then pour it over my head. I stay until my skin feels dry and hot and it starts scaring me to be in the dark.

I lie on my bed and let my eyes drift across the blank ceiling. My thoughts are few and far between but they are sharp. Images of being away from this all, turning myself off, not existing somehow. My palms throb with sadness. I frantically find my phone and type out a message. 'Glad we met up. I love you.' I send it and put it under my pillow. I calm down thinking about the response. Thinking about where our relationship can go if I just keep that stuff to myself from now on. Knowing the powerful relief his reply will give me.

28

As soon as I wake up I grab my phone. I see a notification and my heart contracts, but it says, '3 missed calls' from 'Mum'. It's my own fault for getting excited before I read it.

My chest doesn't relax though because the thoughts kick in: Why has she called me? Why is it three times? I think of who else could be dead now. No one calls three times for a chat.

If I never ring her back, has the bad thing still happened?

I ring her back. Before I can even wish she won't answer, she does. I prepare myself by letting all emotion leave my body.

'Hi, sweetheart, thanks for ringing back.'

'It's okay.'

'How are you?'

'I'm okay.' I feel nauseous with anger. It's disturbing to have such strong feelings that I can't understand.

'Is everything okay at work? Still busy as ever?'

'Yeah, yeah.'

'Are you okay?'

If I'm nice to her I can tell the last thing holding me together will break apart but I don't know why. 'You already asked me that one.'

'Why are you being like that? I'm just ringing you for a chat, didn't realise that was such a crime!' But she doesn't sound angry because she knows she's not ringing for a chat.

'Was there anything in particular you wanted to chat about?'

'I wanted to know how you are, but *yes*, there is also something I wanted to talk to you about.'

'Well. . . we've covered how I am. . .'

'You're so rude sometimes, you know.' Her voice breaks and I can hear her welling up. 'I could really do with a supportive daughter right now.'

The fear rises in me. My skin turns cold. 'And why's that?'

She starts crying. 'Me and dad are. . . separating. I thought I'd call to tell you because you deserve to know now, but we'd like it if you came home to see us.' She collects herself and returns to her normal voice. 'I can assure you nothing bad has happened, it's just sometimes—'

'What do you mean "us"?'

'Well, we're both here together. Dad is here now. We wanted to tell you together—'

'You're not telling me "together", *you're* telling me and he is, what? Sitting in the background in silence?'

'Would you like to speak to him? Mike!'

'No! I would not like to speak to him.'

'Will you come and see us?'

'What do you want from me? I'm not twelve, it barely makes a difference to my life if you're together or not.' I say it but the words don't calm me. In fact, I feel frightened. Like I can't rely on the ground beneath my feet anymore. The room spins around me.

'Dad's moving out this afternoon. He's going to stay with your uncle Steve.'

I let my phone drop onto the pillow so I can hear her speaking in little sounds, but not words, then the pauses between the sounds become longer and the sounds become shorter. I'm too tired to pick up the phone. Pity, she probably thinks I'm too upset to speak. I hear her say something motherly and understanding in a slower tone and then hang up. I bet it was, 'We'll be ready when you want to speak.' Or 'Take your time.' I wish she knew I didn't hear.

I turn on to my back, lie like a corpse and pretend to be dead. I wake up from what was probably a ten- or fifteen-minute sleep. I'm still on my back with my arms crossed over my chest.

It's hard to know what to do next. I can't remember what I do. What am I doing? What are these little moments, the moments in between the main parts? And what are the main parts? What am I doing? I actually can't remember what I'm supposed to do.

If I didn't go and see my parents right now, what would I do instead? Not 'what would I fill the next few hours with?' but 'what do I do? Even if I did go and see them, what do I do after that?' Not to *distract* myself, but what do I *do*? My foot is jiggling so much and I hate it. Who am I trying to show that I'm feeling anxious? I stop moving my leg and it's fine. I'm not anxious, I'm fine. I'm nothing.

I guess what people do is nothing. They eat and watch TV and file their nails and have a beer and kiss someone until it becomes boring and then kiss someone else until it becomes boring, but by then no one else wants to kiss them so they stay together and watch TV and eat dinner until they die.

I get up and walk to the kitchen, still naked. Maybe I will have a tea. I get goosebumps and look down at my body. My breasts look better when my nipples are cold. Even though I can see my ribs, my stomach looks slightly soft, but I'm probably thin enough. Some people might say I was too thin. Some fatter people. I try to let these thoughts make me feel better but they don't.

The kitchen looks so empty without George's things although I'm not instantly sure what's gone. I scream, but it sounds stupid and half-hearted because I did it slightly quietly so my neighbours wouldn't come knocking.

I'm standing still in the kitchen and not making a tea because I don't want one. I look through the cupboards. George has left all the food. I look around and can't see one thing he's taken. I think he has taken a coaster, but then I feel insane for thinking that.

I go back to my room and get my phone and then walk towards George's room, but before I even get near, I realise how completely heartbreaking it would be to go in there, so I back away.

I sit on my bed and notice how small the rolls on my stomach are. Basically just rolls of skin. However thin you are you would still have rolls like this, I think.

I look at my phone's empty screen. What would happen if I just threw my phone away and moved to another city without telling anyone? I find my pants and put them on because I'm done being naked. I sit on the edge of the bed, lay down, and then pull the duvet from both sides over me. What would Patrick think if he saw me doing all this? Does he ever act like this? George doesn't, but maybe *he's* the unusual one. This is the whole reason I like Patrick after all, although now I really think about it I don't feel confident he would understand this any more than George. And potentially even tolerate it less?

Up north is far away and supposed to be nice. It's not that hard to get a job and it's not that hard to make friends if you have a job. Well, not for me; people always like me. I could get a group of friends and do loads of things with them, make proper memories and then after that fall in love with someone. Maybe someone who has never moved out of their hometown and never will. Maybe that was my mistake. Maybe Mum was right.

But this relationship wouldn't be claustrophobic because I'll still have all my friends, and we'll still do things together, even when we have babies. And so even if I did get divorced I'd still have so many people to support me, to see me all the time, people that really *know* me. Because I would have worked out by then which kind of 'me' to be. I would be fine.

The reality though, is that if I went there today I would hate it and freak out and call George and ask him to marry me or something. And if I got a job, I would hate everyone there for a few weeks, then I'd like everyone for a few weeks, then I'd hate them all forever.

I guess none of that would happen though because someone would call the police when they noticed I was gone, and everyone would try and take my 'cry for help' as seriously as they could.

I feel like nothing can get better or worse than this and that thought is relaxing.

I look at my phone again and there is a missed call from Patrick. I take a deep breath in. It's like he knows. He really does love me. It's time for him to be everything I need him to be, everything that George wasn't.

I lie down, right in the corner where my bed meets the wall. It isn't comfortable but I've made my choice now. I ring him back. My heart is beating fast, but my brain is still.

He answers. 'All right.'

'Is that a question or a statement?'

'Both?'

'What about that one?' It's surprising how normal I can make myself sound.

'Neither.'

'What's up?'

It sounds like he is walking and speaking. 'Yeah, sound thanks.'

I won't ask another question. I suddenly wonder if he has purposefully rung so he doesn't have to respond directly to my 'I love you'. There is a slight pause. Now that he has me, is there someone else he wants? No. He's proven himself so many times. I let myself believe it.

He speaks again. 'I was thinking, maybe you could come round in the week sometime? I'd like to see you.' It sounds like he's arranging a business meeting.

'As in, next week?'

'Yeah, next week. Does that work for you?'

'It sounds like you're arranging a meeting.' I forget to make my voice normal. 'Do we have to plan it already? I don't have my diary on me at the moment?' Maybe it was unclear that I don't actually have a diary.

'All right, that's cool. It was just because other stuff gets planned y'know? And if I don't see you next week it'll be like, minimum two weeks, but I get it.'

I guess I'm still not supposed to ask him what he's doing this weekend. 'We can arrange something nearer the time then.'

'Yeah. Cool.' He's going to hang up.

'My parents are getting divorced.'

'What? Sorry, I can't really hear. It's so windy.'

'My parents are getting divorced.'

'What?' It sounds like he's putting his finger in his other ear and squinting. Why do people squint when they're trying to hear?

'It's okay. Don't worry. It's nothing.'

'Your parents are getting divorced? Sorry, I've turned into a quiet alley now. Did you say your parents are getting divorced?'

'Yeah. We don't need to speak now though. Sounds like you're busy.'

'Nah, I've got time. Since when is this then?'

'Since just now.'

'Oh shit.' He elongates the 'I' so it sounds like a reaction to me getting grounded. I don't think I have anything else to say. 'So did they just turn up or what?'

'Well no, I don't think they'll be turning up anywhere together. Anymore.'

'Yeah.' There is a pause. 'How are you?' He can't even pretend to want to know.

'I'm okay thanks. How are you?'

'Yeah, all right cheers.'

Maybe I will hang up. If I threw up lying on my back would some of it go on my face or would it all just stay in my mouth?

'Do you mind?'

'Do I mind what?' I get under the duvet.

'Do you mind they're calling it quits?' I can hear he's started walking again.

'Nah, it's fine.'

'I can hear it's not fine, Iris.'

Can he?

I swallow hard. 'Okay, well no, it's not fine. It feels like I'm in a hot air balloon on my own that's going up and up and up and I can't see the ground anymore. Or maybe it doesn't feel like that. I don't know. I know I shouldn't care that they're getting divorced but the thought of them alone and sad—' I stop speaking.

He's changed tone to a serious one now. It sounds like he's doing his furrowed concentrating face. 'Look. . . maybe I'm not the right person to talk to about this.'

'Yeah. That's all right, you don't need to be.'

'Okay.' There's a pause and I feel so desperately sad. Can he tell that I'm desperately sad? Maybe he can't. Maybe I'm expecting too much of him. Does he really need to be a mind-reader? George certainly couldn't read my mind but that didn't stop him being nice. Nice is an underrated word and personality trait. I remind myself; this is what I chose and this is what I deserve.

No one is saying anything, but I relax because I know he can't just say goodbye.

A slight exasperation in his voice. 'It would be better to speak in person, wouldn't it?'

'Yeah, that would be nice.'

'So when we arrange to meet up, next week or the week after or whatever, we can speak then. And it'll be good. I'll touch your hair when you're talking.'

It's too hot in my bed, so I get out and sit on the edge again. Tears are streaming down my face, but you can't hear it in my voice.

'Okay, yeah, sounds good. We'll speak when we're arranging something. Yeah. Anyway, I'm gonna go. See you later.'

'Okay, see you lat—' I hang up before he finishes his sentence and then throw my phone hard against the wall and it just bounces off and falls down in an anticlimax. I lie down and sob so hard I drool onto the sheets. And then I stop. My eyes are closed and my mouth is open. Reality fades in and out of my consciousness. Sometimes, for a moment, I feel as if I have lost everything and I'm finally free, no longer bound to anyone or anything or being alive. Sometimes I just feel as though the mattress has opened up and I'm falling and falling and falling and.

The terrifying idea presents itself to me again. *If the pain is too much, it's in your power to stop it,* it says to me. I don't know what to say back. I know I can't wait around for Patrick to text me again. I don't have the strength. But without him, without George, I'm completely alone. Two paths open up to me and I make a split second decision.

I reach under my bed for the nice quality travel bag I bought because I thought having nice accessories is what takes you from someone that looks nice to someone who looks amazing. And what's more important than looking amazing? I grab some random clothes and push them into the bag. I stand in front of my mirror and scrape my hair back into a ponytail so tight it hurts my scalp. I press my forehead really hard into the mirror and wonder if I pressed hard enough would it shatter and the glass cut into my face? But I pull away so I'll never know.

I pick up my bag to leave but realise I'm still in my pants. I force a laugh out as I tug on clothes.

I look so bad. Not at all attractive. No one would look at me for a second in a room full of people. My arms look scrawny, but for some reason I don't think it looks good, my eyes are dry and dark and dead. My face is plain, maybe slightly unsymmetrical. What people love about me is just the hours I spend creating myself. Even George. It seems as though he loves me for who I am, but he fell in love with a girl who always looked nice and was interesting and fun and by the time I wasn't her anymore, it was too late, his moral compass wouldn't allow him to leave me just because I have got puffy, dead eyes now. Patrick wouldn't last a second with this reality though. Is one worse than the other? No. It's me who's worst.

I blow myself a kiss in the mirror and take my bag to the kitchen and stuff in some cooking raisins I find in the cupboard. Some people would think that is a healthy snack but eating a whole bag of raisins, which I will, has so much more sugar than any chocolate bar. I take them out of my bag, stuff a handful in my mouth, tip half in the bin, which I notice has a fresh bin-bag, and put them back in my bag. The sweetness of the raisins makes my mouth water painfully.

I walk past George's room, our room, and poke my head in, it's so empty. He's moved back home already. It feels like practically everything has gone although I can already see loads of things he's left that he could've taken. A jacket of his I like to wear when it's really cold, a print his sister gave to him that I love, a lamp we bought together at a market once.

The near silence of the flat is suddenly so unbearable I push my fingers hard into my ears. Then I squeeze my eyes shut and slam the door closed. I will never go in there again and when I move out one day, the next residents will go in and speculate why there is this one room, half full of things, all dusty and neglected. Or maybe in a few years George will come back, and we can pick up where we left off. He'd say something about the lamp and it would probably be funny and the situation wouldn't feel weird even though it's insane. He could make any situation feel like it was normal and funny.

I run out of the house and down the stairs of my block and to the tube station. When people look at me now, what do they think? Sweaty, greasy hair, wrinkled old clothes, big bag of belongings. People would think a lot different of me compared to if they saw me on the way to meet Patrick the other week, all shiny and made-up. Which impression is more accurate? It's not necessarily more authentic just because I'm not wearing deodorant.

At St Pancras, I walk through the station and get on the train, but I feel frozen inside like I'm still standing at the entrance doors.

It feels like time has stopped moving for me or something. It feels like I know something that none of these people know, something awful, and the thought of them finding out makes me deeply sad. It terrifies me, the thought of them finding out.

29

Maybe I should've brought some flowers as a kind of 'commiserations and congratulations' gift. Walking through the town I like to look at everyone and guess what the worst thing that they've ever thought is. It's probably a version of the same five thoughts that cover most of the population. This spotty man in his twenties wearing a cap and a potentially very expensive, potentially very cheap, tracksuit spits on the ground as he is walking towards me and then maintains my eye contact aggressively as he walks past. I bet a lot of bad thoughts stem from the desire for control.

I trip up on uneven pavement and use my hands to steady myself. I roll my eyes at the fact my reflex was to stop myself being injured. Apparently I don't really want to cause harm to myself, I just pretend I want to.

When I reach our house, squeezed in-between two identical ones, I wonder if the neighbours know about the divorce. It's probably the most interesting thing that's happened for fifteen years since someone on the road was arrested for beating up his wife: 'You never would have known. He used to wave at me when I put out the bins.'

I'm standing outside the house because I'm not sure whether to use my keys or to knock. I never usually knock because Mum gets angry and says, 'It's still your home. You'll never be a guest here, madam.' What is she doing in there though? I feel like her life is private now. But I don't want to upset her, so I choose to use the keys with a slight knock as I walk in.

'Hello?' Maybe she's not even in. Dad's coat is still on the hook. Could they have been exaggerating and everything is smoothed over now? The hope hurts worse than the pain. I enter slowly. I feel like I might walk in on her doing something, but I don't know what. Whatever it is, I don't want to see it. I wish for one moment things could just stay still, not frozen, but like how in childhood time seemed to drag, everything seemed repetitive and monotonous but peaceful. I would love that comfort now. This small home with our small family in it was my whole world for so long and now even that is falling away.

I try louder in case she's upstairs. She would never be upstairs in the early evening, but I guess there isn't a 'never be' anymore. I have no idea what she does now.

'Hello? Mum?'

I hear a voice upstairs. 'Iris? Did you come?'

'Take a guess.' I wait at the bottom of the stairs. Nothing could make me go up them. I close my eyes to prepare myself for what's coming down.

'Sweetheart! I wasn't expecting you!'

She looks 98% normal, but the 2% that's different brings a dull ache to my stomach. Her hair, usually in a puffy bob, is still the same but now it's frizzier and flat on one side. The wrinkles on her cheek seem slightly deeper.

She reaches the bottom of the stairs and hugs me. I wish there was a way to make it so nothing was said about the divorce. I feel tense at the thought of dinner with just us two.

'Come on, sweetie. I'll make you some tea.'

Why is it the woman always gets to keep the house? I want to cry thinking about Dad, in his fifties, staying in a house where he has nothing and probably isn't particularly wanted. I actually think I *might* cry, my hands and face start to tingle, but Mum switches the kettle on and turns around.

'Are you only popping in? Put your bag down!'

I hope she can't see my eyes watering. I don't want to bring any emotion to this. I put my bag down.

'Sit down! You're not a guest, you don't need permission to take a seat!'

I sit down at the pinewood table in the middle of the kitchen. Four seats. We always sat in the same three and you can visibly tell that one chair has been used less. I'm not sure if they still sat next to each other or one moved to sit opposite once I'd left. I wonder if she tries to not sit there at all now. I grind my teeth together and push these thoughts away. If I don't think about anything, it can't upset me.

I see half a lemon drizzle cake on the side. She is using old mugs that haven't been used in years. I'm so confused, my head feels dizzy and I know the silence has gone on too long, but I have no idea how to speak.

'It's so lovely you decided to come down. I wish you'd've told me though — I would've got some more food in.'

She hands me a tea but walks back to the counter and holds her mug whilst leaning against the side.

'You don't need to get more food in. I'm not a guest.'

She laughs loudly, and I can't remember if her laugh is usually that loud. Maybe they didn't eat in the kitchen anymore, but I don't see them eating at the large dining table either. It must feel awkward

243

having a whole dining room which is only used once a year. They should've changed it into something else. I can see why you'd get divorced with a depressing room like that in your house.

I've started drinking the tea even though it's burning my tongue. She is drinking hers as well. I'm here to be nice.

'How are you doing?' My voice slightly cracks. Is it unreasonable that I don't want to know how she's doing? I'm sure she has other people she can talk to and I'm the only person who is in the middle of this. Even asking drains every last bit of my energy away.

'I'm doing okay, yes.' She starts to well up, and I have to look into the tea. Thinking of her being unhappy is so deeply upsetting that it makes me angry. Anger is always a more comfortable choice than sadness.

'No, I am okay, really.' She does a 'pulling herself together' inhale and returns to a normal voice. 'It's actually a good thing, for both me and Dad.'

'That's good.' I can see she's desperate for me to ask questions, but I don't know what to say.

'It isn't anything that's happened or anything like that.'

'I know.' I try to sound blank.

'I don't expect you to fully understand, but me and Dad still love each other very much, in a different type of way.'

I can't hold it back anymore. My tone is angry now. 'I really don't care either way.'

The worst thing is that I can see her face is concerned rather than shocked. I want to ask her if she really thinks she's going to find her soulmate now and live happily ever after? She's not going to find someone nicer than Dad. I wonder if she's ever considered that she's the problem. I think about my own life and shame seeps into me.

'I'm gonna put my bag upstairs.' I stand and walk up the stairs, past the hanging pictures of Mum and Dad on various holidays twenty years ago. There is something painful about an outdated yellow hallway. I close my eyes as I walk past their bedroom because I'm worried it will be messy or something.

My room smells warm, and I feel sleepy as soon as I walk in. The sun shines in it during the afternoon and it's always hard not to fall asleep in the duvet-like air. I used to love that, sitting on my bed, feeling the sun on my cheek and then starting to drift off. Having a blissful moment of being aware I was falling asleep. The drowsiness pulling me closer and closer, but knowing it was fine to succumb to it, not a worry in sight. I lie down on the bed and feel like I could go to sleep, but I know it won't feel the same.

I'm kidding myself if I think there were no worries back then. I was probably sitting on my bed writing down what I'd eaten that day, or the things I needed to change about myself, or the reasons people liked my friends more than me. It makes me wince to think of how non-existent and pointless I'd felt without even realising it. How desperate I was to be noticed by anyone.

I was desperate but not despairing though. I thought that getting out of here, having my own money, my own place to live, something fulfilling to do, all that would make me happy. I guess I was wrong.

I reach and get my phone out of the bag. It doesn't seem damaged at all, which I'm, unsurprisingly, relieved at. I turn it on and quickly put it face down on my bed.

I wake up to Mum shouting, 'Dinner's ready, sweetheart!'

The thought of eating makes me feel sick. I check my phone. No messages, no missed calls. Maybe she was right all along. I should just move back here and get a job as a dental hygienist and marry

245

someone from school who I used to wish was my boyfriend. I can see now that there's probably nothing worse about that life than the one I so desperately craved.

I wonder if any of the girls I was friends with still live here. There's something I miss so much about being with girls all day. It's funny because there wasn't one of us who wouldn't drop their friends for a boy, and yet those were easily the closest friends I've ever had. It's a shame we only saw each other as rivals. There was no caring or encouraging. It was all competition and politics. Their successes were my failures. Except they weren't.

'It's getting cold!'

She hates it when I don't come down straight away, so I'm ticking all the good daughter boxes tonight.

She's made Bolognese. If she had looked at a recipe for Bolognese even one time she would know this is not how you make it.

'Do you want some cheese?'

'No, thanks.' I wonder how I can only eat the spaghetti without the sauce. 'Thanks for this, it looks nice.'

'Oh, it's just the same old.'

'A classic.' We eat in silence for a moment, which is intensely awkward.

It's hard, but I can push bits of meat off the pasta and then eat it. Making a little pile on the side so it doesn't migrate back to the middle.

'How's Dad?'

For the first time she looks at me slightly offended, but quickly returns to a neutral and serious face. I notice her portion of pasta is quite small.

'Yes, he's good — he's fine. He's staying with your uncle.'

'I know.'

'Don't play with your food, Iris. You're not a child. You look very pale, you need some iron. Eat up, please.'

She probably expects me to ignore her, but I start eating it normally even though the spongy texture of the mince is making me feel so ill. I try to eat it without chewing too much.

She tries to start a conversation. 'I know this is hard and I understand that. Believe me it's hard for me too. This family is everything to me—' She starts welling up again and it makes me feel even sicker than the mince.

It's all too much, I wish I could leave and never come back, but that neither of us would be sad about it. But where would I go? There are physical places I can go but they're just places to eat, sleep, exist. They're all half-homes now, nostalgic shells of somewhere that used to mean something. But now they mean nothing. Because I'm not part of a couple, not part of a workplace, or school or friendship group. And now I'm not part of a little family. I just have some people I'm related to.

Mum takes some deep breaths to recompose herself. If it's that easy to stop, why doesn't she just stop herself before she starts?

'You don't have to talk about this y'know, Mum?'

She dramatically puts her fork down. 'Well, it's quite a big deal for me, even if it isn't for you. *Twenty-seven years.* That's longer than your whole life, don't you forget. Try and have some sympathy, please.' She picks her fork back up.

'What do you want me to say?' I'm eating all the food now, really fast, but still trying to chew as little as possible.

'Maybe you could just *listen*. I'm just another human, you know? Not only your mum. I have feelings too.'

'Okay, I'm listening.'

'It doesn't mean all of this was fake. We truly had a great marriage. But sometimes you lose sight of who you are—'

I start choking on some meat that I swallowed without chewing. It's a really dramatic, loud, red-faced kind of choke. Mum sits there, holding her fork over the plate and looking at me impatiently.

'Right. Well, I guess we can speak another time then. Unless you're off first thing?' She doesn't leave a space for me to answer. 'It would be lovely if you could wash up, sweetheart. It's fresh sheets on your bed.' She's taking both of our half-full plates and stacking them on the side without even putting what's left into the bin.

'Goodnight.' She walks out and straight upstairs. I wonder if I am a genuinely bad person.

The choking has stopped. I get up, take my plate back and eat the rest. When I've finished and stared into thin air for a while, I lay my head down onto the plate. I thought it would be comfy, but it's not. So I get up and clean the kitchen until it's perfect and then allow myself to look in the dark window above the sink. I am standing very hunched and the Bolognese sauce on my forehead is as funny as I'd hoped. I can't tell if my life is weird or completely normal.

I go upstairs, sighing in the loud way that people do at the end of a hard day. I walk in my room and see myself in another window. But I'm just blurry blocks of colour. Even the blur looks sad. Three times in a row I picture myself jumping out the window, but I never get to what happens when I land.

When I take my shirt off most of the sauce on my forehead gets wiped away, so that will do for now. I check my phone — no new messages. That's fine, that's expected, that's my life now. I decide there's no point in cleaning my teeth.

30

There's a knock at the door. My head feels like I drank a whole bottle of wine last night.

'Can I come in?'

'Yeah.' Even my voice sounds like a lazy teenager.

Mum opens the door, all dressed and clean with a happy smile.

'I brought you a coffee.'

She walks over and puts it on my bedside table, then walks back to the doorway and stands there.

'Look, about last night, I let my emotions get the better of me, and I want to apologise. I know this must be a very confusing and hard—' She stops and stares at me horrified for a moment before running over. 'Oh my god, is that blood? What happened?'

I wonder if I dug my nails into my skin too hard during the night, but she touches my forehead and I can feel the crusty tomato sauce flake off. Apparently she still needs reassuring because she is looking at me and waiting for a response.

'No, it's not blood.'

'Is it. . . Bolognese?' she replies instantly.

'It seems like you already know.' I wish she would go away whilst I'm lying here nearly naked under the duvet.

'How did you get it on there?'

'Is it still concerning you?'

She stands up and walks to the door. 'Okay, well if you're going to be like that, I'll leave you to have your coffee.' She walks out.

I take a sip of the coffee. I haven't had an instant one for over a year and it tastes bitter and watery and it's lukewarm anyway, so I open the window and tip it out. My room's above the dining room so even if it goes all over the downstairs window no one will ever see.

I take ages to get out of bed and even longer to get ready. But once I'm showered and dressed in some faded black jeans that are too big for me now and a sweater with holes in the cuffs, I go downstairs.

She's in the living room watching daytime TV, something I have never seen her do, and I have to swallow hard to keep the pain down.

'Thanks for the coffee.'

'You're welcome,' she says quietly without turning around.

If I get this over with, I can leave. I don't know if some part of me thought I'd be comforted coming back here, but I'm actually feeling increasingly worse. I go and sit down in the small leather armchair.

'Mum, I'm sorry. I know it must be really hard for you.'

She doesn't say anything. I haven't said enough. 'Maybe I'm not the best person to talk to about everything,' I think of my phone call with Patrick and add, 'but I do want to listen if you want to talk.'

She doesn't look at me but speaks earnestly. 'We're still a family, and I'm saying that for myself too. You don't stop caring at fifty. I still want to be happy, as much as you. I've got to give this a go.'

I ask her a genuine question, 'You weren't that young when you got together, how much can change after thirty?'

She still doesn't look at me. 'It's not about change. Or, if anything, it's about how little I changed. When I was in my twenties I didn't quite know who I was, a common feeling for a young adult, I know. I had a notion that a husband, a family, would complete me. But I was wrong, I needed to be a complete person in myself first.'

I try to cut her off but she turns to look at me.

'Do you know what made me realise?' She speaks timidly with a little smile. 'All the meals I know how to cook are ones I know you and your dad like. There were holes in my identity, a relationship paved over those gaps, but eventually it started to crack. And the holes were back. If you're not a fully formed person you can't fill yourself up with other people. People should be additions to an already established life, they should not be there to establish it for you.'

'But you're always going on about how it's selfish to have a career? And how family is everything?'

Her lip quivers but I see her take a deep breath in to hold it together. 'And you know what, I'm really sorry about that, sweetheart. I was completely wrong. A classic case of defensiveness I'd say. But when I say an "established life", I don't necessarily mean a career. Maybe I just mean a personality, a state of mind, some kind of personal contentment.' She glances at me and then away again. 'Do you. . . would you say you have that?'

My mind is blank but an angel must look down on me for a second because the phone rings.

'Oh. Kelly from work has been ringing me every day, bless her.' She gets up and goes to the phone in the kitchen.

I go upstairs and get my bag. I make my bed and look at the room like it's the last time I'll ever see it.

I remember losing my virginity to Lewis who'd been my boyfriend for two months. He came over one Saturday evening after we had both finished work. I remember being at the pub and thinking 'This is the last time I will bring people food as a virgin.' We didn't openly discuss that we would be having sex that night, but we both knew. We'd been kissing and touching each other for a number of weeks and so, following the unsaid social rules of my friends, that night we should take the next step. I don't know if I even wanted to but I thought fifteen was too old to be a virgin. I hoped he would bring up using a condom because I was almost certain I wouldn't be able to do it. The only thing I thought when I was losing my virginity was — thank God I've done it now. One month later I broke up with him because people were saying it was embarrassing that he was the same height as me.

I also remember being eighteen and standing in this doorway, doing this exact thing – thinking. Thinking: I wonder if I'll come back here when I'm thirty, because my parents are moving out or something, and all the memories of being in this room would seem so far away from my current life where I'm a TV presenter or director or columnist, living in a fancy flat in London with an attractive boyfriend and money to spend on getting highlights and jackets and cigarettes.

Now I can't even think of one thing to wish for. I'm not under the illusion anymore that I could do or be anything which would make me happy in any kind of consistent way.

I go downstairs and Mum is standing in the hall, which makes my body pulse with sadness. I want to tell her that I'm lonely too, that I don't know who I am if it's not in relation to someone else, that it's hard to see myself reflected in her like this, that I feel too heavy to take it all on.

I walk quickly past her to the door, so I can have my back to her and let my face drop. To let my eyes water. Just for a second. Then

I turn around back to normal, eyes wider, blanker. 'Do I have to ask Dad if I can go round?'

'He wants to see you, of course.'

'Is it weird to just turn up though?'

I wonder if she can hear I'm finding it hard to swallow. I don't know if I can see something in her eyes but I can't bear it, so I turn around again to pick up my bag.

'Okay, I guess I better be on my way then.' It feels wrong to say goodbye facing away, but it's too late now, tears are falling down my face. My voice sounds normal though, which makes me feel even worse and cry harder.

'Goodbye, sweetie! I put a banana in your bag!' Her voice sounds too buoyant for it to be real too.

My breaths are quick and deep and my face starts to tingle, so I run down the road, around the corner and lean on the side of a house, crying loudly and getting so little air that I wonder if I could die like this. I know I wouldn't die like this, but it's relaxing to think about.

I stop breathing fast and stop crying and trace my fingers over the bricks behind me. They feel rough in this strange subtle way that puts my teeth on edge. I slide down the wall and my jumper comes up so the wall starts grazing my back a bit. I stop and sit down instead. On the floor I push my head back into the wall and clench my jaw.

When I get to uncle Steven's road, I have no idea which house it is because I haven't been here in about a decade. It's hard to know whether to guess which door to knock on, or just ring Dad and ask.

Both seem unbearable. Every time I settle on one, I think: imagine knocking on a door and a random old woman answers and I try to explain I'm looking for Steven's house because my dad is staying with him as he's just separated from my mum and I need to make sure he's still managing to get dressed in the morning.

Or ringing him and he answers like, 'Oh. . . Hey' and then I have to tell him I'm standing outside his brother's house where he now lives and he has no choice but to let me in.

I ring his phone and no one answers. I have to force myself to ring him again.

'Hello?' Does he not have my number saved?

'Hi. Dad?'

'Oh. . . Hi. Sorry, I don't have you in my phone. I guess you don't call this one much!'

Awkward laughter from both of us.

'What are you up to?' I put some feelers out.

'Uh. . . up to. . . now? Or just. . .?'

'Now, as in, are you busy?'

'Yes, yes, I'm busy. You don't need to worry about me, sweetheart.'

'Oh. . . I'm not worried. It's just. . . I came here to see you. . . if you like?'

'Yes, it would be lovely to see you at some point.'

Seconds pass before I can think of anything to say. I'm suddenly very aware that I'm standing outside the house he's in and he has no idea. I walk back to the end of the road.

'What have you been up to? Still at work?'

'Of course!'

Everything I'm saying is wrong because there is nothing right to say.

Just the fact I'm speaking to him without Mum there feels

horribly uncomfortable. I can't remember the last time it was just us two for longer than five minutes.

'Sorry.' I don't know what to say. 'I don't know if you want to talk or not. It's fine either way. I understand.'

'Of course I want to speak to you.' I wonder how much of the same person they are by now. One person split into two.

I sit down on the kerb like you would a step, but it's only around 10 cm higher than the road so my knees are by my face.

'What would you like to speak about? Anything about Mum?'

She was desperate for me to ask that and he gets it for free. I feel awful but it's easier to ask someone how they are when you know they won't tell you the truth.

'You don't need to ask me that. I'm sure you've got bigger things on your plate.'

'I don't mind.'

'Thanks, sweetheart. It is what it is, isn't it?'

I don't say anything.

'Life is never what you expect it to be.' It sounds like he sits down. He sighs and continues. 'No one's at fault here. And it doesn't mean everything is falling apart. You can't appreciate the happy without the sad. It must be hard to see your parents like this, but we're just humans too. Sometimes we find things hard, but we'll get through it.'

My mind is blank with what to say. I press my knees into my forehead.

'I would love to see you sometime, sweetheart. I could take you for a pizza? I know you're busy so don't feel guilty. Everything is fine here, I promise you.'

Hearing someone pretend to be okay makes me want to get a kitchen knife and stick it into my skull. 'I know.' I picture a sharp knife being stuck slowly into my temple.

'Hopefully see you soon!'

'Yeah, definitely, bye.'

'Bye, sweetheart.' He hangs up.

I wonder if he will cry now. I look at my phone. Stare at the screen. I imagine a message appearing from Patrick and deleting it straight away. Two people have fallen in love with me in such a short amount of time, I should just be excited for the next time it happens. I'll probably bump into Patrick one day in the future, and I bet his face will be wrinkly because of all the smoking and his girlfriend will be one of those girls who starts off pretty and then puts on weight and gets a bob and has no idea that their boyfriend doesn't love them anymore. The thought doesn't make me feel better, I just feel cruel. Maybe I should get a bob.

I get up and walk towards the station. Everyone I walk past looks reasonably happy, but I wonder if one day they'll all realise how meaningless this all is.

31

I'm nearly back in town when I decide I should get a drink and maybe a snack for the train home. There's a small Londis on the corner of the road, so I go in and walk to the bright refrigerated wall of drinks. All the drinks, in their colourful cans, are neatly arranged and fully stocked. It's pleasurable to look at, so I stand there for a while considering all the options, when a guy comes and stands next to me.

We both briefly glance at each other and I immediately recognise him even though I haven't seen him in five years. Paul Pike from school. He clearly recognises me too, but we both stand in silence for a second deciding whether we pretend not to. I hope he doesn't think I still live here, but then I realise that maybe it's him who still lives here. I remember that I look disgusting and turn to walk away.

'Hey?'

I surprise myself by turning red. 'Oh. . .' I turn back. 'Hi.' For a split second I consider pretending not to know him, but I don't reckon I can pull it off.

He smiles in the exact condescending way he used to. 'How's it going?'

'Yeah, good thanks. Just back from London to see my parents.'

'Sweet. You live in London?'

'Yeah, have done for a few years.' There is no subtlety in my pride.

'Nice one. I lived down south for a bit, but then came back to live with the 'rents to save up for my own place. Fuck paying off someone else's mortgage.'

'Oh cool, so did you buy somewhere?'

He smiles on one side of his face more than the other. 'Yeah, got this quality place right in town. Well happy with it to be honest.'

'Impressive. I think it's more likely I get struck with lightning than buy a property anytime soon.' I relax with the self-deprecation.

'That's London though, right?' I notice he has three buttons undone on his light blue shirt. I'm pretty sure that's exactly how he's always dressed.

'What do you want then?' He gestures at the fridge.

'Oh, I think I'm just gonna get a water. Was here for about ninety minutes before you came in, just staring at the options.'

He picks up a good quality, but not the glass, bottle of water, a Ribena and an iced lemon green tea and takes them all over to the till. I stand there unsure what he's doing. He calls over, 'Hey – come on. I got you some options.' I walk over and he hands me the two bottles, taking the Ribena and a packet of Silk Cut cigarettes. He sees me look at the packet. 'Only when I'm drinking.'

'Oh yeah, I smoke when I'm drinking too.'

He turns to walk out, and I feel like I could actually stand here with my head in my hands, only now they're full of bottles.

I walk out hoping he's already left, but he's standing outside lighting a cigarette.

'Well, thanks so much for the drinks, you saved me another half an hour.'

As I walk away, he says, 'Iris?'

It gives me a funny feeling that he remembers my name. I imagine how excited I would've been to hear that back in the day.

I turn back. 'Yeah?'

'Me and some friends are going down The Bakers for a cheeky bev if you wanna come?'

'Oh, right. Erm.' I use one of the bottles to point to the bag on my shoulder. 'I'm actually headed home.'

'Suit yourself.' He drops his cigarette even though he's only smoked it for a few seconds and walks away.

That cringes me out a bit, so I'm surprised when I run to catch up with him. 'Oh, all right, let's see what the social scene here has to offer then.'

He takes the bag off my shoulder and walks on.

I know one of the guys, Danny, from school, but not well enough that either of us want to acknowledge that we remember each other. There's two girls, Chloe and Shauna. I don't know if they're people's girlfriends, or just friends of the group, but they're only speaking to each other. And then two other people from Paul's work, Sanj and Nathan. People say hi, but within minutes I feel like I'm sitting next to a group of people rather than with them. Paul pauses the conversation to say he's going to get a drink and asks me what I want, but I insist I'll go get them as a chance to get away and gather my thoughts for a second.

The boy who serves me looks like he could be fifteen, except for the fact he has tattoos all over his neck and face and is serving alcohol in a pub.

'What can I do you for?' He seems so genuine and friendly I feel caught off guard.

'Can I get a Heineken and a double gin and tonic please?'

'Is that just the house gin?'

Again, I feel surprised that a boy with serious acne and 'MUM' tattooed on his face in a dingy pub is making me feel embarrassed about my gin choice and wonder if I need to stop making split second judgements about people. 'Whatever you recommend.'

I wonder if his 'MUM' tattoo is ironic. Seems like a big thing to get an ironic tattoo on your face. He brings over the drinks and gives me a big genuine smile as I hand over my card.

I pass Paul his drink over the table and he gives a quick wink that I remember seeing other people be the recipient of. I use the confidence from knowing the alcohol will soon relax me and sit next to the girls instead of back by him.

'Hey, sorry, I completely forgot everyone's names as soon as they told me. What were yours again?'

They both turn to me with blank eyes and my mind overflows with excuses of why I suddenly need to leave.

'I'm Shauna and she's Chloe.'

'Oh yeah, sorry. I'm Iris.'

'Yeah, I remember.' Shauna has manicured long, red, shiny nails, neat curled hair and enough bronzer to look like she's just come off the beach. But Sara looks more glamorous than her, even when she's just rolled out of bed.

'So, how do you know these guys?'

Chloe smiles. She has very short peroxide hair and small features which make her look like a pixie. Her voice is surprisingly husky. 'I don't even remember at this point.'

'I just wondered if you were their girlfriends.'

Both of them have a big laugh, but it doesn't feel directed at me this time. I take the hint and change the subject to ask what they do. Again I get laughed at for starting 'such a boring conversation', that you 'don't come to the pub to talk about', but one by one they passionately tell me about what they do. Shauna is a life coach. I tell her I've never met a life coach before and she says, 'I bet you've never met a lot of people before, honey.'

She talks about helping people become who they're *meant* to become, rather than who they *want* to become. I ask her if that's ever the same thing and she says, 'Is it the same thing for you?'

I don't really know what she means, it all sounds a bit bullshitty to me, but luckily the question is rhetorical. She tells me that people pride themselves on creating coping mechanisms, but that people who need coping mechanisms aren't living the right life for them. 'You shouldn't have to "cope" with life.'

Chloe is an occupational therapist, and while Shauna goes to get a round of drinks, she tells me of a recent patient she helped move on from a mental illness that had them 'house-bound' to becoming a 'wicked tattoo artist', but she says it's not always about transformations like that, sometimes it's just helping someone spend less time in their wheelchair. Shauna comes back and tells me, 'Chloe works in "coping mechanisms".' I look for a flicker of hurt in Chloe's eyes, but they just laugh. They don't ask me what I do and I'm glad. You don't come to the pub to talk about your job.

By the time I bring back the next round, the group are talking all together about tattoos. Shauna is saying she hates when people ask her what her tattoos mean, but Paul says that the whole point of getting a tattoo is to show other people and anyone who denies that is kidding themselves. Shauna doesn't seem annoyed at his response which surprises me, and I start wondering if they have a thing together.

It would make sense because Paul's type at school was always the most put together girls, expensive new clothes, straightened hair every day, confident but not *too* confident and, of course, big boobs. I remember I look awful, and the thought starts to make me very anxious. Chloe gets up to go to the toilet, so I stand to join her. I think Shauna looks at me judgementally, but that seems to be her reaction to everything I do, so I forget about it.

'Hey.'

Chloe looks at me through the mirror. 'Hey.'

I go and wash my hands in the sink next to her and get ready to say my line. 'Oh god, I look awful. You don't by any chance have some make-up I can use, do you?' I look worse than I remembered. Pale, purple under eyes, lopsided ponytail, grey sweater that washes me out.

She has thick black eyeliner on her lids, but not much else, and so I kind of expect her answer of, 'No, sorry, I don't.'

'I do!'

We turn and see Shauna in the doorway. For some reason I feel defensive and start babbling. 'Oh my god, amazing, I was just saying how gross I look. It's like I haven't slept in weeks or something. And like, what is with this hair? I look like someone who's just finished their first week of Year 7.'

She doesn't say anything, but just reaches in her bag and pulls out a pouch filled with make-up.

'Thanks. I really appreciate it.'

'That's okay.'

I flick through the contents of the bag, wondering what I'm going to do with this dark bronzer and cheap matte foundation, but Shauna reads it wrong.

'Here, let me do it. Funny time to start wearing make-up. You hooking up with Paul or something?' She takes a well-used eyeshadow palette out and dabs some of a light brown shade on a brush. 'Close your eyes.'

'Sorry.' I close my eyes and don't know whether speaking will move my face too much, but she did ask me a question, so I reply. 'No, not at all, we ju—'

'Shh.' She holds my head still and carries on.

I don't want to insult her, but I also don't want my make-up too heavy. 'Honestly just a little bit—'

She holds my head still again. She is so delicate with every touch it sends a shiver across my shoulders. I can't see Chloe, but I know she hasn't left, so I wonder what she's doing.

'Look up.'

I look up and she softly builds up a few layers of mascara. It's so relaxing and calming I feel disappointed when it comes to an end.

'Take a look.'

Before I turn around, I get a sudden worry she's made me look like a clown for a joke. But she hasn't. My eyelids are subtly smoky brown and the thick mascara on my top and bottom lashes makes me look like a doll. She hasn't put anything on my skin, just a little concealer under my eyes. It's the perfect balance of done-up and natural.

'I got the impression you didn't want a full face.' She looks at me through the mirror, and I blush.

'Thanks so much. I'm glad I didn't wear any today, it's much better than I could ever do.'

She stands behind me, softly taking my hair out of its flat pony-tail, and then runs her fingers through it so gently I nearly close my eyes. She turns me around again to face her and pushes her finger through the front of my hair and sweeps it all over to the right side to arrange it over the one shoulder. I turn back and look in the mirror. I look so much better it actually makes my awful outfit look kind of cool in a grungy way.

Shauna stuffs her make-up back in her bag and says, 'Let's get shots.'

When we walk out of the bathroom, all together, I feel like a whole new person. Even if all this make-up was taken back off me, I would still feel more confident and excited.

Shauna goes to the bar whilst Chloe and I sit down. I catch eyes with Paul and feel conscious that I have walked out of that bathroom looking like a completely different person and there's only one reason why.

I remember once, back at work, these three content writers were talking about how fit this PA girl was, and one kept saying how she had 'such a natural look' and how he loves 'natural girls that don't cake their faces in make-up.'

I told them the truth, that even though she didn't wear much make-up, she had undergone a lot of cosmetic work to look that way – nose job, breast implants, lip fillers, teeth straightened and whitened, fake tan, hair dyed blonde, brow tint, and sometimes, lash extensions.

The guy shrugged and said, 'Well, she *looks* natural and that's the main thing.'

What that confirmed to me is that when it comes down to it, as long as you look nice – it doesn't matter how, or why or by when you did it – as long as you look nice, that's what matters. I used to feel glad that I knew all these things but suddenly I'm unsure.

Shauna comes over carrying a black tray filled with pints, a bottle of wine and lots of shots.

'Sambuca's up, bitches.'

A couple of glasses of wine and a few shots later I'm sitting back next to Paul, and he's telling me how his dad won £50k from the lottery. I remember people thought Paul was cute and he used to talk to my friends a lot at social events. I think there was always a part of me that wanted him to, in a surprise course of action, choose me over anyone else. But no one chose me over anyone else. I was always second choice, average, someone in the background of other people's stories. But that just sounds so self-pitying to me now. Maybe I was in the background of my own story, putting everyone else in the spotlight without realising.

'I personally wouldn't want to win the lottery.'

He laughs at me. 'Oh, is that right?'

'Yeah. I mean fifty grand I would probably take, but I've heard there's a high suicide rate in people who win more than that.'

'Right, I better check in with my dad then.'

'I'm only joking. Well, kind of. But I don't mean people like your dad. I mean people that win like, 300 million pounds. You win it and you're like, fuck this is amazing, I can quit my job and do whatever I want, whenever I want. But then you do that, for a bit. Even if that "bit" is like a year. Suddenly it's like, and then what? School holidays are only fun because you know you've got to go back at the end of it. Do you know what I mean?'

'Not really. I think school holidays are fun because you've got nothing to do and it's sunny.'

'Yeah, but it's like, we're so used to the "work for a reward" system. I don't know if it's built into us or drilled into us by society, but pleasure feels best when we've worked for it.'

'Do you remember in the summer holidays when Holly used to have those massive parties in her parents' barn? They were quality.'

'Yeah, and they had all those alco-pops lined up on like, a fake bar? Now I'm like, why did her parents do that?' While I'm speaking he is looking at my face rather than listening. I try to like it.

'Yeah, that was so jokes.'

I smile because I want him to carry on the conversation rather than me having to. He rests his elbow on the table and his head on his hand and looks at me like he's really taking me all in. I resist the urge to speak.

'You're still weird as ever, Ellis.'

It's funny to hear someone call me that again. If a boy had ever called me by my last name it had felt like I'd made it. 'Was I weird?'

'You were just different to the other girls. Had more of a mysterious air to you.'

How can it be that such bullshit is actually making me feel special?

'I don't think I was mysterious, I was probably just constantly worried about humiliating myself.'

Paul gives out a massive laugh and I see Shauna smirk at me across the table.

'You crack me up, Ellis.'

There's nothing guys love more than beautiful girls who dislike themselves.

A few hours later we're in a bar that didn't exist when I lived here. I'm standing at a pillar which has a small shelf for your drinks all the way around it. I'm talking to Danny and it doesn't take long for us to 'find out' we went to the same school. He keeps telling me to 'join him at the bar' and, when I say no, he asks me if I want to 'get out of here' and when I say no to that, he says, 'do you have a boyfriend?'

Paul comes over and gives Danny a disapproving look and takes me over to a table, where a few seconds later Sanj joins us with shots and what tastes like a vodka and Coke. I have a great conversation with Sanj where we ask each other lots of things such as, if I would ever move back to here? If he could do anything in the world what would it be? Do I have siblings? Do I have friends that feel like sisters to me? And does he think politics is failing to engage with our generation? Paul doesn't say much because he probably doesn't understand the concept of asking someone else a question.

Out of nowhere Sanj says he's leaving, and it was lovely to meet me. I feel a mixture of confused, gutted, tempted to leave and excited that I now have Paul to myself. Who tells me to 'wait right here' whilst he says goodbye to Sanj and gets us some drinks.

I glance around the room. Everyone looks like they're moving in slow motion, and I realise I've seen all of these people before. Not these exact people, but they might as well be: three women in their thirties at a table, trying to talk over the loud music, cycling through the emotions of hysterics, shock and empathetic concern. A group of men in their late twenties, standing by the bar, legs wide apart, chest out, tattoos, but well-polished, speaking to each other but mainly looking around the room, wondering where their night will lead them. A group of eighteen- or nineteen-year-olds, the girls speaking to the girls and boys speaking to the boys, their clothes cheaper and tighter imitations of the designer things Sara was wearing last year. A couple, maybe my age, on what looks like a first or second date – he isn't saying much, and is wearing scruffy jeans and trainers, she is saying a lot and keeps trying to pull her dress down as it's become too short now she's sitting, something she wouldn't have realised from looking in the mirror at herself earlier. Another couple who look much further down the relationship line, sitting next to each other in a small booth, her head rested on his shoulder, they don't say much, but sometimes share a peck on the mouth and it looks like they have a little conversation about their cocktails.

This room would be, and has been, and will be, exactly the same without me in it. It's unnerving how familiar this feeling is. I remember work, the people, the pub, the performance of it all, the sense of feeling disconnected. I think of what my mum said earlier. And what I can now see has been a desperate attempt to fill myself up with George and then Patrick. But it didn't work and I suddenly feel a deep sense of calm, because I've finally figured out that there's nothing I can do. I will always be empty. I decide to leave.

But I can't leave because my body won't move. Before this feeling explodes inside me, Paul walks back over with some more drinks. I'm glad to see they're transparent because the thought of another Coke makes me feel sick. I hold the plastic cup which has been designed to look like a real glass but is now scratched and yellowing. The tornado of bubbles in the middle of the drink starts to slow.

'You okay?'

'Oh, yeah, sorry was just lost in my thoughts there for a second. I'm actually just gonna pop to the loo quickly, can you watch my drink?'

'Not as intensely as you, but I can wait here with it.'

There's a four-girl queue for the bathroom. I look, hoping one of them is Chloe or Shauna, but they're not. The girl in front of me is wearing an extremely tight black dress and heels and carries a small clutch bag covered in diamanté. The way she is dressed tells me everything about what this evening means to her. The next woman is probably in her late forties, slightly overweight, in jeans, heels, and a peplum green silky top, she turns around to look at me and Diamanté and rolls her eyes to bond with us over the unappreciated time people are taking in the cubicles.

On the toilet my eyes lose focus for a second and it's only whilst I'm sitting here smiling to myself that I realise I'm drunk. I let the fuzzy feeling wash over me and then read the poster on the door: 'DONT YOU WANT ME BABY? Wednesday Singles Night. 2 4 1 Cocktails'.

I stumble when I stand up to get out. A girl rushes in. The muffled bass of the music comes into sharp focus as the room door swings open and someone else joins the queue. I smile at mirror me. I wash hands and wipe on jeans. I try to say, 'You look so cute' to a girl as I leave but my voice doesn't sound right.

Back into the pulsing music. The dance floor is filling. *Where is Paul?*

'Hey.'

'Hi?'

'What's your name?'

'Iris.'

'You looking for someone, Iris?'

'My friends.'

'Let me buy you a drink?'

'I've got a drink.'

'It doesn't look like you've got a drink.'

'It's not here.'

'You look gorgeous tonight by the way.'

'Thanks.'

'I like your look.'

'Thank you.'

'But I bet you'd look gorgeous in a dress too.'

'Thanks.'

'Did you wear this on purpose?'

'No, by accident. I need to go look for my friends now.'

'Let me get you a drink first?'

'No, thank you.'

'Come on, come with me and I'll get you—'

'Get your hands off her. She clearly doesn't want you touching her.'

'Woah, I wasn't touching her. We were chatting, and I was about to buy her a drink.'

'Do you want a drink with this man?' *Shauna.*

'No.'

'No, I didn't think so.'

'Slut.' And then he's gone.

'Bloody hell he had you right up against this wall. You all right?'

'Yeah. I'm so happy to see you. I missed you.'

She laughs and pulls me. Past the queue. Back into the toilet. People, 'excuse me?' Knocking on a cubicle and we're let in. People, 'erm, there's only one person per cubicle please!'

But we are three. *Chloe.*

'Oh hey, Chloe! I've missed you.'

But she's busy at the windowsill.

Shauna looks over. 'Can we make it three, honey?'

And so she makes it three. 'The only thing my college card gets used for.'

We take our turns and Shauna thanks Chloe with a kiss on the lips. She laughs loudly. 'What are you staring at!'

'Nothing!'

Then she kisses me. And it's funny, this girl's soft lips. Small hands on my face. Then I look straight at Chloe. Not a laugh like I hoped, but a small smile and then she leaves. Shauna next. I wait for a second, embarrassed to leave after two others have. The poster on the door is the same, but someone has written 'Don't force it'. About the door or the singles night or something toilet related? I laugh to myself.

Knock. 'Is someone still in there?'

My face tingles. I take in a deep breath. It feels good.

Out the cubicle, out the bathroom. Every breath feels good. So deep breaths I take.

Shauna and Chloe are on the dance floor. The music is good. Happy. Energetic. We dance in a circle. Shauna sometimes close to me, but I look at Chloe and she looks away.

Close eyes. Listen to the music.

Then open in case people see.

Shauna nudges me and nods to behind me. Paul in a booth with a girl. But I shrug. Lean in. Say loudly over the music, 'All I want is to dance with you.'

She drags us to the bar. Three drinks. I fight to pay. Barman looks exasperated, but I give big smiles and thank yous. The drink tastes dry like air, but not in a bad way.

It goes down easy. My heart pulses.

Outside for a cigarette, I feel the fresh air in my lungs. Deep breaths feel good. Smell of smoke reminds me of Patrick and now my heart hurts. How stupid. Back inside there's a tap on my shoulder.

Paul. 'Hello there.'

'Oh hey.'

'Long time no see.' His sideways smile.

'What have you been up to?'

'That girl over there,' he gestures to someone who I can now see is Diamanté, 'She says I know her friend and boy does she love chatting.' She turns and sees us looking and waves Paul over. Her body's like a short barbie. Definitely fake boobs, but he wouldn't know. I squeeze my eyes shut to get rid of the thought, how can I stop seeing the world this way? It's relentless.

Paul nudges me and leaves. I turn, find Chloe looking at her phone.

'Do you have any more?'

She looks up with blank eyes. 'That's the first thing you've said to me all night.'

'Oh my god. I'm so sorry. I just thought we'd been chatting as a group. I—'

'Come on then.' Walking to the bathroom.

'You don't have to! I just—'

'We can chat in there.'

There's no queue, but as we walk in Peplum walks out of a cubicle.

'Hey!' But she looks at me like she doesn't know me. It's fine because then we're in one and Chloe's back with her card.

'Do you go to college then?'

She does hers first then hands me the note. 'I told you I'm an OT.'

'Oh god. I'm sorry. I don't know what's wrong with me.' I do mine.

'You don't have to say sorry. I don't even know you.'

I feel like crying. I'm boiling so take my sweater off. Now just wearing thin strap top with no bra.

'Yeah, I know it's just, I really wanted to speak to you! I think you look so cool, I love your hair. I just haven't had a chance yet. But I really like you. I'm so lucky I met you guys tonight.' Deep breath and close my eyes.

Chloe. 'Let's go back out.'

I lean in and kiss. And she does for a second but then pulls back, 'You're cute, but I don't need you to do that.'

We leave together but then she's gone.

Behind me, 'Hey you!' Danny with two drinks. He smells strongly of an aftershave people had in sixth form. I watch his acne scars switch between visible and airbrushed as the coloured lights change from yellow, to red, to green, to blue. 'These are for us.'

'Oh, cool. Thank you.' Take it. I hear the repetitive bass and can't help moving shoulders to the beat.

No laugh, no dance back, no smile, just looking at me. He walks us to a pillar with the ledge.

'I can tell you're not from here.'

'Well. . . I am from here.'

'Yeah, but not really.'

'Well, I was born and raised here and lived here for the majority of my life.' I can't taste if the drink is strong. My shoulders move back and forth in a dance.

'Oh, right.'

'What did you mean anyway?'

'You don't look like you're from around here.'

'I feel like I'm being questioned in a village pub in the '80s.'

'No, I'm just saying you look good.'

He looks pissed off, but still keeps looking down at my breasts every few seconds.

The drink goes down easy. 'Do you not like being from here then?'

'Yeah, I do. But that's just me.' Hand on my waist and pulls me close to speak in my ear. 'I'm glad you're here tonight though.'

Look into his small piggy eyes. Is there attraction? I hope Paul is watching. Somewhere. Sip of my drink and slowly move back.

'Where are you staying tonight?'

'I'm going back to London.'

Leans close, hot breath on cheek. 'I think it's too late for that. Come to mine, I've got room.'

Squint at watch to get it in focus. Midnight.

'No, thank you though. I should get going.'

Hand on waist to pull me close again.

But then, 'Mate. What are you doing? Look how uncomfortable she is. We're going back to mine so stop being such a creep if you wanna come.' *Paul*. And behind, like a gang, Shauna and Chloe.

Paul does his side smile at me, 'You coming?'

My body, almost suddenly, feels exhausted. I'm scared of the feeling in my mind, creeping in, making my breaths feel short and sharp, not deep and relaxing. Paul looks ready to leave with or without me so I say, 'I'll go get my bag and meet you outside?'

'Sweet.'

Danny downs his drink and trudges behind Paul and the girls.

Fresh eyes judging my heavy ones. 'Do you have your ticket, love?'

'I can't find it in my pockets.' I look again for the fifth time, but all for show. 'But I know it was 411. It's just a big bag.'

She hands it over and I go stand by the door, take a deep breath. Maybe there is a train back to London? I look behind me, a girl doubling over, her face drooping. People are trying to pick her up, she keeps pushing them away, her dress is falling down and you can see a nipple. I get a twinge in my chest thinking about her waking up tomorrow, what will she feel? I blink away my film of tears. None fall out.

Outside they're all smoking. I go stand next to Chloe. 'Are you coming then?'

'Do you want to know because you want to know if I'll be there or because you want to know if my drugs will be there?'

'Are you pissed off with me? I was genuinely just asking?'

She pauses momentarily to look at me, suss me out. 'Okay, well yeah, I am going.' The cool air touches my skin, and I realise it's not summer anymore. I put my jumper back on. No one is walking yet and I wonder why until I see Diamanté trotting towards us.

'I'm ready!' Her voice has a twang. I like it.

She walks towards Paul and stops, linking arms with him. We head off, and they laugh about something as he supports her precarious walk.

It's only a few minutes till we reach a block of new-build flats just outside the centre. The building is tall and yellow and looks like student accommodation. Danny says he's going to get beers and the rest of us head inside.

Walking behind everyone on the stairs, I start to wonder about all the unexpected moments like this that I have to come. Who knows, in ten years' time will I randomly see Dylan at a cocktail bar in Sydney and end up having sex with him? Or will I end up marrying Patrick's friend Tom? Or will I become famous – Danny watching me do an interview on TV and saying, 'I got with her once.' Even though he didn't.

Paul's flat is shockingly nice. Open plan kitchen, living room, dining area. A mixture between classic high-quality pieces, Smeg fridge, big Sony TV, Mac laptop, on a normal but endearing, dining table with chairs that don't match, half-alive plant, six different types of cereal out on the side. The windows are big and even the town centre looks all right from high up at night.

Shauna and Chloe are sitting on the sofa crushing powder with her college card onto a plate. Diamanté leaves the room so I quickly walk over to the kitchen where Paul is getting some beers out the soft-edged fridge.

'Want one, Ellis?'

'All right.'

He takes the lids off them with a fridge magnet bottle opener and hands me one.

I go to compliment him on the flat, but he walks away and finds a portable speaker to connect to his phone. Luckily Shauna beckons me over and lets me squeeze in next to her.

'I think I'm gonna leave, y'know.'

'I know what'll change your mind, honey.' She hands me a rolled-up piece of torn pizza menu.

Once the taste of coppers has trickled down my throat, with a little help from the beer, I shimmy forward on the sofa so I can look at Chloe too.

'Are you two a couple then?'

Shauna laughs and responds. 'Define couple.'

'Yeah, we're a couple.' Chloe smiles.

Shauna pinches Chloe's waist so she jerks. 'A couple of legends.'

'You're a really sweet couple. You match so well and you're both so nice. Imagine this night without you! Imagine speaking to those guys all night, I don't know how long I can talk about property development for.'

Chloe seems engaged now. 'Have you got a "special someone" then?'

'No. Well. . . I don't think so. I kind of did, but now I don't and it's fine because I think I need to be on my own for a while anyway. Y'know what I mean? Like work on myself for a bit, cause who can love you if you don't love yourself, right?'

Shauna rearranges my hair to the side again. 'Do you not love yourself?'

'I don't know, does anyone love themselves? Wouldn't that

make you a narcissist? Like, I'm in my own head, so I know what a shitty person I am. So, to love myself? That would be pretty fucked up.'

Chloe finishes another line. 'Are you a bad person then? In your head?'

'Not a *bad* person. But like judgemental? Yes. Shallow? Yes. Self-absorbed? Yes. Cruel to the people I love?'

Chloe shrugs. 'That's the first genuine thing you've said all night.'

I can't hide the shock on my face.

Shauna continues for her, 'She didn't mean anything bad by that, hun. Just that you should try saying the truth more, y'know? It's just more enjoyable to be around.'

I go to object, tell her that I've been completely honest all night. But then I think of Sara and I wonder if I've grown so accustomed to being this fake person that I don't even realise I'm doing it. Shauna finishes up, hands me the plate and rolled up paper.

The music stops and an advert for a car plays, bringing an unwanted reminder of reality. Chloe nods to behind me. Diamanté and Paul are in the kitchen. She's standing close to him, hand on his arm, mouth to his ear.

I notice I have finished the beer like it was water. I stand up and go to the kitchen. Diamanté, with a face two shades darker than her neck, introduces herself as Toni.

'You look amazing by the way. I love your dress. I can't stop staring at you!' The words spill out of my mouth. I hope Shauna and Chloe didn't hear.

She looks at Paul and then back at me and laughs.

'Sorry, I just thought I'd say what I was thinking!'

I ask Toni if she's had a good night. Paul's eyes are on me. She gives a brief answer, and then tells Paul she's going for a cigarette and that she wants him to come too.

Amused by her bolshy attitude, I go get a beer from the bright red fridge.

'Help yourself then.' I turn around and it's Paul with no Toni in sight. He sees me looking. 'She's gone for a cigarette.'

'I heard. I thought you had unfinished business to discuss?'

'I thought we did too.'

'Oh, yeah? On what?'

'More importantly, I haven't shown you round the flat yet.'

'Please. Show ahead.'

Back into the small rectangle, which is the hall, he opens what is one out of the three doors that I haven't seen behind. 'Here's the loo.' It's surprising in both the outdated blue decor, and its large size, boasting a full bath, separate shower, sink with cabinets and toilet.

'You a big bath fan?'

'Don't think I've ever had a bath.'

'In. . . your life?'

He shrugs and answers seriously, 'I dunno, maybe when I was a baby.'

I remember a time when I ran a bath and it was cold, but I just sat in it crying, until George came in and found me and took me out and wrapped me in a towel and we both sat on the floor talking while he ran me a hot one.

'The next room is the best.'

He holds the back of my shoulders and walks me to the last door.

It feels like an adult's bedroom. I can't stop looking at a big glass frame with an ugly cityscape print. My eyes feel like they're shuddering.

'Lovely. Didn't know you would be so house proud.'

'Yeah, I even make my bed in the morning. That's what happens when you own a property.'

'I guess I cut my losses and started making mine already.'

He takes my beer out of my hand and puts it down on his bedside table.

'Do you not need a coaster for that?'

He walks back over, grips my waist and starts kissing me. I wonder what my sixteen-year-old self would think of this? She wouldn't know that he is being much too aggressive with his tongue. I pull back. 'What about Toni?'

'Fuck Toni. I wanted you.' He kisses me again, grabbing my bum with both hands. I hope that Toni walks in, but she doesn't, so I pull away for a breath and walk over to get my beer. The room is shuddering unless I take a second to concentrate. Try to focus on the fact Paul wants me. Popular Paul. The ultimate validation. Try to feel good. No. Don't.

'Let's go back to the kitchen a sec.' I turn around and walk out before he can say anything. Shauna is sitting on Chloe's lap. They don't look up when I walk in. Paul hasn't followed me. I walk over to my bag and get my phone out. Take a deep breath in and remind myself that if I have no messages it's fine because you never know what life throws at you, who knew I would be here tonight, who knows where I'll be in a week, what I'll be doing, who I will meet. I press a button to light up the screen. Nothing. Not even anything from Mum or Dad to check I got home safely. I'm glad there's nothing from them though, it would make me sick having to reply to them. Trying and failing to be happy feels worse than not trying at all. I know that now. I should just settle for the lonely life that someone like me deserves. Fake, nasty, pathetic, shallow, selfish, loser.

I stuff the phone back into my bag. 'Where's Toni?'

Chloe responds without taking her eyes off Shauna. 'That girl in the dress? She left I think.'

Shauna, without taking her eyes off Chloe. 'We're probably gonna head soon too.'

The music changes to adverts again. First one for a limited-edition burger at McDonalds, and then the car one again.

My heart hurts to beat. It's difficult to swallow and when I do it tastes of metal.

'You can have the rest, honey.' Shauna points to the plate and they both stand up. 'Tell Paul we said bye and that he needs to keep his dick in his pants for once.'

I feel like I've been kicked in the stomach. Shauna walks up to me. 'I'm kidding. Go for it.' She kisses me on the cheek, Chloe is waiting at the door, and doesn't even look at me.

I go back to the plate and finish off the rest. I love the chemical drip down my throat. I can't make the residue into a line, so I lick my finger to gather it up and press it into my gums. I wash away the taste with some beer and run my tongue over my numb gums because I like the feeling. I start making a plan of what I need to do. Get back to London, find a job, maybe something fulfilling, like a teacher or a counsellor. I can find a part-time job to support myself whilst I study, probably in a café or something and I'd meet such nice people there, because people that work in cafés are so down to earth, and the staff probably all get together and do fun things, and me and my new girl friends will be completely honest, tell each other everything we think, and we'll all be happy if one of us looks beautiful, and we'll say it, but we'll also say who cares what we look like, we don't c—

'What are you still doing in here?'

Open eyes. 'Sorry, I was just about to leave.'

'Where are you going to go? It's nearly 3 a.m.'

'It's fine, I can go stay at my mum's or something.'

'Do you want to stay here?'

'Not really.'

'Look, Ellis. Please stay here, I don't want you walking around this time of night. You can just crash on the sofa.'

'Okay. Thank you.'

He goes to leave. 'You know where the bathroom is.'

'Wait, do you not want to have another drink?'

He turns around and thinks for a second. 'Okay, sure.'

He brings over some brown looking drinks. 'We ran out of beer, sorry.'

'That's fine, I kind of wanted a change anyway.'

The drink is strong.

'Have you got any coke?' I quickly push my finger around the plate checking if there's any more.

'Isn't it a bit late for that? I think the party's over. Have your drink.'

'But the drink tastes better with a little bit.'

'Erm, I don't think I've got any.' He puts his drink down and goes out the room.

He comes back in and drops down a tiny plastic bag on the table. I empty out the contents on the plate. There's barely enough for two lines let alone for a few more rounds.

'Have it all. I don't want any.'

It crosses my mind that this is a depressing situation, but I know that thought will go away after this. I take it and then have a big gulp of my drink. 'I had a good night.'

'Yeah? I didn't think we were on good form.'

'Did you not have a good night?'

'Yeah, I had a good night. Are you all right?'

'Yeah, yeah, I'm good. It's strange to be back y'know? Never would've thought I'd be back here. No offence to you or anything, just that I didn't *love* it here, and when I got out I was so happy. Not that I hated it here or anything, obviously school was fine. It's just not something I ever expected—'

He leans over and kisses me, tongue straight in like post through a letterbox. I straddle him and he slaps my bum, hard.

'Let's go to the bedroom.'

I climb off and he starts walking fast out the room.

'I'll be right in!'

Once he's gone, I lick my finger and run it around the inside of the empty drugs bag and rub my fingers over my gums. I don't feel like I got much out so I stick my tongue in the bag and wiggle it around, and then finish the rest of my drink.

In the bedroom Paul is sitting on the bed looking at his phone. He's taken his desert boots off and lined them up by the door. Turns out he's wearing short socks under his shoes so I can see a bit of ankle in between the sock and his jeans, and it repulses me slightly.

I sit down next to him and take my sweater off. I know you can see my nipples through my top.

He looks at me. 'I think you looked better when you weren't wearing any make-up.'

'Oh.'

'Make-up doesn't impress guys as much as you think.'

'I just need the toilet.'

I quickly leave and go into the bathroom, my heart beating hard and my skin feels clammy, but not sweaty. I go for a wee and notice my pants are cotton and unflattering and I wonder if I should take them off here. So I quickly do, and stuff them in the cupboard under the sink. Going commando is sexy, cotton pants are not.

In the mirror I reassess my make-up. It seems fine at first, but the longer I look the more I remind myself of a child who's been playing with her mother's eyeshadow. But I tell myself that I'm better than other girls he's had, just in different ways. I know it's not true but I try to think it anyway, it's the only way I know to get through this. I pinch my nipples so they're more erect and go back in.

I walk straight over and start undoing the buttons on his shirt. He leans back so I can get to his belt buckle, presumably because he wants me to go down on him. His belt is made up of woven brown diamonds set in a series of rectangles in forest green, sky blue, maroon and beige. I hate it. He's barely erect and I regret not touching him more before I got down here. It feels silly to put a flaccid penis in my mouth and I have to stifle a laugh. Nothing seems to be happening, so I take my top off and sit on him. He grabs both of my boobs like they're stress balls and then sucks on a nipple.

'Bite it,' I say.

'What?'

'Bite it.'

He bites down on my nipple, and its more painful and less pleasurable than I had hoped. I check to see how he's doing downstairs, but it's hard to get a proper grip since his boxers have risen back up. I stand up and pull his trousers off leg by leg, horrifyingly feeling like a mother undressing her child because of the way he holds one leg out after the other, and then both of them together ready for me to take his pants off. I check again and it's at about half-mast now, so I start rubbing it, waiting for things to intensify. But they don't and he's leaning back on his elbows, looking at the whole thing like someone at a Sunday roast watching the turkey being carved up. I take my jeans off and he stares in confusion. I don't address the situation but just climb on top again.

'Let me get a johnny.'

I sit there, naked, waiting for him, whilst he slides it on. And then kiss him again, utilising my tongue as I assume that's what gets him going. That goes on for a while and it surprises me that he is yet to touch my vagina. But then I realise that doesn't surprise me at all. He takes his penis to manoeuvre inside of me, but can't quite find the right place. So he pushes me off him and I lay down on the bed so he can try from a more traditional position.

The reasons it isn't going in easily are: 1. Because there is no lubrication and 2. He only has a semi.

From craning my head up a bit, I can see what looks like him balling his dick up and trying to stuff it in. I try saying 'fuck me' to see if it will heighten the mood but he's too busy concentrating to acknowledge me. He starts rubbing himself and it depresses me so much, I climb back round and suck it again to see if we can finish off this way. After a minute of no luck, I give up and flop down on the bed.

As he stands up to put his boxers back on, I see his butt acne and hairy crack and roll my eyes to myself, thinking about the fact I have to worry about the material of my underwear. I look down at my body and realise I can see it in such distressing detail because the sky outside his window has just started to shift into beige. I make a note to wax my stomach when I'm home because even though I have fine hair it looks dark in this natural light. The thought nearly makes me laugh out loud.

As he goes to the bathroom, presumably to clean his teeth, I realise that I have no underwear to put on and have no idea how to cover myself up. I quickly put my strap top back on and get into his bed. I hear him come in and close the blinds, but I shut my eyes and pretend to be asleep even though there is not a doubt in my mind we both know I'm awake.

I hear a hushed voice. 'Sorry. . . but. . . that's my side of the bed. Do you mind moving over?'

I know I can't pretend to be asleep and not move, but I also can't 'wake up' suddenly and be like, 'yeah sure.' So I do a little pretend groan of someone who's been woken up and roll over.

Despite my grade-A pretending, I cannot sleep, not even slightly. The pillow smells nice like it's been freshly washed and I can't quite work out what makes Paul so domestic. I don't know anything about him, really, and he knows nothing about me, so what does his attraction to me actually mean? Why did I need it? You can't feel pleasure at someone else's desire when it's directed at a mere illusion of who you really are. But isn't this the only thing I ever want? Anyone's lust, as long as it makes me feel alive.

I can tell he's not asleep yet either, because his breathing isn't heavy and he keeps fidgeting. I make sure to stay still and perform some drawn out sleeping breaths because I desperately don't want him to realise we're both awake.

Suddenly I can see through a gap in the blinds that the sky is a cold, sharp blue and I try to work out if I've just been sleeping or not. I slowly turn over and see Paul lying flat on his back, mouth open, gargling breath. My stomach rumbles loudly and for a long time. I squeeze my eyes closed willing him not to wake up, and he doesn't. By the look of his limp face, he's either deeply asleep or better at acting than I would've thought.

I slide out of the bed slowly, creep like a cartoon character out of the room, picking up my clothes on the way. I pop into the bathroom to get my pants, but realise I desperately need a wee. When I sit down my head spins and a high-pitched tone rings in my ears. I wash my hands choosing not to look in the mirror. But then I change my mind and look closely at my face. I look at the faded eyeshadow and the purple circles under my eyes and the black gloop in my tear ducts. My lips are chapped, my hair is knotted like a stray dog. I don't recognise this person but not because she looks bad. She's just one of the many different people I am. But none of them are real.

'You are disgusting,' I mouth to myself. But then I take it back, 'You are not disgusting.' You're just a pillar of moving flesh and blood and how can that be your fault? Why have people made you feel like that's your fault? That you're failing for being this specific bag of guts.

'What a bunch of unoriginal and badly articulated thoughts,' I whisper to myself. My stomach alerts me loudly that it's in pain. I get my unacceptable cotton underwear from the cabinet and also take a couple of disposable razors I see in there.

Back to the living room. I'm not jealous of Paul having to clean up after the pathetic events of last night. Reminders littered across the room. Shoes and bag, and I'm out of here. No need to try and close the front door quietly.

32

I'm in a Burger King on the top floor of the badly ageing shopping mall. I've eaten a 'Breakfast King Meal' and I'm sitting here with a large Coke, bath temperature because they've run out of ice. No judgement noted from the Burger King staff on my appearance or order or just generally being a customer before 9 a.m. Either stuffing myself or eating nothing at all has been the only relationship I've had with food for so long that eating a meal is almost absurd to me now. Like I've forgotten the real use of it. Watching the other customers eating their burgers seems obscene, as if I'm witnessing a dirty secret of theirs. It's easy to forget you have to eat simply to be alive. I guess it makes sense that I'm not good at doing either of those.

Once I read about these two identical twins, one of them was super healthy and ran every day and ate their RDA of vegetables, and the other one was a bit overweight and never exercised. Then one day, the healthy one had a heart-attack and died. People love stories like that because it makes them feel like they have no control over their mortality so they might as well do what they like.

I thought it was stupid, but maybe they're right. Why are people so afraid of dying when it's happening from the moment you're born? Turns out knowing you're completely out of control is the most relaxing state of all. Sometimes it's best to let yourself unravel until there is nothing left. Rather than scrabbling around trying and failing to fix things in place.

There's no window in this Burger King, and the only other people, eating breakfast in their uniforms, are so blank-faced absorbed in their hot drinks and breakfast burgers that they probably wouldn't be able to say in a court of law whether or not they saw me in here. I bite down hard on my straw.

If I killed myself how long would it take for someone to find out? I don't know why people are terrified of being dead for a while before people know. Probably the most lonely, depressed people would be found straight away because they didn't clock into their shift at the call centre. If I killed myself it might take a while for people to notice, but it isn't because I don't have friends, it's because I live an independent lifestyle. I scoff a laugh out. It's pathetic the lies I tell myself. I try to think something truthful instead: I've tried to be happy, and sometimes I've thought I was, but now I realise it was nothing more than stimulation, and I think that's the closest I'll ever get. I know none of it matters now. Not even love can save me from the rotting in my brain.

I don't know if it's my bones or veins or muscles that hurt, but my body hurts so much. The thought that I can choose to die anytime I like calms me. But I know even taking an overdose is agonising and it scares me. It's not like in the films where they just slip away. You can't die without it hurting. The pain is radiating out my wrists and I can't see how it would stop unless I cut them open. I heard that someone once jumped off a bridge and by a miracle they survived, and they said as soon as they jumped, they regretted it.

I float out of the building and along to the old church where I sat on the bench last time I was here. The air has a slight chill to it that feels relieving and I realise how much I've hated the heat and shrieks of people enjoying their summers. I notice that more people are starting to leak out onto the streets now and I don't want them to see me. So I walk up the steps to the door of the church and sit there on the ground. My long hair feels greasy and heavy and I wonder why I've kept it so long all this time. I guess I thought it looked good. What is an identity except a bunch of traits you decided were the best?

The numbness is wearing off and instead a deep ominous despair begins to soak through my body. The thought of getting through the next second and minute and hour and day and week and month and year is terrifying. I feel hysterical. But I'm sitting here motionless, pleading with the universe to evaporate me. I can't even cry because to cry you need to care. Suddenly the endlessness of life becomes intolerable. I need something physical to focus on. I get out one of the razors and fiddle about to try and get a single blade out, it's hard and I cut the top of my finger by accident. I suck it because it hurts and then laugh to myself. Do I want pain or not? Once I get one out, I take my sweater off and drag it along the skin on the top of my arm. It stings, but even when I squeeze it a bit, no blood comes out because I must not have done it hard enough. I understand now what I want. I want to see the blood, to see a physical representation of my pain. I try it again, hard, and this time blood does seep out, but slowly and not a lot. I squeeze it to speed things up, but I know it's shallow. I try again, even harder, and it hurts so much I can't make it as long as the others. I let that one bleed of its own accord. My chest relaxes as I focus on the throbbing pain and the blood. I put my jumper back on and lie down hugging my knees. I press the back of my hands into my eyes. You can't die from an upper arm cut anyway so what am I doing? Is there a plan? I feel like being in reality isn't sustainable. I physically can't endure the feeling of time passing. Panic rises in my chest. I close my eyes and use every ounce of energy to keep my mind on the pulse in my arm.

'You can't sleep here, miss.'

Fear goes straight into my stomach. What has happened? Did I actually sleep here?

'Oh, I wasn't.'

The old man looks angry, and I quickly sit up to check there's people around who can see me.

'Well, you can't lie here then.'

I grab my bag and walk around him, down the steps towards the street.

At the station on the platform I stand and wait even though the next train isn't for half an hour. The terrifying idea presents itself to me again but this time it doesn't seem terrifying at all. It feels right and normal. I take my bag off and slowly put it on the ground. When you are about to die every movement you make feels electric. And calm.

I know I am ready to do this because I'm not thinking about what everyone else's reaction will be. I'm thinking of the relief. When I jump in front of this train, everyone who sees will have a story to tell for the rest of their lives. An exciting reason to be sad really. People will want to hear about it.

I heard once that if tube drivers hit three people who jump in front of their train, they get to leave work for the rest of their life, but still get paid. Imagine if you had hit two. Every station you pulled into would you get a flicker of hope? That would drive you more mental than seeing two people die.

Then a memory pierces through my brain, into my mind, of

me, Mum and Dad sitting in a café eating some warm baguette sandwiches and chips. I must've been about eleven. I thought it was really fancy. It wasn't fancy though. It was a small faux-French plasticky café with circular tables close together and classical music playing. I think it was called Café Français. It makes me want to turn off my brain. I wish I could never remember anything ever again.

Inside the train I find two empty seats and slump into them, resting my head against the dirty window. I wonder if I can't kill myself because I secretly have faith one day I'll be okay or simply because I'm a coward. I guess it doesn't really matter which one. Sometimes life goes on when you don't want it to and there's nothing you can do about it.

I think about what Mum might be doing today, is she seeing her new friend? What do they talk about? I don't think she has anything to talk about, and I'm starting to understand how that was a problem. Sometimes having nothing to say feels like enough of a reason to die.

When the train pulls back into London, I feel such a relief it's almost like happiness.

33

My whole body flushes hot, and I feel sick and faint and deeply embarrassed. Patrick is sitting on a bench at the bottom of the escalator, and he sees me before I'm even halfway down. I have no idea where I'm supposed to look for the next twenty seconds so I look down. My heart is beating so hard it hurts. I look terrible. I've been wearing the same clothes for two days. My hair is puffy and greasy, and my make-up is smudged. I look tired and pale. I get to the bottom of the escalator. He can now see that the person he got to know was a lie.

He stands up and walks over to greet me, grinning. His eyes are bright, his smile is bright. He's wearing a jumper, black jeans and brown shoes, boring, and it looks effortless on him. He's holding a little paper bag. My mind searches around for the reason he might be here but I can't find one.

'Hi.' We don't hug he just nods at me. You would never know we'd touched before. It's making me doubt we ever did.

'Hi. What are you doing here?' My voice sounds more excited than I mean it too. I wish I could understand everything right now. Is he here for me or did I just leave a toothbrush at his?

'I came to see you.'

'How did you know I was here?' Did Mum tell him? I can't

think of any other way he could've found out. People are tutting at me because I'm standing too near to the escalator. He puts his hand on my arm and moves me away a few steps. I almost recoil at his touch but I think it's just because of Paul. Patrick came here to see me. I look at him and try to let it sink in.

'I knew you'd gone to see your parents and I know where you're from, so I knew which train you would have to get back, and just sat here by the platform, waiting. All of yesterday and today. I'm glad you're here cause I'm not gonna lie, it's getting a bit boring.'

He's speaking really fast, I don't know if he's nervous or excited or just stupefied from sitting there for so long, but it's quite nice to see him like this.

'Anyway, I've just been sitting here thinking about how I would survive if I went to prison, and I think I've worked it all out so. . . I'm happy to see your face.'

It doesn't seem like he's properly taken in how bad I look yet. Although, I don't know how he could be missing it. I'm dizzy with embarrassment. I laugh, but I can't get myself to speak.

'Let me take your bag.' He pulls my bag away from me. I must reek of stale alcohol. I have no idea what to do. I'm standing in the middle of St Pancras Station wondering why it has the same acoustics as an indoor swimming pool, and how quickly has he started to regret this?

'Do you wish I wasn't here?' He looks so deflated. Is it possible he loves me? Like George loves me? Maybe I was wrong to be so despairing. I try to cement myself in the moment, absorb the romance of it all, let it cure me. But the relief isn't coming.

'Yeah, no sorry. I don't wish you weren't here. It is a surprise though, sorry. It's been a hard weekend.' Hopefully a good enough excuse for my appearance.

'Yeah, sorry. I shouldn't have done this.' He looks down, a hand clutching the hair over his forehead, his body turning in on itself. 'I just wanted to see you in person to say sorry because over the phone is a bit shit, isn't it? And I don't want to be shit anymore. Let's get out of here, would you come to mine or?' He looks so direct and sheepish at the same time. I try to force out a yes but it's not coming and I realise I'm just staring into space.

'Sorry, I've not really slept this weekend and I have no idea what I'm doing.' Am I testing him? Asking for more? I don't think so.

'Please, Iris. I'm sorry. I want to say sorry properly, at mine. I know I should've been better on the phone and come round to see you and even come back with you or something—'

'Don't worry, honestly it's—'

'I'm not worried, I'm sorry.'

My brain is throbbing. I wish I could go and change and at least put some eyeliner on. I think that's why I'm not feeling it yet. How can I enjoy this moment when I look so bad? His eyes are looking so intensely into mine. I look down on myself in this situation, living my dream – I knew I could do it.

On the way to the tube station I realise how lucky I am, to come back to this, to have something worth living for. He holds my hand and I want to grip it tight but I'm worried it's sweaty.

As soon as we're back at his I tell him I need a shower.

'Yeah, sure, go ahead, you know where it is.'

'Do you have a towel I could use?'

'Yeah, yeah, sorry – have mine.' He goes to where his blue and white striped towel hangs from a hook in the middle of the wall. Although, looking now, I can see it's actually just a big nail that's been hammered in. He hands it to me.

'Do you need anything else? There's shower gel and stuff – I can't guarantee it's good quality or anything, but it dissolves the dirt or. . . whatever shower gel does. . .'

'Thanks.' I start walking out but then turn back and grab my bag. I can't remember what clothes I've brought but I know none are nice.

In the bathroom I think about how intimate it is to wash in someone else's shower, using their things. I try to look forward to getting to know his, the smell of our hair and bodies becoming the same, our toothbrushes next to each other. I look in the mirror, even though it feels like I'm doing a neutral expression my mouth is turned down like a sad smiley face. I wonder if after my shower I should get redressed in here or would that look too shy? I try to psych myself up. Yes, I have bags under my eyes, but my skin is still a consistent colour and texture, my hair is greasy but the ponytail looks better than I thought. Maybe I look bad in a way like a fugitive in a film looks a bit dishevelled, but still manages to look attractive. I'll wash my hair now anyway.

I look in my bag. Lucky I took two disposable razors: multiple razors, multiple uses.

This white and silver bathroom with its free-standing shower would've impressed me when I was younger, but now all I see is that the glass of the shower is plastic and the reason it's silver and white is because no one can dislike nothingness. The shower, which looks like it would be powerful because of its big head, releases water over me at a pressure where I can't feel it hitting my skin. My arm stings and I remember this morning and my stomach contracts. I glance at the cuts quickly as I think it might look shocking but it doesn't and maybe that's even more upsetting.

I can't see the mirror because it's all steamed up, but I know a freshly washed face and clumps of wet hair never look good. I wipe the fog away with the towel and get to work making the best out of a bad situation. I look in the cupboard under the sink for anything to use. It contains a supermarket's own brand toilet cleaner, unopened; half of a toilet roll; Bonjela; an unused aftershave in a white glass bottle; a big tub of Vaseline; a glass; an old-looking packet of generic multi-vitamins; and in the back corner, a used tampon applicator put back in its wrapper that I assume belonged to a girl confronted with the 'no bin in a boy's bathroom' situation. I take out the Vaseline and open it, it's a bit gross and dusty with big finger swoops taken from it. I take a sheet of toilet paper, scrape the top layer off the Vaseline and deposit it into the toilet. I take a little bit from the fresh layer and rub it into the dry patches on my face and lips until it's fully absorbed, and then take the tiniest amount and dab it on to the high points of my cheekbones to give my face the slightest glow. I take the bobble from around my wrist and pile up my hair into a bun which gives my face a little lift. Looking through my bag all I find are old t-shirts, which look like the kind of thing someone would wear who doesn't understand the concept of trends moving on. And I only have badly fitting, faded grey-black jeans I was wearing, or a pair of old, unintentionally sheer leggings that go baggy at the knees, and the only underwear I have is stuff I'd be embarrassed to wear even if I was on my own. I do still have a thong in there from the day I left here and went straight to my parents. . . to Mum's. I consider giving it a little wash, but I decide having it wet is worse than worn. I wrap my towel around me and walk back to the bedroom holding my bag. Patrick is sitting right on the edge and looks up instantly when I walk in.

'How was it?'

'Nice thanks.'

'Can I borrow a t-shirt?'

'Of course, help yourself.'

I put my bag down and walk straight to the drawers at the back of his room and drop the towel. I try to hope he's looking but images of Paul touching my body makes me hate the idea. I open his drawer and pick out a faded t-shirt with the dates of some festival on the back. He will think I look good in this. I put it on and turn around. He is looking. I climb in the bed and sit against the headboard hugging my knees.

He joins me. 'I'm so glad you came.'

'Same.' It isn't feeling right yet. I can't immerse myself in the moment.

'You look beautiful. You always look beautiful.'

But you didn't say that at the station. Do I always look beautiful or do I just always look beautiful when I'm around you? 'Thank you.'

'Even when you're just out of the shower and wearing a random t-shirt you look great.' But I didn't look like this just 'out of the shower' and I chose this t-shirt on purpose. I can't say anything, so I just look at him. I stare at his arm coming out of the sleeve of his creaseless grey t-shirt. I love that he always looks smart somehow, even though he's wearing casual clothes. His pupils are wide and dark, and his eyes look soft and sad. I try to look at us from the outside. Do we look good together? Does it feel good to be chosen by him? No. If someone loves you but you're pretending to be someone else, how can you feel anything other than emptiness? You are essentially witnessing a relationship you've created from the outside. So no matter how much love you get from that person, you will always feel removed from it. I struggle to keep my expression from going flat.

'Iris, are you okay?'

I take my hair down and rub my palms all over my face. I speak into them. 'No.'

'No? What's wrong?' He puts his arm around my shoulders. 'Please. Tell me. I won't be shit this time.'

'It's just. . . I just. . .' I can feel my body start to shake and try to hold it together but then I change my mind. I let go. My voice comes out a little whiney and sometimes it's hard to catch my breath but I say what comes into my head.

'I just sometimes, often, get this pain, like an actual physical pain in my head, but it's not a headache it's connected to my soul almost. Not "soul", I don't know what I'm saying. What I'm saying is that it's excruciating and it barely ever stops and the only way I know how to deal with it is to sleep away the time but time just goes on and on and on and there's only so much you can sleep. I just don't care about anything it's all so. . .' I take a deep breath in and look up to see Patrick staring at me his eyes wet with tears. 'Oh no, I'm sor—'

'Don't be sorry, why are you sorry?' He hugs me so tightly it hurts. 'I know exactly what you're feeling. I know that pain.' He grabs my hand and squeezes it. 'From the moment I saw you, I knew you were different from everyone else, I could see it in your eyes. Sometimes I can see it so clearly, when you look at me.' He smiles and my reflex smiles back, but I feel light-headed with emotional overload. 'I love your eyes. I can't tell you how little any other girl has meant to me since I met you.'

He lets go of my hand, leans his head back on the wall, looks at the ceiling and continues.

'I can't tell you how little *everything* has meant to me since I met you to be honest.' He looks down and his hair flops over his face. I'm finding it hard not to cry.

'I barely care about all the things I usually love. Like film, or music or even my mates really. I'd rather just lie here thinking about you.' The way he is looking down and how his shoulders are hunched makes him look like he's given up. He keeps squeezing the top of his fingers one by one and then starting again. 'It feels like everything positive in my brain has been zapped to make room for thinking about you.' He looks up. 'Anyway, I love you.'

He looks right into my eyes with no discernible expression. Blank, soft, deflated. 'I really, fully love you.' I want the words to go through my ears and trickle into my chest, to soothe it. 'I really want us to be together, properly together, so I can look at your beautiful face all the time and tell you that you're beautiful and I love you. And we can sit around and talk about how everything and everyone is shit. It's you and me against the world, Iris.'

My heart is bursting and it feels like everything I have ever wanted has come true. He actually does love the real me. But I can't stop thinking about Mum and Dad and George and Paul and the pain in my head and how it will never stop and how I can't live with it anymore but I'll never be able to kill myself and I start crying. 'Patrick, the thing is, I want to not be alive. I can't do it anymore, I can't do it anymore. I've tried, maybe not in the right ways, but I've tried to be happy. But it just ends up feeling like I'm fake or everyone else is fake and there's nowhere in between. I'm not sure why but I can't make it through life. But I don't know how to die either. I don't—' I'm pulling at my hair hard and almost squirming and violently sobbing. I feel like I can't breathe so I get up and sit folded over trying to catch my breath but I can't do it. They're getting shorter and sharper. I have to be on the floor. I have to get on the floor. So I do.

I lie on the floor sobbing and rocking. He stands up, shocked into action and grabs on to my arm. 'Get up. Get onto the bed.'

I push him away. 'No. Go away. I need to be here.'

He pulls me again. 'You need to get up. Now. Come on, Iris. You're stronger than this.'

I curl up tighter.

'It's dirty and dusty down there. Get up and we can sit and talk about things on the bed like adults.'

I tune him out and focus on my breathing. It takes a while but eventually it subsides. I sit up against the bed and realise he must be sitting on it. He doesn't say anything. I feel awful. I close my eyes and listen to my breath as it gradually slows even more.

Eventually when I open them I see the paper bag he was carrying earlier next to me. There is a box of chocolates in it. I tilt it towards me. 'Are these for me?'

I hear his blunt voice from the bed. 'Oh. Yeah. I got them for you.'

My mouth waters. I pick them up and sit on the edge of the bed. The atmosphere is strange.

'I'm sorry—'

'Iris, you never have to apologise for that, okay? I just wanted to help and you wouldn't let me. You can't do that.'

I nod and then open the box of chocolates and eat one. They're so sweet it hurts my mouth but also delicious. I start to laugh.

'What is it?'

I turn to him. 'I just think it's so funny sometimes. Have you ever paused your suicidal thoughts to inspect some chocolates? Cause I'll be like, "I want to die".'

I do an impression of sobbing and then pretend to notice the chocolate box and go 'ooo'.

I turn to him and he does a downturned smile like he's humouring me. I pop another chocolate in my mouth and then start switching between pretend sobbing and going, 'mmm'.

He takes the box away. 'Come on, Iris, let's be serious for a second, please. It's not the time to joke around.'

I nod. But then something tells my body to get up. I go to my bag and put my jeans on, trying to look like I'm not doing it quickly, zip my bag up. I think of him five years ago, sitting in his room wishing he was dead. I want to go and sit next to that Patrick, tell him everything will be okay, that I know how he feels and I love him. I do love him. So much it feels like my chest is burning. The pain that never fully goes. When it seems like he loves me and when it seems like he doesn't, I always have the pain.

I turn to him. He is expressionless. He's moved his knees up. Pointy nose and sharp cheekbones and knobbly knees and long fingers and floppy hair. He is so pretty, no make-up or fancy clothes or haircut, just natural beauty. But I think about how the love of this beautiful person has not fixed me.

'Where are you going?' He stares at me, his eyes look wet, his gaze darting from one of my eyes to the other. He looks down and tears fall through the air onto his lap.

My throat hurts to look at him. I open his door. 'I'm so—'

'Don't, Iris.'

I go to leave but then, 'Oh shit, do you want your t-shirt?'

He shakes his head without looking up.

I leave, closing his bedroom door quietly behind me.

34

On the tube I can't stop jigging my leg up and down. My chest still hurts, but it's coming from excitement. I can't help doing little smiles to myself.

When my stop comes around, I stand up and wait by the doors. I change line and get a train to Euston instead.

When the train platform is announced, I walk slowly at the back of everyone because their half-run–half-walk desperation makes me nauseous. This does mean though that the only free seat is next to this guy whose leg is slightly over the spare seat and who is breathing heavily because he has headphones on and probably doesn't realise. On second thought though, I'm not confident he would breathe any different if he took them off. He starts tapping one of his fingers to the music and it makes my blood boil.

Luckily, he gets off at the next stop, so I move over and put my bag on the other seat. For the last part of the journey I close my eyes and rest my head against the window even though the movement makes my head bump up and down and it hurts.

At Hemel Hempstead I don't get up until the last minute and then have to run off the train. I sit on the platform bench and cry for two seconds and then stand up and leave.

As soon as I leave the station the sky gets overcast and it starts to drizzle. I want to put my jumper on, but I know it stinks of smoke. The rain lets up, but the air becomes heavy, and I can feel my hair start to frizz.

It takes me an hour to walk there. It's a semi-detached brick house with a plastic door and a newly paved front drive. I think of remembering this moment in ten years' time. I give a little smile to myself as if I'm in a film, and I'm communicating to the audience that I'm coming to terms with something.

I knock at the door and then realise there's a bell and get a wave of anxiety at the thought of having to ring it but then it turning out that they heard the knock as well and so I seem rude and impatient. I suddenly gasp remembering what I'm wearing and run down the drive and round the corner. I sit down on the floor and put my head in my hands and take deep breaths. I take off Patrick's t-shirt even though I'm not wearing a bra and it's still light and there're houses all around and someone moseying about in their garden down the road. I put on a thin grey t-shirt and the sweater and stuff Patrick's t-shirt back in the bag.

There's no point in wondering what they will think about the knock-and-run, so I ring the doorbell and stand there smiling and waiting.

'Hello, how can I help you?' I recognise her from the pictures, big red hair, wide smile on her face, holding a tea towel.

'Hello, I'm Iris, George's. . . friend?'

'Oh, Iris!' She looks even more shocked than I thought she would. 'Hello. Come in, please.'

I step into the hall, but then we both just stand there finding it harder to pretend this isn't completely uncomfortable. She folds the tea towel in half and then in half again. 'Is George expecting you?'

'Urm, not really. But. . . is he in?'

'Oh, no, I'm afraid he's not. Not at the minute.' She looks around her as if to somehow show he's not here. 'You're welcome to wait here?'

'That's fine, don't worry.'

I'll just travel an hour and a half back to London and message him instead. She probably thinks I'm a stalker considering I haven't even told him in advance that I'm coming. I can't help blushing a bit as I walk out the door.

Just as she's closing the door behind me, we both see George turn on to the drive.

'Oh, it's George!' his mum says in an overly surprised tone to show me she didn't know he was coming back now.

His expression is normal, happy, unperturbed. Maybe a slight eyebrow raise as he looks at me. I turn around, she's gripping the rolled-up tea towel in her hands. 'Iris is here!'

He jumps back. 'Oh shit!'

We all do a little laugh.

'She's just arrived.' Is she confirming her allegiance?

'Welcome,' he says, removing his bag and holding it by the top handle.

'Thanks,' I say, struggling to look directly at him.

'Is there a reason we can't go inside?'

His mum jumps back into action moving to the side. 'No, of course. I had invited Iris in, but. . .'

She looks terrified to finish the sentence, so I say, 'I was only calling by.'

'In the area?' he says, walking in. I stay outside but laugh to try and communicate this awkward conversation has to end and he has to be the one to do it.

'If you're not coming in, then I guess I'm coming out,' he says with a raised voice while he walks into the kitchen. 'Just give me a sec to get some water and a snack. I'm running on empty.'

His mum laughs too much and then takes her cue to leave. She waves the tea towel in hand, 'It was lovely to meet you, Iris!'

'Yeah, you too!' I wave back. She walks up the stairs, still holding the tea towel.

He calls back again. 'You coming in?'

I don't answer because I don't want everyone in the house to hear me refusing to come in. A few minutes later he comes back to the door holding a glass of water and an apple, which he bites into with the side of his mouth very loudly. He holds the glass out slightly, offering it to me.

'No, I'm okay thanks.'

He shrugs and bites the apple again

'Let's go sit somewhere.'

'Where?'

'I dunno, on the kerb somewhere or something.'

He looks relaxed, like a life without me is so simple and carefree that even my presence can't disturb it.

'I'm not keen to sit on the cold, hard ground, I'm gonna be honest with you.'

'Okay, fine. Let's just speak here then.'

He grabs another jacket from the hook and steps out. 'Actually, I know someplace nice, just follow me.'

He walks down the drive and chucks his apple into the food bin and offers out the glass of water again. I shake my head and he drinks it in one long gulp and puts it down on the drive. I look at him for a second.

'What? It's not like someone's going to steal it, or a small child will walk past, decide to go slightly up our drive and then fall on top of it so it shatters underneath them.'

'I didn't say anything.'

He gives me a cheeky smile and starts walking down the road, so I have to run a bit to catch up with him. We walk for a moment in silence and then he hands me the jacket. It feels overwhelmingly kind and I don't want to cry so I put it on and try not to think about it too much.

He glances at me. 'What you been up to?'

'Oh, you know, this and that.'

He doesn't respond but doesn't seem angry. I can't help myself. 'What have you been doing?'

He doesn't pause or seem bothered that I asked him. 'My mate's opening a pizza place, so I've been helping out with the menu. He knows fuck all about food to be honest.'

'Oh, really? That's cool. What have you suggested then? Chorizo and grilled pineapple?'

'You think I'm a pretentious chef?'

We're getting to the edge of the estate where it seems to peter out into a main road. 'No, to be honest, for London, you're a very "down to earth" chef.'

He walks straight down the main road on to a diminishing pavement.

'Is this. . . are you leading me to my death? Because I probably would walk into the road if you led me there.'

'No, no, of course not, I know a lovely spot.'

We keep walking and I'm starting to feel angry, but then when the pavement finally runs out there is a bench, facing out onto the road. It is pretty funny, and I can't help but laugh. I look at him and raise my eyebrows.

He suddenly looks really worried. 'What. . . is this not. . . right?'

I shout, louder than needed. 'I can barely hear you over the sound of the very close speeding cars.'

He looks disappointed. 'But I mean. . . it's a beautiful spot.' His face lifts and he shouts as a car zooms past. 'Isn't it!'

I sit down on the bench and think about a car spinning out of the road and into us. What would people say? Maybe his mum would consider it murder.

He sits next to me and takes a cereal bar out of his pocket and offers it to me.

I laugh. 'No thanks, I'm good.'

He shrugs and puts it back in his pocket. 'I hope you're getting your five-a-day.'

I try and direct my voice towards his ear. 'How's it been? Being at your parents'?'

'Yeah, it's good. Don't have to pay for toilet roll and there's loads of good walks around here.' He gestures to the road we just walked down.

'Yeah, that's good about the toilet roll.'

'Yeah, really good news about the toilet roll.' He doesn't look at me when he speaks. 'What brings you to Hemel Hem then? The attractions or the nightlife?'

'The attractions.'

He nods accepting my answer.

'The one and only George Williams being first on my list.'

He doesn't smile, but I don't think he's angry or sad or cringing or anything really. He's just waiting. He doesn't speak.

'I'm really sorry I came.'

He shrugs.

'I do have a reason for coming.'

Finally he looks at me. 'Oh, yeah?'

I'm so aware of when I swallow. 'I've been finding it hard to look at the world around me – without you to like, look at it with me and show me why it's nice.' I can't help but blush for some reason. 'I just see everything in this bad light, like everything is fake or boring or just sad, and eventually it feels like there's no point in doing anything. Everything is in the dark, and after a while it's tiring to be in the dark all the time, it just makes you want to lie down. It's hard to walk around in the dark. Sorry. . . I don't know what I'm saying.'

Even after all this time it's embarrassing being so earnest with him. 'When I see things, I just want to do them all with you.' I feel like I'm in a poem or something, saying this to someone because I feel compelled to, not because I want a response. 'I probably took that for granted. . . Well, I definitely did.'

Every time a car zooms past I flinch. He is just staring into space. I bet his heart is beating fast though. I want to feel his pulse to check. His skin always looks so smooth and healthy. I love his freckles. I want to tell him they're perfect. 'Are you going to say anything?'

'I don't think you saw the world as happy when I was there. You didn't act like a person who was happy.'

'Can we get out of here? It's so loud and it's getting dark, and I'm kind of cold.'

He stands up. 'Sure.'

We start walking back down the path. I carry on. 'I know I didn't seem happy, I wasn't happy. That doesn't mean you showing me why things are good wasn't important to me. I like seeing *you* like things.'

'You didn't like it enough.'

I stop in my tracks. So he does too. 'I did like it. I do like it. Just because I'm a bad person doesn't mean I didn't like it.'

I burst out crying even though I really don't want to. I don't want to manipulate him. But it's all coming out. I put my face in my hands and try to stop. And then I feel arms around my shoulders, holding me. The smell of his washing powder is the smell of home and that thought makes me cry even harder.

He takes my hair out of its barely formed bun and smooths it out bit by bit. He does it for a while until my breathing slows. Then he moves to the side so it's just one arm over my shoulder and he pushes me softly, so we start to walk. After a few steps he takes his arm away. I wonder if he thinks I've got a bag because I expect to stay the night here.

We start walking towards his house.

I look at him, worried. 'Are you going home now?'

'Have you said what you wanted to say?'

'No.'

'What else did you want to say?'

'It's not something specific really. . .'

He turns right down another road instead of left onto his.

'It's more just. . . wanting to say I'm sorry.'

'It's not something you have to apologise for.'

'It's something that I want to apologise for. I know you probably never want to step foot in that flat again. . . now that you've got all the toilet roll you could dream of. But I miss you.'

'You didn't want me.'

'I was looking for a problem in our relationship where there wasn't one. The problem was me.'

'You made a choice though.'

'Not the right one.'

'Making a choice is making a choice.'

'Do you not think we're good together?'

'You didn't, and it takes two to be good together.'

'I did think we were good together. I do think we're good together. I didn't want a relationship like my parents', where you're with someone just because the other person is. . . there. But I know we're not like that now. If we had a dining room we would use it every day.'

He doesn't say anything, just looks at me confused.

I try to simplify. 'Everyone else is boring.'

'Sometimes you think that about me.'

'I never think that about you. I promise. Maybe I thought my life was boring, but never you.'

He starts walking back to his street. 'If you came here to apologise, I accept your apology, even though it isn't necessary.'

'I didn't come here just to apologise.'

'It's going to get dark soon. Do you want me to call you a taxi? Or I can drive you if you don't want to go on your own.'

'Please, I don't want to go yet. It's nice to be here. Sometimes I feel like I'm on fast forward, and when I'm somewhere like here, with you, it feels like I'm back to normal speed.'

'It's called being bored.'

'I'm not bored. This is the least bored I've been for ages.'

'I doubt it.'

I take a deep breath. 'What have you thought about being on your own?'

'It's fine. I just go to work, see some of my mates that still live here, eat dinner with my parents and watch porn on my laptop.'

I laugh and he smiles. I'm glad he doesn't ask what I've been up to.

'I don't like being without you in the flat. You're the only good thing about it, turns out.'

'Sounds like you need a new housemate.'

'Maybe I just need you.' I don't feel embarrassed to say that, just relieved.

'You don't need me. That's why I'm here.'

'I was wrong.'

'You can't be "wrong" with a feeling. It means something.'

'I don't think straight. I'm always wrong about everything. It's unbearable.'

'Maybe you're "wrong" about what you're saying now.'

'I guess I could be. But it doesn't feel that way, and I have to trust my brain to some extent.'

We reach his house and stand at the end of the drive. 'Why are you here?'

'I really want you to come back. Live with me, be with me. I know you don't trust me, but I'd try so hard to prove that you can.'

'Trust you to what?'

I think of what Mum said, about being a complete person. My voice is full of conviction. 'Trust that I want you because I really, really like you. I like you so much that I love you. It's not because I need you. You're right, I don't *need* you, and I know you won't fix what's wrong with me, I will have to find a way to do that myself, but I still enjoy being around you and. . . I'll even pay for the toilet roll.'

He doesn't say anything for a while. 'There's no way you can afford that.'

'Please, George.' I take a risk and put my hand on his arm, but it's just far enough away to feel a bit strained. His hair has grown, standing a bit further off his head. It makes him look even taller. 'You never tried to fill in and pave over my holes, I see that now.

All you did is let me be myself, and I hate myself, so I hated you for doing that. But it's not your fault.'

'Can I just check, are we still talking about you and me or have we moved on to roadworks?'

I can't help but beam up at him. 'Have you missed me at all?'

'Yeah, I've missed you. Things are dull without you.' He looks casual like he doesn't think what he just said was a big deal.

'That's what I meant.'

He looks at his watch. 'What time is it?'

'Please don't make me leave yet.'

'When do you plan to leave?' He looks serious this time, and I get a sudden hit of fear.

'I don't know, but I don't want to leave yet. We need to finish this conversation.' I swallow and take a deep breath. 'I'm not asking to stay here. I just—'

'Where are you going to stay then?'

He picks up my bag.

I'm breathing fast, but I'm not going to cry. I don't want to pressure him anymore. He deserves better than that. I want him to be as happy as he possibly can be. He gets his keys and comes back out. The car door clicks open. I am weak.

'I love you. So much. Do you believe me?'

'Yes, I believe you. I love you too.' He goes to open the car door, so I move out the way. He stops and puts his hands on my shoulders instead.

'I'll never not be there for you. You always have me there for anything serious.'

'Life is serious.' I look up at him.

He raises his eyebrows.

'I don't want to go back to the flat alone.' I start crying. I give up trying to be strong. He pulls me in to give me a hug. I rest my head on his chest and cry harder. The hug feels like everything I could ever want.

'Do you even want to stay here? You can barely step in the hall. You gonna sleep on the drive?'

I do a breathy, half-crying laugh and calm down, but we stay hugging. 'I guess not.'

He pushes me away slightly to look at my face and I feel such a surge of love, so I stand on my tiptoes and kiss him. He kisses me back. I put my hand on his face and kiss him more, but I've barely taken a full breath in minutes so I pull away. 'Do you really want to call it a day on us? Forever? Just because I'm a fucking idiot?'

He breathes in and exhales deeply and looks down again, scratching his cheek. 'No, I never wanted that.'

I'm still crying, but I want to kiss him, so I kiss him and cry at the same time and he pulls back laughing.

'Not that I'm not enjoying that, but I feel a bit uncomfortable kissing a girl who's crying.'

I stop and rest my head on his chest again and hug him as tight as I can until I stop crying. I don't feel excited, I just feel calm and happy.

There's something so relaxing about being a passenger in a car. Especially at night. No part of me feels like I have to be watching the road. It's not even that George drives particularly slowly or at 'ten and two', but I think it takes a certain level of bad luck to crash a car. And I don't feel unlucky today.

On the motorway I can see all the white headlights from the cars going the other way to us and all the red ones of the cars in front. I squint my eyes so the lanes become blurs of colour. I think about

George doing things around the kitchen, his eyes and mind focused on the task at hand and how much I love to watch him. I picture the little smile he gets when he concentrates hard. I feel myself going to sleep, and it's nice to have a few minutes to appreciate the sensation before I fall fully under.

35

Every day George wakes me up with a tea because otherwise I sleep until the afternoon. But I don't take this act of kindness for granted. Our new routine has specifically evolved to prove there's equality in the relationship. At first things feel delicate, and I try to prove to him that things have changed, keeping the flat immaculate, attempting to meditate, turning down Sara's invitations until they fade away. But he sees what I'm doing and tells me this isn't a trial. 'Just treat me like someone you love, not someone you want to make love you.'

The rest builds naturally from there. I do the washing up after he does the cooking. He goes to work, I put a wash on and go to the supermarket. I buy a little garden table for the living room as a surprise and we eat every meal at it. Sometimes when I feel up to it, I make a cake after dinner and we have a slice of it with a cup of tea the next day before he leaves for work at 2 p.m.

In the afternoons I try to do something productive like having a bath, but then I realise that's not really productivity, that's just basic hygiene. I lie in bed looking at the ceiling instead. It's unmarked and hard to focus my eyes on anything. So I close them. I'm usually sitting up in bed at 1 a.m., waiting expectantly to greet George. He lets me follow him around the flat talking about nothing. And he just stands there, nodding, his eyelids heavy. We brush our teeth in silence, but I can't stop smiling looking at his half-closed eyes. I feel a swelling of love in my chest.

'I like you and love you,' I tell him when we're done.

'Thank you,' he says, putting his hand on my shoulder and looking at me earnestly. 'I. . . appreciate you saying.'

I raise my eyebrows and we laugh.

And when we're in bed, and I'm kissing him and stroking his chest, he never pushes me away and says, 'I've been standing on my feet all night, why don't you get a job?'

His skin is always warm, and I like burying my face in his neck and smelling his comforting neutral smell.

Sometimes I think about going into my old room. Just to do something. Like when you squeeze all your pores even though you know nothing good will come from it. The door is always left open, to make the room look casual, like a room people go in and out of. But they don't. As far as I know, neither of us have been in there for months. Probably not since the day I moved the last of my stuff back into our room. It feels as if we have moved on from everything now, and yet that room seems to say there is something left unsaid, hanging over us. Sometimes I swear I know what it is, it's on the tip of my tongue, it's saying that this could happen all over again, it's the fact that I don't know who I will be in six months or a year or ten, it's because what has actually changed, it's provoking me, it's saying 'I'm here waiting for you to succumb and return to me.' Or it's nothing and I'm overthinking things.

My alarm goes off at 8 a.m. because I planned to run down to the shop and buy some pastries to wake George up with. But my body really hurts, and I want to sleep so much more than I want to get up.

The next thing I know I'm woken up by George giving me little kisses all over my face. 'I made you a tea.'

'Oh, for fuck's sake.' I push myself to sit up and he climbs in next to me.

'Sorry, that was pretty out of order from me.'

I rest my head on his shoulder. 'No, sorry. It's just I was meant to make *you* a tea.'

'That's nice.' He kisses me on the cheek.

'It's not nice if I didn't do it.'

'Either way, we've got a tea and we're in bed so that's the main thing.'

I smile and shuffle even more close to him. 'You're so nice.'

I run my fingers over his chest and stomach. 'How come it looks like you go to the gym three times a week?'

'Because I secretly do, to impress you. Don't want to seem too keen, but got to keep you interested, y'know?'

'Well, it's working. I should be secretly going to the gym.' I push my stomach rolls.

'Everyone's stomach does that when they bend over.' He puts his tea down and starts kissing my stomach. Then he takes my mug and puts it on the bedside table and works his way down.

I wake up to the smell of hollandaise sauce. I walk into the living room and see two plates of perfectly presented eggs Benedict on the garden table. I go give him a kiss on the mouth.

'I love you. I should probably put some clothes on.'

'This isn't that kind of establishment.'

I run into the bedroom and throw on the t-shirt he was wearing yesterday before he went to work. It's black with a drawing of a bowl of spaghetti on the back, and it just covers my bum. I'm not sure it gives me the 'girl who is sexily only wearing her boyfriend's shirt' look, but I love wearing it because it's soft and smells like George.

I eat the eggs and the muffin and afterwards we sit on the sofa and he puts his arm under my t-shirt and around my waist and I feel full and cosy. He gives me a squeeze. 'I think we should go do something.'

'Yeah, it's just. . .' I lean forwards and put my head in my hands. 'Ugh, I don't know why, but the idea of going outside and seeing everyone, walking around living their lives, it just gives me this feeling of despair.'

He leans forward to join me. 'We don't have to see anyone else.'

'I literally mean just seeing people walking down the street.'

'Yeah, I'll make sure you don't see them. Trust me.'

I can't stop shaking my leg. The thought of going out makes me feel a bit sick but then the thought of staying in and wasting this precious time with him is almost worse. This is always a problem and there is never a good outcome.

'Do we have a deal? You come out with me, and I guarantee you won't see anyone?'

'All right but if I see anyone. . .'

'Yeah. That's the end of it. You're free to go.'

In the bedroom I put my hair in a bun and throw on my comfy grey jeans and a jumper, keeping on his t-shirt. I don't bother looking in the mirror and I wonder if this is what being better would feel like. In some ways I think I'm wonderfully happy but then it can switch so suddenly and I can feel completely empty again. And then there's the lingering worry, that if this all carries on endlessly, what's to stop me running back to Patrick for the pathetic ecstasy of his validation?

I go and flop on the sofa and wait for George. I like it that his days off are usually Tuesday and Thursday. It makes no difference to my 'schedule' when his days off are, and it's never busy when we go and do something. It feels like we're a couple of tourists. But when I don't make it out, I just sit here feeling the crushing pressure of time running out for me to change my mind. Trying, and often failing, to persuade myself that if I could just get up and go see something other than this flat, before I go back to sleep again, I would feel better.

George comes into the room with a quiet excitement in his eyes. He goes and rustles in the kitchen cupboards for a second and then comes back to the sofa. 'Come on.' He puts his hand out, so I grab on to it and let him pull my full weight up.

'Where are we going?'

'You leave that to me, okay?'

As soon as we get walking on our street, I see a woman pushing a pram and a man on a scooter and so I stop still. 'Right, I'm going back. I can't. . .'

'Sorry, sorry. Wait.' He takes me to the side and stands behind me.

'You going to do some kind of magic?'

He puts something on my head and pulls it over my eyes. I take it off again. It's a silk eye mask I bought for sleeping a while back when I heard it helps to prevent wrinkles.

'What is this?'

'I don't know. That thing you sleep in to keep the light out, isn't it?'

'Yeah, but why have you brought it?'

'You can't see what you can't see.'

I give him little smile. 'What am I actually supposed to do now?'

'Come on, give it a go.' He takes it off me to put it back on my head, so I help manoeuvre it to sit properly.

With it over my eyes I immediately tune into the sounds, mainly cars, near and far and general unidentifiable white noise.

'Hold my hand then.' I can hear he's smiling.

'Nah, I think I can do it on my own. Just tell me if I'm going to bump into anything, or like, if someone is walking towards me.'

'Yeah, okay.'

'This is a trust exercise, okay? Don't fuck it up.'

'You have my word.'

I start walking. 'Can you just confirm I'm walking straight?'

'I can confirm. No crab walking yet.'

'No, I mean like, not veering off one way or anything?'

'Yeah, you're walking straight.'

'Okay.' I can only walk in tiny steps and even that is terrifying. I stop and laugh. 'Oh my god, I have no idea why this is so terrifying, but it really is.'

He's cracking up too. 'You've gone about a metre.'

'I'm just getting my bearings, all right?' I start walking again with my hands a bit out in front of me for some reason. 'Please actually look at the pavement to see if there's anything I could trip over or anything, cause I could actually fall on my face.'

'Believe me I've got the time to scout the whole area in detail before each step.'

I walk a few more steps.

Then I hear a, 'Sorry, excuse me.'

So I pull the mask up and see a woman trying to walk past us.

'George! What the hell! I told you to tell me if there was anyone coming at me!'

He's laughing a lot and it's making me laugh too. 'She was like a full metre away from you!'

'Right, that's it, you've broken the trust. Forever. You think I'd ever fall back on you to catch me? Think again.'

'But what are we going to do at office training days? It will be humiliating for us. Give me another chance.' He puts his hand on his hip and nods his head to invite me to link arms. I pull my mask back down and link like I'm clinging on for my life.

We walk a few more steps and it's actually becoming easier. 'I think I'm getting the hang of this.'

'Yeah, it's pretty easy. Especially considering I've closed my eyes too.'

I stop and take the mask off and we both laugh, but I disapprovingly raise my eyebrows. I hand him the mask to put in his pocket and continue to cling on to him as we walk along in a pleasant silence.

I don't ask where we're going because it doesn't matter. Soon he slows down as we arrive at a little park that's as big as a large garden. But it's very nicely kept with benches studded along a neat path. He leads us to sit down on one of them. The sky is purely clouds.

'Won't it be chilly to sit still?'

'I'll keep you warm, come on.'

So I sit next to him and he pulls me close towards him. People walk past us, but they're looking forwards and usually on their phones and so it feels like we're on our own. He's stroking up and down my neck, and I can't help but close my eyes in relaxation. But then he taps me on my shoulder. 'You having a nap?'

'Maybe. What of it?'

'You're on a date.'

'What?'

'We're on a date, right now. But sitting here is not the whole date.'

'We moving to a bench up there?' I gesture up the path.

'You'd be so lucky.' He reaches into his jacket pocket and pulls out two Lion bars. I'd mentioned the other day that I hadn't had one in years, but it was a favourite of mine when I was a child.

'Oh my god!' I take one and look at it, getting nostalgic at the packaging, even though they still sell them in every shop. We open them and he holds his out to 'clink' it against mine.

'Cheers.'

'Cheers,' I say back and bite into the delicious chocolate. Just as good as I remember. 'I'm already sad for when it ends.'

'There's plenty more Lions in the sea,' he says, basically three quarters of the way through his already. I try to take little bites to savour it but I reassure myself that I can always get another one.

'Thank you so much.' I snuggle back into him when I've finished.

'My pleasure. Literally. I got a lot of pleasure from that as well. Great choice.'

'Best date ever.'

My heart feels full and I can't stop smiling but I can never fully enjoy these happy feelings, because I'm always waiting for the next sad one.

A couple of days later we're sitting on the sofa, both not watching the news when he pinches my shoulder.

'Let's go out. Not *out* out, just outside.'

'But we've already been outside today?'

'There's no limit as far as I'm aware.'

'But there's societal norms,' I say, trying to be funny, but I don't think it lands.

'I'm gonna pop out then.'

'Good idea.' I give him a little kiss on the cheek.

After he's gone, I sit there for ten minutes wanting to run out after him but worrying because I feel so empty when I'm not with him. I know that can't be healthy but five minutes after that I'm pulling on my jacket and ringing him.

'Hey. Where are you? I've just left. I want to come meet you.'

'You don't need to do that. I'm just having a nice walk.'

'I know I don't need to, but I want to. That can't be bad. Surely?'

'Meet me outside that Portuguese bakery where they sell pastries and beer.'

I can't help walking fast. When I get there he's sitting outside at a little metal table with two Pastel de Natas and two bottles of beer. There's a soft autumnal sun on his face.

'You look beautiful in the sun,' I say as I sit down.

'So I look good for a couple of weeks a year then?'

I smile, but don't say anything. My senses feel so tender, almost raw. The feel of the hard bottle pressed on my lips, the cheerful sounding conversation in a different language on the table next to us, the look of George as he bites into his pastry, happy and present. My throat hurts knowing a miscellaneous dread could so easily overwhelm me at any moment.

'I'm worried about feeling bad just sitting here.'

'I know.' He looks at me like he really does know.

'Sometimes I feel so ashamed. I know I have so much more than most people, I'm so privileged and yet I'm not okay. . . I can't manage to be okay. I haven't even got anything to cope with – no responsibilities, no problems, no trauma. And yet it's a constant struggle – just being alive.'

He looks slightly uncomfortable in a way that I've rarely seen.

'Let me tell you something.'

I tense up expecting bad news.

'You know my mum and dad have been on and off? Well, when I was younger they always had these massive rows. My mum would be sobbing and my dad seemed cold. So I usually took my mum's side.

'Because, like you, even though her life had been fine, much easier than my dad's in fact, she always felt so down. I guess I could have thought, "get over it. You have nothing to be sad about" or whatever. But, to me, she seemed to give my dad such simple instructions of what she needed, or what he needed to do to help her, to make her happy.'

He looks up as if to remember. 'Stuff that was reasonably easy to change. It seemed to me like my dad didn't listen.'

He takes another bite of his pastry and I can't help but smile with love for him. 'And then they would break up. But looking back, it wasn't as straightforward as all that. He saw her easy life and didn't understand why she couldn't be happy. She saw easy fixes and didn't understand why he wasn't helping her. Now I can see neither of them were in the wrong.'

He rolls his shoulders back and sits up straight again. I know he's been getting a bad back from standing up at work all night, but he never mentions it. I make a mental note to ask about it more.

'So they would call it quits and I would think, maybe there's some way I can help her get all the things she wants. More alone time, more money, less chores etcetera, etcetera.'

'You're such a goo—'

'And sometimes I would manage. I'd look after my sisters. Pay rent when I was a bit older. Cook healthy dinners. Stuff like that—'

'Well, I think you—'

'Can you just listen for a sec? I'm trying to say those things never made her happy. Or maybe that's wrong. Maybe they did make her happy, temporarily and like, superficially. But they didn't make her content. She would get the things she felt so desperate for but it never worked. Sometimes it even made her feel worse. It's disconcerting when you realise that getting what you want doesn't make you feel better.

'She was either excitedly pursuing something or feeling empty and hopeless. A healthy mind feels happy when something good happens and sad when something bad happens, but in between those moments it just feels settled. She couldn't enjoy a month of her life without craving "progress".'

I nod, trying to take this all in. He takes another second to gather his thoughts.

'Do you know what that feels like? To feel a nothingness that's pleasant? A neutral feeling?'

I nod without thinking, but then shake my head.

'She didn't either. And it took me a long while to understand that. Maybe I didn't want to see because it made me feel like I could do nothing to help. It was easier to tell myself I'd be able to make her feel better if I tried hard enough.' He picks up the remainder of the pastry, but then puts it down again.

'And. . . so. . . with you too, it seems like you think that there's something you could get or be that would make you finally feel great. But then you get it, and you don't feel better so you assume it's because you wanted the wrong thing. When someone thinks "I'll be happy as soon as I. . ." then the chances are whatever's at the end of that sentence won't make them happy.

'So what I'm trying to say is, nothing has to be "wrong" or

325

"missing" in your life at all to feel what you feel. Sometimes people can feel unbearably sad and there is no obvious reason. And it doesn't make you less worthy of sympathy or help.'

I try to swallow inaudibly.

I let his words rotate in my mind, like I'm learning them as lines.

'Is your mum okay now?'

'Well she's not "okay now" because she didn't have the flu. It will always be part of who she is,' he says with the slight smile of someone who has come to accept something.

'But I think it felt like a relief. Not searching for an environmental problem or reason for what she was feeling. And getting the proper help she needed. From a doctor.'

Neither of us speaks for a second. My head is whirring but I'm struggling to form them into thoughts.

'How come you've never mentioned this before? I'm not saying that confrontationally, I just—'

'Maybe I didn't try hard enough, it wouldn't surprise me if I just wanted to "solve" the problem instead, like I did with my mum. It makes me feel more in control, telling myself that it's possible. But I also did try to tell you sometimes. You don't often listen to me so. . .'

My face flashes from a guilty smile to a guilty frown. 'I know. I'm sorry. I had this wrong idea of you in my head, that you were so happy and that was your only perspective so you wouldn't be able to understand. A huge flaw of mine is that I tend to see everyone through this very simplistic arbitrary lens. I'm so caught up agonising over my stupid little thoughts that I fail to see the complexity of everyone around me. There is no excuse but I won't be like that anymore. I want to know everything you have to say ever.'

I take a sharp breath in hoping that I keep to that. How is he supposed to trust me when I can't trust myself? But I'm taking responsibility for this now, I decide.

'I'm not saying you have to take no accountability for your actions but don't beat yourself up about it too much. I've seen you struggle to get through the day alive. You weren't always able to consider me in that way.'

Suddenly I see myself through his eyes. 'Do you ever look at me and think 'thank god I'm not like that'?'

He looks hurt. 'No. Do you think when I see what you're going through I feel nothing? I'm not comparing what we feel, but I've felt helpless, I've been desperate, I've wished so hard I could just take the pain away from you.'

I want to apologise again but know that's the wrong reaction. Before I can think of the right one, he carries on.

'But that wasn't the point of this whole story. I guess my point is, I should have tried harder to tell you this, that you are like her, so you could—'

'Please can I just say something?'

'Yeah.'

I try to look behind his eyes, to something deeper. 'There was nothing you did wrong. You are my happiness, remember?'

He tilts his head down. 'That's not how it works.'

My heart clenches.

'Happiness is more than another person loving you,' he says quietly.

I go to ask him what I should do now then but stop myself. That's for me to find out. Instead I just squeeze his hand across the table.

Later that night, when he has gone to work, I lie down

the centre of our bed and let the tears silently flow out of my eyes and down my temples. A pleasant nothingness. I picture it. It doesn't come from what you are or have or do. It just is. A neutral feeling.

If anyone else had described that to me I wouldn't have believed them. I would have thought they were exaggerating, simplifying, kidding themselves.

36

I can't cure myself or find that equilibrium overnight though. If only a shift in mindset was the finish line rather than a first step. It's afternoon already and I still can't get out of bed. I know there's nothing I want from the shop. The day feels so long I could scream. I try screaming a little, but I feel silly, so it ends up sounding like a loud version of the noise you make when the doctor is checking your tonsils.

I'm just deciding whether to try and go back to sleep again when I hear my phone buzz. Sometimes George calls me if he takes a walk on his break. But when I check, it's Sara. Her calls had eventually petered out but recently they've started up again. I get ready to decline, my willpower unwavering these days, but then wonder if it's necessary to protect yourself from something that is no longer dangerous to you.

'Hey, Sara.' My voice sounds like the voice of someone lying down.

'Hi.'

'How's it go—'

'I thought you might like to come to drinks tonight?'

'Oh, right. Urm, I dunno, I'm actually feeling a little. . .' I don't know how to finish the sentence.

'Come on! It'll be fun! You always disappear off the edge of the world and I miss you.'

'I'm not sure—' I haven't had time to work out what the right thing to do is and I regret answering.

'Please! I've got to speak to you. It's been *ages* and it's important.'

A part of me hopes that things could be different, now that I'm different. 'Maybe. Where is it?'

'Just the normal pub, near work. We're headed there now.'

'Okay, cool. I'll let you know soon. Bye!' I hang up before she can reply.

I grab my towel and head to the shower wondering how to know if I want to do something or not. I'm almost entirely certain I could never be drawn back into that world, that dynamic, again. But there is always an element of me that is unsure. Am I different now or am I just away from it all? There is a tension inside of me that will never relax until I find out.

Sitting on the edge of the bed in my towel I consider what to wear. Should I try to make myself look as nice as possible in case I bump into old colleagues? Or wear the worst thing I can find to prove a point to myself? I decide it doesn't matter what I wear or don't wear. Just wear something, I tell myself, and so I choose black jeans and a big warm cord jacket that Mum bought for me as a present when I first moved to London.

Walking up to the pub I feel anxious about what version of me will come out. Disconnected and despondent or effervescent and charming? Both feel so heavy and intolerable.

Inside, it's full, and I have to look around to find Sara.

'Iris! Here!' By herself at a table right in the corner, Sara stands up waving. Her hair has grown long, and the ends have lightened like she's been in the sun. But she looks gaunt and her golden eyes are dull.

I give her a tight hug. 'Hey! How's it going? Are you okay?'

'Good! Yeah great, thank you. I got you a G&T.'

'Oh, thanks.' I sit down. 'So, what did you want to talk to me about?'

'What? Is that the only reason why you're here? I just wanted to catch up!'

I laugh, embarrassed how quickly I feel out of practice with socialising. 'Oh, sorry. You just made it sound like. . . it doesn't matter. How are you?'

'Yeah, things are good. The rennos on my flat are nearly finished, and I've been seeing this guy with an *incredible* penthouse, twenty-fifth floor, looking over the city.'

'Wow, what's he like?'

'He's a COO. Used to go out with Princess Diana's niece. We had sex in the rooftop garden the other day. We were just chatting and suddenly he took off all my clothes and we had this crazy sex. He likes to *choke* me.'

I realise that being open isn't the same as being vulnerable. But we've never been like that with each other because no one encouraged it. I try, 'Do *you* like it?'

'Well. . .' She thinks for a moment. 'Honestly, he's exactly what I need right now so I'd like anything!'

I laugh with her but I can't help thinking that her answer isn't the whole truth. Though I guess I'm expecting something of her that I've never offered myself.

The tension has eased and she asks me, '*So*, how have you been then?'

I notice I'm jigging my leg and try to still it. 'Well, me and

George are really good. But. . .' I take a deep breath, thinking suddenly of Shauna and Chloe, and try to be honest, 'I'm struggling a bit, I suppose.'

Sara leans forward, 'With what? Settling down? I can totally get that—'

'No no, nothing to do with George. Nothing in particular. That's actually the problem. Just. . . life. . . I find it hard sometimes. And, well, sometimes, I feel pretty down.'

I laugh awkwardly and she laughs with me, but still looks confused. 'Oh, right.'

Just then I feel a hand on my shoulder and jump. I turn around, but I already know who it is. Patrick, his bright eyes lit up with energy.

'Iris.'

'Oh, hey.' I pause, waiting for Sara to jump in, but she doesn't so I grasp for something to say. 'You've had a haircut.'

'I've had a few.'

It's short. Very short on the sides and barely floppy on top. But it looks good. He looks good. I need to end this quickly before my thoughts can spiral into what ifs. I laugh and gesture to Sara, 'I'm meeting Sara.'

Sara takes that as her cue to stand up and hug him. She speaks marginally quieter, but loud enough so I can clearly still hear. 'Did you get my message? Let's do something on Saturday instead?'

'Yeah, fine.'

Patrick looks down at me again. 'Come for a cig?'

'Oh, I don't smoke anymore.'

He raises his eyebrows. 'Really? Well come out for a chat then.'

'Sorry, maybe another time, I'm here to see—'

'Sara, you wouldn't mind Iris keeping me company for a minute, would ya?' He looks at her with his dimpled smile, and she looks at him both charmed and frustrated.

'Okay fine, I'll be over there.' She gestures to where a group of people I don't recognise, presumably colleagues, are standing. 'Don't be ages please!'

We walk outside together, but to my surprise my heart isn't racing. I feel a stillness, in fact.

He leans against a wall and starts to roll a cigarette. 'Is it all right if we have a chat?'

'No actually, I came out here to stand in silence.'

He stops and squints, clearly not in the mood to take things lightly. 'Are you okay?'

I can't help blushing. 'Yeah, sorry, that was meant to be funny, but just came out more. . . grumpy teenager?'

He breaks into a little smile and then puts his finished cigarette behind his ear. 'First things first. It's really nice to see you.' He moves over to me and pulls me into a hug. I get a surprise flash of nausea, it feels wrong to be this close. I try to wait for him to move back first, but I can't stop a reflex that pulls me away.

I attempt to distract from how awkward that was. 'So how are you?'

'I guess "it's nice to see" me too then. . .' He says sarcastically.

'Oh sorry. . . it's—'

'Calm down, you're fine. I'm messing with you. You're looking well. Hair back and no make-up is your best look I'd say.'

Feeling self-conscious that he's only seen me without make-up in our more intimate moments, I try to make my reply seem unfazed. 'Your new haircut is a good look too. Brings out your cheekbones.'

He runs his hand over his hair and smiles. 'D'ya think?'

But I still feel uncomfortable with the way the conversation is going. My confidence at being able to keep a distance is waning. I remind myself, *yes he can make you feel like you have a reason to live but the reason is just trying to be perfect for him*. I'm about to change the subject to something trivial when his face gets an intense expression. Direct eye contact, slightly raised eyebrows, and just the beginnings of a smile. It feels so earnest and it's making me cringe.

His voice is serious. 'How have you been? I feel like we left on a bad note, and I've been wanting to tell you how you'll always be an important person to me. And that I'll always be there for you as a friend.'

'Oh, well, thank you. And yeah, I'm good.' I'm not sure how much he knows about George, and I don't want to rub it in. 'Obviously life is always a struggle because. . . well. . . being alive is just awful, right? But yeah, other than that, good,' I say smiling, trying to keep the mood light.

'Are you working at all?'

I do a jokingly disapproving look. 'I thought you weren't one of those people who ask questions like that?'

He finishes his cigarette looking hurt. 'You know I didn't mean it like that. I just want to know about you. I miss you.' I want to tell him that we don't need to be so intense all the time. Life is heavy enough as it is, let it be silly and relaxed whenever you can.

'Sorry, I'm just being defensive because, of course, I'm not. . . doing anything.' I can't bring myself to say that I miss him, because the truth is, I don't. He doesn't seem to notice.

'I'm glad you're doing all right. Sometimes I see people talking about stupid shit that means nothing, and I think about how much you would hate it. It's nice to know I'm not the only one out there thinking like that.'

'Yeah, people are shit. That's never going to change.'

He looks down to bite his nails and his short hair tries to flop down. He looks so good when he's like this, in his own head. But I know now that just because he looks good doesn't mean I need him to think I look good. And just because someone might think I'm attractive, doesn't make me happy. I leave him to think for a second.

'I love you.' He doesn't look up when he says it.

I realise now, clearer than ever, that what I loved about Patrick is something I projected on to him, an ideal, someone who made me feel seen. And him loving this version of myself I had fabricated based on what I thought he would like best? That is not love; that is appreciation. I struggle to come up with a response, but he looks up and carries on anyway, 'You're the only one that gets it. Gets how shit everything is. It's hard to enjoy things with people who actually think what's going on is fun.'

I realise I'm nervously biting the inside of my cheek.

'You never loved me, did you?' He looks like he might cry.

I want to tell him our relationship was based on little more than a common distaste for life and mutual attraction but maybe I'm downplaying it now. 'I know you think you love me but—'

'Are you being fucking serious?' He looks furious, his eyes glassy with tears.

'Sorry.'

He looks straight at me, and I feel like he's about to walk away, but he doesn't. I don't want to be a bad person, so I find some words. 'I didn't mean that. I'm sorry. Do you think things end for a reason?'

'Yes. But maybe that reason isn't permanent.' His eyes look even more blue when they're filled with tears.

I try to take a second to really think about it, find something true I can say. 'Do you think we're compatible?'

'Do you?' He's looking down and shaking his head like he can't quite believe it.

Before I can reply, he rolls his eyes. 'What is "compatibility" anyway?' He air-quotes the word, almost seething with sarcasm. 'Sounds like the bullshit you hear in couples therapy or something.'

'What if two people don't bring out the best in each other?'

'Okay, so tell me why we don't bring out the best in each other? I'm not encouraging you to live your dreams enough or something?'

'Maybe we're too similar? Like. . . you just said about us agreeing on how shit everything is. . . well like, isn't that potentially just gonna lead to us bringing each other down? Maybe we both need people who will help us see that everything. . . isn't always shit.'

His anger looks desperate. I try to take a minute to gather my thoughts, but he moves on. 'Do you not have any feelings for me then?'

'Well. . .' I think of George. 'I'm out here speaking to you?' My heart is beating now, why can't I just say no? This is not a time to be cowardly.

His face relaxes at that response, which makes me even more tense.

I quickly add, 'You said you'd always be there for me as a friend? That goes both ways.'

He closes his eyes and takes a deep breath. Just then Sara comes out the pub door looking around. I go to wave her over, but then say, 'Sorry, Patrick, I can't stay long, and I really should spend some time with Sara.'

He looks at me with a blank face. Bloodshot eyes. I give him a quick sad-eyed smile and go back inside with Sara.

As soon as we're sat back down Sara says, 'So can we speak for a sec? I need to tell you something.'

I start to feel nervous and she instantly notices. 'Nothing bad has happened! Well. . . something bad *has* happened. But it's fine. Well actually, it isn't fine. . .'

'Okay. . .? You're worrying me now.' I hope it's nothing serious but I also wonder if she's about to open up to me. Maybe she's also ready for this friendship to take a different shape.

'No need to worry.' She giggles again but more nervously. 'Right, okay. I know you're back with your old boyfriend now, right?'

'Yeah, George.'

'Well, it just seems like you're really happy with him.'

'Yeah. . . I am.'

She does an affected exhale. 'So, when you were with Paddy, or whatever it was between you two, I saw him a bit less cause I guess we were both busy and stuff.' She keeps glancing up as if to check he's not near us.

'Okay.'

'But then he contacted me, and we met up and it was so great to see him and everything.'

I stop filling in the silences.

'And me and him have always been really close, you know that.' She keeps sighing at the end of her sentences, and I find myself feeling irritable. 'I know what you two have is completely different, but I think we're just close in another way. And I guess. . . in that moment, it manifested itself differently.'

'In what moment?'

'We slept together. It was only a few times though.'

I pick up my drink, just to have something to do, but realise I don't want alcohol. 'I'm just going to get a Coke instead.'

She nods and looks deflated, sighing again.

I walk to the bar, trying to gather my thoughts, but all I can feel is my brain bypassing any thoughts and my body tensing up. I try and work out what I feel. Sad? Betrayed? Angry? Unfortunately, not surprised.

My mind races through my options: argue with Sara, run back to Patrick, run back to George, or go and cry by myself. None of them feel quite right. I take my new drink back to our table and she starts speaking before I'm even sat down.

'I'm sorry. It doesn't take anything away from what you two had, or have. . . We just made a mistake that one weekend. It's never happened before or since.'

'Which weekend?' I give up on trying to sound calm.

'Just a weekend this summer.'

I'm trying to work out when this could have been when she adds, 'I think it was a weekend you went to visit your parents or something? He said you weren't together at the time. So it was nothing like that.'

I picture it. Me at Mum's, dealing with their divorce, my phone with no new messages, checking it again and again, my brain slowly melting, and him stroking his fingers over Sara's perfect skin, her pushing his hair back off his face, him telling her she's beautiful, how he's always thought that, how he knew this would happen one day. His phone on the floor, forgotten about. Sara, lying there naked, asking, 'How's things with Iris?' Him replying, 'She's gone to her parents.' Nothing more. He kisses her. But she hasn't forgotten me – the fact that she can take him from me is all part of her desire. But I don't feel angry. I'm not better than her. We've both been addicted to the same thoughtless narcissism. Making constant comparisons to other people for the fleeting self-gratification of superiority. A few tears fall down my face. I feel guilty for being

338

part of this cruel interplay. But mainly I feel relief. Released from it all. More certain than ever that this is behind me.

'Oh no. God, I'm so sorry. I didn't think it would upset you this much.'

I wipe my nose, which is already running. 'I'm not even upset. With either of you. I just cry at anything these days.'

I laugh, wiping the final tears away, and Sara laughs a little too, her brow still furrowed.

We sit in silence for a moment and then, in a strained tone I haven't heard before, she says, 'I actually *can't* cry. Like, this guy with the penthouse that I'm seeing. He was supposed to be coming to dinner at my mum's, I'd arranged it all and was so buzzing for it, but then a few hours before we were meant to go he said he couldn't be bothered! I was super upset, but I couldn't cry. I really struggle to cry for some reason. So I went to the bathroom and smudged my own make-up and pinched my cheeks to make it look like I had.'

Her eyes are wide staring straight into mine. I notice she's squeezing her thumb.

'Shit, that's horrible, I'm sorry. He should be taking you seriously without you having to pretend to cry.'

Suddenly her expression transforms into a bright grin and she rolls her eyes. 'Oh, it was nothing really. Just me being dramatic. He took me to Nobu instead and it was *amazing*. We got the Wagyu steak.' She flicks her hair to one side and takes a long sip of her drink.

I wonder if one day we can be more sincere with each other. Who knows if we would still be friends if we found out who the other person really was, probably not, but it's nice to think it's possible. And if not, at least I know that's what I want now. To be truthful and trusting. To have friends that I elevate and respect, not envy and resent. To find fulfilment in relationships that aren't exclusively romantic.

Back at home I feel tired and happy and sad. I sink into the sofa, my unrelenting inner monologue about to intensify when the sound of the key in the front door distracts and soothes me. George walks in and without a word said between us, sits on the sofa right on top of me.

'Oh my god,' he fake startles, 'I didn't see you there.'

I push him off, laughing, and nuzzle into him. We don't ask each other about our days, yet, because right now all we want to do is be close together and watch rubbish TV. Thinking about myself a year ago, I feel sorry for the girl who would have found this pathetic. Back then I wanted to be someone who didn't spend their time doing these unglamorous things, when really I should have wanted to be someone who found joy in them.

37

I slowly wake up the next day to George stroking my hair.

'How are you feeling about your doctor's appointment today?'

I find his hand and squeeze it hard. 'I mean, I'm scared. I don't know what they're going to say. But I suppose also just, ready.'

'I'm so proud of you, you know.' He looks a bit emotional, which takes me by surprise, and I'm about to become overwhelmed myself when he taps me on the thigh twice and says, 'Teas?'

I crawl down and out of the bed. 'Yes, teas, but I'll make them. You must be exhausted.'

By the time I get back with our drinks, George's lips are parted and his angelic face soft with sleep. My mind fills with love for him, but I know now that love isn't going to fix what is broken in me. Using George as a crutch, looking for the value in life by watching him enjoy it, was never going to truly help me.

And neither was tying all my self-worth to the opinions of others – it seemed to me as if the world was rewarding me every time I made myself more attractive, more productive, more elusive. I thought I was simply a successful person but I was actually getting caught up in stuff that doesn't even matter. Your most superficial aspirations often have the loudest voice. They call out to you offering satisfaction from easy to define results. But it wasn't healthy, the relentless searching for goals and striving for achievements. Being able to enjoy life without needing constant confirmation from external sources that I'm doing well at it, that is what I want now. I don't want to manufacture happiness anymore. I want to unearth it.

I hold George's hand softly so not to wake him. I know the best thing I can do now is take responsibility for my own life and work towards being the person he deserves to be with.

I walk to the GP surgery. The sky is still halfway between dark and light. There is a chill in the wind so I pull my jacket tighter across me. I try to mentally prepare for what is about to come but struggle. A negative voice in my head says this appointment probably won't help.

As I near my destination a familiar feeling of dismay envelops me. Attached to nothing, bobbing around the shores of my mind looking for any reason to land on. I try to tell myself that it's just my brain grabbing in the dark for something to justify this melancholy wave of emotion. But there is no reason – I know that now.

I sit down on the crumbling wall surrounding the doctor's surgery to take a breath and ground myself by watching the reddening leaves on the trees shiver in the wind. I used to think you needed a reason to be alive, I was flailing around waiting to be seen and validated, but maybe I'm just alive like this tree is alive: simply to be here. Life doesn't need reason or purpose to be valid.

I remind myself of what George said, I'm not less worthy of help because this pain doesn't stem from some specific cause or trauma. It's just there, both a part of me and separate from me, and I need to learn how to live with it. I've been obsessively searching for new, better ways to live my life, but what I needed was to work on being comfortable as I am. Being able to find pleasure in the mundane, in the daily rituals, in the simple things, that is a worthwhile aspiration.

Listening to snippets of conversations from the people as they walk past, about their upcoming days at school and their breakfasts and their shopping lists, I close my eyes and exhale. I realise how much world there is, outside of the one in my mind, and feel impatient to see it in a new light. But first I have to do this, I think, as I walk over and open the door.

Acknowledgements

Thank you to my incredible agent, Rachel Neely, for her constant help, advice, wisdom, encouragement and belief. Without her I have no idea what I'm doing.

I'm forever grateful to my editors Katie Seaman and Clare Gordon. Thank you to Katie for sharing my vision and helping this book become the best version of itself. I feel very fortunate to have had an editor who was so talented, kind and passionate. Thank you to Clare, for her remarkable expertise. And for making the process exciting, enjoyable and less intimidating.

And of course the amazing team at HQ: Rachael Nazarko, Kate Oakley, Vicki Watson, Emily Burns, Becci Mansell, Angie Dobbs, Halema Begum, Tom Han. And beyond: Mayada Ibrahim, Linda Joyce.

This book wouldn't be possible without:

My dad, Gary, and the infinite positivity and encouragement I received from him growing up. He taught me why books are magical and made me believe I could do anything.

My mum, Suzanne, and the limitless support she gives me. I wouldn't be here, or anywhere, without her.

My sisters, Hannah and Charlotte, for reading my writing

religiously, speaking about my work relentlessly, cheering me on continually, inspiring me constantly, educating me perpetually and entertaining me endlessly.

My partner, Ben, who has been patient, caring, hilarious, fun and brings joy to even the most mundane of days.

To everyone that helped me along the way: Dr. Elza Eapen, Lavinia Greenlaw, Kate Murray-Browne, Natalie Wright, Derawan Rahmantavy, Ollie Gretton, Francis Elvans, Kathryn Lacey, Swithun Cooper, everyone in the Royal Holloway creative writing workshop and the best dogs in the world: Tina & Teddy. And, of course, the rest of my friends and family that I'm so lucky and grateful to know because who am I if not an amalgamation of all of you!

And, finally, to all my favourite writers who've made me feel less alone and more alive.

ONE PLACE. MANY STORIES

Bold, innovative and
empowering publishing.

FOLLOW US ON:

@HQStories